STORM'S INTERLUDE

A Rosefire, Texas Romance

Vonnie Davis

This is a work of fiction. Names, characters, places, and incidents are either the product of the author's imagination or are used fictitiously, and any resemblance to actual persons living or dead, business establishments, events, or locales, is entirely coincidental.

Createspace Paperback Edition
ISBN-13: 978-1544621906
ISBN-10: 1544621906
Cover & Formatting designed by Kelly Moran
Photo courtesy of DepositPhoto
Published in the United States of America

Check out these other titles from Davis:

Santa Wore Leathers
Her Survivor
Hers to Heal
A Highlander's Obsession
A Highlander's Passion
Bearing It All
How to Seduce a Fireman
For the Love of a Fireman
Pin-Up Fireman

Storm's Interlude* was the winner of the *HOLT Medallion Award of Merit* and nominated for *Book of the Year* at *Long and Short Reviews.

Dedication

To cowboy romance lovers everywhere who love the code these men live by, their swagger, and the women who ride rein over their hearts. I mean, surely I can't be the only one who loves these swoon-worthy, muscle-hardened men.

Chapter One

Someone swaggered out of the moonlit night toward Rachel Dennison. Exhausted from a long day of driving, she braked and blinked. Either she was hallucinating or her sugar levels had plummeted. Maybe that accounted for the male mirage, albeit a very *magnificent* male mirage, trekking toward her. She peered once more into the hot July night at the image illuminated by her headlights and the full moon. Sure enough, there he was, cresting the hill on foot—a naked man wearing nothing but a tan cowboy hat, a pair of boots and a go-to-hell sneer.

Well, well, things *really* did grow bigger in Texas. The man quickly covered his privates with his Stetson. Rachel sighed. The extraordinary show was evidently over. Should she stand in her Beetle convertible and applaud? Give a couple of catcalls? Wolf whistles? Maybe not.

She turned down the music on the car's CD player. Sounds of crickets and a lonely bullfrog in the distance created a nighttime symphony in the stillness of this isolated stretch of country road. Lightning bugs darted back and forth, blinking a display of neon-yellow glow.

The naked man strode toward her car, and Rachel's heart rate kicked into double-time. Common sense told her to step on the gas, yet what woman wanted to drive away from such a riveting sight? Still, life had taught her to be careful. She reached into her handbag and extracted her chrome revolver. Before he reached her car, she quickly slid her gun under the folds of her skirt.

Just let him try anything funny—I know how to take care of myself.

Both of his large hands clasped his hat to his groin. His face bore annoyance and a touch of chagrin. "I need a ride." By his bearing and commanding tone of voice, she guessed the man was used to giving orders and having them followed.

Her gaze took a slow journey across his face. Even in the moonlight, she could see traces of Native heritage. His shoulder-length ebony hair, too long for her tastes, glistened against his bronzed skin. Proud arrogant eyes sparked with aggravation.

Because Rachel believed in indulging herself, she allowed her gaze to travel over his broad shoulders, muscular chest and tight abdominal muscles. She saw a thin trail of dark hair starting below his navel, and, knowing full well where it ended, she fought back a groan. Her gaze slid back up to lock on his. "You need a pair of pants, too." Knowing her voice hummed with desire, she cleared her throat, hoping the naked man hadn't noticed.

He leaned his head back and studied the sky for a beat. "Just my freakin' luck! A few friends tried to get my mind off a long overdue break-up." He snorted. "Hell, guys don't do that. They were just hunting for an excuse to get drunk and steal my clothes in what they thought of as a joke." He scowled at her. "Now, to top the evening off, I'm being ogled by some horny kid with damnable blue eyes."

What the heck was wrong with her eyes? She quickly glanced in her rearview mirror and saw nothing amiss. She narrowed those "damnable blue eyes" and sneered. "Look, buster, I'm not the one prancing around Texas naked as a jaybird. I'll have you know I'm hardly a kid." She glanced at the tan cowboy hat. "And, furthermore, stop hiding behind that big ol' Stetson. From what I saw, a French beret would do the job."

There, let the arrogant fool stew on that while he strutted back to whatever rock he'd crawled out from. She slammed her car in gear and sped off.

She swore she wouldn't look in her rearview mirror. Nope, she would *not* look. As if the mirror were a magnet emitting a powerful homing signal, her gaze slowly slid to the glass surface. He was standing where she'd left him, his Stetson tilted back on his head, his hands fisted on his narrow naked hips and his mouth moving. He was no doubt cussing her out.

A smile blossomed; a French beret would never hide all that. Wait until she e-mailed Grace, her best friend. She'd never believe her story of a naked man on a narrow, deserted road in the hill country of Texas.

Rachel exhaled a long sigh and accepted the inevitable. She couldn't very well abandon him, the caring part of her insisted. *Nurse Rachel to the rescue...again.* She mentally shrugged at the conflict of emotions. It was nearing ten o'clock. Where would he get help? Where would she get help if he attacked her? Men couldn't exactly be trusted. Hadn't she learned that?

She made a wide U-turn, her revolver still safely tucked under her skirt. When she stopped next to the naked stranger, a tanned hand emerged from the darkness and grasped her arm. Fear sprinted up her spine. Her right hand instinctively slid under the pink and purple plaid skirt of her sundress to touch the cold, hard steel of her gun.

The man was hiding his impressive family jewels behind his hat again. "Look, I apologize for the kid remark. I'm much obliged you've come back. My appearance being what it is, I understand your reluctance to give me a ride. Do you have a cell phone I could use?"

His voice was like black satin—deep, silky and darkly sensual. For a second, fantasies danced across her mind, spinning and leaping to some wild, soundless passionate beat. An involuntary shudder went through her.

Dark eyes narrowed and his grip tightened on her arm a fraction. "Do you or don't you have a cell?"

The size of the man was intimidating enough, but when he aimed those midnight eyes at her, his power nearly doubled. Showing fear wasn't an option. Not anymore. She'd learned displaying weakness made one vulnerable. "Yes, I have a cell. First, would you kindly let go of my arm?" She smiled, trying to hide her anxiety. Her tongue licked her lower lip, a nervous habit, and she saw a change in his eyes.

Her breathing increased. What if he meant to harm her? She tightened her hold on her revolver, releasing its safety. This wouldn't be the first time she'd held a man off with a gun. Relief flooded her system when she felt his grip loosen.

With a feather-light touch, he trailed his fingers down her arm, leaving a track of heat as if blazing red flames propelled from his fingertips. All her female parts softened and trembled, except for her nipples which gave their typical hardening response. His gaze spoke of sexual awareness and prowess, sweeping over her face as if he were gauging her reaction to his touch. His nostrils flared and, that quickly, his eyes shuttered and he pulled back.

She couldn't take her eyes off his face. Her nerve endings were humming a slow, sultry song. *Get a grip, Rachel.* She let go of the revolver and tugged her cell phone from a side pocket of her purse.

Silently she handed it to him, then slid her trembling hand under her skirt again to touch the security of her gun. The man was too compelling for his own good, and most certainly for hers.

The stranger thumbed in a number and placed the phone to his ear. "Jackson, you miserable som'bitch. Get your smartass out here and bring me my clothes! Stop that damned laughing. You'll find me along the road. I'll be the nude pissed-off man with smoke blowing out his nostrils." He swiped the phone and extended it to her.

"You never told him where you were."

"He knows." The man fairly vibrated with annoyance.

She lifted an eyebrow in question and waited.

"Jackson, me and two of our old high-school football buddies went to the swimming hole we used as kids." He looked up at the sky and scanned it. "Ever notice how a full moon brings out the idiot in most people?"

"There are studies to that effect, yes." God, he was gorgeous. Bet he'd be even better looking with a haircut.

"Had some beers. Passed a couple whiskey bottles around. Got the bright idea to skinny-dip like we did back in the day when we were full of piss and vinegar. I dove in and before I knew it, Jackson and the guys had run off with my clothes. All they left me was my hat and boots." He glanced at the starlit sky again. "I'm gonna kill 'em all."

She smiled. He evidently had some crazy friends.

A siren wailed in the distance, growing steadily closer. "Guess I should move my car out of the middle of the road."

"No need." He lightly placed a hand on her shoulder. "It's just Jackson, the *venerable* police chief of Rosefire, Texas." Sarcasm tinged his voice.

"Your friend, the one who stole your clothes, is the chief of police?"

He nodded, and then his attention shifted to the back of her car. "You a gardener? See you got plants on your backseat."

"They're herbs. Healing herbs for a new friend who's sick."

She thought she saw a flash of pain in his eyes. His hand slowly moved across her shoulder to her braid, sending shivers down her spine.

"You've got mighty long hair. Guess braiding it keeps it out of your eyes while you're driving with the top down." There was a quick smile, white teeth flashed and dimples winked.

Rachel swallowed. Dimples. He just *had* to have dimples. If she didn't soon get away from this man with his muscles, his deep voice and those prominent dimples, she'd be nothing but a puddle of femininity on the front seat of her new car.

He raised the braid, looping it around his fingers before letting it fall. "Bet all that blonde hair is glorious when it's loose."

She blinked twice. Just how was she supposed to react to *that* remark?

"Anyone ever tell you you've got full, sensuous lips that make a man wonder? I've seen those same blue eyes before, too. Been driving me crazy, in fact." What the heck was he talking about? He curved his large hand around her neck. The rough calluses on his hand and fingers sent shivers up and down her spine. Her eyes connected with his and her mind took a momentary joyride on one of those adjustable mattresses—she'd have to set it to firm. Her gaze dropped to his lips. Oh, yeah, most definitely firm. She imagined sex with him would be wild and passionate.

His voice deepened as he groaned, "I have a feeling I'm going to regret this, but I'll be damned if I'm going to live the rest of my life wondering..." Ever so slowly, he leaned toward her. Dear God, was he going to kiss her? Her heart rate jumped into triple-time, and a flock of crazed bumblebees dive-bombed in her stomach. Oh yeah, he was definitely going to kiss her—and irresponsible or not, she was definitely going to let him.

His dark, powerful gaze slid from her mouth to her eyes. "If you say no, I'll stop." Her tongue slipped out and wet her lower lip. He evidently took it for the welcome it was and captured her lips.

Firestorm—his kiss, gentle nips at first, quickly turned potent and fierce. He tasted of spice, whiskey and beer. There was a faint scent of lime-based cologne mingled with the dank smells of creek water. Her toes curled in her pink sandals. Oh God, she was in big trouble. Thank goodness she'd taken her hand off her gun or she'd have shot her car dead.

Heat flooded into every cell of her being as his lips and tongue gave and took. Begged and commanded. Whispered and roared of more male potency than she'd ever experienced. He groaned and pulled back just a tad, his eyes heavily hooded with desire. "Like I said, *that* was a mistake. Madness of the full moon." With his Stetson still firmly held in place, he kissed her gently on the forehead and stepped away from the car into the darkness.

She fought the urge to beg for more. Her body was whimpering for completion. She detested her response, appalled she was aching for a stranger. What was wrong with her? Hadn't knowing Kyle taught her anything?

The siren was increasing in volume as it grew closer, a wailing backdrop for her warring emotions. She was so engrossed in her thoughts, she jumped when the stranger's voice caressed her senses in the darkness. "No need in staying. Leave, kid. You can take that gun or knife you've been hiding under your skirt and put it back where it belongs. I'm not going to attack you."

"How...how did you know?" Rachel removed the pistol from its hiding place but decided against putting it away just yet. After all, this man was dangerous on so many levels.

His sensual voice stroked her again. "Put some aloe on your sunburn tonight. Your skin's hot." He slapped at something. "Damn mosquitoes."

The police cruiser crested the hill, the same hill the stranger had appeared on minutes earlier—a lifetime ago.

Chapter Two

Storm Blackhawk was *not* a happy man. What he was at that exact moment was mosquito bait—a six-foot-two mass of sexually aroused, naked, mosquito bait. He looked up at the full moon, swatted at a mosquito buzzing around his ear and snarled. Like most males, being impassioned without a willing female had put him in a seething mood. The additional indignity of being nude along the road, eaten alive by gnats, mosquitoes and chiggers, only fueled his temper.

He glared at Jackson Cole slumped on the ground, leaning against the side of the police cruiser. The drunken man, chief of police no less, had fallen out of the cruiser laughing at the sight of him standing there, wearing nothing but a pair of hand-tooled cowboy boots and his tan Stetson. For two cents and a cheap cigar, he'd kick Jackson. An audible sigh of disgust escaped. Why bother? He'd still be in a pissy-assed mood.

What was supposed to be a carefree night of booze and "remember when's" to ease Storm's confused emotions after breaking his engagement to a spoiled, sexy rich woman went sour in a hurry. Maybe it was just too soon. He'd dated her exclusively for over two years and, damn him to hell, he still cared for her, spoiled and demanding, or not. Hell, deep emotions didn't stop on a dime.

Jackson had called two of their old football buddies, who were still single, and bought the required cases of chilled beer and a few fifths of Jack Daniels. The night went from teasing to a major episode of embarrassment.

Storm's first dose of painful humiliation had been walking the road naked in hopes of reaching home before anyone saw him. The experience was akin to one of those disturbing dreams where you suddenly found yourself in a familiar place naked, like at a barbeque or a rodeo. Of course, he hadn't been able to sneak home undetected. *She'd* showed up in that little excuse of a car, baby blues beckoning, full lips beguiling.

Granted, he should have hidden behind some bushes when he heard the sound of her approaching car, but he'd been so provoked by that point, he didn't give a good damn whose headlights illuminated his naked state. He'd mustered what dignity he still retained and kept on clomping along.

Had he known the driver would be an intriguing paradox of wide-eyed innocence and sexual-fantasy lips, he'd have hidden all right—hidden for his *own* safety. What in God's name had possessed him to kiss her?

He swatted at gnats flying around his face. One could place part of the blame on the dream he'd had for the past three nights. Since his dad's death, several years ago, Storm had inherited his Native-American father's capacity for vision dreams—short, vivid ones where he saw into the future. Little flashes of forthcoming light, his dad had called them. For the last three nights, he'd dreamed of large blue eyes and a deep, sultry laugh almost like a siren's song calling his name.

The dreams were unsettling. So when those baby blues, the ones that haunted him in his dreams, gazed up at him from that sweet face, he kissed her just to see what would happen. He'd been foolish enough to think one taste of her would banish the dreams forever, banish them and leave him in peace. He swore softly. The woman was trouble with a curvy figure and lips made for kissing. He groaned at the memory, his mood darkening even more.

Jackson made some inane remark and giggled. Storm was in no state of mind for his best friend's taunting laughter. He yanked Jackson from the dirt and shook him. "Look, you drunk, simple-assed, poor excuse for a friend, give me my damn clothes."

Jackson laughed that hyena laugh that told of too many beers.

"You're not fit to be out on the highway, you damn fool. You're drunk!"

"So? You're bare-assed naked." Jackson's smile slipped and his face sobered. "And Sunny's gonna die. Our Sunny." He exhaled a moan of pain as if it came from the depths of his soul. "My Sunny."

Storm released Jackson and shoved him out of the way. "I'm not talking about this with you. Not in the mood, man. Give me my clothes." He slapped his bare backside. "Mosquitoes are eating me alive." He reached into the backseat of the cruiser for his clothes Jackson had evidently thrown into a pile.

"I keep thinking of her long black hair and how it's gone."

Storm jerked off his boots, tugged on his black jeans and zipped the fly. "It'll grow back." He sat on the seat of the cruiser and yanked on his socks. "Thought you were over her."

Jackson tipped a bottle of beer to his lips and took a long drink. "I can't get over her. Lord knows, I've tried. I've loved that woman since we were six years old." He motioned to Storm with his beer bottle. "You know that. We were the Texan three musketeers—you, me and Sunny. Wasn't I drunk for a month after she married that no good Abbot?"

"That you were." Storm dragged on a boot.

His friend took another drink and then belched. "Got drunk for two weeks when I found out she was pregnant."

"You were downright pitiful. Like you didn't think married people had sex."

Jackson drained the bottle and reached into the cooler for another. "Sawyer should be my son. She should be my wife. And, *dammit*, she should be healthy."

Storm dragged a black T-shirt over his head. "Give me the keys. No way I'm letting you drive."

"My Sunny..."

He stuck out his hand. "Keys, Jackson." He'd drive the cruiser home, drag Jackson's sorry butt inside and pour him onto one of the sofas. The last thing he wanted to do tonight was play nursemaid to a drunken lovesick pup, even if the pup had been his closest friend since first grade. For sure he didn't want to hear someone lament about his twin sister losing her hair and maybe losing her battle with leukemia. He refused to accept the pain of that reality.

Jackson handed his keys to Storm before pulling the last bottle of beer from the cooler of ice in the cruiser.

****

Rachel still reeled from the effects of that sizzling kiss when she turned off Longhorn Road at the two yuccas next to a large, gnarled live oak. Her little red Beetle bounced on the dirt road that led to the Triple-S Ranch.

The naked stranger, whoever he was, packed quite a sexual punch. She hadn't responded like that to a guy in, well… She glanced in her rearview mirror. "Never. I've *never* reacted to a guy like that. And a stranger, to boot. Oh, Rachel-girl, what were you thinking back there? You weren't thinking, were you? You were having a taste of full-moon madness."

She grinned. “And a taste of macho male.” He was cherry cheesecake and caramel-swirl ice cream and double-fudge brownies all rolled into one. As a diabetic, she avoided all three. Even so, she still fantasized about them, just like she was in hormonal fantasyland over this stranger. Avoidance was the key here. Thank goodness she’d never see him again.

She’d kissed him back, for heaven’s sake—a stranger—and she’d enjoyed every second of his lip lock.

His ramblings about her eyes were more than a little odd. Since she’d never been to Texas, there was no way he could have seen them before, not *her* eyes, anyway. Maybe he’d just had too much to drink. Still, he was a hunk. The trite phrase tall, dark and dangerous most definitely described him.

She felt downright pitiful. Ten minutes after his kiss, and she was still humming with desire. She lifted a slender shoulder in defiance at that thought. After all, it was better to be alone—safer to be alone.

When she eased her car to a stop at the security gate, she leaned out and punched in the security code Sunny Abbot had e-mailed her. The double wrought-iron gates, bearing three large intersecting S’s, creaked open. Rachel drove on, relieved her long journey was almost over. A mile and a quarter of private dirt road and she’d be there.

As promised, Sunny had left the outside lights on for her late arrival. Sunny was Rachel’s new patient. The twenty-nine-year-old woman had acute lymphoblastic leukemia.

When Sunny’s first round of chemo failed, she’d researched online for alternative treatments. Sunny told Rachel she’d read her article on the emotional benefits of treatment at home and how that edge often tipped the scales toward remission. Intrigued, Sunny had checked out Rachel’s credentials with the Leukemia and Lymphoma Research Society and, finding them to be impeccable, contacted her.

Rachel held a master’s degree in nursing. She was also trained and certified in acupuncture, massage and other holistic training methods. She’d carefully and expertly combined the two disciplines, making a name for herself in the private nursing field for critically and terminally ill patients.

Sunny had hired her to come to her home, the Triple-S Ranch, saying she needed a miracle. Rachel prayed God would grant one to her new patient.

Before being contacted to come to Texas, she'd taken two weeks in the mountains of Colorado to rejuvenate emotionally from Kyle's abuse and to complete more research. Being so far away from her home in Yazoo City, Mississippi, had distanced her from the dangerous man who'd haunted her dreams and made her waking moments a nightmare.

On Rachel's third day at the beautiful mountain lodge with its hushed cool serenity and long hiking trails, she received her first e-mail from Sunny. After a flurry of emails and phone calls, she'd accepted the job. Rachel decided to come directly to Texas from Colorado. By taking this extra layer of caution—not going home to Yazoo City before coming here—she hoped to throw her ex-fiancé further off her trail. She'd also asked Grace, who was taking care of her plants in her absence, to overnight the title to her SUV so she could trade it in for a new car before she left Colorado. That SUV held some painful memories.

Perhaps, while in Texas, she could decide where she'd relocate. Going back to Mississippi, where she'd be subjected to Kyle's continual harassment, was no longer an option. His violent tendencies had increased—thus her need for the gun. She didn't like living in fear. Nor was she proud of herself that during her period of mourning for her father, she'd allowed Kyle to take over her life. While in the mountains of Colorado, she'd vowed she'd never let another man tell her what to do again. From that point forward, her life was hers to control.

This job had come at an opportune time for her. For some reason, she'd formed a quick connection with Sunny. The two women had e-mailed often during the past week, building a level of trust before her arrival. She found forging friendships with all her private patients helped in her treatments—and, eventually, their recovery.

She parked her car near a crepe myrtle in front of the large ranch house and raised the Beetle's tan canvas top. Bending and stretching once she got out of the car, she worked some of the kinks out of her body. Not the sexual kinks, of course. A smile played on her lips. Who *was* that man with the midnight eyes and skilled lips?

She'd never know. Perhaps that was for the best. Men seemed to equal trouble.

Visions of a hot shower and comfy pajamas propelled her. She hefted two suitcases and her laptop from the trunk and headed for the wide steps leading to the large front porch. White rocking chairs and potted plants graced the covered veranda. When she reached the carved wooden door, adorned with a gleaming brass knocker shaped like a Texan longhorn, the door suddenly opened.

An older Mexican woman, her salt and pepper hair combed into a large bun at the nape of her neck, held one finger to her lips in a gesture to be quiet. "Miss Dennison?" Her Mexican accent tinged her words. Rachel smiled and nodded. "Miss Sunny is trying to get little Sawyer asleep. He's having a bad night. Welcome." She waved her inside and smiled.

Rachel could hear the fitful cries of a little boy upstairs. Sunny had written little vignettes about her son in many of her emails. She was divorced and the single mother of an active three-year-old, which only made her disease more heartbreaking. Sawyer needed a healthy mother. Rachel was determined to see he had one.

"I'm Noella, the housekeeper and cook. Follow me. I take you to your room. I can see you are tired." The woman, wearing a green dress uniform and white apron, took the largest of the suitcases from Rachel and lead the way toward the curving staircase. Just then the child upstairs began screaming for a drink of water.

Noella paused on the bottom step, shook her head and once again whispered, "I think I should take care of little Sawyer when he's like this. It's too much stress for Miss Sunny, but I say nothing."

At the top of the steps, Noella turned left. "This is Miss Sunny's wing." She gestured with her hand as she tiptoed down the thick carpeted hallway. "You have the room across from Miss Sunny and little Sawyer," Noella whispered before opening the door and tiptoeing into the room.

Rachel followed the housekeeper into the bedroom illuminated by lamps on either side of the white bed. The walls were covered with yellow and pink daisy wallpaper. The drapes at the two windows were white. "This was Miss Sunny's room when she was growing up." Noella turned on the lamp on the white desk, further illuminating the room. A yellow love seat welcomed. So did the vase of yellow and white daisies on the desk between the windows.

"The room is lovely."

The housekeeper's eyes softened. "I made everything fresh and welcoming for you. *Sí?* A box arrived for you yesterday. I took the liberty of unpacking it and placing the books and journals on your desk."

Rachel thumbed through the medical journals and books, making sure Grace had packed all she'd asked for and, of course, her dearest friend had. There was an envelope she'd open later, when she was alone. "Thank you, Noella. I've worked very hard doing extra research about Sunny's leukemia." She pivoted in the housekeeper's direction and smiled. "I have hope."

Noella crossed herself. "*Sí,* we need hope. I pray for my Sunny every day."

"I've been praying, too. Praying and developing a wellness plan to make her stronger for the next round of chemotherapy."

The housekeeper nodded and wiped a tear. "Good…good. She's not as weak as she was two months ago when her chemo ended. Even so, she's like a shadow of our Sunny."

"I've helped other patients become stronger. My goal is to do the same with her."

"Thank you. She's like my daughter, you see. I carried her into this house when her parents brought her home from the hospital. Her proud papa carried in his son." Noella blinked several times as if trying to gain control of her emotions. She cleared her throat. "Miss…Miss Sunny gave me your dietary requirements. I have food in the refrigerator labeled with 'sugar free' notes. My sister, Juanita, is diabetic, too. She struggles with her sugar levels. She eats too many tortillas, but I say nothing."

"You're most kind. I'm sorry to put you to so much trouble. I can do my own cooking while I'm here."

Noella appeared insulted. "I have cooked for this family since Mister Sawyer Blackhawk and Colleen were expecting the twins. No one has complained in the twenty-nine years I've been here."

Oh dear, wrong move. "I'm sure you're a fantastic cook. Why else would the family have kept you on all these years? I only offered to cook to save you some work. This large house must keep you quite busy."

The snubbed woman wiped a tabletop with her white apron. "I am very organized. You will see in your time here."

"I'm sorry, Noella. I didn't mean to cause offense." Getting off on the wrong foot with the family's longtime housekeeper wasn't the best way to create a harmonious atmosphere for her patient.

"I will cook for you. *Sí?*" She fixed her determined gaze on Rachel.

Ah, here was a defining moment in what she hoped would be a friendly, working relationship. Rachel smiled. "I love Mexican brown rice and chicken."

"Tomorrow I make for you." The housekeeper nodded, seemingly appeased. "You will eat it. *Sí?*"

"Absolutely. I'll be looking forward to it. I usually eat a light snack before I go to bed to keep my glucose levels even throughout the night. Would you mind if I raided the refrigerator later?"

Noella headed for the door. "My kitchen is always open. Just clean up after yourself. I want no dirty dishes in my sink. Miss Sunny is usually up by nine. I think she should sleep later, but I say nothing."

Rachel unpacked her clothes and put them away before heading for her longed-for shower. Her adjoining yellow bath was stocked with lots of plush towels and pretty soaps. In the shower, hot water sluiced down her body, stinging her sunburned shoulders.

The naked man's words came back, the sensuality of his voice haunting her. "Put some aloe on your shoulders tonight. Your skin's hot." She leaned her head back, rinsing her hair and recalling the sensations of that kiss. Mercy, the things that man's lips and tongue did to her mouth. Would she ever be kissed like that again?

****

Getting the cruiser to the Triple-S Ranch was simple. Getting more than six feet of drunken deadweight out of the cruiser, while staring at that red Beetle convertible parked under the crepe myrtle, wasn't. What in blue blazes was *she* doing here?

An uneasy feeling niggled at his gut. Why would the young woman with the big baby blues be parked in front of his house? It wasn't as if she'd picked his address from his pants' pocket, seeing as how he wasn't wearing any at the time. Plus, she'd need the security code to get through the gates. He closed his eyes, muttered a curse and accepted the inevitable: Sunny's new nurse.

After depositing Jackson on the sofa in the den, he knocked on Noella's door. The housekeeper clasped the lapels of her ancient chenille robe together when she opened her door. *"Sí*, Master Storm, what is it?"

"I brought Jackson home. He's sleeping in the den."

She straightened her shoulders and crossed her arms into her usual stance of annoyance. He'd seen it many times growing up. "Drunk?"

"Yes, ma'am. He was crying in his beer about Sunny."

Noella crossed herself and shook her head. "They should have married, our Sunny and Jackson Cole. His love for her is strong. He's ten times better than that worthless *mofeta* she married. Thank you for telling me. I'll take care of Jackson in the morning. Poor man. He's heartsick, but I say nothing."

"Whose red car is out front?"

"Rachel, Miss Sunny's new nurse."

Storm swore and ran a hand through his long black hair.

"Is that any way to talk?" Noella slapped his side with her robe's fabric belt and then crossed herself again. "You be polite to Rachel. You show that young lady the manners Noella teach you. *Sí?*"

"Do I have a choice?" He reined in his temper at Noella's sour expression. "You know I had reservations about hiring her. All that holistic mumbo-jumbo. Massages for cancer." He snorted. "Acupuncture, for God's sake."

So her name was Rachel. Yeah, the name fit—feminine, soft, delicate. He could still feel the softness of her lips and did a mental head slap. He'd kissed Sunny's nurse. Just how was he going to handle this fine state of affairs?

Noella's eyebrows shot up. "I don't care for your attitude, young man. How would you like to fix your own meals?"

"Blackmailer," he grumbled.

"Miss Rachel brought hope into this house tonight. She told me herself she has hope for our Sunny. I feel it already. It radiates from her like heat from an oven. There's something about her. You will sense it, too, once you meet her. She has…" Her hands fluttered as if searching for the right words. She patted her heart. “She has deep kindness, a goodness of the soul. I sense this.”

He leaned a shoulder against the doorjamb and studied the housekeeper’s face. She’d nail his hide to the barn door if he shared what happened earlier. Worse, she wouldn’t cook for him for a month, and he did enjoy eating. Noella was right. There was definitely *something* about the woman he’d kissed on Longhorn Road, but he doubted it was the same worthy quality the housekeeper was referring to. “I hope she’s good for Sunny. Hope she takes care of her the way she should.”

Noella put her hands on his forearms. “That’s the real issue here, isn’t it, my son? You think it’s *your* job to take care of us. Especially, your sister and her child. You resent that someone else might take over your job as caregiver.”

“No, that’s not true.” He looked over her shoulder to the television playing in her sitting room, trying to calm himself. How did she know? Noella always identified what was going on in his mind, almost before he did. It was eerie and damned annoying.

“Isn’t it? From the time your mother left, you became everyone’s protector. Almost as if you took care of us, were perfect for us, we wouldn’t leave you the way she did.” Her dark eyes bore into his, making him feel prickly in his own skin.

“That’s bullshit.” Noella’s eyebrows rose when his vocabulary turned too colorful for her tastes. “Sorry, ma’am…nonsense.”

She squeezed his arms and smiled. “Oh? And is it nonsense that from the time your mother left, I never had to carry in the groceries by myself? Hmmm? Even now, you always manage to be nearby when I come back from shopping.”

He shrugged as if it were no big deal. She was right, of course, but he’d never admit it.

“When I am sick, who brings me a cup of tea? Who drives me to the doctor?”

“That’s only because you’re too stubborn to go.”

“Son, don’t deny your caring nature. It doesn’t make you weak for one moment. You are as strong as any two men. You are intelligent and you keep this place profitable. Your ranch hands hold you in high regard. No one takes care of his animals like you do. These are qualities to take pride in. *Sí?* Take pride also in that you care deeply for those around you. Too many men are self-centered. You, my handsome one, are not."

She'd chipped away at his exterior, and his defenses came down. "It's just that I've taken care of Sunny all my life, especially since she left that cheating husband of hers."

"Yes, you brought her home two days before she delivered little Sawyer. Her spirit was broken, wasn't it?" Noella shook her head and clucked her tongue. "So sad to see her suffering, but you forced her to go on. Also, her little *bambino* brought her happiness again."

"He's brought us all happiness. Something we needed after Dad died. Guess it's no secret little Sawyer is more than my nephew. He's like my own son. I was with her in the delivery room. The doctor put that squalling, wiggling child in my hands, and it was instant love."

"You'll make a good father one day."

Storm shrugged. "Not since I've broken things off with Pilar." A jab of painful regret aimed straight for his gut. He still cared for her to a degree, even though he couldn't handle her tirades and cheating. "Besides, she didn't want to have children. She was afraid it would spoil her figure."

"Hunh! How can you spoil the shape of a nasty stick?"

"Let's not argue over my ex-fiancée...again. I believe the topic of our conversation was this new nurse of Sunny's." Noella had never made her feelings toward Pilar a secret. She thought Pilar was spoiled and self-consumed. Too bad it had taken him so long to see it himself.

"Rachel will be good for all of us. You'll see." She favored him with a smile and a pat on his cheek.

"I doubt she'll be good for me." Then, just as he'd done since he was young, he gave her a hug and a kiss. "Good night, Momma Noella. Sleep well."

Chapter Three

Rachel was in yellow cotton pajamas, combing out her wet hair when she remembered Grace's envelope. She tore it open and sat on the desk chair to read it.

Hi Rach,

Bad news, I'm afraid. Kyle broke your dining room window to get inside your house. I reported it to the police, who dusted all over for fingerprints—including the commode lid the idiot left up. They got a little pissy with me when I refused to tell them where you were, but I was being honest since I knew you were traveling.

Kyle tossed everything from your desk, no doubt looking for clues to where you'd gone. Good thing you'd put all your important papers in a lockbox at the train station, where only I can get to them. I'm sorry to tell you, he broke your Grandma Emma's blue vase and matching bowls you loved so much and slashed your favorite chair with a knife. That's how I know it was Kyle in one of his rages.

Text me when you get to the ranch and read this. Love you.

Grace

Rachel's heart sank. Oh, Kyle, when will you leave me alone and move on to someone else? She tugged her cell phone from her purse and sent Grace a text telling her she was safely at the ranch. She asked if Grace had the window replaced and how much Rachel owed her. Laying her cell on her nightstand, she scooped up her comb to finish untangling her hair. There was a soft knock at her door.

Comb in hand, she opened the door and came face-to-face with her new patient, Sunny Abbot. As expected, she was bald, thin and pale, but her wide smile beamed her inner warmth and beauty. Her dark eyes, now devoid of lashes, held what appeared to be pain and dread.

Sunny took Rachel's hands and squeezed them. "I'm so glad to finally meet you. I know it's late, but I wanted to welcome you to the Triple-S." She strolled into the room. "Did you find everything you needed?"

"Yes, thank you. You have a lovely home."

"It's a tomb." Sunny shoved her hands into the pockets of the white terrycloth robe that nearly swallowed her and shrugged. "Sorry. Don't mind me. I'm in a mood tonight. I think that's why Sawyer couldn't relax enough to go to sleep."

"Children sense our moods. I'm sure with you being sick, he's become more intuitive."

"Yes, and it breaks my heart to put him through this." Her thin hand fluttered to her scalp. "Having a bald mother has to be scary for him."

Rachel placed a hand on Sunny's arm. "When you hug him and whisper words of love, do you think he cares you're bald?"

Sunny shrugged and swiped at a falling tear.

"So tell me, why did you call this house a tomb?" She meant to get to the bottom of Sunny's negative remark.

Her patient started roaming around the room. "Because everyone in this house whispers now, as if my diseased body can't handle normal noise." Pulling back one of the white drapes, Sunny gave a quick glance to the darkness of the night. "It's so damned quiet here that I almost welcome Sawyer's tantrums." She smiled and tilted her head. "Almost.

"This was my room growing up. I was pregnant with Sawyer when I moved back here, so I took the suite of rooms across the hall since it had a nursery on the other side of the bathroom." Sunny pulled the drapery back again and looked out. "I used to climb out this window onto the branch of that big ol' live oak and shimmy down to meet Jackson, my childhood sweetheart."

She turned to Rachel and smiled. "Oh, the antics we used to pull. My daddy threatened to tan my hide many a time, but he was more bark than bite, especially with me. My brother's just like Daddy in that regard. He explodes and simmers, but he's harmless. Don't let his bluster intimidate you."

"I won't. I'm a nurse, remember? I'm used to male doctors flexing their egos."

Sunny laughed. "Fewer men have egos as big as my brother. He thinks he can boss everyone around. Still, for all that, he's a loving man. I depend on him more than I should, I suppose, but he's one of the few men in my life who's never let me down. Although he can be a bit of a tyrant. 'Rest,' he commands. 'Keep the house quiet for Sunny,' he orders."

Sunny turned and strode to the love seat, picked up a yellow and pink-striped throw pillow and fluffed it before flinging it back onto the love seat. "I *swear* the quiet in this house will drive me batty. Noella won't even play her mariachi music anymore. I grew up dancing and stomping to that lively beat." A harsh bark of laughter escaped Sunny's lungs. "She's even taken to tiptoeing through the house. Can you believe it?"

Well, Rachel's first order of business was certainly evident. She'd dispel the tomb image tomorrow. No matter what this brother and the housekeeper said, she'd fill the house with music and laughter.

"They're all natural responses when you don't know what to do or how to handle a situation. I gather Noella loves you very much." She was pleased to see a show of spirit. If Sunny could complain, she could fight.

"Yes, Noella raised my brother and me, especially after Mother left. Storm and I were loud, rambunctious twins, and Mother was too high-strung to put up with us. Thank God we had Daddy. He was the best."

"Mine was, too." A stab of pain pricked her heart. Thinking of her father, who'd died a year ago, still brought sadness. "I'm sure your mother's leaving was hard on you."

"It was hardest on my brother, I think. He had nightmares for a long time afterward."

"How old were you when she left?"

"Five." Sunny fussed with the daisies and pulled one out of the vase to smell it, twirling it in her hand. "I barely remember her. My only image is of her being all dressed up, hurrying out the door and blowing us kisses. She spent a lot of time elsewhere." She shrugged her narrow shoulders. "My fear is I'll leave my son before he's old enough to form lasting memories of me. Will Sawyer suffer the way Storm did, I wonder?"

Rachel's heart twisted at Sunny's words. She *had* to do all she could to help Sunny. "Then we have to work doubly hard to see that doesn't happen."

Sunny swiped at a tear and nodded. "You'll meet my brother, Storm, tomorrow. He runs the ranch."

"How is he handling your illness?"

"Not well. Everyone around here acts as if this were the land of the walking dead. I hate it. I want my life back." Finally, as if she'd run out of steam, Sunny flopped onto the love seat. "You've looked at my medical records. What do you think?"

"Well, I've studied your records closely. Your doctor's office was very cooperative in faxing me everything I requested—lab reports, biopsies, bone marrow reports and peripheral blood smear reports. From what I see, your specialist has followed proper protocol." Rachel sat cross-legged on the bed, facing Sunny.

She ran the comb through her damp hair. "I want to change your routine and diet. You know this. We've discussed it."

Sunny nodded. "We have an appointment with my oncologist at nine tomorrow morning."

"Good. I'll want him to go over the treatment plan I've developed. I'm not a replacement for your medical team. I'm an addition. I do nothing without the approval of your doctor."

"That was one thing my brother insisted on. He's a little leery of your methods."

"Understandable, I'd say. There are a lot of quacks out there in the nontraditional medical field. One does need to be cautious. I've always insisted the doctor knows what I'm doing with the patient at home."

Sunny aimed worried eyes on her. "I'm afraid I'm running out of time. What's your opinion?"

"Well, I might have thought that initially, but"—she shook her comb at Sunny—"if you can come into my room, stomp around and throw a bit of a tirade, tossing pillows and bitching about things around the house, I'd say you're a fighter."

At Sunny's widened eyes, Rachel smiled. "Sunny, a fighter *always* wins. Two boxers step into the ring. Two emerge. Both are victors because both had the guts to fight the fight. You're in the boxing ring of life with cancer. Do you have the guts to fight the fight?"

Her patient shoved up the sleeves on her robe. "Believe me, I'd love to fight someone right now. To feel alive again." She tilted her head to the side and smiled. "I did throw a bit of a temper tantrum, didn't I? God, it felt so good! You never once told me to sit down or be calm. Why was that?"

"All women need to bitch now and then. We were born with the bitch gene, after all." She shot Sunny a wry look.

Sunny laughed. "Oh, I'm going to enjoy having you here. I can tell we're going to be great friends."

Rachel walked over to Sunny and knelt by her knees. "Training for the fight won't be easy. You'll have days where you'll hate me for pushing you so hard. I've found the stronger a patient becomes, the better they can handle the fight. When I've pushed you too hard, I expect you to tell me. I need to know exactly how you're feeling."

She took Sunny's hand in hers. "Promise me. Promise me you'll give me honesty every moment of every day, so I know how you're feeling both emotionally and physically. In return, I promise I'll be honest with you. I promise you'll feel alive again."

Sunny blinked several times, her eyes locked on Rachel's. A slow smile curved her lips, and her face shone like the star she'd been named for. "Girlfriend," she purred, her Texas twang especially pronounced, "you've got yourself a deal."

****

Storm stepped onto the back porch, leaned against a wooden pillar and thought about the fancy nurse Sunny had hired. Rachel Dennison had more initials after her name than a bowl of alphabet soup. He'd checked her out online and then asked Jackson to do a background check. No disturbed quack was going to mess with his frail sister's health.

However, the squeaky clean nurse had checked out. Of course he'd had no clue what she looked like, no idea she had eyes as big and blue as the Texas sky or lips that... He groaned. God, those full lips were a guy's fantasy.

What did that recurring dream mean? She'd come to him, this petite woman who stirred his nighttime libido. He'd been so aroused the last three mornings he'd been in pain. Maybe that accounted for his behavior earlier out on the narrow road that ran past his ranch.

If only Nurse Rachel had the foresight to post a picture of herself on her Website instead of pages of information framed with flowers or palm leaves, maybe then he'd have known whom he was dealing with on Longhorn Road. He'd have kept his urges in check. He rolled his eyes. She'd seen him naked. That whole scene had to go down as one of life's most embarrassing moments. Parading down the road, damn near naked as the day he'd been born.

He ran a hand through his hair. He'd kissed her, for God's sake. Did more than kiss her—he'd nearly devoured her whole. Fact was, he'd been two heartbeats away from hauling that little morsel from her bug of a car and having raw, standing-up-against-a-tree sex. He felt himself harden and cursed. Why would a sane man respond to a strange woman like that? It had to be some odd lingering effects of that dream, that *damnable* dream.

Pistol, his overweight Basset hound, stood at his feet and whined. Storm took pity on the long-eared dog and scooped him up. "Come here, short stuff." He scratched behind Pistol's ears, earning him a canine lick. "Let's take a walk." With the dog held in his arms, he walked toward the orchard.

Near a plum tree, he set Pistol down and scooped up a handful of dry earth and smelled it. This was his land, his and Sunny's and little Sawyer's. However, Sunny was dying, growing weaker and paler. He slung the handful of dirt in anger.

Permitting himself the momentary weakness of panic and pain for what lay ahead, he drew a ragged breath. It wasn't often he allowed himself to feel like this, to hurt so deeply. Sunny, his sister, his twin, the person he'd shared the secrets of the womb with, was dying. He glanced up at the full moon and the bright clusters of stars. "I'd give up this ranch in a heartbeat to keep her alive." He made a fist and shook it at the sky. "You hear me, God? Why her? Why not me?"

Six months ago, in a tear-filled conversation, his beloved sister had begged for his promise to raise little Sawyer after…after….hell, he couldn't even think it. He thrust a hand through his hair. Life without his twin? Unthinkable. Unbearable.

Sunny feared her ex-husband, Mitch Abbot, absentee father of the century, would try to gain custody of Sawyer and his trust fund. He ground his back molars together. *Over my dead body. Little Sawyer belongs here on the Triple-S Ranch.*

Storm leaned back against a plum tree, reached up and plucked a ripe fruit. He sniffed the plum appreciatively before biting into it. Juice ran down his chin and he wiped it away with the heel of his palm.

One day soon he'd show his nephew how to climb one of these

fruit trees. He planned on teaching Sawyer everything about the ranch. The boy had been ten months old the first time Storm set him on a saddle in front of him. They still rode like that, nephew and uncle astride Lightning, while he pointed out things to Sawyer about the ranch. With every ounce of his being, he'd keep this child he loved here where he belonged.

To further secure Sawyer's future, the two siblings had their family lawyer draw up the proper papers and update their wills. Still, a sympathetic judge might overrule Sunny's wishes in favor of Sawyer's natural father. Mitch was good at playing the victim. Wasn't that how he'd ensnared good-hearted Sunny?

Less than a year after their hasty marriage, Sunny was pregnant, but the bloom of her pregnancy was soon erased by the shadows of a wandering husband. When their father suddenly passed away, she came home alone for the funeral.

Late on the night of their father's burial, Storm had pried the truth from Sunny. She was miserable. Mitch was taunting her with details of his affairs. Promising not to beat her husband to a pulp, Storm moved his sister home the following day, two days before Sawyer was born.

In many ways, Sawyer was his son. He'd walked the floor with him many a night when he was fussy. He'd held the child's chubby hand when he made his first awkward steps. Promising to raise Sawyer was no great sacrifice, for he dearly loved his nephew.

Even so, Storm's promise to Sunny had put him in an unpredictable situation with Pilar. Pilar Fontaine, the woman he'd been casually dating for two years, had suggested if the two of them were married, the courts would look more favorably on Storm's claim to Sawyer. Mitch was single, after all. If Storm had a wife, they could provide a more stable environment for Sawyer than Mitch. So they'd planned to marry.

While Storm enjoyed Pilar's company, his love for her wasn't as deep, as all-consuming as a man's should be for his wife or fiancé. That knowledge eventually made him regret his promise to Pilar, which was one of the reasons he ended their engagement—that and her cocaine using circle of rich friends, plus rumors of her seeing other men.

Granted, Pilar was used to a glossier lifestyle where she lived in

Austin—parties, plays, and oodles of expensive boutiques. That had him somewhat concerned. However, she assured him in many little and sensual ways he was the man for her. But could she give up her chrome and glass condo to live an isolated life on a ranch that generations of Blackhawk's had owned?

He hoped in time, she'd come to understand his reasons for breaking off their engagement. That she would find someone else who loved her lifestyle for he didn't.

Storm had already postponed the wedding once when Sunny was hospitalized with complications from her chemo. She was so weak, the doctors weren't sure she'd survive. Pilar accused him of always putting his twin first.

Then there were the vision dreams of a blonde with sky blue eyes. The woman in a little red car, who had snagged his attention.

He laughed, recalling Rachel's quip that a French beret would be enough to hide his manhood. Nurse Rachel had spirit. He'd give her that. Recalling the way her trembling hand kept sliding under her skirt, probably in search of a hidden weapon, he'd guess she was cautious, too. Not with her kisses, though. No, she wasn't cautious with them. She'd been sensually devastating.

While he, on the other hand, had been reckless for kissing a complete stranger. Up until four days ago, he'd been engaged. If he ever married, he had every intension of being a faithful husband. There would be no affairs for him. He wouldn't be like his mother. No, what happened out on Longhorn Road was the foolhardy action of a man on the rebound—merely an interlude.

He pushed himself away from the tree and glanced toward the house. Pistol, who'd been sleeping at his feet, stood and yawned as he stretched. Storm bent to scratch the Basset's ears. "No use hiding, Pistol. Some mistakes you just have to face." He headed for the house, hoping he wouldn't have contact with the blue-eyed mistake until morning.

Storm heard off-key singing when he opened the back door. He quietly toed off his boots in the mudroom before stepping into the kitchen.

An open laptop sat on the wooden kitchen table. Beside it was a mug of steaming tea. On the counter, a loaf of wheat bread rested next to a jar of peanut butter. Protruding from the opened refrigerator was a cute behind, covered by baggy yellow pajama bottoms, wiggling to the beat of the song she sang. *"Shot through the heart and you're to blame, you give love a bad name."*

The off-tune singing switched to humming, but that perfectly rounded bottom continued to wiggle. "Pickles...pickles. Surely there are pickles in this huge refrigerator. Maybe some of those sweet little Gherkins. Oh, look, cottage cheese. *You give love a bad name..."* The off-tune singer extracted a container from the crowded contents of the refrigerator, absently reaching out to set it on the counter.

Sneaking up behind her in his stocking feet, he placed a hand on the top edge of the open door of the refrigerator and leaned over her bent body.

She moved a pitcher of orange juice. "Okay, pickles, where are you hiding?"

"Check behind the milk."

Rachel yelped and spun around, her hand to her heart. Her big blue eyes opened impossibly wide. "You! Wha...what are *you* doing here?"

He held out his hand. "Hello, Rachel. I'm Storm Blackhawk, Sunny's twin brother."

"You…you're Sunny's brother? No freakin' way! Don't you *dare* touch me." She made a fist and had the audacity to shake it under his nose. He didn't know whether to laugh or paddle that cute behind she'd been wiggling earlier. "You…you just keep your hands and your lips to yourself. You…you naked, kissing bandit."

Storm leaned his head back and laughed. "Well, I'm not naked now. And just how do I classify as a bandit? I didn't steal anything from you."

Rachel fisted her hands on her hips, leaned in and narrowed her eyes in such an appealing way he was overcome with a keen desire to kiss her softly and slowly, the kind of kiss that made you sigh partway through it. "You *stole* a kiss from me." Her eyebrow arched. "Or have you forgotten?"

He smiled, his hands itching to touch her. What man walking the face of this earth could forget a kiss like the one they'd shared earlier? "Is it called stealing when the woman gives as good as she got?"

Rachel shook her fist again. "Back up, buster. I'll not be kissed like that again."

"I was right. All that hair is glorious hanging loose and free." He reached out, twirling a long strand of silk around his fingers. God help him, but she was a charmer. He held a long curl to his nose and inhaled her floral shampoo; a sexual vision slowly stroked his libido.

Why did this woman heat his hormones as if he were some randy teenager? He had to get himself under control. She was his sister's nurse. He figured a reminder about sexual harassment was due right about now. While he'd never resort to such predatory behavior, the urge to take one step toward her was overpowering. One step and he could capture those soft, luscious lips. He felt himself harden and, thinking better of the idea, he stepped back.

She skittered around him and away from the refrigerator. "I don't believe this! Of all the men for me to see naked on the road, it just had to be my patient's brother? *Un-beee-live-able!*"

"You see many naked men walking along the road?"

She narrowed her eyes again. "You kissed me."

"Yeah, well, every man makes a mistake now and again. Guess I should have at least waited until we were properly introduced." He winked. She sneered. "Look, all joking aside, I owe you an apology for my impulsive behavior earlier. I never should have kissed you." He could have sworn he saw steam roll out of her ears. Had he said something wrong?

Moving the gallon of milk aside, he reached in for the jar of pickles. He extended them to her. "Your pickles." She yanked the jar from his hand, pressing them to her chest. Her movement caused his gaze to drop.

He'd had a sense, out on Longhorn Road, of her having full breasts. Now that she was standing before him, braless and in thin cotton pajamas, his tongue nearly rolled out onto the floor. His gaze slowly traveled up to meet hers.

She must have understood his expression for she slowly shook her head, set the pickles on the table and turned to bolt from the kitchen. "I'm going to get my bathrobe. When I get back, Mr. Storm Blackhawk, you'd better be the hell gone."

Chapter Four

The sun gentled the Texas sky awake with her show of pinks and oranges intermingled with the dark grays of dawn, promising another hot day. Storm was talking to Red Pelton, his foreman, and three ranch hands, Ben, Eduardo and Randy, giving them orders for various projects.

Suddenly the crew's heads collectively swiveled to the left. Low whistles and snide remarks warmed the air already heating up for the day. Even Pistol panted louder than normal.

Storm narrowed his eyes. Rachel was jogging down the driveway wearing a tight red midriff-skimming top and black running shorts that should have been declared illegal. Damned if he could figure how a woman so short could have legs so long.

"Gentlemen, the woman you're gawking at is Sunny's new nurse. I'll expect you to keep your distance. She's here to take care of my sister." Their lewd responses did nothing to improve his mood.

Nor did hearing Jackson give a wolf whistle. Storm's narrowed eyes ricocheted off Rachel to his best friend. Minutes earlier, he'd seen Jackson stumble out of the house, grimacing at the sunlight and holding a hand over each ear, probably in an attempt to keep them from falling off his hungover head. Now Jackson's arms were extended across the roof of the cruiser, and he sported a mile-wide grin as he ogled Rachel, obviously enjoying the view.

Storm turned his irritated attentions back on his men. "Stop drooling over Rachel and get the hell to work. You're burnin' daylight." At their raised eyebrows, he barked, "Go on, now. I'm in no mood to be fooled with today."

Storm headed for Jackson and shot a dark look down the long driveway. He'd tossed and turned most of the night thinking of Nurse Rachel and that lush body of hers. Those eyes, those lips, and that long, silky, curly hair had haunted him in his sleep. Strange part of it all was she wasn't his normal type. He usually preferred tall, slender women—women more likely to do his bidding.

Rachel, the spirited little minx. He snorted. Imagine that spitfire shaking her fist under his nose, warning him to stay away. This was *his* ranch, by damn, and he'd do what he pleased. He'd never met a woman who both irritated and intrigued him from the instant he'd set eyes on her—until Rachel. He didn't like it one bit.

Jackson turned at Storm's approach. "*Who* the hell is that?"

"Sunny's new nurse." He stood next to his best friend.

"Damn. Makes a man want to get sick just so she can nurse him. She's one fine-lookin' woman." Jackson's eyes narrowed. "What's got a burr under your saddle? You've got that look."

"What look? How's your head? Figured you'd still be in the den, sleeping it off."

Jackson rolled his eyes and winced, the gesture obviously causing him great discomfort. "Sleep? With Noella jerking the drapes open in the den so the bright sunlight liked to fried my eyeballs? Then she set to running the vacuum around and around the sofa like she was some shark circling in for the kill."

Just to irritate his best friend, Storm hummed the famous *Jaws* beat.

"Mind turnin' down the volume on that?" Jackson shot him a dark look. "Between the Jack Daniels, the Coors and Noella's vacuum, my head is throbbing like a som'bitch. To say nothing of the dressing down she gave me about getting drunk...again."

He regarded Jackson, noting the sadness in his eyes. "She's got a point."

"Woman put me on notice. Me, the chief of police!"

"Don't sound so shocked. You know how Noella can be. What'd she say exactly?"

Jackson leaned a hip against the cruiser, folded his arms across his chest and studied the tops of his boots. Storm waited. This was Jackson's thinking pose. "She told me to stop feeling sorry for myself. That my problems were my own doing. If I hadn't been sowing my wild oats while Sunny was away at college, maybe she would have taken me seriously."

"Guess she was referring to Brittany Daniels."

"Yeah, and Katie Lyn and April." Jackson exhaled an audible sigh. "And all the rest."

"You *were* a dog." Storm's behavior hadn't been much better. He'd taken two years at Texas Tech along with Jackson. The wide supply of cute girls notwithstanding, both had decided the college life wasn't for them. By then the elder Sawyer Blackhawk's heart problems were slowing him down, and he welcomed Storm's return to take over some of the ranch operations. Jackson entered the police academy, hoping to make a career in law enforcement. Sunny finished her degree at University of Texas at Austin, graduating with honors.

The distant rhythmic pounding of running shoes caught Storm's attention. He laid his arms across the roof of the cruiser and watched Rachel come around the bend. She'd evidently run to the gates and turned around, giving her a two-and-a-half-mile run. Pistol whined, and for once Storm understood what the dog meant. The woman had a way of turning a man's head.

Jackson glanced Rachel's way and then back at Storm. "You got your eye on her, buddy?"

"I'm not ready for another woman," he replied absently, his attention totally focused on Rachel. She ran effortlessly; the sweat on her pale skin glistened in the bright morning sun. He wondered what it would be like to lick off that sweat. A man could spend hours...

Hell, he had to quit looking at her and fantasizing. It was so wrong. "Sunny has an appointment with her oncologist this morning."

"You takin' her?"

"No." He jerked his head in Rachel's direction. "She is."

"She's not married, is she?"

"You know she's not. You did the background check."

Jackson laughed. "Man, you can't take your eyes off her."

"Go to hell, Jackson." He turned and stalked off.

****

Problems plagued Storm all day. First, a needed shipment of high-grade barley for his private blend of horse feed didn't arrive. The water pump went out on the old pickup used for various chores around the ranch. He ordered a new one, but the pump wouldn't be in until tomorrow, which meant he'd have to let Red use his personal truck. Then, three head of cattle he'd bought at auction earlier in the week were diagnosed with Coccidiosis, a parasitic disease causing diarrhea and sloughing off of the lining of the intestine.

Storm popped two more antacid tablets and checked his

watch—five after four. Rachel and Sunny should have been home from the doctor's three hours ago. Where in the blue blazes were they? He snatched his cell from his belt and thumbed the screen—no messages and no missed calls.

The bright sun beat on his back and sweat rolled off him as he dug another fence hole. He wanted to enlarge the corral before the shipment of wild mustangs arrived. When he swung the pickax again, he cursed himself for not buying a new fence-hole digger after the old one stopped working last year. Three more holes. He had three more holes to dig before he started mixing concrete and setting in the posts.

When he swung the pickax again, his mind went back to his sister. If Sunny needed more tests, she'd call. She knew how he worried. Rachel's car looked new, so they shouldn't have had car trouble. He dialed Sunny's number for the fourth time. No answer.

"Boss, got two more steers down." Red took off his sweat-brimmed hat and wiped a forearm across his face.

Storm bit out a string of profanity, swinging the pickax into the rocky soil one more time. "They part of the bunch I just bought?"

Red nodded. "Good thing the new stock is still isolated from the rest of the herd."

"I called the vet earlier. He's on his way. Ought to be here in about thirty minutes." He stopped, then checked his cell again, even though he had it on vibrate. "I'm sorry I was so abrupt with you and the men this morning."

"Hey, if I had my eye on a gal, I wouldn't take kindly to guys starin' and disrespectin' her, neither."

Storm stared at his foreman for a few beats. "What gives you the idea I'm interested?"

"You ain't?"

He reached for the thermos of water sitting nearby and took a long swig. He poured some over his hair and shook it, hoping the water would help cool him off. Then he turned his gaze on Red. "Hell no, I'm not." The sound of a vehicle caught his attention. "Hope that's Rachel and my sister."

Red scratched the back of his neck. "I'd'a figured you was hopin' it was the vet, seein' as how you ain't got your eye on that pretty little gal."

"Go to hell, Red." He picked up his discarded T-shirt, shook it out and tugged it on.

Rachel parked her car under the crepe myrtle. Before she could open her door, Storm descended on her like a swooping falcon on his prey. "Where have you been?" He glanced at his sister, sound asleep in her seat, a pink scarf around her head.

Rachel got out of her little convertible and reached into the backseat for bags. "Shopping."

He took off his black work Stetson and slapped it against the side of his leg. Pistol, who was standing next to him, whined. "You mean to tell me you dragged my sick sister through stores?"

Rachel leaned over her car to retrieve another bag from the backseat, showing more than a little of her long, shapely leg. "Yes, I did." She turned and had the audacity to bat her eyes at him. "After all, someone had to push me around in a wheelchair so I could get my rest."

He grabbed her arm and hauled her up against him. "Don't give me that smartass attitude when you're dealing with my sister." His gaze automatically focused on Sunny. Quite simply, she was his mirror image—only her image was smaller, paler and frailer than he'd like. Her cancer was eating him alive, too. Worry over Sunny withered the landscape of his soul.

"I'm sorry. That was thoughtless of me. You love your sister very much. I can see that."

Storm released Rachel's arm, somewhat appeased. "From the moment of conception, it's been the two of us. My job in life is to protect her. Her job is to brighten my world. She is exactly as her name implies." He jerked his head in Sunny's direction. "How long has she been asleep?"

"About an hour." Rachel leaned across the car for one last package. He tried to avoid looking at the way her green skirt hugged her bottom like a pair of lover's hands. The thought made his palms itch and his mood darken.

"You must have bought out the stores." His gaze raked over her, taking in her appearance. Her long braid was tied with green ribbons, woven into the braid somehow. She wore a green sleeveless sundress that showcased her cleavage and trim waist—and firm backside. Red toenails peeked from white high-heeled sandals. Even in the heat she looked fresh and cool—and she heated *him* more than he liked to acknowledge.

He knew he was scowling when Miss Cool-as-a-Cucumber turned and had him in the grasp of her blue eyes, as if she were taking his measure. He set his Stetson back on his head. "If you'd have thought to call, I wouldn't have worried about her." He walked around the Beetle, opened the door and lifted his sleeping twin.

Sunny stirred in his arms as he carried her into the house. "I had a fabulous day, brother."

Rachel set the bags down so she could open the door to the house, and he carried Sunny inside.

"You could have called to tell me you'd be late. I was worried."

"I think Sawyer must have gotten in my purse and traded his toy phone for my cell. Kind of hard to call on a Mattel." Sunny's face was flushed. She'd probably gotten too much sun from riding so long in that damned convertible.

"What did the doctor say?"

"Lost six more pounds." She yawned and smiled. "My vitals are good. My cancer is still there. And I need to get drunk and have raw sex."

"Yeah, right. I'll take care of the getting drunk and having raw sex. Nurse Rachel is here to take care of the cancer. All you have to do is eat more and gain back those six pounds." He lithely carried her up the stairs.

Sunny poked him in the shoulder with a finger. "You're a bossy man." She held out her hand. "We got manicures."

"Great! I'm here worrying about you and you're getting your nails done."

She smiled again, and he took pleasure in seeing it. She'd been too serious of late; so had he. "We got pedicures, too." Sticking out her feet, she showed off blue toenails.

"Nice color." He wiggled his eyebrows, and she giggled.

"Oh, Storm, it was so good to do normal things again. Rachel insisted I ride in a wheelchair at the mall. We shopped, had fruit smoothies and got our nails done."

Rachel hurried around him to open the door to Sunny's room. She breezed in, dropping the bags and moving some of the throw pillows on Sunny's bed so he could lay her down. When she opened the drapes, afternoon sunlight poured in. "I want you to rest until dinner. I'm going to get you something to drink. Storm, can I get you anything cold?"

"Water would be fine. Thanks." He turned his attentions to his sister. "What did the doctor think of Rachel's treatment plans?" He sat on the edge of Sunny's bed, and she scooted over to accommodate him.

"Dr. Frey asked her oodles of questions. They talked a lot of medical jargon. Then he nodded and told me I was lucky to engage her. She has a way of making me feel alive."

"Then all the money we're paying her is worth it. I'm glad to see you smile again." He cupped her cheek. "You got some sun." Retrieving a light blanket from a chair, he covered her. "Tell me what you bought on your big shopping trip." He closed the drapes to put the room into darkness.

"A red bathing suit. All of mine are too big. Some shorts and tops. A cute pantsuit. Oh, and a remote control car and some books for Sawyer."

Rachel came in carrying a tray with two glasses and a steaming mug of tea. "Here you are, Miz Sunshine: green tea sweetened with honey and guaranteed to fill you with vim and vigor. Storm, here's your water." She sat the tray down and promptly opened the drapes.

"I just closed those." Storm wanted to irritate her. She sure as hell was irritating him.

She put her hands on her hips and shot him a defiant look. "And I just opened them. Sunlight is good for your sister. It helps elevate the mood."

He took a long drink of water. "By the looks of her face, she's had enough sun for one day."

Rachel walked over to examine Sunny's skin. "Yes, I see what you mean. I should have insisted she put on sunscreen. I won't let that mistake happen again."

"It better be the only mistake you make with my sister." He didn't like her cavalier attitude. Sunny needed protection from everything. Time to show Nurse Rachel who was running things around here. He set his empty glass on the tray, walked to the windows and closed the drapes. "Sunny needs the room dark so she can fall asleep."

He could read in Rachel's facial expression she wanted to tell him what she thought. Her eyes narrowed. That sensual mouth of hers was pinched. Her arms crossed under those full breasts, and one foot tapped in obvious annoyance. Why, he could swear steam was coming out of her ears. That fact pleased him greatly. Lordy, but she was a beauty with her cheeks flushed in high anger.

If glares could kill, he'd be stretched out on a marble slab at Van Snoot's Funeral Parlor. Rachel snatched her shopping bags, turned and stormed out of the room, her pointy chin angled high and that tight skirt switching and sliding so sensually over her hips, he wanted to groan.

"Why, brother, I think she turns you on." Sunny smiled as if she'd just uncovered some confidential information.

Chapter Five

Noella's promise of Mexican brown rice and chicken was the only thing prompting Rachel to get ready for dinner. Since the housekeeper was making it especially for her, she couldn't very well stay locked in her room or drive an hour for some pizza. No, she'd have to suffer through a meal with that overbearing, dogmatic, insufferable Storm Blackhawk. Until five days ago, he'd been engaged. No doubt he'd kissed her last night on the rebound.

Good Lord how she'd like to pop him in the jaw—and she abhorred violence.

Had the cowboy Romeo kissed every woman he'd come in contact with the last few days? Was he trying out women for a temporary replacement for the ex-fiancé? *The jerk.* She slammed her hairbrush on the dresser and sprayed on perfume. One word out of his mouth, and she was going to slug him.

Storm and the man she'd seen earlier turned from a large window overlooking Noella's rose gardens when Rachel entered the dining room. She was nearly bowled over by the combined power of their testosterone. Coming back from her run this morning, she'd seen the pair talking next to the police cruiser. She'd chosen to ignore them. Now, observing them up close, the pair seemed formidable, as if they felt they could handle anything or anyone.

Storm's eyes swept over her red silky blouse and tight black skirt. When his eyes landed on her new red strappy heels with ties that wrapped around her ankles and crisscrossed up to her calves, his eyebrows shot upward. "Well, don't you look lovely tonight?" She hadn't been expecting that, nor was she prepared for his smile and winking dimples to fluster her.

He looked handsome and virile in a black golfing shirt and tan khakis. It was an outfit that would have gone unnoticed on any other man. However, his build, his muscles, his power of movement made it eye-catching. His shoulder-length hair, combed straight back from his wide forehead, glistened blacker than his shirt. Dark eyes bore into hers as he lifted a glass of amber liquid to his lips.

"Thank you." She cleared her throat, hoping her voice didn't sound too breathless, too interested, which, of course, she wasn't.

Storm winked, almost as if he'd read her mind—the scoundrel.

"I'd like you to meet Jackson Cole. We've been best friends since we were riding tricycles. Jackson, this is Sunny's nurse, Rachel Dennison."

Jackson stepped toward her and extended his hand. His smile didn't reach his eyes, and for that reason she sensed sadness about him. Although he was slightly shorter and thinner than Storm, he gave one the impression of an old watch wound too tight, as though he kept his power tightly leashed. His blond hair was cut in a short military style. So this was the chief of police. Bet the crime level stayed low in *this* county.

"I'm honored to meet you, Miss Dennison, especially since you're here to help Sunny."

"Call me Rachel, please."

"I'd be honored, ma'am." Jackson's handshake was warm and firm. "You took Sunny to the oncologist today. What did he say? How's she doing?"

"I'm still alive and kicking." They all turned to watch Sunny enter, wearing the aqua pantsuit she'd bought earlier at the mall. She'd taken extra pains with her appearance, wearing large dangling aqua earrings, makeup and the fake eyelashes Rachel had talked her into buying. A white lace scarf was artfully tied around her bald head. "I heard you were coming to dinner. My, if you aren't a sight for sore eyes, you handsome rascal, you." She winked, and he offered a smile that reached his eyes.

Almost as if they were the only two people in the room, he went to Sunny and cupped her face with his hands. His eyes searched hers, speaking silent volumes of affection before he kissed her forehead. Then he enveloped her in his arms. His eyes closed and he breathed her name.

The scene was so painfully poignant, tears filled Rachel's eyes. Storm placed a hand on the small of her back, and she gazed up at him. "How long has he loved her?" she whispered.

"Since we were riding tricycles." He wiped her falling tear with the pad of his thumb. "You're very gentle-hearted, aren't you?" His voice was deep, sensual. Her stomach fluttered.

He was standing so close to her, his male scent eliciting a very female response. For the briefest of moments, she wanted to lean into him, which was *not* a good thing. Hadn't she promised herself not to get entangled with a man again? She glanced at the embracing couple, choosing to ignore Storm's question. "Then, why..."

"Life gets complicated. People make bad choices and pain happens." He studied his sister and then focused dark eyes on Rachel. "I take it the fake eyelashes were your idea."

By the tone of his voice, he wasn't being critical. She'd been prepared to handle critical and rude and overbearing, but not his gentleness. Rachel searched his face. Warmth shone from his eyes and, for the first time, she noticed wrinkles at their corners, no doubt from spending so much time in the hot Texas sun. She fought the urge to reach up to smooth them with a touch.

"Yes. The better a woman feels about her appearance, the stronger she feels. For cancer patients, feeling strong about *anything* gives them an added boost. In time, her hair and eyelashes will grow back. This is just a stop-gap measure until then."

He glanced at his sister again. "I see."

"Happiness makes us stronger. I talked her into buying some clothes that fit, too. Wearing clothes that hang on you is only a constant reminder you're sick. Better to feel pretty and alive, don't you think?"

Storm studied Rachel for several beats. "You focus heavily on the emotional side of the patient, don't you?"

"Aren't we ruled by our emotions?" She certainly was, especially at that moment, with the heat from his warm hand pressing into the small of her back. The smell of his cologne wafted over her, and his dark eyes regarded her intently.

He smiled and leaned over so his mouth was near her ear. "Great shoes, by the way."

She chuckled and looked in the opposite direction, hoping he wouldn't see her blush. "Sunny called them 'ho-red.' We laughed so hard when the shoe salesman fumbled, trying to tie the laces around my ankles and calves."

Storm glanced at her shoes again. She could have sworn she heard him mutter, "Lucky bastard."

Sawyer ran into the dining room from the kitchen. "Unkie Jackson!"

Jackson released Sunny and stooped to scoop the boy into his arms. "Hey, tiger."

"Mommy got me a 'mote contwol caw and two new books."

"Wow! You hit the mother lode!"

Noella carried in a salad bowl. "Oh, Miss Sunny, you look so pretty tonight."

"She looks beautiful." Jackson wrapped his arm around Sunny's waist, holding Sawyer in his other arm. How perfect the three of them looked together. Rachel had never played matchmaker before, but if Sunny had the attentions of a handsome man, what a boost that would be for her emotionally. Now, how could she bring these two together?

"You're smiling, and I swear it's positively dangerous." Storm's remark, next to her ear, feathered her hair. His hand swept up her back a few inches. A shudder went through her. His eyes narrowed and darkened at her response. Lord, but he was perilous to a woman's self-control.

Rachel stepped away from Storm's overwhelming presence. "Need some help carrying in the food, Noella?"

"Help is always appreciated. We're having Mexican brown rice and chicken tonight, especially for Rachel." Noella breezed through the kitchen door and Rachel followed.

Dinner was a festive occasion. Sunny was buoyed by Jackson's presence. Jackson could barely take his eyes off her. Several times he brought an empty fork to his mouth and never once seemed to notice he'd taken a bite of nothing. Storm was polite and genial, a side of him Rachel found charming. Bubbly Sawyer, king of the booster seat, entertained everyone.

Rachel took a sip of water. "The three of you seem close."

Jackson smiled and nodded. "We're the Texan version of the three musketeers. Have been since the first grade."

"Jackson practically lived here during the summers. He and Storm picked on me terribly. Me, the weak little female." Sunny's eyes twinkled.

Noella shook her head and chuckled. "I say nothing."

"Now, sister, you lie. I remember garter snakes in our beds. Worms in the toes of our sneakers. And salt in the Kool-Aid."

Jackson nodded. "I recall how she cut the back seam of my swimming trunks the day of a big pool party. I had no clue I was baring it all for the rest of the kids."

Rachel laughed. This was a new side of her patient. A good side. A strong side. Now all she had to do was resurrect the ornery girl who'd done these things.

Sunny's face turned wistful. "A party. We haven't had a party in so long. Not since my diagnosis."

"I think a party is an excellent idea. If I recall from your medical records, you have a birthday in a couple months or so." Rachel swung her eyes to Storm. "Why don't we plan a small party for the two of you to celebrate? Food, music, dancing, swimming."

"A Texas barbeque for our thirtieth birthday." Sunny looked at Storm. "Wouldn't that be fun?"

Storm's eyebrows furrowed in obvious concern when he looked at Rachel. "You don't think it would be too tiring for Sunny?"

"I think it would be great for her to be around family and friends. She'll be stronger by then. I'll see to it." If she had her way, Sunny would be much stronger, maybe even a few pounds heavier.

"Still, all the excitement of the preparations and…"

"Storm, please. A party!" Sunny pleaded with her eyes as well as her words."My life's been on hold for so long. I want to feel alive again."

"*Sí,* Master Storm. If Miss Sunny wants a party, she should have one. I think we should ask Pepe and his band to come play." Noella snapped her fingers over her head. "We could wear pretty clothes and dance. Oh, I'll let my hair down, *sí?*"

Storm raised his hands in surrender. "All right, I give in. I can't fight three determined women at once. No man's that strong."

Rachel held a spoonful of chocolate mousse in front of her lips. "Gee, not only is the man handsome, but he's smart, too." She quickly dropped her eyes and shoved the dreamy dessert into her mouth, if for no other reason than to keep her mouth from prattling on again. *Great!* Why had she said he was handsome? Maybe he hadn't picked up on it. Please let his mind be elsewhere.

"Well, well," Sunny purred. Rachel shot her patient a look universally understood by females, silently screaming *drop it, please!*

"You know we could always use a fourth musketeer, Rachel," Jackson said. She pivoted her blushing face on Jackson. He winked at her, causing her to blush more.

“Can I wear a mask, Unkie Jack? I wanna be a musket-ear, too.” Everyone’s gaze landed on little Sawyer. Laughter filled the dining room; the child’s lips and teeth were covered in chocolate mousse.

****

After dinner, Jackson, Rachel and Storm went outside to the patio to enjoy their coffee while Sunny gave Sawyer his bath. Rachel stretched out on a chaise lounge, obviously enjoying the easy banter between the two men.

Pistol waddled over and, after making three attempts to get his tubby tummy off the ground, jumped onto the foot of the chaise. He licked Rachel’s ankles, and for the first time in his life, Storm wished he were a dog.

Rachel laughed, a deeply lush, sensual laugh that stirred him. He closed his eyes for an instant as the memory of that dream flooded back. The blue-eyed woman laughing in the dream had touched him, not just physically, but all the way to the depths of his soul. He opened his eyes and watched her scratch behind Pistol’s ears. The dog rolled over, giving her access to his belly. When the dog groaned, so did Storm.

Realizing he needed a diversion from staring at Rachel, Storm stood to light the citronella candles and tiki torches. The sunset beyond the stables momentarily drew his attention. It was his favorite kind—bright reds and oranges with streaks of purple. There was nothing like a Texas sunset with the sky so close and so large even a man born and bred here was made speechless by its grandeur. He loved it here, where his soul dwelled.

“Where are you from, Rachel?” Jackson slapped at a gnat. Storm regarded his best friend. He was a cool one, Jackson was. He knew very well where Rachel was from, having done a thorough background check on her.

“Yazoo City, Mississippi, known as the gateway to the Delta. Although I’m looking for a new home base.”

Jackson leaned forward, his hands dangling between his knees. “Yeah? How come?”

She lifted a shoulder. “I just feel it’s time to move on. My dad is gone now, and his estate is finally settled. My folks were divorced. Mom lives in Las Vegas with her new husband.”

“So, you thinking of moving there?”

Rachel shook her head. "No, my stepdad's not one of my favorite people. He's a mover and a shaker, very self-centered. Although being nearer to Mom would be nice. I'm a small-town girl in my heart. Six lanes of traffic snarls and garish lights aren't my style."

Jackson reached for his coffee. "I know what you mean. Rosefire is plenty big enough for me. Good place to raise a family."

"Do you have children?" Maybe he was divorced like Sunny.

"Never been married, so there are no children I know of. I have dreams of kids, though, and a great love for a certain three-year-old."

"I see."

Storm looked at Rachel. "How long ago did your dad die, if you don't mind my asking?"

"A little over a year ago. Car accident." She turned a woebegone expression on him.

"Losing a parent is tough. I'm sorry for your loss. Sunny and I mourned greatly when Dad died. We leaned heavily on each other." He jerked his head toward Jackson. "And we had Jackson and Mama Noella. Soon we had little Sawyer to help us. Did you have someone to help you through the grieving process? Family?"

"Some friends." She looked down at her clasped hands. "Also a friend who turned out not to be a friend." She pushed her hair back. "If that makes any sense."

"I see." Although he really didn't. Was there some mystery there? "What about family?"

She shook her head. "No. My older brother, my only brother, was killed in Iraq. Drew's death changed my parents. Dad turned into a bit of an anti-war activist, making speeches about it at the dinner table every night. Mom was so heartbroken she turned into a person I didn't recognize, for a while. She left us six months later to 'find herself.' I'd just graduated from high school and chose to stay with Dad. He and I were very close, and I miss him terribly." She looked at Storm, and a measure of pain and understanding passed between them. Both had been left behind by a mother who valued freedom more than family obligations. Both had cherished their fathers.

Storm ran a hand through his hair. "Are you and your mom

close now?"

Rachel nodded. "We're getting there. We went through a rough spell for a while. I was angry. Felt she'd turned her back on us when we needed her. As I matured, I realized she was merely coping with her grief over losing Drew. She just chose to grieve in a destructive way, but she's doing better. We're doing better—she and I. Mom has many regrets, but she has to live with them."

"Living with regrets can be tough. It's good the two of you have reconciled. I'm sorry to hear about your brother. We've lost a lot of good men and women in Iraq and Afghanistan." Storm gulped a few sips of coffee. "Lives have been changed forever. I'm sure losing your brother was a hard thing for your family to endure."

"For sure." She swiped at a falling tear and drew a ragged breath. "Drew and I were close. He was a very protective older brother. Much like you are with Sunny. First Drew, then Mom, for a while, and now Dad. My coping mechanisms are rather beaten and dented. I simply fell apart when Dad died so suddenly in that car crash."

"I'm sorry, Rachel. Loss, no matter the form it takes when comes into our lives, takes something away from us. Not just the person we've lost, but a part of us, too. A piece of our souls. I miss my dad, too. He was a good man. Taught me a lot about life and this ranch."

"Sunny holds your dad in high regard, too." Rachel turned her attention to Jackson as if she couldn't bear to continue their vein of conversation. "Sunny looked great this evening, didn't she?"

"Fabulous. She's still thin though." Jackson raised his coffee cup to his lips.

"Give me a couple weeks with her. I've changed her diet. You know, I think you're very good for her. She's more animated with you here." Rachel swung her shapely legs off the chaise. Storm tried not to stare at her thin ankles in those "ho red" heels…or those siren red toenails…or those shapely calves.

Her voice tore his fantasy-hazed mind from her legs. "The happier a patient is, the stronger they fight. They've got more reasons to live. You could be a big help. Women love a little romance."

"Jackson here has a way of flubbing up romance."

"Kiss my ass, Blackhawk." Both men chuckled, good friends that they were.

"Make sure you seek Sunny out before you go. Cancer patients need the healing of another human's touch, a hug, a kiss." She favored Jackson with a dazzling smile.

"She keeps pushing me away. I keep actin' like an ass."

"That you do." Storm raised his coffee cup in a mock salute. Jackson made a crude gesture. Both men chuckled again. Their history ran deep.

Rachel scratched behind Pistol's long ears. "Be gently insistent, Jackson. Show her how much she means to you. She's just scared. This cancer is enough to scare even the strongest person."

"I'll try. I've got a lot of makin' up to do with that woman. Don't know if she'll give me the chance. I didn't handle the news of her cancer well. Went on a drunken binge. Acted ten times the fool." He rubbed a hand over his face before turning to Storm. "Those mustangs still comin' tomorrow?"

"Yeah, around noon or after. Finally have the corral enlarged."

"Need some help?" Jackson took another sip of his coffee.

"I'd welcome another pair of hands. The mustangs are bound to be scared and full of unexpected moves when they're unloaded."

"Mustangs?" Rachel had Pistol on her lap, still scratching behind his ears. The Basset was in dog heaven.

"Yeah, after countless phone conversations and a hellacious mountain of governmental paperwork, I'm taking a delivery of ten head of wild mustangs for the Bureau of Land Management. Some parts of the state are having a bad drought, the free range being one of them. I offered to let some graze here until fall, maybe longer if needed. Rain's been good to us here this year. Grass is plentiful."

"Fascinating. I can help if you're shorthanded. I've ridden for years. I wouldn't know all your ranch hands do, but I'd be better than nothing. I follow directions well."

Jackson chuckled. "I just bet you do. Hear that, Storm?"

He scowled at his best friend before looking at Rachel. "Do you have jeans and boots? I don't want you around my men in those skintight clothes you wear for running."

She beamed a smile. "Sure do. I'll get my run in early, shower and change. I'll work with Sunny for an hour and make sure she's fine. Wild mustangs, how exciting!"

Not nearly as exciting as thinking of her in a shower. His libido had snagged on that vision and refused to let it go. He narrowed his eyes and glared at the woman who'd had him in knots since she'd made that remark about the French beret out on Longhorn Road. Why her? Why not Pilar? Even the times he'd showered with Pilar, he hadn't been as aroused as he was at this moment. Damn the blonde-haired minx anyhow.

"Unkie Storm! I'm all clean fwom my baf." Sawyer streaked onto the patio wearing Sponge Bob pajamas, a book in his grasp and his hair still wet. Storm held out his arms for his nephew, who shot into them. He loved the comfort of this child on his lap.

If he'd married Pilar and she'd had her way, Sawyer would have been the closest he came to being a father. Pilar made it quite clear getting "big with child" and "changing disgusting diapers" was not in her future. Thank God, all that was no longer as issue. Eventually, he'd meet someone else who wanted children and him exclusively.

"Mommy got me a new Georgie book." Sawyer wiggled and grunted and settled into Storm's lap. He held the book in front of Storm's face, waving it back and forth. "Will you wead it to me?"

"I didn't hear the magic word." Storm gave the child a stern look.

"Oops. Sowwy. Will you *please* wead it to me?"

Sunny lowered herself into a chair next to Jackson. "Does Unkie Storm have a choice?" She laughed softly.

Jackson reached out and took her hand, bringing it to his mouth for a kiss. "You always were beautiful in the moonlight."

Sunny's eyes opened wide. "Well, aren't you just full of compliments tonight?"

Jackson winked. "Darlin', you ain't seen nothin' yet."

"Okay, grown-ups. Time to be quiet while I read *Curious George Goes to the Beach.*"

Sawyer laid his head against Storm's chest. "I wuv you, Unkie Storm."

Storm kissed the child's dark hair, inhaling the smell of the child's shampoo and savoring that sense of contentment he always felt when holding this little fellow. "I love you, too, son."

Chapter Six

Sawyer fell asleep during Storm's second reading of the new book. The child's gentle, nasal breathing brought a sense of peace to the summer night. "Want me to carry him up to his bed, sister? Give you and Jackson some time alone."

"Yes, please. I think it's about time Jackson and I had a long talk." Their hands were joined and both were smiling.

Storm stood, holding the sleeping boy. "Rachel, I've a hankering for a moonlight ride. How long has it been since you rode a horse? Could I interest you in joining me?"

"I haven't ridden since Dad died. Yes, I think I'd enjoy a ride." She stood also, a feeling of excitement fluttering in her belly. Time alone with Storm…was this a good idea or not? "I'll need to change clothes."

"Me, too. I'll meet you at the stables then." Storm flashed a smile, obviously pleased she'd agreed to accompany him.

"Sounds great." When they reached the top of the steps, she turned to Storm. She pressed a gentle kiss to Sawyer's forehead. The child was limp as a ragdoll in his uncle's strong arms. "Need any help tucking him in?"

"No, thanks. I've got the drill down pat."

Rachel hurried into her room and changed into jeans, a pink shirt and boots she'd bought earlier that day. The boots were a little stiff, being new, but she figured they'd loosen up eventually. She bent over at the waist and ran a brush through her long hair, brushing out tangles. She was tired of taking care of it. Maybe the next time she took Sunny to the doctor, she'd get it cut and donate it to Locks of Love. She sprayed perfume on her neck, out of habit, surely not because she expected to get close enough to Storm Blackhawk for him to get a whiff. She rolled her eyes. Perish the thought.

When Rachel passed through the kitchen on her way to the stables, she grabbed a handful of sugar cubes for the horses. Outside lights were blazing at the stables, softly illuminating the tall man who was deftly saddling a mare. She stopped for a minute to watch the way Storm interacted with the horse. Their exchange seemed like a gentle conversation, as if he were catching up with an old friend. She smiled at the charm of his actions. A man who loved animals and small children couldn't be all bad.

Storm turned to watch Rachel as she approached. He'd changed into jeans and a white T-shirt, his black Stetson was settled on his head. He handed her the reins. "Rachel, meet Princess. She's a good, gentle mare, but she's responsive. She'll keep up with the best of them if you give her a chance."

She extended an open hand with a sugar cube on it. "Hello, Princess. My, aren't you pretty."

Storm chuckled. "Flattery and sugar—you know how to get to a horse's heart."

"Well, all girls love flattery and sugar. Right, Princess?" She patted the mare's neck, and the horse nickered and nodded. What a mundane remark to make. Now he probably thinks you're fishing for compliments. She cut her gaze to Storm and was relieved to see he was busy with his horse. She needed to relax. This was merely going to be a short ride.

"Princess's eyes are unusual, quite beautiful." She cocked her head to the side and rubbed the horse's velvety soft nose. "Her eyes have an almost human quality to them. They're blue. She's Appaloosa, isn't she?"

Storm was smoothing a blanket over his mount, a large midnight black stallion with a jagged sliver of white on his forehead. "Yeah, she is. Her breed was almost wiped out by the U.S. Calvary years ago." He lifted a saddle off a rack and slung it across his mount's back as if it weighed nothing.

"Why would the Calvary kill off horses?" She glanced at Princess and rubbed the mare's face. "I mean, wouldn't the Calvary *need* horses? Seems rather counter-productive. Like, well, like if I, being a nurse, killed off my patients."

Storm yanked on the cinch. "Yeah, I get your point. You're right about it not making much sense. From what my dad told me, the Calvary chased the Nez Perce Indians into the Bear Paw Mountains up in Montana and then slaughtered many of their Appaloosas. He was half Nez Perce and half Comanche, my dad was."

"I thought I detected traces of Native American in you and Sunny."

"Our cheekbones give us away, don't they?" He flashed her a smile.

"Yes, that and your dark straight hair and dark eyes. Although you have a fierceness about you. I don't detect it in Sunny, maybe because she's ill."

"Sunny is very gentle in her own way. I'm more like my dad. Focused. Determined. Hell bent on having my way. Just like he was. My dad had dreams. Visions. I've started having them, too, now that he's gone. Can be damn disconcerting at times."

She'd read about this while she was treating a patient in South Carolina with Comanche heritage. The patient was very focused on walking the Red Way, as the Elders called it. As his nurse, she'd needed an understanding of Native American philosophies and traditions to effectively treat the whole person. She'd found their culture fascinating, spiritual and very connected to the earth.

She stepped closer. "Really? You mean you dream things and then they happen?"

Storm reached out and skimmed his knuckles down her cheek. A gentle gesture so in conflict with the fierce expression in his eyes. Her stomach quivered in response and her breathing quickened.

"Yes," he whispered. He quickly turned his back to her, and she was sure she heard him mutter he'd dreamed her. Surely she'd misunderstood.

"What about your mother? Was she Native, too?"

He turned to face her again, his facial expression different this time. "No. Irish. Dad went to Ireland to buy a prize stallion. He met our mother while he was there. Didn't buy the horse, but he brought her home to marry." He expelled a harsh bark of laughter. "He'd have done better with the horse. The woman broke his heart."

"Yours, too, I gather." She reached up and laid a hand over his heart. Touching patients this way was second nature to her, but the charge that went through her system just now was unexpected. She meant to pull away, but Storm's callused hand covered hers as if he didn't want to break the connection.

He stared into her eyes for a long time. She tried to gauge his stern expression, imagining she saw pain and dejection there. This man was hurting; she responded to that, healer that she was. "You have a way of touching a person's soul, Nurse Rachel. I'm not sure if I like that."

She'd made him uncomfortable. In working with patients, she'd learned when to back off. Now was the time to do so with him. She turned and placed a hand on his horse's muzzle. "Tell me, who is this handsome fella?" She held out a cube of sugar. The horse made one step toward her and took the cube from her outstretched hand.

"Mind your manners now, Lightning. Show the lady your good side." Lightning nudged Storm's shoulder. "Hey, careful!" The horse nudged the man again and backed him up a couple steps, and then the horse turned to Rachel, gently nuzzling her neck.

Rachel laughed and wrapped her arms around Lightning's neck. "He's gorgeous. What a personality he has."

"He's trying to claim you for himself, the big-feeling bag of bones." The horse nodded and whinnied as if he understood Storm's remark. Rachel laughed and returned to her horse, picking up the reins.

Storm asked, "Need me to give you a leg up?"

"No, I'm fine." She hoped she'd be fine; it had been a year since she'd last ridden. A sigh of relief escaped her after she settled somewhat gracefully into the saddle.

"I tried to adjust the stirrups for your height. How'd I do?" Storm wrapped a warm hand around her calf and checked the angle of her leg. "I figure you're about five four. Right?" He looked up at her and she nodded. "Stirrups are still too long, aren't they? Hold still. Gimme a sec." He made some adjustments and walked in front of her horse to do the same to the other side. "Better?" His hand slid up her leg a few inches, and her eyes closed with pleasure as warmth jolted up her leg to her core. Princess danced sideways a few steps. No doubt the horse was picking up on Rachel's hormonal vibes. When he asked if she was okay, she merely nodded.

Storm swung onto his horse in one easy, fluid motion. Old leather creaked. "Ready?" He smiled at her and resettled his hat on his head.

"Yep. You lead. I'll follow."

His smile broadened, deepening those dazzling dimples. "Now those are words every man wants to hear."

She laughed. "In your dreams, cowboy. I follow no man."

Holding his reins in his left hand, he clucked his tongue to set his mount in motion. "Most of our horses respond to verbal commands. I don't abide spurs being used on horses."

"Gee, guess I'll have to save my spurs for better things, then." Oh Lord, *what* had possessed her to say that? Like she even owned a pair of spurs; like she'd think to use them on…on… She shot a sideways glance at Storm. He'd stopped his horse and stared at her as if he'd been pole-axed or something. *Please, Lord, just let the earth open up and swallow me whole. It can spit Princess back out, but keep me and my big mouth buried in some deep cavern.*

"Woman, you have a way of making a man wonder." He looked at her for a couple more beats, shook his head once and set Lightning to walking. Princess obediently followed. Even though the moon was shining and the sky was filled with stars, Rachel figured the glow from the blush on her cheeks would illuminate their path. Storm leaned over and unlatched the gate leading to open pasture. "Where'd you learn to ride?"

"Camp Conohatchee, a children's camp. I worked there as a counselor for three summers during college. I gave classes in gymnastics and swimming. Carol Sue Linninger was the riding instructor. We became friends, and she taught me."

Princess matched Lightning's steps. Storm looked at Rachel. "Did you enjoy working with children?"

She smiled. "I loved it. Kids are so honest and eager to enjoy things. Like Sawyer and his new book tonight. You're very good with him."

"He's the bright spot in my life right now." He shook his head and laughed. "He's a handful at times, but then all Blackhawks are. It's in the genes. Let's pick up the pace a little. Lightning's getting antsy." The black horse began to cantor, and Princess followed suit.

"How old were you when you started to ride?" She glanced at Storm, who certainly rode as one with the horse.

"As soon as I started to crawl. Dad said if my legs were strong enough to crawl, I was ready to set a horse. Been riding ever since."

"How big is the Triple-S?"

"Sixteen hundred acres and change. We raise cattle and horses. Some grains, mostly for our animals."

She glanced around in the semi-darkness. "So much land. How do you handle it all?"

"It's all I know. Dad had me across every inch of this land by the time I was six. I'm a rancher and proud of it. Love every tree, every blade of grass, every rock of this place. Dad loved it, too. Made me promise on his deathbed I'd never sell it. As if I could. Although I'd defy his final request if it meant Sunny had her health back."

"She'll get it back if I have anything to do with it."

He shot her a glance. "You sound sure of yourself."

"I'm sure of Sunny. Inside where it counts, she's strong. Her desire to live is her best weapon. Granted, things don't always go the way we hope, but I've got a strong plan of attack in mind for her. I never give up." She thought of her desire to be rid of Kyle. "Never."

They rode in companionable silence for a few minutes. "It's hard for me to imagine how large sixteen hundred acres is. The house I grew up in is on a quarter of an acre. Seems like a lot to me when I have to mow the yard. I put it up for sale last week."

"I sense sadness in your voice. Is that what you really want to do with the property?"

She shrugged and fought back tears. No, she wasn't sure. Fact was she was selling to break ties with Yazoo City and Kyle Benson. She was selling her home for safety and peace of mind; the home with all the memories of her childhood and her dad. Kyle made her feel vulnerable, and she hated every nuance of that emotion. Perhaps she'd keep her emotions under control if she engaged more in conversation. "You know we hear all the time about Texas being the largest state in the union. Until you're here, you have no concept of what that means."

Storm shifted in the saddle, causing the old leather to creak. "You'll find most forms of geography in Texas. We have plains, low mountains, prairies, desert, marshland, wooded and bushy areas, beaches, rivers, lakes and the Gulf of Mexico. Won't find a prettier state, Rachel."

"Gee, don't you sound like the proud Texan."

"That I am. You couldn't pay me to live anywhere else. I love this state, this ranch." He looked around as if he were surveying all that lay around him. "My dad might be dead, but I see him everywhere on this ranch. I only wish he'd lived long enough to meet his grandson. Man, would he have spoiled that ankle-biter. Dad would've busted with pride to learn his first grandchild was named for him. This land is dad's legacy to Sunny and me. It'll be Sawyer's one day."

"Y*our* children's, too. When you have them, that is." For some reason that thought saddened her. She looked away; what right did she have to be bothered that he'd have children with a woman he loved?

His silence unnerved her. Had she said something wrong? Oh, right. His recent break-up with his fiancé. Their awkward silence stretched on.

After several minutes, Storm asked if she was getting the feel of her horse. She nodded. "Think you can keep up with us?" His white teeth shone in the moonlight. He tugged on the brim of his hat and kneed Lightning, who took off like a bullet.

"Let's go, Princess! The race is on." She leaned over the Appaloosa's head and enjoyed the exhilaration of the wind blowing through her long hair as her mount ate up the ground. To her credit, Princess did her best to catch up to Lightning as the black stallion galloped across the range and then up a hill.

Storm reined his mount to a halt when they reached the top of the rise. Several large live oaks and cottonwoods dotted the landscape. Storm was laughing, obviously pleased with the ride. He leaned down and patted his horse, murmuring praises to Lightning, who nodded and snorted in response.

Rachel was laughing, too. She hadn't enjoyed herself this much in ages. Oh, the freedom of riding a horse, she'd forgotten the exhilaration of the ride.

Storm took his hat off and resettled it on his head. "Pretty good riding for a Mississippi Mouse."

She felt her smile slide off her face as if it were ice cream melting off the cone. Was she really so mousy? First Kyle. Now Storm. Her stomach twisted and sank. She bit her lower lip and looked away. First, the sad thoughts of her selling her home depressed her, and now this. Her emotions were too close to the surface tonight. They had been since their earlier conversation about Drew.

Storm brought his horse around so it was facing the opposite direction from Princess, which put him side by side with Rachel. "What's wrong?"

She raised and lowered a shoulder in a half-hearted shrug. "Just coming back to reality, I suppose. I was feeling rather attractive earlier tonight in my new clothes and 'ho-red' heels. Your remark about my being mousy brought me back to earth."

Storm muttered an oath. "I never said you were mousy. Good God, woman, you have to know you're a knockout."

"It's okay. It's something I've heard plenty of times before from a guy I used to date. You only reinforced his opinion." Didn't she feel like the fool? What possessed her to confide in this man?

He stared at her for a moment and then reached out to place his hands on her waist. "Come here."

"What?" She felt a sense of panic. What was he going to do?

"Slip your feet out of the stirrups. Come on, now." For reasons she couldn't explain, she did as he asked. He lifted her from her saddle and settled her in front of him. Lightning danced to one side a couple of steps, and Storm calmed him with a few words. His strong arms held her against him as she sat sideways on the horse. "Who was this yahoo who said you were mousy?"

He brushed her hair from her forehead and peered into her eyes. Oh Lord, she was in big trouble. If she hadn't made a big enough fool of herself earlier, her reaction to him just now was practically virginal, which she was not. Yet the force of his blatant sexiness made her feel inexperienced. "Tell me, now." His voice was gentle, yet commanding.

She looked away and sighed. "I recently broke up with a man who insisted I was plain and mousy. It's no big deal."

Storm's one arm was around her back, supporting her. His other hand went to her neck and pulled her face closer. "The man was twenty times a fool if he didn't appreciate what he had, who he had. I've always had a hankering for mice, myself. Had several as pets when I was growing up. Believe me, I meant no disrespect by calling you a Mississippi Mouse. On the contrary."

His dark eyes glistened in the moonlight, and his gaze dropped to her lips. "You pull at me, Rachel. God help me, I can't resist one more taste." His lips touched hers, and fireworks went off. A groan escaped. He turned her so they were chest to chest and his arms banded around her, holding her tight. His tongue flicked at her lips. "Open for me, mouse."

"No, I'll die if I do." She'd known men before, but this one was too powerful, too magnetic, too…sexy.

"I'll die if you don't." He captured her lips again and kissed her slowly, so slowly she felt the earth rotate or her heart turn over, she couldn't tell which. His hand went to her breast and covered it. Her nipple rose to make acquaintance with his palm. He groaned and pulled her closer. How could anything be so perfect? Wonderful didn't begin to describe how she responded in the security of his arms. Mercy, this man knew his way around a pair of lips.

"My mouse," he groaned as his lips breathed a trail of delicate kisses on her cheek and down her neck. Shivers fueled the fire burning inside her—a contradiction in terms, but that's what this man did to her. Nothing made sense or mattered, but being in his arms. Yet things did matter. She would not be a woman on a man's rebound.

She pressed a hand to his chest. "You've…you've recently broken off an engagement. Sunny told me. I suspect this is just a rebound thing for you. It's too soon to move onto another woman. I won't be used this way."

He pressed his forehead to hers and drew a shaky breath. "I'm sorry, Rachel. I honestly don't look on you as a rebound allure. I have a lot of respect and attraction for you. I want to get to know you better. You have to decide if you want to give me that chance." He set her back on Princess, who'd obediently waited by Lightning's side. "I hope you do."

While she positioned her feet in her stirrups, he walked Lightning a few feet away as if he needed some space to collect himself. Should she join him? Or should she just head on back to the stables? Would she remember the way?

No, she'd rather take the bull by the horns. She cleared her throat. "Don't get me wrong, Storm Blackhawk, I find you very attractive. However, I live by a personal set of codes. I don't cheat on exams. I don't do anything to harm my patients. Nor do I take things that don't belong to me, like a man another woman loves. You two might still work things out and get married. It's only been a few days, after all."

Storm didn't look her way. He kept his head turned. "If I didn't feel lower than a rattler's belly before, that speech just made me feel lower." He shook his head once as if he'd come to a decision of some sort. "You're a good woman, Rachel Dennison. I can't say what force draws me to you, but something does." His horse started prancing and he gentled him with low, calm murmurings. "It's time we get back. Sunrise comes early." He reined his horse and started to descend the hill.

They were almost to the stables when his cell phone played a tune. "Hello. No, Pilar, I really don't want to talk." He turned Lightning and walked him away a few steps. "We're just getting back from a ride, and I'll need to rub the horses down. Please don't cry. You know I can't take that…"

Rachel and Princess rode on toward the stables. She really didn't want to hear his private conversation. In her opinion, the two would be back together within the week. Damn, if she didn't want to cry herself.

Chapter Seven

Early the next morning, Storm was leaning against the corral fence, feeding pieces of apples to the horses. "Here, Beauty." He presented a quarter of an apple in his outstretched hand. Sunny's palomino daintily nibbled. "Ever the lady, huh?" Storm chuckled, and Beauty nodded and nickered. "You miss Sunny, don't you, girl? Maybe she can ride again one day soon."

He rubbed her muzzle. "I'm starting to have some hope about her illness. That she might have a chance at beating this cancer." He prayed she would, hoped and prayed with every fiber of his being.

Lightning butted his head against Storm's elbow where it rested on the top rung of the fence. "Okay, okay, don't be so impatient." The large horse blew through his nostrils, and his tail switched. "You're being bossy again." Storm cut another piece and presented it to his horse. "You're too spirited for your own good. You know that, don't you?" Lightning shook his head as if he understood, and maybe he did.

Princess jostled between the two, vying for her piece of the apple. "I didn't forget you, little girl. Did you like Rachel? I think she kinda liked you." Lightning nipped at Princess's ear. "Now, be nice and share." He fed the Appaloosa some apple and gave another piece to Lightning.

"I'm not spoiling you just 'cause you're my horse." Lightning nickered. Storm chuckled. "It's just that we men have to stick together. Can't let the fillies get control of us. You've got these two to contend with. I've got Rachel and Pilar. Gotta admit I don't much care for the way Rachel stirs my blood. I can't seem to keep my hands off her." He rubbed his hand down Lightning's forehead, and the horse stepped forward so Storm could bury his face in its neck. It seemed to Storm as if the horse were commiserating with his owner.

"Dreamed about her again last night, Lightning." The horse whinnied. "At least the dream was different, but just as unsettling. Just as arousing. In case you're wondering, I'm *not* waiting for another glimpse of Rachel on her run. Did you see that get-up she was wearing this morning?" Lightning nodded and blew out through his nostrils again. "Almost made me sit up and beg for buttermilk."

He patted the horse's neck. "God, I don't know how much more my heart can take. She was probably right last night. I might just be hunting for a quick substitute for Pilar, a rebound thing. Got no business fantasizing about Rachel, but everything about her churns my hormones. She turns me on when I'm awake and taunts me in my dreams. Feel like I'm losing control."

She'd been wearing a neon-yellow midriff top and blue short shorts this morning. Storm found it disturbing her legs looked as fabulous in sneakers as they had in those "ho-red" heels last night. He hardened at the thought and muttered a curse. How soon could Nurse Rachel get Sunny strong and healthy again and get the hell off his ranch—and out of his life? Did he really want her to leave until he got a chance to know her better?

His cell rang and he looked at the display. Pilar calling again. He let it go to voice mail. She'd called late last night, promised him she'd be more faithful and leave the cocaine alone if only he'd take her back. The woman had whining down to a fine art. All the while she was making her promises, Storm could hear his dad tell him over and over, "If a woman will cheat on you once, son, she'll be prone to do it again."

Rachel came around the bend in the long driveway, her sweaty skin glistening in the peach glow of sunrise. Ben, one of his ranch hands, astride his pinto, galloped over to the fence and called out a greeting. Rachel ran in place, waving and smiling at the rider.

Storm's eyes narrowed in annoyance when Ben, who should have been checking the fence line to the south, got off his horse and leaned against the white fence, obviously checking out Nurse Rachel and her sweat-glistened skin. Storm heard her husky laughter and his mood darkened. Fool woman had no right being so friendly with his men.

Rachel waved a farewell and started running again. Ben didn't get back on his horse but stood there grinning and watching. Storm whistled a shrill two blasts, and Ben glanced his way. When Storm motioned for Ben to get to work, the ranch hand saluted and got on his horse.

Storm figured now was as good a time as any to tell Nurse Rachel to stay away from his men. The last thing he needed was some ranch romance gone bad. Not when her job here was to focus on getting Sunny stronger. He stalked toward her, calling her name.

She stopped and pivoted. "Morning, Storm. I was on my way to get some orange juice."

"Not just yet. I've got something to get straight with you." He knew he was sounding gruff, but he hadn't slept well since she got to the Triple-S, and he was in a piss-poor mood.

"Oh? Can you tell me while I get some juice? I really need…"

"What you need, young lady, is to stay the hell away from my ranch hands. I want them working, not ogling you in that spandex get-up."

She fisted her hands on her hips, her expression incredulous. "Excuse me?"

His eyes swept over her. "Don't you have any decent clothes to run in? What happened to sweatshirts and sweatpants? What in hell were you and Ben so chummy about over there?" His chin jerked in the direction she'd been talking to Ben.

Sweat poured off her skin. She trembled and had a faraway, glazed look.

"I've got a ranch to run here. I can't be worried about some…"

"Orange ju…" Her eyes rolled back in her head, and she slumped to the ground.

Storm's heat stopped, then stuttered back to life. Good God! He scooped her into his arms. "What in God's name?" He gently shook her. When she didn't respond, he ran for the kitchen door. "Noella! Noella!"

The housekeeper came running. "*Sí,* Master Storm. What is it? What's wrong with Rachel?"

He charged into the cool of the kitchen. "She passed out." Maybe if he hadn't been ranting at her, she wouldn't have fainted, but now wasn't the time for recriminations. "She kept talking about getting orange juice and started trembling."

"Ah…her sugar has dropped." Noella rushed to the refrigerator and pulled out a pitcher of orange juice, reaching for a glass. "I know what to do."

Storm stood there holding his unconscious burden. He stared at her pasty, clammy skin. "Sugar? What are you talking about?"

Noella bustled over with a full glass of juice and a spoon. Removing the lid from the china sugar bowl, she added two spoonfuls of sugar to the juice and stirred. "Set her in a chair and try to get her awake enough to drink this. She is diabetic. Her sugar levels have dropped too low. This juice will help."

"A diabetic? You mean to tell me we've hired a sick woman to take care of my sister?"

"Stop yelling. Set her down, please." Noella motioned to the chair with the spoon.

When he placed Rachel on the wooden chair, she moaned and nearly toppled off. He grabbed her arms and settled her in one spot. Then he gently slapped her cheek. "Rachel. Rachel, honey. Wake up."

Her long brown lashes fluttered on pale cheeks. "Wha…?"

Noella shouldered in between him and Rachel. "Little one, drink this for Noella." She placed the glass against Rachel's lips. "Drink now."

Rachel sipped and choked. Then sipped again.

"More. Drink more, little one." How many times had Noella cooed those same words to him when he'd been little and hurting so badly after his mother dropped out of his life? He'd stopped eating and refused to talk to anyone. Storm forced those painful memories from his mind. Instead he focused on the attractive woman in front of him.

Rachel sipped again, taking longer gulps. Her eyes fluttered open. "More," she croaked.

"*Sí,* you drink for Noella. You should have eaten before you ran, but I say nothing." The housekeeper clucked her tongue.

"Wanted…wanted to be ready for…" Rachel took another drink. "For mustangs."

"Next time, you'll know better. Eat first, then run." Noella held the glass away from Rachel's lips. "There's a couple sips left. You drink it all, *sí?*"

Rachel nodded and reached for the glass. When it was empty, she handed it back to Noella. "I'll be all right now. It only takes a couple minutes for my levels to rise." She leaned her head back, closed her eyes and sighed.

He couldn't take it another minute. The woman had fainted right in front of him, taking twenty years off his life. When she'd crumbled to the ground, his heart had crumbled with her. He stood in front of her, grasping the back of the chair on both sides of her shoulders, and leaned in so they were nearly nose to nose. "Why in hell didn't you tell us you were sick?" He hadn't felt this helpless and angry since he'd heard his sister's diagnosis.

Her blue eyes popped open and then narrowed. "I am not sick. I'm a diabetic. Rarely does this happen. I put my excitement over the arrival of the mustangs before my customary routine. Normally I have a container of yogurt before I run so my sugar levels don't drop so low. It won't happen again."

"You're damned right it won't happen again!" He was shouting at her and couldn't seem to stop himself. "Maybe if you hadn't stopped to flirt with Ben, you'd have gotten back to the house before you got so damned sick."

"Are you deaf? I am *not* sick. I had a reaction to a low glucose level." Rachel straightened and shoved at his chest. He leaned all the closer, and his gaze dropped to her mouth. She shoved at him again. "Besides, who do you think you are to yell at me like that? I wasn't flirting, I was merely being friendly."

"Oh? Like you were friendly with me out on Longhorn Road? Like you were being friendly with me last night?" He straightened and charged for the door. Stopping, he shot her a fierce frown, the one that usually sent his men scurrying. "When those mustangs come, I don't want you within spitting distance of them. Is that clear?"

"Crystal clear, your eminence!"

He spun on his heel and shot her another dirty look. She hiked that pointy chin of hers and glared in defiance. Damn, but the woman had sand. A man could depend on a strong woman like that. Not him, of course, but someone else. Some lucky bastard. His eyes narrowed. For the first time in his life he had the urge to kill a man he didn't even know.

"I'm going to town to pick up a water pump for the old truck. Need anything, Noella?"

"I can have a list ready in five minutes, and I hope your mood improves while you're gone." Noella extended both hands in a stop gesture. "But I say nothing."

He shot both women a scowl before he stormed out of the kitchen.

When Storm returned from town, he was still in a sour mood.

He'd had another argument with Pilar over the phone and ordered her never to call or text or e-mail him again. The water pump cost twenty dollars more than he'd been quoted over the phone yesterday, he'd broken some eggs when he'd tossed the grocery bags into the truck, and damned if he hadn't done something utterly stupid. He'd bought Rachel an angel.

What possessed him to buy it, he hadn't a clue. The thing had caught his eye when he passed Amanda's Antiques. He'd stopped to admire the angel, thinking it reminded him of Rachel with its long, flowing blonde hair and pretty blue eyes. The angel was holding a golden scroll upon which were painted the words, "Angel of Hope."

Before he knew it, Amanda, owner of the antique shop, was handing him back his charge card and a pink floral gift bag with tissue paper artfully sticking out of the top. Tucked inside all that tissue paper was a note card he'd signed without thinking. What a *damn* fool.

He'd set the bag on the front seat of the pickup before going in the grocery store to get the items on Noella's list. Making his way through the store as quickly as he could, he mentally kicked himself for making that impetuous purchase. What in God's name had he been thinking? More than likely she wouldn't accept a gift from him, anyhow, after the way he'd yelled at her earlier. When he'd returned to his truck after buying the groceries and seen the bag again, he'd been so disgusted with himself he'd tossed the groceries onto the floor—thus the broken eggs.

Later, Storm was in his office talking to a supplier on the phone when he heard Sawyer's chatter coming from the pool area. He spun his swivel chair around to look out the window and make sure the boy wasn't near the pool alone. To his surprise, both Sunny and Rachel had Sawyer in the water. Pistol's short legs ran back and forth along the edge of the pool as the dog barked in excitement. Storm hadn't seen his sister swim in almost a year. Yesterday when she'd mentioned buying a new swimsuit, he'd figured she planned to lounge around the pool.

He barely heard the person's response on the other end of the phone line. Should Sunny be in the water? What was that fool nurse thinking? His sister should be resting, conserving her energy. For that matter, Nurse Rachel shouldn't be in the water either after passing out this morning.

He slammed the receiver and charged down the hall to the door leading to the patio and pool. Fool women. Did he have to watch them every minute of the day? Between the two of them, they didn't have enough common sense to choke a gnat.

****

Rachel was treading water next to Sunny and her excited little boy. "Today you're going to play in the pool for ten minutes with Sawyer. In three days, we'll increase it to twenty minutes. You'll swim a lap across the pool next week. You'll do that for three days before we increase it to two laps. We'll make small increases until your stamina builds up. Promise you'll tell me if it's too much for you, okay?"

Sunny was beaming. "You're sure I can do this?"

"You need sunlight and exercise to get stronger." She cast an eye at the excited child. "Plus, Sawyer needs his mommy to play with him."

Storm snapped off the CD player Rachel had set on one of the umbrella tables. The strains of Kenny Chesney's latest CD died. "Rachel, get out of that pool!" His order reverberated off the tall redwood fence surrounding the pool area.

"Unkie Storm! Unkie Storm, wook at me! I'm swimming wif Mommy and Wachel."

Storm took his angry, piercing gaze off Rachel and smiled at his nephew. "I see, buddy. Don't make Mommy tired. Okay?"

Rachel glanced over her shoulder at the child's deflated face. She was going to have to lay some ground rules with this man. He couldn't interfere with her treatment plan. She hoisted herself out of the pool and reached for a towel from the pile next to the CD player, wiping her face and blotting her hair.

Storm stood in front of her, fuming, clearly gaining steam for a battle. Well, she'd give him one. She was still ticked off from the way he'd acted earlier, accusing her of flirting with Ben. Storm Blackhawk had no right to tell her what to do. Wasn't that how the abuse with Kyle began? First he'd criticized her friends, slowly alienating her from them. Then the name calling started, followed by the shouting and finally the hitting. She'd not go through that again with anyone.

She tilted her head and looked at the arrogant man. "You're interrupting my time with my patient. What is it?"

The tall man with his authoritative presence jerked his head toward his sister. "She shouldn't be playing around in the water." He shoved his hands into the back pockets of his jeans. "What if she takes a chill?"

"Chill? It's ninety-four degrees and it's barely eleven o'clock." She wouldn't let this man intimidate her. "I have a regimen of treatment scheduled for your sister, based on my training and experience with cancer patients." Just for emphasis and to show him she meant business, she punctuated her words with finger jabs to his hard chest.

"Her doctor approved every item on my detailed plan yesterday. Sunshine and exercise are part of the regimen, as are massages and naps and healthy eating. Don't interfere again." She pressed the button to turn on Kenny's singing.

Storm slammed the button, ending the song. "Who in the hell do you think you are? You've been barking orders at me and her since you got here."

Once more, she punched a finger into his hard chest. "I'm a medical professional your sister hired to do a job. I work for her, not you."

Storm grabbed the finger she'd been poking into his chest. "You go too far, Nurse Rachel. I don't want her overextending herself."

She jerked her finger away from his firm grasp and glared at him, understanding his concern, yet knowing she had to stand her ground. "Neither do I. That's why she'll only be in the water for ten minutes. My waterproof watch has an alarm on it in case I lose track of time." She held her watch for him to see. Then, she looked away for a heartbeat, searching for a way to make him understand. "You said last night you enjoy running this ranch."

"Yes."

"How much of your day is spent outside, doing physical work?"

"Sunup till sundown most days. Some days I'm trapped inside, like today, entering figures in the computer." His eyes narrowed. "What're you getting at?"

She shrugged. "Just wondering. Suppose you got sick and couldn't work the ranch. Imagine how you'd feel. Wouldn't that be stressful for you? How would those stresses impact your recovery?"

"I never get sick, so it's hard for me to imagine that." He waved a hand in a dismissive gesture.

She fisted her hands on her hips. "Don't you have an imagination?"

His eyes swept down her body, over her sleek, lime green one-piece swimsuit. A slow smile spread across his handsome face and his dimples flashed. She felt her nipples tighten in response—damn them anyhow.

His gaze swept to lock on hers. "Oh, believe me, I've got a *very* vivid imagination." He reached out and lightly ran a fingertip up her arm. A frisson of desire flooded her system so fast it nearly buckled her knees. For one second they were oblivious to their surroundings. Storm stepped closer. Her breathing quickened. Her tongue licked her bottom lip in nervousness, and she swore she heard him groan.

Sawyer shot past, jarring them from their private sensual cocoon. "Gotta go bafroom!"

Storm stepped back, shaking his head. "Kid's got perfect timing."

Rachel needed to get control of this situation and of herself. "As you so succinctly stated earlier, I'm here in a professional capacity, not to be friendly with anyone. My work here is very important. Sunny's health is paramount."

A muscle bunched in his jaw and his eyes turned cold. "You'll get no argument from me on that."

She nodded once. "Good. Now, if you'll excuse me, I have work to do. One more thing, stop putting pressure on that little boy to protect his momma. He's a child. Sunny needs him to be a child, not a protector. That's what you and I are for." She turned, dove into the pool and swam two laps before she calmed down enough to return to her patient.

Sunny's allotted time in the pool was over. She spent thirty minutes reclining on a chase lounge watching Rachel and Sawyer play in the water. Her serene smile told Rachel she was greatly enjoying the normalcy of the morning, listening to the squeals and giggles of her little boy.

Later, when two long horse trailers rolled in the dirt driveway, creating large clouds of dust, Noella was serving drinks to three people on the front porch. Sawyer was jumping up and down with excitement. Sunny was holding a bouquet of red roses and wearing a dazed smile. Rachel, well, Rachel was mad as hell.

Disregarding the order Storm had barked at her earlier in the day, she'd donned jeans, a navy T-shirt and boots after her time in the pool, determined to help unload the mustangs. However, when she joined the ranch hands at the paddock, Storm had ordered her, in no uncertain terms, to get back onto the porch—the bossy jerk.

"Lunch will be later than usual today. Master Storm needs extra time with the wild horses." Noella set a plate of raw vegetables and fruit on the stand between Sunny and Rachel. Then she handed Rachel a frosted glass of lemonade. "If you don't slow down on that rocking chair, you'll rock yourself to Mexico. Master Storm was right to insist you stay on the porch out of harm's way. Wild horses can be unpredictable."

"Yeah, well, Storm didn't have to bark at me that way. He can be so *damn* bossy." She grabbed a carrot stick and chomped into it. Noella and Sunny both shook their heads and pointed to the child. Rachel slapped her forehead. "Sorry."

"Yeah, Unkie Storm can be *so* damn bossy." The child proceeded to stuff his mouth with grapes.

"Damn is a word you can't say, young man. Only two grapes in your mouth at a time. You'll choke." Sunny picked two grapes from the bowl. She pointed to them. "One…two. That's how many you can have. One…two. Now, show me how well you can count two grapes."

The child, eager to show off, beamed a grapy smile and plucked two grapes from the bowl. "One…two." Sunny and Rachel both applauded. Sawyer giggled and bounced around the porch like a ball. "One…two…one…two."

Sunny tugged a rose from the bouquet and handed the rest to Noella. "Put these in some water, would you, please? I still can't believe Jackson thought to bring me roses."

Noella took the flowers and smiled. "You know how that man feels about you, but I say nothing." She turned and stepped inside, humming "Her Comes the Bride."

Sunny held the rose to her nose and sniffed. "The day that woman says *nothing* will be the day they hand out ice water in"—

she cast her son a sideways glance before spelling the word—"h-e-l-l." Both women laughed.

Men hollering in the paddock drew their attention. The first of the mustangs charged out of the trailer, ears laid back, hind legs kicking. The trio on the porch watched as the wild horses were unloaded. Rachel had never seen such beautiful, spirited creatures. "Oh, they're breathtaking, aren't they? Look at how they hold their heads. Like they're proud of who or what they are." She munched on a stem of broccoli.

"Some are descended from Spanish Conquistadors' horses."

Rachel glanced at Sunny. "Really?"

Sunny nodded and took a sip of her drink. "Their ancestors were called 'dawn horses.' From what I understand, they were a much smaller creature back when they roamed here fifty million years ago. For some reason they disappeared from North America. Then when the Conquistadors reintroduced them, they were larger animals. They became a vital part of life here. Indians and settlers all depended on them. Columbus brought horses, too. Sleek, desert-bred horses."

"Wonder why they disappeared from here in the first place? Ice Age? Lack of food? Aliens?"

"I haven't a clue." Sunny studied the mustangs and smiled. "You're right, though, they do have an innate pride about them."

They were gorgeous. So was the authoritative man on the black stallion, but she refused to acknowledge that. Still, her eyes seemed to search Storm out, and she became angrier every time her gaze landed on him—*damn* the attraction.

"Mommy, I like the white one with the brown spotted neck. Can I have him?" Sawyer was pointing and jumping up and down as if on a trampoline.

"They aren't ours to keep, sweetheart. We're just taking care of them. Didn't Unkie Storm promise you a pony for your fourth birthday?"

"Uh-huh, and I want that one." He pointed with his chubby finger and his lower lip stuck out in a pout.Sunny slapped a hand over her eyes and groaned. "Oh no, I feel a tantrum coming on. He's over-stimulated, which tends to make him demanding." She leaned her head back and sighed.

"Tired?" Rachel reached out to take Sunny's hand, checking her pulse.

"Yes, all of a sudden I am." She was pale and a little breathless.

"Why don't you lie down for a quick nap? Rest some before lunch so you can enjoy Jackson's company. I'll see to Sawyer."

Sunny stood and swayed for a second. Rachel jumped up and took her arm. "I don't know if I can make it up the steps." Sunny's voice was weak.

"Sawyer, come take Mommy's hand, would you please?" She led her patient inside, past Storm's office and down the wide hall toward the den. "Why don't you lie down on the sofa in here? Save you from going up those steps." Sunny settled onto the leather sofa. Rachel covered her with a brown and orange afghan. "Kiss Mommy so she can have sweet dreams." Sawyer smacked a loud kiss on Sunny's lips.

Rachel scooped Sawyer into her arms. "Come on, tiger. Let's go back outside and watch Unkie Storm herd the horses onto the range." She turned to her patient. "You sleep. He'll be fine." Sunny nodded and closed her eyes.

Rachel carried the eager child down the porch steps and near the fence, stopping about four feet away. The delight on his chubby-cheeked face was visible. Unfortunately, so was the displeasure on Storm's.

He whirled his horse toward them. "Keep him away from the fence."

Moron. Overbearing, bossy man. As if she would do anything to harm this adorable child. She hiked her chin a notch and glared at him. She'd not move closer to the fence, but she'd not move back, either. He had to learn she wouldn't follow his orders. Never again would she bend to a man's will. Hadn't she promised herself that as she hiked the mountain trails in Colorado? One mistake with the male gender was enough.

The child turned to Rachel and sighed. "Unkie Storm being damn bossy again."

Before she could correct him, a chestnut-colored mustang with a black mane arched her back and kicked her hind legs into the loins of Storm's horse, causing it to rear up. Rachel's heart caught in her throat as she watched Storm struggle to gain control, talking to his horse and patting its neck. If he hadn't been glaring at her, he'd have seen the chestnut approaching. Maybe she'd better step out of his field of vision before the daggers his eyes were shooting found a home in her hide.

"What color is your new remote control car, honey?" She turned and carried Sawyer toward the house, hoping her question would distract the child from the horses.

"It's wed wif black stwipes. Wanna see it?" He beamed a smile.

She kissed him. "Sure. Will you show me how it works?"

Chapter Eight

When they finally gathered around the table for their late lunch, Rachel's food stuck in her throat. She'd been seated next to Storm and could sense his displeasure. Although he'd washed the dust, grime and sweat from his face and arms in the mudroom and tugged on a clean, faded yellow T-shirt, he still smelled of sunshine and horses. She was trying very hard not to notice him or his anger…or the way that worn T-shirt stretched over his muscles.

Jackson had stayed for lunch. He was sitting next to Sunny, and the two seemed lost in their own world. The nap had revived her. The color was back in her cheeks again, and she seemed more animated.

Sawyer's incessant chatter about the mustangs helped ease the tension radiating off Storm. Sawyer wanted to know the names of all the horses, and Storm was obviously making them up on the spot to please the child. Some were goofy to make him giggle.

"Is that all you're going to eat? Rabbit food?" Storm motioned to her salad with his fork.

"Since I'm a diabetic, my dietary needs are different. I avoid most breads and high-carbohydrate foods." She shrugged, indicating it was no big deal.

"I think you should eat more than a puny salad." His jaw was set in obvious determination. He extended a bowl of sliced peaches to her. "Here, eat."

"Unkie Storm, you can be so damn bossy."

All heads swiveled toward the little boy. "What did you just say, young man?" Storm set the peaches down, a shocked expression on his sun-weathered face.

Jackson laughed out loud, and Sunny elbowed his ribs. "Don't encourage him." She gave her son the stern-mother look. "Sawyer Dalton Abbot, didn't I tell you earlier you couldn't say that?"

Storm stared at his sister. "He said the same thing about me earlier?" He sounded hurt.

"It's my fault." Rachel reached out, laying a hand on Storm's work-roughened one. "I was angry with you for sending me back onto the porch, and I mouthed off before I remembered little pitchers have big ears. He was only repeating what he heard from a thoughtless adult."

Storm glanced at his nephew while unconsciously turning his hand over, entwining his fingers with hers. "I see." A jolt of heat shot up her arm. He must have felt it too, for his head slowly turned, and he stared at their joined hands. His gaze rose to hers. She started to pull her hand away, and his grip tightened. "I was right to send you to the porch. That paddock was no place for a sick woman."

"I'm *not* sick. My body just doesn't process glucose or sugars like most people's." She shrugged and smiled. "So I monitor my glucose levels, exercise and watch what I eat. I lead a perfectly normal life." *Except when I kiss strange, naked men on quiet country roads, falling in love at first sight.* Her cheeks heated. Her heart pounded. Where? Where had that thought come from?

Storm put Sawyer and Pistol down for a nap while Rachel finished giving Sunny her first acupuncture treatment. Now Sunny, too, was resting. This would be a perfect time to e-mail her mom and Grace. Rachel silently closed Sunny's bedroom door and walked across the hall to hers. That's when she saw the pretty pink floral gift bag hanging from her doorknob.

What was this? She removed the bag from the brass doorknob. A gift? She glanced around to see if anyone was waiting for her to find it; a silly gesture, she knew. Still…

She walked into her bedroom and closed the door behind her, resisting the urge to peek in the bag until she was alone. Who would have left it? Settling on the love seat, she gently pulled away the tissue paper, wanting on one level to prolong the sweetness of the gesture, yet fighting the urge to dive in to see what was in the bag. There was more tissue paper wrapped around something hard. She removed it with care, laying it on her lap to peel the pink tissue paper away.

She gasped in delight. An angel. She held up the figurine to examine it. A beautiful porcelain angel with long hair and flowing robes tinged with pale blue at the hem. "Angel of hope," she whispered, reading the notation on the golden scroll. She gingerly ran a finger across its face. What a sweet expression the angel had. How charming.

What a kind gesture, but who was it from? She picked up the tissue paper on her lap and turned it over and then peered into the bag. That's when she saw the ivory envelope.

"Amanda's Antiques" was printed in gold in the corner of the envelope. Rachel's first name was scrawled beneath in a bold hand. She turned the envelope over and removed the ivory, gold-edged card. *"I'm sorry I yelled at you this morning. Thank you for bringing hope to our family. S."*

She lifted the angel from her lap. Storm? Storm had gotten her this angel? Had to be him. He was the only one who'd yelled at her this morning. She turned the delicate angel over in her hands, admiring it from every angle. Still, an angel from him was so out of character. The man was an enigma. He could go from caring to cross, gentle to gruff. Who could keep track? She glanced down at the angel pressed against her breast, next to her heart where the perplexing six-foot-two enigma had found a home.

Rachel had just sent her mother an e-mail when someone knocked on her door. "Yes, come in."

Noella opened the door, her breathing rapid. "Come quick! One of the ranch hands has been hurt."

"Not Storm? Tell me he's okay." She couldn't bear it if Storm were hurt.

"It's Eduardo. Master Storm is with him. He sent me to get you."

Rachel was already tugging her well-equipped nurse's bag from her closet. "How bad are his injuries?" She ran down the steps behind the housekeeper, who had an armful of clean sheets and rags.

While Storm and Red carried Eduardo into the stable under Rachel's supervision, Noella spread a couple pristine sheets on the clean floor. Eduardo's face was white and he was sweating profusely. He'd tried to separate a sick calf from its mother. The mother had chased him, causing him to take his eyes off the new bull. He'd been gored.

Storm ran a shaky hand through his hair. "That ambulance should soon be here. What's taking it so long?"

Rachel gave Eduardo three extra-strength Tylenols, not nearly enough to take care of the pain, but they would take off the edge. She cut away Eduardo's shirt, exposing the wound.

"Madre de Dios." Noella crossed herself. "Tell me how I can help."

“Open the packages as I hand them to you.” She snapped on latex gloves and began cleaning the wound. “Talk to me, Eduardo. Tell me about *la novia*.” She wanted to distract him from what she was doing. He had a deep, nasty gash in his abdomen from the bull’s horn. There were definite serious internal injuries.

“My Maria. *Si*, she loves me.” His breathing was rapid. Sweat rolled from his face. He winced as she ministered to him.

“Think of all the TLC you’re going to get from her because of this. Lots of hugs and kisses.”

He groaned in pain. “I certainly hope so! ’Cause this hurts like hell.”

“She’ll bring you this and bring you that. *Mi amigo*, you’re going to get all kinds of loving out of this little injury. Might as well milk it for all it’s worth.” She held a pressure bandage to his cleaned wound. “There, the worst is over with. You can tell her how brave you were. I never heard you scream like a *llorica.*”

He nodded, his teeth gritting. Ambulance sirens sounded in the distance. “*Gracious*. You’re an angel,” Eduardo proclaimed and then clenched his teeth and moaned.

“Just a little longer and the paramedics will give you something stronger for the pain. Hold on, Eduardo.”

By the time the EMTs loaded Eduardo into the ambulance, he was unconscious. For now he was out of pain. Rachel snapped off the gloves and pushed her hair back from her face.

“You did good, Nurse Rachel.” Storm wrapped his arm around her waist, drawing her to his side. “I’m going to follow the ambulance. Make sure he gets everything he needs and inform the hospital the ranch will take care of the bill.” He turned to Red. “You want to call Eduardo’s mother? Find out if she needs a lift to the hospital. I’ll swing by to get her.”

“Sure thing, boss. I’m sure Mrs. Ruiz will appreciate the ride. Can you handle her wheelchair okay? Getting her in and out of it?”

“Shouldn’t be a problem. I do know how to be gentle.” Noella smirked at Storm’s remark. “What? Do you know me as anything *but* gentle?” By now Noella and Red were laughing. In short order, Storm was, too.

He shot Rachel a look. “Wise guys. I’m surrounded by ’em. Make your call, Red, while I wash up and put on a clean shirt.

Wouldn't do for Mrs. Ruiz to see her son's blood all over my clothes." He hurried off to the house.

Rachel wrapped her unsanitary things in a towel and placed other items back into her well-ordered nurse's bag. She'd been impressed by Storm's consideration for Eduardo and his mother. On the surface she thought him a hard and demanding boss. Perhaps she'd been wrong.

When she stepped into the mudroom that was also a laundry area, a shirtless Storm was at the sink washing. He was tanned and muscled. Her mouth went dry, while her fingers itched to slowly touch those firm abs—so slowly she could memorize every cell's contour.

She set her bag on the dryer. "I wanted to thank you for the angel. She's beautiful."

He dried his face and chest with a towel. Then he reached above her head for a clean T-shirt from the pile on a shelf over the dryer. As he reached, his other hand went to her waist and his thumb rubbed her midriff in slow, tantalizing circles. Her stomach fluttered. He smelled of soap and sunshine and leather. As he pulled back, their gazes locked. "The angel reminded me of you."

"Me?" Mercy, but a girl could get lost in those dark eyes. He had a way of looking at you as if you were beautiful, as if he couldn't bear to tear his gaze away. Her lungs wanted to collapse as if his thoughtfulness sucked the air from her lungs.

"Yes." He stepped closer. Their thighs touched. Her body responded with feminine desire. He trailed a finger down her cheek and along her jaw. "You see, she called out to me from the store window with your long hair and blue eyes. Your innate beauty."

Rachel tore her observation from his and searched for someplace else to visually devour. She found his naked chest was so near her face, she could kiss those prominent pecs if she chose. Realization dawned. She *really* wanted to touch and kiss his hard, muscular torso. Her hands fluttered to his rippled abdomen and slid upward. He groaned her name, and she snatched her hands back.

Then he leaned closer and kissed her neck. "The angel was lovely and fragile looking just like you." He kissed her neck again. She shivered. "I couldn't resist her, just like I can't resist—"

"Hey, boss." Red opened the screen door and stepped inside.

"Mrs. Ruiz said..." His eyes took in the two of them standing close. "Oops...sorry."

Storm stepped back and tugged on a black T-shirt. "Mrs. Ruiz want me to pick her up?"

"Yeah." Red's eyes slid from Storm to Rachel and then back to Storm. "Sorry, I didn't mean to barge in on you two."

Rachel grabbed her bag. "I'd better go check on Sunny. Give Eduardo my best." She hurried through the kitchen and headed for the stairs. What must Red think, seeing them like that? They were practically kissing. Storm Blackhawk could make love to her soul with a look, a touch, a word. She was in over her head, and it was about time she admitted it.

Rachel was making a bedtime snack of peanut butter and celery when Storm stepped into the mudroom. "Hello to the house." He toed off his boots before coming into the kitchen.

"Hello to the boss."

"Hey, mouse. You still up?" He ran a hand across the back of his neck, and his eyes held weariness. He'd whispered his question. The only light burning in the large kitchen was over the sink, casting the room in intimate semidarkness that seemed to lend itself to whispers.

"How's Eduardo?" She took a bite of her celery. Her voice, too, was lowered.

"Like you told us after they put him in the ambulance, he needed surgery. Doc said his small intestines were punctured, just as you suspected. They took out a five-inch section." He wrapped his hand around her wrist and took a bite of her celery.

"Hungry, cowboy?" They stood close. He still held her wrist, poised to take another bite.

"Starved. Haven't had peanut butter and celery since I was a kid. Forgot how good it is." He took more of her celery, then helped himself to the couple sticks she already had on her plate.

"I'll make you an omelet." She pulled fresh vegetables from the refrigerator and began chopping. "Tell me about Eduardo. How long was his surgery? Did you talk to him afterwards? Did his color look better?"

Storm poured a glass of milk, leaned his hip against the counter and talked to her while she chopped vegetables and leftover ham, whipped eggs and made his omelet. When she slid it onto a dish, he winked and told her she was a girl after his own heart.

She sat with him while he ate, her chin resting on her palm with her elbow on the table. "I gotta give you one thing, cowboy. You do eat with gusto."

He fed her a bite. "Great omelet. I had some crackers from a vending machine but couldn't face the hospital cafeteria. Believe me, this really hits the spot. Thanks, mouse." He took her hand, rubbing his calloused thumb over her palm in slow, gentle strokes. She tried not to respond to his touch. At least she told her heart not to, as for her body, well, it was beyond taking advice where this man was concerned.

"Did you really have mice as a kid?" He fed her another bite, his eyes watching her lips close over the fork.

"Sure." He scraped the last bite from the plate. "Homer and Marge."

Rachel groaned. "*The Simpsons*." She stood and took his plate and glass, heading for the sink.

"You didn't watch *The Simpsons*?" He pulled a clean dishtowel from a drawer while she ran water to wash the dishes and pan.

"Oh, sure. I loved them." She stuck her hands into sudsy water. They whispered about their favorite movies and books. They compared tastes in music. Before long, the kitchen was clean enough even for Noella's critical eye.

Storm turned out the light and followed Rachel out of the kitchen, their whispered sharing drawing to an end. "Sleep well, mouse. Think I'll check my e-mail before I head up to bed."

She paused on the steps, relieved and yet disappointed he wasn't following her upstairs. There'd be no chance for a good-night kiss at her bedroom door.

When Rachel yanked on her running shoes the next morning, eager for the day to begin, it was still dark. Once her laces were tied, she stepped into the hallway and found a CD lying on the floor.

She picked it up and stepped into the light of her room to read the computer-generated cover: "Mood Music for Mouse." She flipped the case over to read the list of songs from Storm's collection he'd burned on the CD for her. A smile crept across her face. He knew how much she liked music. She'd told him so last night. What a sweet gesture.

Humming quietly, she slipped down the steps, through the dining room and into the kitchen for her yogurt. Storm must be up and gone already. A half-empty carafe sat at the coffeemaker. She'd seek him out later to thank him for the CD.

The aroma of fresh coffee made her stomach growl. Although she yearned for a cup, she'd wait until after her run. A reward. She smiled, taking her first bite of yogurt.

While she ate, she mentally reviewed her schedule for the day. She'd have Sunny plant herbs and spend time in the pool with Sawyer. Then she'd give her a massage. After lunch, she'd get Sunny to walk outside for a little while. She was concerned her patient tired so quickly.

She finished the yogurt and threw away the container. That's when she noticed the back door was open. Stepping into the mudroom, she saw Storm through the screen door. He was leaning against a post, obviously staring off into the wide Texas horizon and sipping coffee.

He had one hand shoved into the pocket of his jeans, which looked buttery soft with age. His dark, straight hair hung over the collar of his faded red T-shirt. Broad shoulders stretched the material. She yearned to reach out and rub her hand over his strong back.

What was it about him that attracted her? After all, she'd met many handsome men in her life. Kyle, for one. Damian, the guy she'd dated in college, was another. She smiled. Dr. Isaacs at Kings Daughters Hospital, back home, was drop-dead gorgeous, but then he was openly gay.

Still, what was it about Storm? He was arrogant and opinionated. Bossy. Yet he could be incredibly caring and gentle. Evidently, he was prone to giving little gifts. He was devoted to his sister. His love for his nephew was very touching. She imagined he'd make a great father.

What was she going to do about her attraction to him? What was behind it? Could his magnetic pull on her simply come from his ability to kiss her into sensual overload? If they were to kiss again, would his effect be just as potent? God help her, but she'd love to find out.

"You might as well come out and join me." His deep voice caressed her senses and beckoned. How did he know she was watching him? She wiped her hands over her shorts in a nervous gesture. Did he know how long she'd been standing there, staring, dreaming…yearning?

Embarrassed, Rachel stepped onto the porch and stood next to the man who had moved into her mind—lock, stock and saddle. "Good morning."

He saluted her with his mug. "Mornin'."

His eyes were so intent on her that, for an instant, her mind went blank. Her attraction to this man had to be channeled into friendship—*merely* friendship. "Thank you for burning me that CD. I can't wait to play it."

"You're welcome." A faint blush crept up his neck.

She took pleasure in his discomfort. If she was uneasy around him, she was glad he was obviously suffering from the same emotion. "How long have you been up?"

"An hour, give or take. Did you have your yogurt?" He drained his coffee and set the mug on the porch railing.

"Yes."

"Good. I don't want any low-sugar episodes like yesterday morning." He jerked his head toward the horizon. "This is the best place to watch the sun come up. Our best views of sunsets are on the patio, but here, right here is the spot you get a great view of the sunrise. Nothing like a hill country sunrise."

The curve of the golden sun peeped above the mountains in the distance. Shimmers of apricots and reds undulated like dancing rays celebrating the birth of a new day. Birds began singing as if to welcome the sun. "Oh, you're right. It is beautiful. I guess you do this every morning? Drink your coffee and watch the sun come up." She looked up at him.

He never spared her a glance. "Yup."

His freshly shaved face was relaxed. The smell of his soap and aftershave filled her nostrils. She wanted to bury her nose in his neck and inhale his masculine scent for hours.

She smiled again. "You always so talkative in the morning?"

"Yup." He turned slightly and smiled at her. She laughed. Lordy, but he had a disarming smile. His dark eyebrows wrinkled.

"Why do you wear such revealing clothes to run in?"

She glanced down at what she was wearing. Frankly, right this minute, she couldn't remember what she'd put on. "What do you mean? It's just a white running bra and red shorts."

"Running bra?"

"Not that kind of bra." She slapped his arm. "Running bras are made for women to wear in public. They provide more support for…for…our…ah…the running female."

"Yes, and more eye candy than the average guy's heart can take." He looked over her shoulder at her derriere. "Damn if those shorts shouldn't be declared illegal."

She'd had enough. "If you don't like the way I look, then don't look at me."

"Easy now. Never said I didn't like it."

She huffed an irritated breath. "Then what?"

He grabbed her upper arms and hauled her to him. "Then, this…" His lips crushed hers and sparked a response like two electrical wires arcing, sending showers of white-hot flashes. Fireworks. Oh, yeah, there were most definitely fireworks. She fisted her hands in his long hair.

His tongue swept across her lips, a silent request. She opened her mouth and accepted. He moaned and moved a powerful hand to her bottom, pressing her to him.

When he lifted her, her arms wrapped around his neck and their hungry lips fused, seeking what they both needed. Oh, God, this was even better than the first kiss, even better than his kisses the other night on the horse. He turned and pushed her back against the pillar. She wrapped her legs around his waist. "Rach…God, honey." His teeth scraped down her neck, and her eyes crossed.

Shivers ran down her spine. Her nipples peaked in response. His hands, strong and firm, ran from her hips up her back. She moaned his name, and he captured her lips again. Their tongues touched and tortured and tamed.

Storm broke the kiss and slowly lowered her down the length of him. She felt his erection straining. He lowered his forehead to hers. "We can't keep doing this. As you so rightly reminded me the other night, I've only recently broken off an engagement. It hasn't even been a month, and Pilar hasn't accepted it. Just because I'm mad as hell over her behavior doesn't mean I want her hurt. She's been an important part of my life for over two years."

"I know and I respect your consideration of her. I broke off an engagement about a month ago. It's not easy." Especially when your ex-fiance stalks you with threats and beatings. She stepped away. "I better do my stretches and then run."

He nodded, and for a minute she thought he was going to say something. Running a hand through his hair, he looked away for a beat. "I just don't get it. It's like you're a magnet and I'm powerless to resist." He turned and walked toward the stables.

Chapter Nine

Storm stood at his office window, staring out at the trio in the pool. Sawyer's delighted squeals swept over him. He shook his head a couple of times and grinned. The kid sure knew how to have a good time. The child hadn't had much fun lately with his momma being so sick. Maybe he'd take him riding later. Give Sunny a chance to rest.

Rachel crawled out of the pool, taking his breath away. Trim, muscular legs, rounded hips, narrow waist and God, those large, firm breasts. He'd barely been able to think of anything else since he'd held her to him that morning, two weeks ago, kissing her with her legs wrapped around his waist. He felt himself harden. Just how long could a man live with a perpetual hard-on?

He turned from the window and slumped into his office chair. Frustrated on many levels, he ran both hands through his hair. The woman was driving him insane. It wasn't as if she were the prettiest girl he'd ever seen. Pilar was equally as attractive, in her own way. For sure he'd dated his fair share of beautiful women in college and afterward. Tessa O'Dell came to mind. He tapped a pen against his desk. Still, none of them had affected him so instantly and deeply like Rachel Dennison. None of them had invaded his dreams.

The woman had an intriguing layer of defensiveness about her, as if she felt she had to protect herself. She certainly had no problem expressing her opinions or arguing with his. He'd never expected he'd enjoy an argumentative woman, but he took pleasure in seeing her in a pique, her cheeks flushed in anger. Every time she got miffed, he had an irresistible urge to kiss the irritation right out of her. She was also fun to be with, charming and interesting. He felt different when he was around her. On one hand, he was aroused, and on the other he felt at peace. He shook his head once. It was the strangest thing.

The sounds of more laughter and water splashing seeped through the open window, as did the music Rachel was so fond of playing. It was good to hear Sunny giggle again. Maybe that was part of the attraction. Gratitude. Was part of what he felt for Nurse Rachel purely gratitude for her helping Sunny?

With Rachel there, much of the tension that had permeated the house for so long had evaporated. Noella's claim that Rachel brought hope was correct. It was like they'd all been given a new lease on life, not just Sunny. He tossed the pen down and stepped to the window again.

"Master Storm, I bring you some coffee and two banana nut muffins." Noella set the plate and steaming mug on his desk.

"Thanks, Momma Noella. You know the way to my heart." He glanced over his shoulder and smiled at her.

She stepped beside him and looked out the window. Rachel was holding Sawyer's hands and dancing with him to a song playing on the CD player. The delighted child was giggling. "*Sí,* I know one way to your heart." Her head jerked in the direction of Rachel. "Maybe she knows another, huh? But I say nothing."

"She confuses me. Besides, I've only known her a few weeks." His gaze stayed focused on Rachel.

"*Sí.*" Noella patted his chest. "But your heart, my child, does your heart know that?" She turned and started to walk out.

"Are you taking Mrs. Ruiz to the hospital this afternoon?"

Noella stopped. "Her neighbor's taking her. I ordered a basket of fruit for Eduardo's room."

"Good. Good. I talked to him a few minutes ago. He was tired from physical therapy. Walking and bending are still painful for him, but he seemed in good spirits. I bet he'd enjoy a call from you, momma."

"*Sí,* this I will do. Eduardo is a good man."

"Yes, he is. The Triple-S takes care of its own. We'll look after him and his mother until he's back to work."

She nodded. "*Bueno.* Your poppa always looked after his men. It pleases me you do the same." Noella patted his cheek and bustled out.

Storm sat, determined to get the rest of the figures entered on the computer. He bit into the warm muffin, rolling his eyes in appreciation. Keeping computer records was the bane of his existence. He lifted the fresh cup of coffee to his lips, sipped and choked. In half of the entries he'd posted minutes earlier, he'd entered Rachel's name. *Dammit!*

****

After Sunny's time in the pool playing with Sawyer, Storm came out onto the patio. Gone were his relaxed features Rachel had seen earlier at breakfast.

He hunkered in front of Sawyer. "Want to ride with me for a while? We'll go check on those new mustangs."

"Yeah! Can I go wif Unkie Storm, Mommy?" The child was doing his happy dance.

"You'll have to put on dry clothes. Jeans and a T-shirt." Sunny was breathless as she collapsed onto a chaise lounge. "Whew, I'm tired."

"You rest. I'll get him dressed. Come on, partner." Storm spared Rachel an irritated glance. "I hope you haven't overextended my sister. She's out of breath."

"She just swam two laps across the pool for the first time. Naturally, she's out of breath."

He grabbed Rachel's arm and yanked her to him. "Laps? You have my sick sister swimming laps? Are you nuts?"

She winced at the pain. Her heart was beating like a bass beat on a rap song. She didn't know if it was anger or fear. Whichever, she didn't like it. Her gaze went to his calloused hand squeezing her arm and then quickly swept to his hard, black eyes. "Kindly remove your hand."

When it tightened, she glanced at Sawyer, who had slid from his uncle's hold to crawl onto his mother's lap. For his sake, she whispered, "Not in front of the child."

Storm's dark eyes blinked twice and his grip loosened. He turned to his nephew. "Are you ready to get dry clothes on, buddy?"

"Is you being damned bossy to Wachel again?" Sawyer's eyes were big as he cowered against his mommy.

"Sawyer Dalton Abbot!" Sunny shook a finger at her son in admonition.

Storm hunkered down again in front of the boy. "It's all right, sister. I *was* being damned bossy. Don't growl at him." He reached out to take Sawyer's hand. The child pulled back. "I'm sorry if Unkie Storm scared you."

"You haf'ta say 'sowwy' to Wachel." Sawyer crawled off his mother's lap and ran to Rachel, wrapping his little arms around her knees.

Storm stood and sighed, his hands on his hips. "You're right, partner. Rachel, I'm sorry I snapped at you. I've always protected Sunny and, well, I'm just worried about her."

"That's okay." Her voice held no warmth. When she had him alone, she'd tell him she didn't like his grabbing her in anger. She'd tell him how she saw it as abuse. Not now in front of the little boy she'd come to love, but soon. She refused to put up with abuse from another man. One trip down that road had been enough.

"Now, kiss and make up." Sunny beamed a mischievous smile.

Sawyer clapped his hands. "Yeah, Unkie Storm, kiss Wachel. I kissed her before. It was fun. Go 'head. She don't bite."

Storm chuckled. "No, but I might."

A duet of "Kiss her, kiss her," erupted from Sunny and Sawyer.

Storm rolled his eyes and stepped closer.

Rachel shook her head. "No." The last thing she wanted right now was a fake show of affection from him. *The jerk.*

He cupped her face in his hands, his eyes locked on hers and he lowered his head. Warm lips pressed a kiss to her forehead. She reached up and placed her hands on his forearms, torn between pushing him away and pulling him closer. He laid his forehead against hers. "I'm sorry I was so rough earlier."

Perhaps now was the time to tell him how she felt, when he seemed open and receptive. "I don't like abusive men. They frighten me. I avoid them at all costs."

Storm stilled, a muscle bunched in his cheek. His voice was barely a whisper when he spoke, so sensually tender it spun a web of privacy around them as if they were the only two souls in the vast, beautiful hill country of Texas. "You think I could be abusive?" He stepped closer so their thighs touched. Her stomach fluttered in response.

Their gazes locked. Their breaths mingled. One of his hands lightly stroked her neck, and warmth rushed through her. "Never, honey. Especially, never with you. I don't abuse my animals and I don't abuse women. God treasures both, and so do I." He cupped her face. "I'm finding I treasure you." His gaze swept to her open mouth. "Treasure you more than I have a right to, my sweet mouse." He brought his mouth to hers and showed her how sweetly gentle and tender he could be.

Her jelly-boned legs showed her how vulnerable she could be

with him.

"Wow, Unkie Storm, you kissed her a weally long time. You must be weally, weally sowwy."

After thirty minutes of sunning themselves, Rachel took Sunny upstairs for a massage.

Strains of Marc Anthony crooning "You Sang to Me" filled Sunny's apricot and aqua bedroom. The drapes were opened wide to let in the sunlight. Rachel was determined to erase the tomb image from Sunny's mind.

"This morning was wonderful," Sunny cooed, lying on her stomach on the massage table, waiting for Rachel to begin the massage.

Rachel rubbed a special lotion onto her hands to warm it before applying it to her patient's sun-warmed skin. "I was so proud of how well you did in the pool today. Your endurance is increasing. Two whole laps across the width of the pool. That deserves some chocolate. I hope you're not too tired?" She used her thumbs in rotating movements over Sunny's neck.

"A little. Oh, that feels so good."

"Sawyer loves the water, doesn't he?" She wanted to keep her patient's mind off herself and her illness. She suspected too much time had been relegated to that. To help Sunny fight, she had to change her patient's mental outlook and help her focus on the joys of living.

"He's like a fish. Just like Storm and I were at that age."

"You and your brother are very close." She moved down to Sunny's shoulders, finding some kinks and applying pressure to work them out. "He's very protective."

"Twins usually are." Sunny groaned. "I'll give you two hours to stop that."

Rachel chuckled. "Who's the oldest?" She applied more lotion and moved further down her patient's back, applying pressure in special spots.

"God, that feels fantastic." Sunny cooed. "To answer your question, I'm the oldest by two minutes. Daddy used to say I came out beaming like the sun 'cause I'd beaten my brother in the race to be born. Storm was so mad I'd gotten here first he was born scowling and howling, raging like a storm."

Rachel smiled at the image, nodding. "Thus, the names?"

"Yup. Our parents had Christopher and Caroline picked out, but we didn't fit them."

"No, I guess not." She poured more lotion in her hands and massaged Sunny's arm, thinking about Storm for the umpteenth time that day. Who would have believed the arrogantly sexual man she'd found on that road, weeks ago, would be her new patient's brother? "I can't imagine anyone calling your brother Christopher." No, the name Storm most definitely suited this man with his mercurial, passionate moods.

"Are you still angry with him for the way he acted earlier by the pool?"

Rachel walked around the massage table so she could do Sunny's other arm. "Your brother was just being protective. Even so, I don't like his manhandling me."

"Seemed like more than that. I mean, sparks were coming off you two." Sunny turned her head and aimed her dark eyes on Rachel, eyes identical to her brother's. "You know, it's almost as if you two knew each other before you came here."

"If I told you, he'd kill me."

Sunny rose on one elbow, her face animated. "Well, then you *must* tell."

The nurse, who was pleased to see her patient show an interest in life, warred with the woman who wanted to keep a chance meeting with a hunky magnetic male a secret. Still, it wasn't exactly a secret. She'd e-mailed Grace all about it.

Sunny's eyebrow shot up. "Well?"

She sighed. "Your brother and I met on my way here, on Longhorn Road."

"Really? Why hasn't either one of you mentioned it?"

"If I share the details, you have to promise not to tell him. Storm would be angry if I told." She bit her lower lip. His only mention of their run-in had been in the kitchen the morning her sugar levels dropped. He'd thrown it in her face then. As though she'd instigated everything that moonlit night. As if she made it a habit of enticing men, and that's what she'd been doing with Ben. Heck, she couldn't even remember what they'd talked about.

"Ouch! Must not be a good memory the way your touch has

roughened."

"Oh, Sunny, I'm sorry. Did I hurt you?" See how that man made her? He made her nuts. More than likely Storm hadn't given that first kiss another thought, while she hadn't been able to get it out of her mind. Perhaps, for him, it had just been an amusing moment in time. An interlude he'd quickly forgotten.

"Are you going to share?"

She bit her bottom lip. "It would have to be kept between you and me. A confidence."

Sunny smiled; her chin quivered, and huge twin tears threatened to spill. "Do you know how long it's been since a friend shared a secret with me? It's as if a person with cancer can't handle a secret or is no longer worthy of confidences."

Rachel took a deep breath, absorbing what her patient said, knowing she would have to share a confidence to gain the intimacy of Sunny's trust. She scrutinized Sunny's eyes. "Promise you won't tell him?"

"Cross my heart." Sunny crossed the right side of her chest.

She placed her forehead against Sunny's. "Your heart is on the other side, dummy." They laughed like teenaged school girls.

"Okay, I'll tell you, but first lie down while I massage your legs." She walked to the other end of the massage table and pushed up the sheet. Squeezing lotion onto her hand, she began her story. "Well, I was driving here that first night, minding my own business when a naked man…"

"Naked?" Sunny's head whipped around. "You don't mean..."

"Yup." The corners of her mouth curled up, and she winked. She massaged Sunny's legs while she shared every detail about meeting Storm.

"My brother kissed you? So, the kiss he gave you down by the pool wasn't his first?"

Rachel shook her head. "Nor was it the second." Drats, she shouldn't have said that.

Sunny's eyes were alight with surprise and excitement when she rose on her elbows to look over her shoulder at Rachel. "How many times have you two kissed?" Rachel kept her head down, her hands massaging her legs. "Rachel?"

"Once on the road that night." She sighed audibly. "When we

went for a ride the day you saw your oncologist, and again one morning when we watched a sunrise together. Neither time meant anything to him, I'm sure."

"He's kissed you several times then? Interesting. I can't get over his kissing you before he knew who you were." She shook her head. "I really can't imagine his doing that. He's always so in control." Her eyebrows furrowed. "If only he weren't still being harassed by Pilar. The spoiled bitch takes his 'no's' as a challenge."

"He's told me he hates hurting Pilar's feelings. To me, it's a strong indication he's not completely over her. Given enough time, I think they might get back together." Through long, restless nights of reliving every shared kiss, every shared word, she'd focused on that fact—he still cared for this other woman.

She could not, would not become a man's rebound fling. Besides, until Kyle Benson lost interest in her, her personal life remained in turmoil, which was why she needed to remain perfectly entrenched in her professional life. Plus, she had to keep her whereabouts a secret.

"Rachel...Rachel?"

"I'm sorry. Did you ask me something?" She pulled the sheet over Sunny's legs and patted her shoulder. "All done."

"Thanks. That was great. I asked if you were attracted to my brother." Sunny sat up and hung her slender legs over the side of the massage table, her eyebrows arched as if waiting for an answer.

Rachel walked to a window and wrapped her arms around her waist. "What woman wouldn't be attracted to Storm? But then, Storm's not emotionally free, is he?"

Sunny stood behind her, laying a hand on Rachel's shoulder. "I don't want to see you hurt. But I do need to warn you Pilar is used to getting what she wants. She knows how to pout and cry until she gets her way with her indulgent Daddy, or any man. And she's not above using trickery."

Rachel turned, blinking away the tears. "And I've never been one to play games. I'm out of my element with that kind of conniving feminine behavior. I'm just plain old me." Her hands rose and fell.

"Oh, honey. Sometimes I could kick my brother."

Rachel wrapped her arm around Sunny's shoulders. "Thanks for the loyalty. Luckily, Storm spends most of his days on the range or working in the stables. We only see each other at mealtimes. Some days we're like old friends, engaging in gentle conversation. On others, we're like gasoline and a match."

Either way, I feel like the moth and Storm the all-consuming candle.

Never one to kid herself once the truth had become painfully clear, Rachel had accepted she'd fallen in love with Storm Blackhawk.

Chapter Ten

Sunny pulled panties from her dresser, raving about how great she felt after her massage. She was heading for a shower when Noella carried in a basket of clean laundry.

"I had to remind Master Storm to put a hat on little Sawyer before taking him for a ride. It's good to see that child riding with his uncle. Reminds me of when your poppa took Master Storm on rides. Goodness, but he hadn't started walking yet."

Sunny stopped, her hand on the doorknob to the bathroom. "I remember Daddy taking me riding on the range. He made everything an adventure. He'd have adored my little cowboy." She opened the door and entered her bathroom.

Rachel began dismantling the portable massage table. "Sawyer is such a cute kid."

Noella placed clean items in Sunny's dresser. "Little Sawyer has his mother's disposition. Her illness has been hard on him." She turned from the dresser. "Usually Miss Sunny spends the morning reading or gazing out her windows, but you had her in the pool playing with her child. I worry she'll overdo, but I say nothing." She turned large, anxiety-filled eyes on Rachel.

"I've only been here for a few weeks, but I've already learned you are the heartbeat of this house." She gauged the housekeeper's reaction before continuing. "I'm going to need your help."

Noella stopped, her arms full of clean towels. "Help doing what?"

"To fight cancer, a patient has to be as healthy and strong and happy as possible. That's why I have Sunny doing exercises, spending time outdoors and eating certain foods. She needs to laugh and dance. To hear music. The more she enjoys life, the more she'll fight to keep it."

"*Sí*, but she must not overdo."

"She'll still take naps, but since she'll be tired from her increased activity, the quality of her rest will be improved. Too much sleep is not good for anyone. It makes them lethargic. My job is to get Sunny strong enough to undergo another round of chemo. She's still weak from the first round, even though it ended months ago."

"She got so sick." The housekeeper sat on Sunny's bed and crossed herself. "She was like a shadow, my Sunny. And the throwing up. My heart hurt so bad, but I say nothing."

"Thank God she had you to help her. Most women don't have anyone to rely on the way Sunny relies on you. Their husbands go off to work day after day, and they spend the day alone—sick and scared."

"*Sí.* I've always taken care of Miss Sunny and Master Storm. And now, little Sawyer."

"Storm isn't happy I'm here. He thinks I'll do Sunny more harm than good. We've already had several arguments over my treatment plan."

"With Storm there are always arguments. He's an extremely passionate man when it comes to those he loves and for this ranch. He feels too deeply, that one. He thinks his job in life is to protect whoever he cares for." She ran a hand over the bed's coverlet. "He got very upset the morning he thought you were sick."

"I think you misunderstood. He wasn't upset over my fainting. He was accusing me of flirting with Ben."

Noella tilted her head. "Ben's a good-looking man. He enjoys charming the women, from what I hear."

"I'm here to help Sunny, not to find romance." Would she ever allow herself to find romance again? There were beginnings of a romance here, but not with Ben, with a man she felt powerless to resist. Could she ever respond to another man—someone other than Storm? Would any man measure up to the one with the midnight eyes and dazzling dimples? She suspected her heart would always yearn for him.

The housekeeper stood and approached Rachel, patting her cheek. "You say you're not hunting for romance, but maybe it find you. *Sí?*"

Rachel shook her head. Why would any woman be interested in Ben when there was Storm? Granted, the man she'd spoken to briefly seemed nice enough, but he didn't appeal to her. She almost wished he did; then maybe she could get over Storm Blackhawk.

Everyone was seated at the table when Rachel joined them for lunch. Jackson was there, sitting next to Sunny. "Hi, Jackson. Nice to see you again. Sorry I'm late, everyone. I was on the phone with

Dr. Frey. He was giving me the results of your labs from yesterday, Sunny. For now, things are stable and that's very good. I want to impress upon you how good that is."

Sunny's face brightened. "Remission?"

Rachel didn't want to disappoint her, nor did she want to mislead her, giving her false hope. "Not yet. But, with the levels of leukemic cells in your blood and bone marrow staying consistent for a month, we're seeing a stabilizing effect. Granted, the numbers are still high. The good news is they're not increasing. You know how pleased he was you'd gained eight pounds. He raved about much better you looked."

Storm laid his hand over Rachel's. Pain warred with hope in his features. "You…do you and the doctor consider this a good thing?"

She nodded. "Yes. With our doing everything we can to make your sister stronger—healthy eating, exercise, sun, and positive emotional reinforcement—this stabilization levels the playing field for a span of time. A span of time for Sunny to get stronger, so she can undergo the second series of chemo. I'm feeling very good about this."

He sat back, closed his eyes, and nodded in silence. Rachel tried to ignore her body's reaction to his thumb making small circles over her knuckles as he held onto her hand like a lifeline.

Tears glistened in Sunny's eyes. "Hope," she whispered, her chin quivering.

Jackson drew Sunny into his arms. He kissed her forehead. "Everything good begins with hope, sugar."

Noella crossed herself, her lips moving, and then blotted her eyes with the hem of her apron. "Wouldn't it be wonderful if Miss Sunny wasn't sick anymore?"

"I not sick," Sawyer chimed in, obviously not quite sure what was happening.

Rachel opened her eyes wide. "No, you're strong. Show me your muscles." She held up her arm and flexed it. The child mirrored her actions, and everyone laughed. "I bet you could be Superman."

He shook his head, grinning with a mouth full of peanut butter and jelly sandwich. "I need a cape."

"I'll make you one," Rachel promised.

His eyes got big. "You will?"

"Sure. I'll even put a big 'S' on the back for Superman Sawyer." The boy giggled, and Rachel realized she was falling deeper in love with the impish child every day.

Rachel poured oil and vinegar on her salad. "Suddenly, I feel ravenous."

"We should celebrate." Storm was grinning. A jovial air had permeated the kitchen.

"No booze." Jackson held his hand up in a stop gesture. "I promised Noella I'd slow down, and I have. Been gettin' drunk on love lately." He gazed at Sunny and winked. She beamed a smile.

Storm glanced at Noella, who was giving him a warning look. "No, I was thinking of that apple pie I smelled when Sawyer and I got back from our ride. I say we live dangerously and have it for lunch, not dinner."

"Wif ice cream!" The child's smile was wide, his sweet enthusiasm infectious.

Noella laughed. "*Sí,* my darling boy. With ice cream. Your Unkie Storm has a good idea. Now eat all your lunch so you can have the special dessert."

Storm turned to Rachel. "I'm sorry, I didn't think of your diabetes. Can you have pie and ice cream?"

She shook her head. "I'd love it, believe me, but I shouldn't have more than a bite."

"I'll share a bite with you. You're part of the reason we're celebrating, after all. Besides, no one makes apple pie like our Noella. She uses apples grown here in her orchard." He turned to his sister. "How are you feeling? Not too tired, I hope."

"Are you kidding? For the first time in months, I feel alive. Rachel and I potted some plants after breakfast. Healing herbs, she calls them. I swam. Got some sun. Had a marvelous massage. You should have Rachel give you one." She smiled at her brother, and Rachel could have sworn there was a tinge of mischievousness in her patient's eyes. "Rachel has *fabulous* hands. Bet she could do wonders with your body."

Storm had just taken a drink of iced tea. He choked.

"Goodness!" Sunny teased, spearing a cherry tomato with her fork and holding it in front of her mouth. "Was it something I said?"

The pie à la mode was served. When Storm laid his arm across the back of Rachel's chair and brought a spoonful of the dessert to her mouth, she held up one finger. "Okay, but one bite is all I can eat." She closed her eyes and opened her mouth. The sweetness of sugar, the tartness of apples, cinnamon, nutmeg and the cold of ice cream landed on her tongue. It had been ages since she'd indulged. The tastes mingled and melted.

She savored, swallowed and moaned. "Heaven. That was so good it made my toes curl." She slowly opened her eyes and stared into the piercing gaze of midnight eyes. Storm was watching her as if he were measuring and mentally recording every nuance of her reaction. "Why…why are you staring at me like that?"

His gaze never left hers as he extended a long finger and swiped a chunk of apple from her lower lip. "I've never seen anyone enjoy something so much." He held up his finger. "Here, you missed a piece of apple."

Rachel coiled her hand around his wrist and brought his finger to her mouth. She sucked the fruit from his finger, twirling her tongue around his skin. Storm's eyes swept shut, and he groaned. For a brief second, she enjoyed the sensual power her mouth exacted over him.

His cell rang and he swore under his breath. He snatched it from his belt and checked the display before answering. "The woman just won't give up." He held the phone to his ear. "Okay, Pilar. What is it now?" His gaze slid to Rachel. "An art exhibition? Tonight?" He sighed and closed his eyes. "No, I don't remember promising to be your escort. We no longer date. Ask someone else to take you. We're finished." He turned his fork over and over while the woman on the other end of the phone talked.

Rachel stood and gathered her plates. Reality check: there was another woman in his life. A woman who wasn't going away without a fight. The bitch was obviously obsessed with Storm.

"Of course I'm a man of my word, Pilar." By the tone of Storm's voice he was getting angry. "Don't start crying. What time do you want me there? You got it." Storm slapped the phone on the table.

Noella pushed Rachel away from the sink. "Go sit down. I'll load the dishwasher." When Rachel shook her head, the housekeeper placed her hands on the younger woman's shoulders, whispering a command as she turned her around. "Don't give up on him. He cares for you." Noella turned her eyes to Storm. "Will you be here for dinner tonight?"

"Yeah. I'll be heading out soon afterward, though." He watched Rachel sit next to him and regarded her closely. "You okay, mouse?"

She wanted to kick him. To call him vile names for toying with her as if her feelings were inconsequential. She was a woman, caring, intelligent and educated. Damn him for touching and kissing her. Damn *herself* for loving it.

Her hands were fisted in her lap. He laid his hand over them. "I'm sorry."

Pilar's call was the end of a dream. A dream she wasn't aware she'd had until now. She fought tears. She fought humiliation and she fought anger—anger at him and herself.

"Look at me." His command was gentle.

She lifted her head and turned hardened eyes on him. She was struggling, trying to hang on to resolve and anger. "I think you're kidding yourself if you think your relationship with Pilar is over. She still has control over you and your emotions."

He removed his hand from hers and appeared to be struggling with a response. Then he turned his attention to his sister. "Sunny, are you napping this afternoon? Or does Nurse Rachel have plans for you to go mountain climbing instead?"

Sarcasm. Rachel could handle his sarcasm. "Actually, cowboy, I was saving that for tomorrow." She took a perverse pleasure in seeing the muscle in his jaw bunch. "Do you always grind your back molars like that? With your temperament, your jaw must ache by the end of the day."

Storm shot Sunny and Jackson a dark look when they laughed. "Nurse Rachel, you'll find I am the most amenable of men."

She lifted her phone, tapped the calendar app, and poised her index finger above the keyboard. "What day of the month does that usually occur? I'll be sure to mark it on my calendar."

"Oh, Master Storm, she gonna be good for you. You take yourself too seriously, but I say nothing."

"Yes, we all know how you say nothing around here, Momma

Noella." He stood and cleared his place setting, taking his dirty things to the sink. "You push us around with that flour-covered fist of yours. The minute we think about stepping out of line, you threaten to stop cooking."

He walked to Sunny and leaned over, kissing her bald head. "Sleep well, sister." The depth of affection in his voice and eyes nearly took Rachel's breath away. How would it feel to be loved and adored by this man? She'd never know.

Sunny reached back and patted Storm's hand where it rested on her thin shoulder. "Have a good afternoon, brother."

Storm laid his large hands on his nephew's shoulders. "Drink the rest of your milk, partner, and it's off to bed with you." Sawyer quickly complied, favoring his uncle with a milk mustache. Storm scooped the boy from his booster seat and held him close. "Mmm...milk mustache!" Sawyer started to squeal and giggle as Storm carried him out of the kitchen. "Me kiss milk mustaches..." The uncle made loud kissing noises amid the delighted squeals of the child.

"If you want to see the softer side of Storm," Noella said, "watch him with that little boy. He adores his nephew. So much so he was willing to marry a woman he didn't really love, but I say nothing." She gathered the remaining dirty dishes and carried them to the sink.

"What does she mean?" Rachel looked at Sunny.

"Before you ladies tear apart Storm's love life, I have to get back to town." Jackson took Sunny's chin in his hand, turning her face to his. "How would you and Sawyer like to go to the movies with me tomorrow night? That new animated flick is playin'." He kissed Sunny's cheek. "I'll buy you popcorn, little girl." He wiggled his eyebrows.

Sunny's face glowed with a faint blush. "Make it a large, Mr. Policeman, and I'll even let you hold my hand during the scary parts." She batted her eyes. "I know how you hate violence."

Jackson stood, laughing. He hugged Noella in farewell and waved to Rachel before he left. As soon as the door closed, he opened it again, popping his head back in. "You won't forget our date, now, will you?"

Sunny laughed and blew him a kiss. After the door clicked shut again, she sighed. "That man has always known how to touch my heart." She turned to Rachel. "You asked what Noella meant by Storm marrying a woman he doesn't love. It's a long story...a divorce story...a cancer story." Sunny opened her pill box and dumped her midday dosage into her hand. She placed them in her mouth and washed them down with water. Rachel waited.

"You see, I have a consuming fear of Sawyer's dad trying to gain custody of my son and his trust fund after I die." She sat back and sighed. "Storm and I went to our lawyer and had custody papers drawn up. Went through all the legal steps to make him guardian when the time comes."

Noella snorted. "Then Pilar started telling Storm things. Started saying how if they were married, he'd stand a better chance of keeping little Sawyer."

Rachel looked from Noella to Sunny. "He fell for that?"

"Yes, he fell for it." Noella poured herself a cup of coffee. "He loves that little boy more than his own life, and Pilar knows that. She's an opportunist, that one." Noella sipped her coffee and smiled. "But you are not."

"Me?" Rachel pointed to herself. "What do I have to do with any of this?"

"I see how he looks at you. I saw the look of terror on his face when you passed out that morning. I also saw you two out by the pool earlier." Noella waved her hand in front of her face as if it were a fan. "The heat of his gaze. The way he kissed you, his feelings tender and true. He touched you. No? And you melted. *Sí?* I see wonderful possibilities, but I say nothing."

"Whatever heat you saw was his temper. I don't get involved with men who are in relationships." She looked at Sunny's raised eyebrow. "Okay, I *try* not to get involved. Obviously I've been a little lax in that department lately." She stood and carried bowls and platters to the sink. "Besides, I have rotten luck with men. Thanks for lunch. It was great. Your apple pie…" She brought her fingertips together and touched them to her mouth, making a smacking sound. "Superb!"

Noella's smile was pure delight. "You're very welcome, little one."

"'Little one.' My father used to call me that." She hugged

Noella. "Thanks for calling forth a sweet memory."

The housekeeper smiled and patted Rachel's hand. "From now on I call you little one. *Sí?*"

"I'd love it." Rachel turned to her patient. "Sunny, let's take a short walk before your nap. Just one trip around the house."

Sunny followed Rachel outside, and the two started strolling through the yard. "What Noella said was right, you know. My brother's definitely interested in you. You keep him on his toes. He needs that. He must have been attracted to you at first sight to kiss you out on Longhorn Road. You mustn't forget that first kiss."

No, Rachel would never forget that kiss as long as she lived. How *could* one forget that firestorm of feelings he ignited? The things that man did in the space of one kiss. She took a ragged breath and pretended to admire Noella's flowerbeds.

Storm's ex-fiancée was still pulling his emotional strings. She sounded exotic. Pilar was probably beautiful and sexy, while she was short and top heavy and plain. Mousy. A stab of new feeling pierced her, twisting her stomach. She took it for what it was: jealousy.

Everyone would be better off if she ignored the man and focused all of her being on her patient's recovery. Both Sunny and a darling child depended on her to extend their time together. She wouldn't fail.

She linked her arm in Sunny's as they walked around the end of the house. "Let's get two things straight. One, you're not going to die just yet. You've got too much orneriness in you."

"True." Sunny tilted her head and nodded. "Although I never realized it until you came."

"Second, your brother's still emptionally attached to another woman, no matter how much he denies it. Now, you and I are going to forget about *that* kiss and the others. We'll both be better off if we do."

"Rachel, you are so full of it."

She batted her eyes at Sunny. "Of what, girlfriend?"

Sunny chuckled. "You mentioned earlier you had rotten luck with men. What did you mean?"

"I was engaged for a while." In many ways her engagement seemed ages ago. So much had happened since that awful period of her life.

"Was?"

"Yes. He was my best friend's cousin, so I knew of him. Just not about him, if you know what I mean." She glanced at Sunny, and Sunny nodded. "After my father died suddenly in an awful car crash, Kyle started coming by the house. You know, just to see how I was doing."

"You mean he made his move when you were most vulnerable."

"Gee, you're beautiful *and* astute. Before long, Kyle asked me out on a date. He started doing things around the house, making himself indispensible. I was floundering without my dad. Losing him was extremely hard. I was also busy starting my business, taking extra classes and studying for certification." She shrugged. "Too much turmoil and pain at one time. Before I knew it, the man—and I use that term loosely—had ingratiated himself into every aspect of my life."

"I hear that. We lost Dad a few days before Sawyer was born. I lost my father, left my cheating husband, and gained a son all in the span of five days."

Rachel stopped and turned to face Sunny. "No! How...how did you survive?" She pointed to the front porch steps. "You need to rest. Your breathing's labored."

Sunny nodded and sat on the nearest step. She placed her elbows on the step behind her and leaned back to watch a golden butterfly flit from flower to flower. "I haven't a clue how I survived. Storm willed me to, I guess. He passed some of his strength and toughness on to me. Of course, there was the wonder of my new baby. He was so beautiful."

Rachel sat next to her, took her wrist and checked her pulse. "He still is."

"Yes, that child's my whole world. Enough about me. Tell me more about you and Kyle."

Rachel looked away for a beat, tamping down the pain of the memories. "Once we were engaged, the putdowns started. When I'd object, he'd say I was paranoid or neurotic."

Sunny straightened and stared at Rachel for a beat. "Paranoid? Neurotic? Girlfriend, you have *got* to be kidding me! You're so not any of those things."

She swiped at a tear. "No, but I was in such a sensitive state over losing Dad. The suddenness of his death." She looked at her clasped hands. "Some teen texting and driving hit him head on. Dad and I were so close." She cleared her throat, trying to regain control. "Initially, when Kyle's insults started, they didn't register. Guess I was in the emotional fog of mourning. Every time I didn't see things his way, he accused me of being paranoid or neurotic."

Sunny took Rachel's hand and squeezed it. "That's so cruel. The manipulating bastard."

She squeezed Sunny's hand in return, their emotional bond strengthening. "That's how the abuse started. With his undermining my mental stability, I actually started to doubt myself. Can you believe it? Long story short: he wore me down emotionally so the remaining steps of the abuse seemed normal." She shrugged again. "Like I deserved it or something. The temper rages started. He beat me several times, broke my wrist. I got scared and ended the engagement. Took me a while, but I finally came to my senses."

"Smart girl." She pointed her finger at Rachel. "Now I understand. That's why you reacted the way you did earlier when Storm was rough with you, isn't it? Oh, honey, if Storm knew…"

"There's no reason for him to know. You ready to go the rest of the way?" Sunny nodded and stood. They started walking again, arms linked.

Sunny patted Rachel's hand. "Honey, I think the two of you are kidding yourselves about the way you feel. If you could only see how you look at each other, hear the sound of your voice when you address one another…" She wiggled her fingertips in the air. "…see the sparks between you two, then you'd know what I know."

Rachel shrugged. "I've accepted how I feel. I've also accepted the man I care for is attached to another woman no matter how much he denies it. They'll work things out and she'll have her hooks deeper into him than she did before. I refuse to bemoan how much it hurts, 'cause frankly, it hurts like hell."

"What am I going to do with you two?" Sunny stopped and looked at Rachel, who crossed her arms and regarded her with one eyebrow cocked in defiance. "Okay, okay, I can see you don't want to talk about it. So, tell me what your ex-fiancé did when you broke off the engagement."

They started walking again. “He slashed my tires.”

“Bastard.”

“I replaced them. He slashed them again.”

“Oh, a determined bastard.”

She looked away. “Yes. Next he smashed a window in my SUV and slashed the seats. When that didn’t make me come crawling back to him, he broke into my house and cut up all my clothes.”

“Oh, see, now we’re gonna have to kill him. A man doesn’t mess with a woman’s wardrobe and live to tell about it.” Sunny smiled wryly.

“Of course, there were harassing phone calls and emails. Terrible texts.”

“Did you go to the police?”

She nodded. “Oh, yeah. Repeatedly. Got a restraining order against him after he beat me and broke my wrist, making it illegal for him to come within five hundred feet of me or my house. He wasn’t allowed to contact me by phone or text or e-mail.”

“I gather that didn’t stop him.”

“No. He broke in one night.” She bent to smell one of Noella’s peach roses, giving Sunny a second or two to rest. Their walk around the house was tiring her.

Sunny plucked a yellow rose and ran it over her cheek. “What happened?”

“At the time, I was taking care of a patient in a little town about thirty miles from Yazoo City, where I lived. So I commuted every day. Got home after dark every night. One night he was waiting on me, sitting in my living room, big as you please. Said he wasn’t leaving. Claimed we were getting married within the month.”

Sunny took her arm, and they started walking again. “Oh, that gives me the chills. What a sick creep. What did you do?”

“I surprised him. I pulled a gun out of my purse and ordered him out of my house.”

Sunny stopped and looked at her with a shocked expression, one tinged with respect. “Really? You had a gun?”

“Yes, I had a permit for it and everything.” They’d finished their trek around the house, and Rachel held the door open for Sunny. “He left, but not before threatening to kill me. Said I had two options—marry him and live or die without him.”

They stepped inside to the coolness of the mudroom and then entered the cleaned kitchen, where the hushed noise of the dishwasher created a humming background. Sunny collapsed in a chair, her breathing labored again. "And?"

"And I figured I had another option. I hid from him. A coward's way out, I suppose. He didn't know where I was working."

"He never followed you?"

"No, I made sure of that. Once my patient was in remission, I went to Colorado for a few weeks to relax and decide what I was going to do about Kyle. That's where I was when you contacted me. Since I came straight here, he has no idea where I am. I got a new cell phone number and e-mail address. No one in Yazoo City has it except Grace. She's the only one who knows how to get in touch with me other than my mom. For the first time in months, I feel safe."

Rachel went to the refrigerator and poured them both a glass of a carrot juice concoction she'd made earlier that morning. "Here, drink this before you lie down."

Sunny accepted the glass of orange liquid. "What will you do when you're through here?"

"You mean once you're in remission?"

Sunny lifted her glass in a mock salute. "I like how you think." She took a sip and shuddered. "What the hell is this ghastly stuff?"

Rachel laughed. "It'll grow on you. As for what I'll do once you're in remission, I don't know. I'll figure something out. I'll do some online research and find a good place to live. Somewhere warm, I think. I've never driven much in snow."

"Why not stay near here? I'd hate having you go away. We've grown so close. I could help you house hunt."

Stay here in Rosefire? Near Storm and his new wife, if they do marry? No way. She couldn't bear it. "I was thinking Arizona or New Mexico. Now, finish your juice and lie down for your nap. Leave your drapes open. The only time I want you in a darkened room from now on is at night."

The corners of Sunny's mouth twitched into a smile as she looked into her glass. "Yes, doctor."

Chapter Eleven

Storm knew he should be out checking on the sick cattle or the new mustangs. The vet was here giving them a good going over, seeing to their inoculations. Red, his foreman, was helping the vet. Still, he ought to do his fair share, especially with Eduardo in the hospital. He just couldn't seem to drag himself away from the house. He assured himself it had nothing to do with the magnetic allure of Nurse Rachel.

Pulling the navy drapery away from the window, he watched Sunny and the nurse slowly walk around the house. He was glad to see she didn't have Sunny running laps.

He ran a hand through his black hair. The infernal woman was like a tick. She bored under his skin, irritating him one minute and turning him on the next. He desired her so badly, craved her, in fact, that he thought he'd die for the wanting of her.

Damn if she hadn't been a glorious sight the day the mustangs arrived, holding Sawyer and giving him a go-to-hell glare after he told her to stay clear of the fence. Of course, if he hadn't been so taken with the image she'd presented—rebellious woman holding a child—he'd have kept Lightning away from the attacking mustang.

Sawyer moaned and rolled over. Storm glanced over his shoulder at his nephew. Back when Sunny was so sick from the chemo, getting Sawyer to take a nap was next to impossible. The child seemed to sense his mother's extreme discomfort. Storm came up with the idea of offering a treat—the boy could take his naps in Unkie Storm's big bed.

They'd made it a special private time, the two of them. Three, if you counted Pistol. Sawyer could choose two of his books for Storm to read. Sometimes he'd read the same book three and four times before the little fella finally closed his eyes. Today, it had only taken one reading of *Curious George Goes to the Beach* before he'd fallen asleep.

Storm peered out his window again, hands in his pockets. Just look at the two of them, arms linked and heads tilted toward one another, chatting as if they'd been friends forever. What were they talking about? Or whom? Had Rachel told his sister about seeing him naked or about his kissing her?

He ran a hand across the back of his neck. Would he ever stop wanting the blonde spitfire? The kiss at dawn, a few weeks ago, with her arms tight around his neck and her legs wrapped around his waist was a memory he'd have until he inhaled his final breath. He felt himself tighten again and softly swore. He'd go crazy with her staying here for another month or two until Sunny was strong enough for another round of chemotherapy.

The dreams weren't helping, either. Course right now, he had no clue if they were actual vision dreams or sexual dreams. Whichever they were, they were damned unsettling. Those blue eyes staring up at him while he made love to her.

His dad had talked about his dreams from time to time. During his teenage years, Storm had felt a sense of embarrassment over his Native heritage. When his dad had spoken of such things, he tuned the old man out. Now he wished he'd paid more attention. After college, when he sensed his dad was getting weaker, he'd listened more, asked more and remembered more. Even so, many of the gems of wisdom his dad shared during those rebellious teenaged years were lost.

Sunny and Rachel stopped walking, and that change of movement caught his attention again. Rachel was so animated when she talked. He smiled. He surely did enjoy watching her; doing so calmed him in a strange way. Calmed him and coaxed him to draw closer to her.

Pilar's call earlier had upset Rachel. She'd never admit it or make a big scene the way Pilar would in the same situation, but the pain was there in her eyes. Damn, he hated hurting her. But it looked as if he had to have another blow-up with Pilar, tell her once more he didn't want to see or hear from her again. This time he'd be more adamant and unyielding. He'd make damn sure she knew they were through. Maybe he'd even tell her he was interested in someone else.

Without a doubt, Rachel affected him. He didn't think his heart could stand another look at her in a tight bathing suit. With her figure, she made a conservative suit look obscene. If one of his ranch hands saw her, he'd have to shoot the bastard. Imagine what she'd look like in a skimpy bikini. He groaned.

Seeing her talking to Ben that morning soon after she'd arrived touched off something so elemental, it scared him. She'd only talked to the ranch hand for a few minutes, yet he was ready to tear something apart in a rage so deep, so dark he barely recognized it for what it was—jealousy.

He ran a hand down his face and gazed longingly back at the bed. For two cents, he'd lay down with Sawyer and take a nap, too, especially now that he was taking Pilar to an art exhibit full of weird paintings he didn't understand or like. Getting gussied up in a tux and driving the hour plus to Austin was the last thing he wanted to do tonight. Still, he had to make sure Pilar understood they were no longer a couple.

Now his desires raced toward Rachel which was odd, for she wasn't his style. She was too opinionated and, at times, too plucky. He smiled. He didn't think she'd back down from anyone. He had to respect that quality in her. The girl had nerve.

She'd also brought the house back to life, demanding everyone talk in normal tones again and that music fill the home. He and Noella had only tried to create a home environment where Sunny could rest. According to Nurse Rachel, they'd turned it into a tomb.

The vet's van slowly drove away from the paddock where the sick animals were kept. No use to hurry outside now. Storm turned away from the window. More ranch records waited for entry into the computer. He'd sooner take a beating. Before he left his room, he tugged the sheet over Sawyer's shoulders. The child mumbled in his sleep, "Wachel..."

"Feel sorry for ya, kid. Know just how you feel. I dream about her, too."

Over an hour later, Storm rubbed his forehead, wishing he could ease the pounding. He searched through his desk drawers for aspirin. Nothing. He was sure Noella kept some in the kitchen. Striding down the hall, he heard humming coming from the den. He poked his head in and found Rachel sitting, with her feet tucked under her, sewing. Her glorious hair was loose, curling and cascading around her shoulders and down her back.

"What are you doing?"

She jumped, jabbing her finger with the needle. "Must you always scare me like that?" She sucked her finger in those luscious lips of hers. More male fantasies grabbed him by the throat, making breathing difficult.

He entered the room. "You never answered my question." Remnants of T-shirts lay on the coffee table. "What are you sewing?"

She held up the project she'd been laboring over. "I'm making a Superman cape for Sawyer, just like I promised." The body of the cape was royal blue. She was sewing on a big red "S." "I didn't have any material, so I used two of my T-shirts. What do you think?"

He was touched. "I think he'll love it." He fingered the red T-shirt, noting the hole shaped roughly like the letter she was attaching to the cape. "You didn't have to ruin your shirts."

She shrugged and made a few more stitches. "They're just clothes. I've learned not to get too attached to things. Life is about people, not objects." She knotted the thread and cut it. "There, all done. I can see him running through the house wearing it. Can't you?" She chuckled in obvious delight, holding it up and inspecting her handiwork with a critical eye.

Storm watched her excitement over making something for a child. Pilar was just the opposite. Clothes ranked high on her priority list, more so than people. During their engagement, he often wondered if he made enough money to keep her in silks and satins. A pain jabbed his head, and he reached for his temples.

"What's wrong? Headache?" Rachel lay her sewing aside.

"Yeah. I was on my way to get some aspirins. Three or four ought to knock out the worst of it." He rubbed his temples some more.

"Uh-huh. Sit down, cowboy." She motioned to the sofa, and he sat. "Where does it hurt? We can't have you going to see your main squeeze tonight with a headache, now can we?"

"Look, you think I want to go? I promised Pilar over a month ago I'd go to this stupid art event. A friend of hers is having a showing."

She looked away and sighed. Did she really want to have this conversation? Wouldn't it be better to let sleeping dogs lie, as her daddy used to say? "Let's not argue. Just show me where your headache hurts. I'll see if I can help."

He sat and then pointed to the areas of pain with his index finger. "Up the back of my neck into my head. Around my head.

Behind my eyes." He'd long since associated his heartburn with stress, now he was wondering if the headaches came from the same source, too.

She stood behind the sofa and started massaging, using her trained thumbs at pressure points. "You get these often?"

"Yeah. Anytime I'm stuck in front of that computer for hours." Or when I think about spending time with Pilar. He blinked several times at that personal revelation. Why hadn't he made that connection before?

"Maybe you need glasses to wear when doing computer work." She slowly ran her fingers up and down his neck and then across his shoulders, pressing in hard with her thumbs and gently rippling with her fingers. "You've got knots of tension back here. Big knots."

She leaned over him and dug her elbow into his shoulder. He didn't know which felt better—her massaging or her breasts pressed against his back. Scents of her perfume wafted in the air, luring and beguiling like a floral siren. Her breathing had quickened in his ear as she ministered to him. His had quickened in like manner. Every one of his senses homed in on Rachel. She was consuming him.

"My God," he moaned.

"I know I'm being rough, but this is the best way to get these subscapulari muscles to relax. Your trapezes are so tight, too. Goodness."

Her voice was deep and breathless with exertion, which only fueled his arousal. He closed his eyes. While her massaging and pounding of his muscles sent chills up and down his spine, the smell of her perfume, the sound of her voice, the feel of her breathing against his neck and his ear was inflaming his manhood to near madness. The warmth of her sensual touch was killing him. If he lived through this, he was heading for a cold shower. Hell, a dozen cold showers couldn't undo the effect she was having on him.

"Tilt your head forward, Storm. I've never seen anyone so tense. Even your rhomboids are knotted." She pressed against him more, rotating her elbow into his knotted muscles. "It's almost as if the harder I massage, the tighter your knots get."

No fake! His whole body was a mass of sexual knots. He glanced over his shoulder, taking in her determined expression, her teeth gritted as she pounded and elbowed his muscles into submission. She was clearly in nursing mode, clueless as to what she was doing to his libido.

"Rachel."

She leaned forward and increased her pressure on his shoulder. "Can't...talk...now," she grunted.

"Rachel."

"Maybe...maybe if I try from the front." She hurried around the sofa. To his utter amazement, she crawled onto the sofa, straddling her knees on either side of his lap. "Lean down and put your head against my chest. Let me attack those knotted subs and traps from this angle."

If she wasn't the cutest thing, hell-bent on ridding him of his headache. If he leaned his head between her breasts, he'd be a goner. No male, unless he was six feet under and had been there for twenty years, could take this.

"Rachel."

"Come on, lean against me. Wish I had one of my wooden rollers to run over your muscles. Maybe I should go upstairs and get one."

"Rachel."

She finally stopped talking and peered into his eyes. He watched her slowly shift from nurse to woman. Saw her blink as awareness surfaced. Her blue eyes, wide with shock, shifted to his mouth. "I...ah...should...get off your lap."

He placed his hands at her waist and shook his head. "No, you're fine." He slowly ran his hands up her back and sighed a kiss to her neck. She shuddered when his warm breath caressed her skin.

"This isn't a good idea. I…I should move."

"Stay...stay." Storm's hands sifted through her long hair. "Silk and curls. I've thought of running my hands through your beautiful hair." She pulled back, her gaze searching his face, her lips parted. "I keep thinking of kissing you again." His hands clenched in her hair and ever so slowly, he brought her face toward his. "Come here, mouse."

His lips massaged hers, touching and sipping until a sigh escaped her lips. "You've been driving me crazy." He groaned the words against her lips before he captured them, pouring all his desire and needs into the kiss.

She ran her hands up his chest, around his neck and into his hair. When she moaned, he pressed her closer. He'd meant only to kiss her one time, to taste her lips once more, but that objective was gone. Now he needed more, sought more and, by damn, would have more.

He bit her lower lip, gently tugging it out and running his tongue inside the warm flesh of that luscious lip. She shuddered, and he was lost. Lost in kiss after kiss. He spiraled toward sensual oblivion, lost in the essence of her. She'd taken possession of his soul—a conquest he was powerless to resist.

Rachel's fingers trembled over his face, her eyes cloudy with desire, her lips swollen.

He covered her face with countless delicate kisses as if she were an elusive dream he meant to detain. His hands fumbled for the hem of her shirt and slowly explored her back, forging a trail upward. Velvet—she was warm human velvet; he could spend forever touching her. She quivered and locked her arms around his neck. "Storm." His name was uttered on an exhale of desire.

She took his earlobe into her mouth and nipped it. He groaned, tightening his hold on her. Pulling back, she tugged at his T-shirt. He leaned forward and she pulled it off. She ran warm hands over his shoulders and pecs, murmuring words he couldn't quite hear over his own heavy breathing. She bent her head and ran her tongue from his neck to his chest. He gasped when she bit his nipple.

"My God, Rach." He grabbed her arms and pulled her upward, capturing her lips again. He delved his tongue into their sweet moistness.

Sensations—he was immersed in the glory of sensations; at once he wanted to drag them into eternity and rush to completion. He tilted his head to gain deeper access with his lips and tongue. She rubbed her breasts against him, driving him totally out of his mind.

Obsession—she'd been his obsession from the first dream, before he laid eyes on her. He wanted to touch every part of her, needed to touch every part of her. His hands moved under her shirt to unsnap the front clasp of her bra, and her breasts fell free. He groaned, marveling at the feel of her. When he ran his thumbs over her beaded nipples, her head fell back as if in total surrender as she moaned his name.

Enough—he couldn't get enough of her. An ecstatic madness overtook him. He leaned down and placed his lips around her nipple, licking, tugging, sucking. Closer, he needed her closer. So close that they, though two, became one, separate, but united. The madness of wanting her, possessing her, and, yes, surrendering to her consumed him. He brought a hand to her bottom and rocked her against his hardness, wanting her to know how she affected him.

He rocked against her in a gentle rhythm over and over, a prelude to the dance of love—slowly, very slowly, whispering her name with every intimate connection of man to woman. She fisted her hands in his hair and shuddered. "My God! It's too much! It's too strong! Storm...Storm." She'd climaxed in his arms, on his lap, fully dressed. He held her close as she shattered and trembled. He tattooed a ribbon of kisses to her neck. The woman was magnificent.

He had to be inside her, needed to feel her surround him. The madness of desiring her was burning his very soul. He slid a hand down the back of her jeans and once more brought her in intimate contact with the hard length of him. "Rach...Rach, I need you..."

"Little one, Noella bring you some ice..."

"Oh, my God!" Rachel jumped from his lap, trying in vain to straighten her T-shirt, tugging it over her exposed breasts. Her face was blushed, her eyes languid, and lips swollen from his endless kisses.

Storm closed his eyes and leaned his head against the back of the sofa, breathing hard, trying to regain control. What had he done? He'd been so maddened for her he'd lost all restraint. In his twenty-nine years, he'd always been in complete control. He opened his eyes and focused on his flesh and blood desire.

"What...what is going on here?" Noella looked from him to Rachel, both obviously embarrassed.

Rachel's eyes sought his, pleading for help. Her face, already flushed with desire and completion, blushed a deeper red. She never made eye contact with Noella. "Nothing...nothing is going on." She hurried from the room.

"Storm Sawyer Blackhawk!" Noella slammed the tray of refreshments she'd prepared for Rachel onto the coffee table. "You cannot dally with that girl. She's too sweet."

He rubbed his hands over his face. "I know how sweet she is. It just happened. It meant nothing." It meant *everything*.

His mind was still crammed with the sweet sensations of Rachel; his fingertips still tingled with the touch of her, and his mouth was still full of her taste. His body ached for her like he'd never ached for another woman, including Pilar. He sat forward, dangling his hands between his knees, and shook his head. Just how did a man get over a woman like Rachel Dennison?

Noella fisted hands on her hips. "Are you still dating Pilar or not? Either you break it off with Pilar or stay away from Rachel. You cannot have both." She snatched his discarded shirt, tossed it at him and stormed out.

Storm leaned back and closed his eyes, willing his body to calm. The time had come to accept the inevitable. He loved and craved Rachel with his whole being.

Chapter Twelve

Rachel slid down the closed door of her bedroom onto the carpet. She was trembling and sobbing, so humiliated she never wanted to set foot out of her room again. She'd allowed Storm to do things to her, and she'd reacted to it all.

What did Storm say to Noella? "It just happened. It meant nothing." She swiped at the tears coursing down her face. Nothing. It meant nothing to him. While...while it had meant *everything* to her. At the age of twenty-seven, she'd just had her first climax, fully dressed in the arms of a man who couldn't emotionally let go of another woman.

She was by no means a virgin, having lost that status in college. Sex was something she enjoyed even if she never reached the summit, so to speak. She appreciated the kissing, the touching, the closeness and that special enjoyment two people could bring each other. Toward the end of her relationship with Kyle, however, sex had become a chore. How could a woman begin to respond to a man who brought her so much misery? Just now, with Storm, with all her senses heightened, she'd had her first climax. The experience was a beautiful moment for her, but a meaningless one for him.

If she hadn't stopped in the hallway outside the den to refasten her bra, she wouldn't have heard his remarks to Noella, wouldn't have known that was how he truly felt.

She raised her knees and pressed her forehead to them, wrapping her arms around her legs. A wave of self-hate went through her. Noella had walked into the room while she was still climaxing. She saw. She had to have known what was happening.

The sobbing began anew. How could one go from the ecstasy she'd felt in Storm's arms to the depths of disgrace she felt now? A long time passed before the crying jag ended.

The last thing Rachel wanted to do was face Storm and Noella again, but the reality was she had a job to do here. What little pride she had left propelled her to face them both, no matter how difficult.

Fresh from her shower, she braided her wet hair and added one last swipe of mascara to her swollen eyelids. Her tan linen pantsuit, with square black buttons down the front, was boxy enough to camouflage her ample bosom. She added black square earrings and slipped black bangles onto her arm before stepping into black strappy heels.

One quick turn in front of the mirror told her she looked presentable—for a wanton woman who couldn't seem to stay away from her patient's brother. A man she barely knew, no less. Well, that ended right here, right now. She was not ruled by hormones or by Storm's magnetic maleness or the power of his kisses. What was called for was grit and determination.

She would walk down those steps and into the dining room. Her head would be held high and her face emotionless. She'd be coolly polite. Once she made it through dinner, she would plead exhaustion and retreat to her bedroom—for round two of a major crying jag.

Her gaze traveled to the desk where she'd written and discarded two letters of resignation. Sunny needed her; she couldn't turn tail and run. The needs of her patient always came first. She was a nurse, and nurses lived by a special set of codes, both personal and professional.

Reaching for her glucometer, she pricked her finger to check her sugar levels before eating. With all the stresses she'd had these past few months—Kyle's harassment, hiding from him, and meeting Storm—her glucose levels were jumping all over the place. Knowing this, she was checking her levels more often. A higher sugar reading meant adjusting her diet and increasing her exercise routine. When her reading flashed eighty points higher than what she liked, she resigned herself to stricter portion control and sit-ups and push-ups after dinner.

With one hand on the doorknob, she pressed the other to her stomach, trying to still the butterflies. She could do this. She *would* do this.

Halfway down the steps, she heard Storm laugh. The sound of his voice washed over her like warm honey, and her traitorous stomach lurched. She was too raw with emotion, her system still on overload with sensations. She turned to go back to her room, admitting there was no way she could do this.

"I thought I heard your footsteps."

She stopped and slowly looked over her shoulder. Storm was standing at the foot of the curved stairway, a hesitant smile causing his dimples to flash. He was dressed in a tuxedo, ready for his date with Pilar.

Gorgeous hunk didn't begin to describe him. His white shirt was a stark contrast to his tanned face. Shoulder-length black hair was brushed behind his ears. Obviously, his tuxedo was tailor-made to fit those broad shoulders and chest muscles. Chest muscles she'd touched and kissed earlier. She closed her eyes at the memory, and her stomach twisted again.

"You're not going to run from me, are you, mouse?" his voice taunted. "Noella's serving grilled salmon. Would be a shame to miss it."

So, this was how it would be. He'd goad her and delight in her reaction. Well, she could handle it. She'd handled Kyle, hadn't she? Just to show him she wouldn't cower, she kept her gaze focused on his as she descended the stairs. No smiles were wasted on him; she wore a stony mask.

"You've been crying. Your eyes are swollen." He reached out and cupped her face. "Tell me, love. Tell me, why you were crying?" His gaze searched hers for something, but she hadn't a clue what. The pad of his thumb slid across her lower lip. His eyes darkened.

Rachel jerked away. "Don't touch me! I'm your sister's nurse, not your plaything."

"Rachel. Mouse."

"Leave me alone." She turned on her heel and headed for the dining room. A steely hand snaked out, spun her around and hauled her back to the hardness of his chest. His arms tightened around her. Angry eyes locked. Wills warred. The muscle in his jaw bunched.

"How would you like to go see your main squeeze tonight with a black eye? Get your hands off me, or so help me, God, I'll..." She shook her fist at him.

"Storm, Rachel, what's going on?" Sunny stood in the doorway to the dining room, her eyes wide with concern.

Storm released his hold on Rachel, holding his palms out in a "holds-off" gesture, his eyes cold. "Tell Noella I'm sorry to miss dinner, but I need to see my *main squeeze*." He turned and strode out the front door. Both women jumped when it slammed.

Sunny walked toward Rachel. "Honey? What happened between you two?" She glanced back at the door. "What's gotten under his craw?" She waved a hand in the direction of the kitchen. "Noella's in one of her door-slamming moods." Then she rubbed Rachel's arm. "You're crying. *What* in blue blazes is going on in this house?"

Rachel swiped at a tear, still trembling from seeing Storm, feeling his anger, reacting to the potency of his masculinity. She glared at the door. No way in hell would she allow him to ruin her evening.

Her smile was rueful. "Well, at least you can't say you live in a tomb anymore."

Noella stormed out of the dining room. "Where is everyone? My dinner's getting cold." She looked around. "Where's Master Storm?"

"He left in a huff," Sunny replied.

"Said he was eager to…eager to see his main squeeze." Rachel choked out a sob and placed a trembling hand to her mouth. "I'm sorry. He just makes me so mad, and I have no clue why."

Noella took her in her arms. "There, there, little one. A woman is always more vulnerable when she's falling in love. Come. You eat, *sí?* Everything will work out. Master Storm is too passionate a man. It is his Comanche heritage, but I say nothing."

****

Storm pressed the doorbell to Pilar's upscale apartment. He could have used the key she'd given him over a year ago, but that would only send a message of hope.

She opened the door, her forehead wrinkled and her lips pinched. "You're early. You know how I hate that. You can see I'm not finished dressing." She pivoted on her bare feet. "Zip me up, would you? Why didn't you use your key instead of making me answer the door? That wasn't very considerate of you."

He took her wrist and pressed the key onto her palm, closing her fingers over it. "Since we're no longer engaged, I won't be needing it. Nor will we be seeing each other again after tonight. I'm only here because I promised to take you to this event."

Pilar's expression changed from annoyed to persuasive. She straightened his bow tie and ran her polished fingertips down the lapels of his tuxedo jacket. "Darling, certainly it wouldn't hurt for us to date every once in a while. What would be the harm?"

"I see you're still wearing my engagement ring. We ended things several weeks ago."

She faked an innocent response when she held up her ring finger. "Oh, am I? I'm just so used to it being there. It feels so right, I hate to take it off. Don't be a grumpy soul, Storm. Surely we can work this out." She looped her arms around his neck. "I know a hundred ways to make you change your mind. Besides, I haven't told Daddy yet. You know how testy he gets when someone hurts his little girl." She batted her eyes at Storm.

How had he ever felt any attraction for this spoiled, fake woman? "We're through Pilar. Tonight is the last night we're seeing each other."

She stepped back a pace, her face contorted with rage. "What did you just say?"

"This is our last evening together. Now finish getting dressed so we can get this over with." He slipped a roll of antacids from his pants pocket and popped two into his mouth.

Pilar reared back like a boa constrictor, ready to strike. "Why you vile, mean bastard! How dare you treat me like this?"

He leaned toward her and narrowed his eyes. "From what I've heard, you've been cheating on me and doing drugs."

"Oh pooh. Only at parties, which hardly counts."

"Which at parties? The cheating or the drugs? Look, we don't have enough in common to maintain a relationship. You're silk and champagne. I'm denim and cold beer. I blame myself for not realizing it earlier. Your beauty blinded me. It took me a long time to realize how spoiled you are. I run a large ranch and don't have time or the endless finances to accommodate your many whims."

She threw a few more insults and hurled some expensive vases and figurines. But when he turned to leave, she calmed down and begged him to go through the evening.

Pilar was in a major pout when they returned to her condo building earlier than she wanted. When they stepped onto the elevator, she complained. "I still don't see why we had to leave so early. The party wasn't even in full swing yet." She shot him a disgusted look when he depressed the button for her floor. "Was it because some people were doing coke? I've told you, it's no big deal. It's a way for people to relax. Yes, I did some, but only a couple lines."

"I don't approve of drugs. They make slaves of people." They were from two different worlds, he and Pilar. Why hadn't that obvious fact slapped him between the eyeballs ages ago? Man, a Q-Tip displayed more smarts than he had over this woman.

"Sometimes you can be so uptight, darling." The doors of the elevator whispered open. Pilar sashayed down the carpeted hallway, removing her key from her tiny bag. "You never even commented on my new purse." She pouted. "It's Louis Vuitton, and you never even noticed."

"Do I look like I give a rat's ass about a woman's handbag? Good night, Pilar, and good bye. Don't call. Don't text. We're through."

He smiled when she slammed the door in his face. One hurtle down. He'd made it damn clear their relationship was over. Now, he had to work at winning over Rachel. Just how he would do that would take some major planning. He'd really hurt her this evening by seeing Pilar.

Chapter Thirteen

Storm and Rachel politely ignored each other for the next four days. The tension of their silent warfare strained Rachel's nerves. At times she wanted to toss her clothes into her suitcases, grab her laptop and kiss the Triple-S good-bye. Then little Sawyer would come charging into a room wearing the cape she made him or she'd see Sunny making progress, and she knew she had to stay. She was settling into a routine that revolved around Sunny and the little boy.

Every morning, Rachel would rise early, eat a container of yogurt and run two trips back and forth to the gates, totaling a five-mile run, something she needed with her sugar levels jumping all over the place. Storm evidently got up earlier, ate his breakfast and busied himself around the ranch so he wouldn't come in contact with her. Which was fine by Rachel.

After her run, she'd shower and dress, then she'd place a card bearing an inspiring thought on Sunny's breakfast plate. When Mother and child came downstairs for breakfast, Sawyer would clap his hands, begging his mommy to read him the card. Sunny would read it aloud, explaining it to the child in simplistic terms. Rachel admired Sunny's gift of being a good and patient mother.

Sawyer, sweet child that he was, had giggled and charmed his way into Rachel's heart. He'd worn her hand-sewn Superman cape faithfully from the time she'd put it on him. Echoes of his running and shouting, "Supa-man Sawyer! Here to wesque you! Here to fight ebil. Supa-man Sawyer!" filled the house.

For the first time in her life, she was thinking about having a child of her own. In the future, of course, after she married. Still, for a woman who'd been obsessed with her education and career, dreaming of being a mother one day was a giant leap. The problem was every child she envisioned holding in her arms, nursing at her breast, had straight dark hair and proud black eyes.

After breakfast, she'd have Sunny tend to her pots of healing herbs, pinching and watering. She was growing peppermint, lemon balm, rosemary, valerian and sage. Rachel also helped Sawyer plant two little offshoots of the plants in clay pots. Mother and son fussed over their herbs together. When Sawyer consistently drowned his plants with too much water, Rachel looked the other way and smiled. He was such an exuberant child; she adored him.

Much as Sunny hated taking more pills, Rachel added many vitamins and high-quality supplements to her regimen. Her patient didn't complain—much.

In addition, Sunny was adjusting to the changes in her diet. Noella was now cooking with olive oil and serving more fresh fruits and vegetables.

Sunny's time in the pool, followed by sunning on a chaise lounge, gave her some color. Water aerobics and swimming laps were slowly increased her strength and endurance. Playing in the pool with her son was adding joy to her life. During her a daily massage, she and Rachel exchanged secrets and shared dreams. Her patient was allowing herself to hope for a future with Jackson. Daily applications of special lotions Rachel blended softened Sunny's scaly skin again, adding a healthy glow.

Preliminary plans for Sunny and Storm's birthday barbeque were listed on a notepad Sunny organized over and over. The thought of being well enough to have a party had her so excited. Noella was in charge of hiring caterers and engaging the band. Storm hired a bartender and rented canopies and chairs. Sunny designed and printed invitations for thirty friends while Storm hovered nearby, scowling and fretting over his sister's time in front of the computer. He wanted her resting. She'd never seen a man so protective of those he loved. Rachel's job, it seemed, was to mail the invitations in town at the post office and then stay out of the way, or so Storm silently implied with an imperiously raised eyebrow.

Fine. She could do that. Never let it be said Rachel Irene Dennison stuck her nose in where it wasn't wanted. Still, the man confused her with his mixed signals. At times he avoided her and at times he was everywhere, watching her with those dark eyes.

One afternoon when she was carrying a tray of steaming green tea and homemade cookies into the den for Sunny, she stumbled. She'd known Storm was behind her in the hall and was paying attention to his footsteps following her. Perhaps that's how the toe of her shoe got caught under the edge of the Oriental carpet.

Storm's strong arms swiftly went around her waist, drawing her back to the hardness of his chest, steadying her, unnerving her. "Careful, mouse. You okay?" he breathed against her ear. Her stomach did that crazy flip-flop thing it did whenever he touched her. *God, but I miss his hands on me.*

She nodded, afraid if she turned to look into his eyes, she'd be lost. To her delight and displeasure—she didn't know which, her feelings were so jumbled these days—he brushed her hair back with his fingertips and kissed her neck, keeping his lips pressed to her as if he couldn't bear for the connection to end. "You smell like heaven, sweetheart." Then he silently turned and left the room. The man had her so confused with desire and irritation, she wanted to hurl the tray of teacups against the wall.

When Rachel handed Sunny her freshly brewed cup of green tea, Sunny rolled her eyes and droned on about her eyes starting to turn green from so much of the brew. Although she'd observed the scene between Rachel and Storm, Sunny didn't mention it, thank goodness. She'd have burst into tears if the woman had.

Sunny was the model patient. She'd read the Mayo Clinic report Rachel showed her, which stated that green tea extract helped reduce the number of leukemia cells and shrink swollen lymph nodes. Thus, green tea had become Sunny's drink of choice.

Everyone was pleased with Sunny's small steps of improvement. Every day brought new challenges and ever increasing degrees of hope. However, Rachel had to admit the biggest impetus to Sunny's progress was the blooming relationship between her and Jackson Cole.

The old cliché that the road to true love was never smooth certainly applied to those two. Sunny shared all the ups and downs, the passionate times and the arguments, the mistakes and misunderstandings that had kept them apart when they were so clearly perfect for each other. She confided to Rachel her hope that this time, they'd get things right.

Their feminine delight was phenomenal when they discovered signs of dark hair growth on Sunny's scalp. Sawyer ran his little hand over his mommy's head. "Mommy, your haih is as soft as Pistol's. Are you gwowing doggie haih?" Both women pealed with laughter. The basset hound barked at their exuberance, adding to their joyous melee.

Rachel had taken to riding Princess in the evenings after dinner. Red always rode along to keep her company and to "relax," he claimed. She figured he was afraid she'd get lost, and perhaps she would have. The ranch was immense but vastly beautiful. No wonder Storm—jerk that he was—loved every inch of it.

Red seemed to enjoy showing her the property. He'd spent a good part of his life there, working first for Mr. Blackhawk and now for Storm. He expressed great respect for his boss, bringing his name up at every opportunity, which wasn't something Rachel needed to hear when she was so angry with him. Even so, Red was teaching her things about the ranch.

Some sections of the land were flat, so flat you could see for miles and miles. Hundreds of heads of cattle grazed on the range. Other sections contained hills and wooded areas, all teaming with wildlife. She especially liked riding along the creek, listening to its calming song as it rippled and surged over rocks.

Red pointed out wildlife and vegetation. Along the creek were bald cypress trees with needle-like leaves, Yaupon, an interesting evergreen, Parsley Hawthorne and many more varieties Red knew, but she'd never remember. He showed her cottontail rabbits, raccoons, fox squirrels and white-tail deer. Last evening they'd seen a pair of coyotes watching them from a hill. He taught her to listen for armadillos, which you heard digging for food long before you saw them. She found it fascinating that momma armadillos always bore four pups, all of the same sex.

Time seemed to stand still when she rode Princess. For in those fleeting moments, all of life's problems disappeared. Because of its emotional benefits for Rachel, she planned to start Sunny riding again next week. This added pleasure was sure to boost her patient's mood.

Rachel had to admit she chose to ride after dinner because Storm spent most evenings locked in his office. She was avoiding him as best she could. For that reason, she'd taken to eating her luncheon salad out on the patio by the pool, saying lunch should be family time. When Sunny objected, Storm flatly stated the nurse should eat her lunch wherever she damned well pleased. Evidently, he didn't want her near him any more than Rachel wanted to be near him.

Once Storm carried Sawyer to his room for the child's afternoon nap, Sunny would join Rachel on the patio. Their after-lunch walks had increased to two trips around the ranch house, followed by acupuncture and Sunny's nap.

When Sunny was rested, Rachel led her through her yoga poses. Her patient was gaining strength and feeling more alive.

She, on the other hand, was feeling restless and lifeless with the absence of Storm's company, his touch, his kiss—and she didn't like it. Nor did she like the fact she constantly relived that sensual session on the sofa. How could any other man possibly erase those few moments of intensity with Storm? Moments that clearly meant nothing to him, but everything to her.

To Storm's credit, he was sickeningly polite on the occasions they ran into each other. It galled her. Still, wasn't that what she'd told him? She was at the Triple-S solely as Sunny's nurse, and nothing else. Hadn't she insisted he leave her alone? Still, he didn't have to go to such extremes. Where was he tonight? With his girlfriend...ex-girlfriend...whatever Pilar was?

She pierced a piece of steak and grumbled under her breath that Storm Blackhawk was a heartless bastard.

"You always attack your food like that? Or does eating red meat bring out your violent tendencies?" Jackson leaned back in his chair, holding a glass of iced tea. "I believe you could be downright dangerous, little lady."

Rachel blinked twice, bringing the present into focus. She'd been so wrapped up in her mental venting that she'd withdrawn from the dinner conversation. Jackson had dropped by earlier with more roses for Sunny. She'd invited him to stay for dinner.

"Sorry. Guess I was zoning off." Deep in thought about Storm Blackhawk and how he'd ruined her life.

Sunny placed her elbows on the table and folded her hands, resting her chin on them. "Do your thoughts revolve around my brother? My *missing* brother, I might add? I haven't seen him all day. Have you, Noella?"

"*Sí,* earlier. He's been very busy. Ranch stuff, you know." The housekeeper shrugged.

Sunny gave Noella a strange look, her expression still quizzical when she turned to Rachel. "Is it my brother who's upset you?"

Rachel shot a look at Jackson. He was Storm's best friend. She doubted he wanted to hear her tear him apart. Fact was, tonight she didn't have it in her to make polite chitchat. Her muscles were jumpy and her mood dark. She needed something. Maybe an after-dinner run to deplete her store of nervous energy. Her cell phone rang.

"Sorry, I thought I'd turned it off." She slipped the jangling phone from the pocket of her white slacks and checked the display. "Oh, it's Grace Palmer, my best friend." She swiped the screen. "Hey, girl. What's happening?"

"Rachel? Rachel…my apartment was broken into." Grace was crying.

"Are you serious? Were you hurt?" Rachel's throat tightened and her stomach twisted. The two of them had been roommates at the Southern Mississippi School of Nursing for four years. They'd forged a quick and lasting bond.

"I'm fine. I'm on night shift this week, so I was at the hospital when it happened. Whoever broke in came in through the sliding glass doors on my balcony."

"Your balcony? You live on the third floor." She shoved her hair back from her face. How awful for Grace to have the safety of her home violated like that. She must be very frightened.

Grace scoffed. "Yeah, so much for Dad's philosophy of being safer on higher ground. Look, the thief took my grandma's diamond and pearl ring, my new TV and"—she sighed—"my laptop."

Rachel sipped her tea, hoping to steady her nerves. "Oh, honey, they're just things. Except for your grandma's ring, they can all be replaced. Thank God you weren't home. You could have been hurt."

"Mom keeps saying the same thing. But as for the ring…at first glance, Grandma's ring doesn't look valuable. It was in my jewelry box along with my high-school ring and the heart-shaped sapphire ring I bought on that cruise you and I went on two years ago. Remember? Only someone who knew the ring would see it was more valuable than the other two." She cleared her throat. "Someone like a relative, Rach."

Rachel frowned. Everything came to a standstill for a beat, including her breathing. No. No, she couldn't mean her cousin, Kyle. "Are you implying what I think you're implying? You…you think Kyle broke into your apartment?"

"That's the theory the police are working on. The thing is, if he has my computer…"

A cold chill clawed its way up Rachel's spine, like a prowling, menacing panther. "You…you had my contact information on your computer, didn't you? And all of my emails."

"I'm sorry, but yes, I did. They're all under a file I labeled as BFF. I thought you should know, just in case." Grace sounded full of regret.

Rachel's gaze darted around the dining room, coming to grips with the cold, hard truth. Kyle knew where she was. Memories of the beatings, the yelling, the threats came rolling at her like the proverbial snowball on a hill, ever increasing in size as it silently barreled toward her.

"Rachel, I'm sorry." Grace was crying again.

"It's not your fault." Her voice sounded wooden. "Where are you staying? Do you want to stay at my house? I can contact the realtor, tell her you're using it should she want to show it."

"No, my folks are insisting I come home until this whole mess gets settled."

Rachel ended the conversation and placed her cell on the table next to her plate. Her heart was racing and her palms sweaty. Calm, she had to remain calm. Logical, she had to think logically. Had the thief been Kyle? Would Kyle break into his cousin's home? He'd broken into hers. If he stole Grace's computer, then he could access her emails, he'd find her address and new phone number. Her phone rang, and she jumped.

Chapter Fourteen

"You gonna answer that thing or just stare at it?" Jackson broke through Rachel's fog of trepidation.

She flipped the phone over and closed her eyes a beat, pleading a silent prayer before looking at the display. Her heart sank—Kyle Benson. She couldn't go through this all over again. Now he had her number, he'd call her relentlessly. She'd have to get it changed.

"Rachel? Is it Kyle?" Sunny's voice was full of concern.

Before she could reply, Jackson reached across the table and snatched the phone from her hand. "Kyle Benson, this is Chief of Police Jackson Cole. If you're stupid enough to call this number again, I assure you, your next phone call will be from a jail cell to your lawyer." He tapped the end call icon and slid it back across the table.

Rachel sat back in her chair and folded her arms. "Okay, Mr. Chief of Police. How did you know Kyle's full name? I never told Sunny what it was."

Noella picked Sawyer out of his booster seat. "Miss Sunny, I'll give him his bath tonight while the three of you talk. Come on, my sweet boy, what toys do you want in your bath?"

Sunny waited until the housekeeper and child were out of earshot, then turned to Jackson. "I never told you a thing about her ex-fiancé. How did you know his name or that he'd be threatening her?" Both women glared at him, waiting.

"Man, can't believe I screwed up like that." Jackson sat back in his chair and rubbed both hands over his face.

"Jackson, out with it." The tone of Sunny's voice clearly indicated she expected a reply. "Didn't we just promise each other honesty?"

Jackson sighed audibly, then nodded. "Yeah, sugar, we did. I did a background check on Rachel before Storm agreed to you hiring her. There were police reports of domestic violence incidents and vandalism, followed by a restraining order against one Kyle Benson."

"You investigated me? Me, *personally*, not professionally." Of all the nerve. Suddenly, she felt violated. This man knew all her personal stuff. Not that she had anything to hide. Still…

Jackson's gaze on her was steady. "You have to realize this woman sitting next to me is the most important person in my life. Storm's, too. So when he asked..."

"This was Storm's idea?" She snatched the phone, stood and shoved it into her pocket, fairly trembling with outrage. "I expect people to check out my professional credentials, demand it, in fact. But to delve and probe through my personal life makes me feel like you've rummaged through my panty drawer to see if I prefer thongs to bikinis. The next time I see Storm I'm going to give him a piece of my mind." She picked up her plate and silverware and carried them to the sink.

Jackson followed. "Look, I don't see anything wrong with what we did. Would you invite a total stranger to live in your home without first making sure he or she wasn't a criminal? A child molester or a thief? Even educated people, credentialed people do unspeakable things. Storm was only protecting his family, as any man worth his salt would do."

She turned to face him, angry, hurt and embarrassed that her personal life had been picked and prodded through. "I see your logic, but I don't have to like it. Does Storm know about Kyle, about the abuse?"

"Storm's concern was that you had no police record, no history of wrongdoing. Since you were the victim, a squeaky clean victim, I saw no need to divulge any information about the attacks on your property or your person. Now, you gonna tell me about that phone call?" He looked every inch the lawman. Brash. Determined. Fierce.

"Someone broke into my best friend's apartment and stole her laptop." She exhaled a long sigh, then shared the details of Grace's break-in. The uneasiness over Kyle returned. He'd read all her emails to Grace; she was sure of it. E-mails where she shared her true feelings about Storm. She turned and stared out the window. She had to get away. Had to.

Jackson gently laid a hand on her shoulder. "You can't keep running."

"Gee, a lawman who's psychic." She turned and gazed into his concerned eyes. "Sunny, you're a lucky woman to be loved by a man like this. He may appear gruff, but he's got a good heart."

Sunny approached and stood behind Jackson, wrapping her

arms around his waist. "I've always known what a good man he is, even when he was acting like an ass. That's behind us now."

He turned and wrapped an arm around Sunny, kissing her forehead. Their love was so palpable, the room nearly filled with it. His attention returned to her. "Rachel, you'd better call Grace. Tell her you've gotten a call from Benson. If he has your new number, then he's the one who stole the laptop. She needs to relay that information to the police in Yazoo City."

She nodded. "Yeah, guess you're right." Just then her phone chirped, indicating the arrival of a text message. Her stomach twisted. Her hand trembled when she swiped the text key.

"no where ur at. coming 2 get u bitch. maybe I'll hurt that man u got hots 4 or snatch that kid."

Terror! Every muscle in her body tensed. Hurt Storm? Snatch Sawyer? No. Dear God, no. She started trembling. She had to get away. Had to remove the danger from this ranch, from these people she'd come to love so much.

"Rachel, you're trembling." Jackson took the cell phone from her hand, laid it on the kitchen counter, then helped her to her chair. "Sugar, get her some brandy or somethin'."

"Sure." Sunny returned a minute later, extending a squat glass containing amber liquid. "Drink this now."

Rachel sipped, choked and raised the back of her hand to her lips. "What…what is that?"

Sunny chuckled. "Some of Storm's best whiskey. Aged to perfection, or so he claims. Take another sip."

Rachel sipped. Warmth burned in her throat and stomach, spreading outward. She'd need a gallon of this stuff to dull the fear. Kyle had threatened to take Sawyer, to hurt the man she loved. How could she remove the danger from them? How could she protect them? There was only one way. She swallowed and closed her eyes; a shudder went through her. She'd have to give herself to Kyle.

Jackson held her phone. "What's Grace's number? I'll call her. Tell her what information she needs to pass onto the police there."

"It's on speed dial. Press three." She took another sip. The trembling had subsided. While her mind focused on what she had to do, she vaguely heard Jackson's conversation with Grace. She had to keep Storm and Sawyer safe. Kyle was capable of anything. She had to get away from the ranch. Her eyes slid to Sunny, who was standing next to Jackson. She could hire a replacement to work with Sunny. Give the new nurse her notes and treatment plans and schedules. Until she hired that person, everyone would be safer is she stayed somewhere else.

She set the glass on the table. “Is there a motel in Rosefire?”

Sunny turned to her, eyes wide. “You’re leaving me?”

“No. I’ll still come here during the days, but I don’t need to live here to do my job.”

“No, you’re not going.” Sunny hugged Rachel. “You’ll be safer here.”

True, but Storm and little Sawyer wouldn’t be. Visions of that sweet child sleeping in his bed upstairs floated to her. For now, he was safe; she’d do whatever was needed to keep him that way. She had to deflect Kyle’s attention. She’d move into a motel and send him a text, telling him she wasn’t staying here anymore. While she was seeking her replacement, she’d convince Sunny it was for the best and that her care wouldn’t be compromised.

“Do you think Kyle will come here? Is that why you’re doing this?” Sunny’s face was shadowed with worry.

Rachel shrugged. “The last thing you or little Sawyer needs is the drama Kyle can create. It’ll be better if that drama happens away from here. He’ll show up, rant and rave and then he’ll leave.”

Sunny hugged her harder. “What if he hurts you? I couldn’t bear it. Stay. Between the four of us, we can fight him off.”

“The four of us? Surely you aren’t including Storm. He avoids me. He’ll be glad to see the back of my head as I make that final turn in the driveway. I wish he didn’t feel that way about me, but he does. He’s barely spoken to me since…since we had that argument.” She could hear the pain in her own voice, the tremble of it. She cleared her throat and looked into Sunny’s eyes. “It’s just as well I spend less time here on the ranch, don’t you think?”

“Maybe it’s better she goes.” Jackson placed his hands on Sunny’s shoulders. “I’ll keep an eye on her. Post one of my deputies at the motel.” Sunny shook her head. “Sugar, you’ll still see her every day.”

****

Storm had been in a foul mood for days. He wiped down

Lightning after their long, strenuous late-night ride. "Enjoy that extra ration of oats, buddy. You earned it after that ride tonight." The horse nickered and nodded. "I needed the ride more than you'll ever know. Felt good to charge into the wind, be at one with the elements. It felt good against my battered face." He kept up his rhythmic brushing.

"Dad used to take a lot of late-night rides. Now I know why. He was trying to outride the memory of Mother, just like I was trying to ease my need for Rachel." He kept brushing while his monologue continued. "Been a hell of a week, Lightning. Made me think of Dad. What a good man he was, even with a broken heart. They don't make many men like Sawyer Silverfeather Blackhawk anymore. Always hoped I'd measure up to the old man. Haven't of late, but figure I'm on the right track now.

"I've been worried about Rachel. She looked so wounded that evening when she came down the steps for dinner after our interlude in the den. Had she regretted our time on the sofa? That I'd brought her to climax? Her eyes had been swollen from crying, which really bothered me. If she'd been crying, I should have been holding her in my arms. A man comforts the woman he loves—and God help me, I do love her."

He relived her massage and the feel of her hands on him, the feel of his hands on her. She'd been like sweet liquid fire in his arms. Responsive. Incendiary. The spitfire had branded his soul for all of eternity.

For the first time, he understood why his dad could never get over his mother, even though she'd left him high and dry with two little kids to raise on his own. Sometimes, if a man was lucky enough, he met a woman who not only stirred his libido but touched his heart and embraced his soul. Colleen had been that woman for his dad. Rachel was that woman for him.

He loved that she was so patient with Sawyer. The child had been whiny and fussy before Rachel's arrival at the Triple-S. Tension from Sunny's illness no doubt affected the little fellow.

However, Rachel had that take-charge quality that dispelled the pressure. Her philosophy was to make a plan and stick to it. Find out what worked and mold it to fit the patient and the family. He'd watched her infuse her education, determination and hope into his sister. Hell, into the whole household. She had a noble way of giving of herself. He'd never met anyone like her.

If he were honest, he wasn't a hundred percent sure Rachel would give him a chance, even now that he'd made damn sure Pilar understood they were really and truly finished. Rachel might still refuse him. A man should love his wife so much he'd lay down his life for her, and there was only one woman he felt that way about.

For the first time in his life, he understood what his father meant all those years when he rebuked suggestions from friends to find another woman. "There's only one woman for me," Sawyer Blackhawk would say. "Even if Colleen has moved on, my love goes with her, stays with her."

"Dad sure did love our mother," Storm grumbled to the horse. "Lord knows she didn't deserve it." Lightning nickered and nudged Storm's pocket. "Yeah, I got a cube of sugar. What'cha gonna do about it?" He chuckled as the horse stepped closer, obviously smelling the sugar. He offered Lightning a cube on his open, outstretched hand.

"I shouldn't have taken Pilar to the art exhibit the other night. Should have refused her when she called, instead of hurting Rachel." He started grooming the horse again. "Some men don't mind if they hurt a woman. Not me. Oh, I can be blunt. Maybe even a tad rude. We both know I've got a hell of a temper, but I take no pleasure in hurting a woman.

"Bad enough I had to look at all those paintings that looked as though they were painted with someone's feet, but then Pilar dragged me to a party. Loud. Glitzy. Glamorous. Boring as hell. Know what I mean, Lightning?" The horse nodded and nickered. On the way home that night, too weary to make the long drive, he'd pulled under a grove of live oaks and slept.

Rachel was just starting her run when he pulled in the long gravel driveway the next morning, his tuxedo shirt wrinkled and his black bowtie undone. The look of pain and scorn she shot him made him feel like the underbelly of a slug.

He spent the day agonizing over how to stay out of her way until he could tell her he'd broken things off completely with his ex-fiancée. Then he and Rachel needed to have a long talk about their feelings.

The next afternoon, Pilar called—groggy, incoherent—rambling about not wanting to live without him. She told him she'd taken an overdose of pills. Although he refused to go to her, he did call 911 to have them send an ambulance to her condo. After that, he blocked her number.

Two days later, Storm was helping a mare foal a colt when Tanner Fontaine, Pilar's father barged in the stable, red-faced, his fists curled and barreled chest heaving. "Blackhawk, you coldhearted sombitch, I'm going to beat the hell outta you. My little girl is just now out of danger. You drove her to do what she did."

"I'm sorry you feel that way, Tanner. But I am glad Pilar's doing better."

Tanner's eyes narrowed. "You miserable, self-centered bastard!" His clenched fist landed squarely in Storm's eye. He'd been braced for it. Even so, he staggered back a step. "Pilar's been fighting for her life because of you." Another fist landed to Storm's jaw. Pain exploded.

Ben came running behind old man Fontaine and banded his arms around him. "I'll hold him while you hit him, boss."

"No." Storm wiped the blood from his face. "He has a right to defend his daughter. I told Pilar I never wanted to see her again. In the process, I hurt her feelings. Tanner, you've made your point. I haven't fought back because I figure I owe you a few pounds of my flesh." Storm jerked his head toward Ben. "Let him go. His business here is done. Tanner, get off my property."

The old man stomped to his Esclade. He slammed his door, threw gravel as he made a wide u-turn and sped out the lane.

"That man is trouble," Ben said.

Storm wiped his face with his handkerchief. "Yeah, and his daughter came by her temper honestly. She'd damn spoiled." The mare nickered in pain and Storm dropped to his knees, by her side, speaking in soft tones. "Thanks for diffusing the situation, Ben. I'm not afraid to fight my battles, but sometimes you earn an ass pounding. At least in a protective father's opinion. Hell, my dad would have reacted the same way over Sunny."

By the time Storm stepped into the house later that night, the house was dark. He knocked on Noella's door.

"*Sí, sí*...I'm coming." The door slowly opened, her hands

tugging the ties of her worn robe. "Child, what happened to you?" She wrapped her arms around him and held him to her. Comfort. She always brought him comfort. From the time he'd been little, he'd sought out Noella for comfort. "You tell Noella. *Sí*?" He nodded. "Come, you need ice."

Storm sat on one of the kitchen chairs while she rummaged in the freezer for bags of peas.

"Here, hold this to your face. I'll make coffee and we'll talk." She shook a finger at him the way she'd done countless times in his life. "You'd better not lie to me."

He held the bag of frozen peas to his eye. "The night I took Pilar to the art show, I told her I never wanted to see or hear from her again."

Noella crossed herself. "Thank God! It was hard on you, *sí*? I know how you hate hurting people. I change my mind. I think we'll have some of that good scotch your father always favored late at night when he needed to talk."

Storm watched her move gracefully around her kitchen. She returned with two thick glasses containing amber liquid. One she placed in front of him. With the other glass in hand, she took a chair directly opposite him. "I've never known you to indulge, Mama Noella."

"Sawyer insisted on it. Claimed he didn't want to drink alone." She smiled as if lost in a favored memory. "He said a man who drank alone was on his way to becoming an alcoholic."

Dawning registered. Why hadn't the thought occurred to him previously? "You loved him, didn't you? Why didn't I see that before?"

She shrugged. "It was a love that was never returned. For your father, there was only Colleen."

He reached out and took her hand. "I'm sorry. I think you would have made Dad very happy, just as you've made us happy. You made a great deal of difference in the lives of two abandoned kids. You had our love. You still do. I hope you know that."

Noella nodded. "*Sí.* You two were my *bambinos* from the time Colleen brought you home from the hospital. What a joy you both were. You mustn't hold onto ill feelings of her. She was a troubled woman, never meant to be a rancher's wife or a mother. She was homesick for Ireland."

"You gave us everything our biological mother wouldn't or couldn't." He sipped at the scotch and studied her. "Did Dad know?"

She stared into her glass. "What? About my feelings?" She shrugged. "Perhaps, but it was something we never discussed. He would never betray his wedding vows, and I would never accept a married man's advances. So I said my confession religiously for loving and desiring a married man." She crossed herself. "May God forgive me. Now, tell Noella how you got that black eye and swollen jaw."

"Pilar called a couple days ago, sounding disoriented and weak. Said she'd taken pills."

"Madre de Dios! She tried to kill herself?" The woman made the sign of the cross again.

Storm nodded. "I wasn't sure if she was being honest or playing another one of her tricks, so I called an ambulance. I never went to her. I meant what I'd said. Our relationship is over."

Noella leaned toward Storm, concern on her face. "Is she okay?"

Storm nodded again and drained his glass in one long swallow, hissed at the burning, the numbing. "When her father showed up here this afternoon, he wanted some revenge." Storm pulled the bag of peas from his bruised and swollen face, replacing it with another frozen bag.

"He's her father. Of course he'd be upset, but to attack you?" Her eyes narrowed. "What did you do in retaliation?"

"Nothing. The man deserved his pound of flesh, don't you think?"

"You did the right thing. Noella is proud of her boy. When will you talk to Rachel? You care for her, *sí?*"

"I love her. Must admit the enormity of it scares me. I never felt this way about Pilar or any woman, for that matter. I plan on staying out of Rachel's way for a day or two until my face looks a little better. Plus she's upset with me right now. We both need a little time."

So, Storm rose early and avoided his family throughout the day, figuring the condition of his face would get back to Rachel if he didn't. Right now he wanted a bath and the chance to hold the woman he loved in his arms. By his estimation, they'd both had enough time to think things through.

Lightning was bedded down for the night. The horse had been groomed after their long ride earlier. Storm ran a hand down Lightning's face. "Thanks for the ride, fella. Thanks for listening to my ranting, too. Sure am glad you know how to keep a secret." Storm turned out the lights in the stable and headed for the house. Battered face or no battered face, the time for talking was now.

Chapter Fifteen

After toeing off his boots in the mudroom, Storm stepped into the kitchen where he heard voices. Sunny and Jackson were talking to Noella. Sunny was holding Sawyer in her arms; the child was sleeping.

"I can't believe she's gone. The house feels empty already." Noella wiped tears from her eyes. "She'd be safer here with us."

Storm felt a sheet of ice freefall through his body like an elevator snapping its cables. "Who's gone?" Everyone turned.

Jackson was the first to react. "Holy shit! Whose fist did you run into?"

"Did Kyle find you already?" Sunny held her son closer to her. Her face seemed pinched with worry.

"Someone better answer me. Who's gone, and who the hell is Kyle?" Storm's determined glower swept over the three adults in the kitchen.

Sunny was the first to speak. "Sit down, brother. Noella, would you mind making a fresh pot of coffee? I think we're going to need it."

Storm pulled out a chair, turned it around and straddled it. He crossed his arms over the back of the chair and emotionally braced himself for what he feared.

"Rachel moved out." Sunny unconsciously rocked Sawyer just as she had when he was a baby.

The light in the room narrowed to a pinpoint. "What?"

"Rachel left about an hour ago. She says she'll be back to work with me tomorrow, like always, but she felt it was time for her to move out."

"Because of me?" First his mother and now Rachel; both women he loved had left him.

"No. Yes. Well, not exactly." Sunny looked at Jackson. "You tell him."

"Long story, I'm afraid. You're not going to like it."

"I'm not going to like much of anything if Rachel's gone." He'd have to bring her back. Once he talked to her and told her how he felt, he'd do whatever it took to convince her to come home, to come back to him.

Jackson leaned forward in his chair. "Seems she was engaged, at one time, to an abusive man."

"Engaged?" A wave of hot fury flowed through him. She'd loved someone else. Did she still have feelings for this guy? "She mentioned an old boyfriend but never said he'd been abusive. Did you know about this? You did the background check." His eyes narrowed when the words truly sunk in. "Abusive. You mean he put his hands on her?" Anger rushed in, burning and destroying his hold on composure.

He remembered that day by the pool, when she'd told him she didn't like abusive men. Now he understood. What stress had his angry outbursts put on that sweet woman? Did she fear him, too?

Noella set a mug of coffee in front of Jackson. "Thanks, Noella." He took a sip and focused his eyes on Storm. "I found several reports of domestic abuse. But everything I learned about her indicated sterling quality on her part. She was evidently a sweet kid who got mixed up with the wrong kind of man. I saw some pictures of bruises. Emergency room report of a broken wrist."

"You didn't think that was important enough to tell me?" He stood and slung the chair against the table. "Bruises!" He clenched his fists. "A broken wrist!" He would kill the bastard. A rage like he'd never known grabbed him by the throat and squeezed with a vengeance.

"Sit!" Noella barked. Sawyer whimpered in his sleep. She glanced at the child and lowered her voice. "Rachel doesn't need your anger. She needs your protection."

"Oh, she'll have my protection all right. Whether she wants it or not!" Storm raged for a few moments, making threats and promises. His anger so strong, so explosive, he trembled. No one. No one would ever put his hands on his woman again. No one would hurt her. He'd protect her with his dying breath.

Noella fisted hands on her hips. "Calm yourself! You haven't heard it all. You have to calm down." Storm whirled on her. "I mean it! Save your temper for the man who's after her. For now, you must settle yourself and listen."

After her? This man was after his Rachel? Acid rolled in his stomach, burning and cramping. How much worse could this get? He strode to Jackson, rested a fist on the table in front of him, leaned in and met his stare. “Is she in danger?”

Jackson nodded. “In my opinion, yes. This man poses a definite threat. When she broke off the engagement, he slashed her tires. Twice. Broke into her house and cut her clothes to shreds.”

“My God, what she’s been through.” He sank into a chair. Now her remark about clothes being “just things” made sense. Had she gone through all this alone?

“She got a restraining order against Kyle Benson, but he violated it. She went into hiding. The only person who knows she’s here is her best friend, who is also Kyle’s cousin. He broke into his own cousin’s apartment and stole her laptop. He read Rachel’s emails and found out where she was.”

Noella set a steaming mug of coffee and a plate on the table in front of him. “Master Storm, I make a sandwich for you. Eat.”

“Food? I can’t think of food now. I’m going for Rachel.” He started to rise, and Noella placed a firm hand on his shoulder.

“You eat and calm down. Think this through.” Noella had always been the voice of reason to his tempestuous nature. She’d spoken like this to him when he was a child. He hadn’t liked it then. For *damn* sure, he didn’t like it now.

Her eyebrows shot up. “Your poppa would have used his head. You will use yours, too, *sí?* Make plans. Take precautions. Bring her home. But first, you eat. You had no dinner.” She folded her arms and glared.

Storm rolled his eyes and took a breath. “Okay. Okay, I’ll eat the damn thing.” He bit into the sandwich and nearly had it devoured when he saw private looks exchanged between Sunny and Jackson. “What?” He drained his coffee.

This time Sunny shared the news. “When Rachel got the call from her best friend tonight, warning her, you should have seen her face.” She shook her head once. “Then…then her phone rang again. When she checked the readout, she just froze.”

Storm went still. “Was it him?”

She nodded. “It was like she was frozen with fear. Jackson snatched the phone, identified himself and warned Kyle not to call her again.” Sunny shot a look at Jackson. “Then she got a text. She tried to hide it from us, but eagle eyed-policeman here noticed.”

Jackson sipped his coffee. “Buddy, the color drained out of her face when she read that text, and she started trembling. I've never seen anyone *that* frightened before in my life. She laid the phone on the counter. When Sunny comforted her, I snuck a peek at her phone and read the text."

Jackson leaned forward, eyes intent on Storm. "Bastard said he was coming here. That he would either hurt you or snatch Sawyer if she didn't go back with him. That's why she left, man. To protect you both."

Storm's eyes swept to the child, the child he loved more than life itself. "That's why you're holding him." He looked at Sunny. For the first time this evening, the worry and fear in her eyes registered. So did her protectiveness as she held her child next to her breast. He'd stayed away from his family for the day, and all hell had broken loose. Protecting them was his job. "I'm sorry I wasn't here, sister."

She kissed her child's head. "I needed the feel of him in my arms. Needed to know he was safe. Are you going to tell me about your face?"

"Not much to tell. I told Pilar I never wanted to talk to her again and she overdosed on some drugs. Her father took offense." He shrugged. "No big deal. Not compared to all this. Where's Rachel? Do you know?"

"She promised she'd call with her cottage number when she got checked in at the Dew Drop Inn. I'll have one of my deputies set up surveillance. Make sure she's safe."

"No need." Storm stood and went to his sister. "I'm taking a shower and then going for her." He kissed his sister on the head and then placed his hand on Jackson's shoulder. "You staying here with Sunny?"

"Yup. Wild horses couldn't drag me away. Until this matter is resolved, looks like we'll both stick close to our women. You gonna finally admit to yourself that you love Rachel?"

"Oh, believe me, I've already faced that fact. Now, all I have to do is convince her." Storm placed a hand on the child's head.

Sawyer stirred and opened his eyes. His little arms stretched upward. "Unkie Storm." He took the child in his arms, kissed him and held him tight. Sawyer wrapped his little arms around Storm's neck and snuggled closer."I wuv you, Unkie Storm."

"Love you, too, son. Go back to sleep now." He carried the child to the window, ran a gentle hand up and down the boy's back and looked out into the night. A mixture of love and alarm and protectiveness engulfed him so hard and fast he nearly staggered with it. His eyes clasped shut. He would protect the boy. Rachel, too, by damn. He carried Sawyer back to Sunny and laid him in her lap. "I'm going for Rachel. I want us all here while we figure out how to make this man see he has no claim on her." He ran a hand through his hair. "Lord, this is like something from a movie."

****

Rachel stepped into her room at the Dew Drop Inn. She'd rented it for the week. Although it didn't begin to measure up to the room she'd had at the Triple-S, it was clean and the mattress didn't sag. When she checked in, Nora Mae, the gum-snapping woman with a teased hairdo, claimed Rachel was getting the deluxe suite. Rachel looked around and smiled. Evidently, the velvet portrait of Willie Nelson elevated the small room from regular to deluxe. It couldn't have been the orange and pink floral bedspread or the tattered aqua drapes.

In all honesty, the condition of the room was the final straw to a trying day. She made sure all the locks were in place, set one suitcase on the floor and the other on a table and flopped across the bed for a good old-fashioned crying jag. What was she going to do? She was in love with a man who avoided her and, conversely, she was being hounded by a man she was avoiding. A very dangerous man. She removed the pistol from her purse and laid it on the pink nightstand.

For all of her careful planning, her life was in a dangerous, depressing state of flux. She was a highly educated person, respected in her field and virtually on the run. How could one man destroy her well-ordered life? Why, oh why, had she ever accepted his advances? He'd been so charming, so attentive, trying to gain her favor.

Until Kyle was no longer in the picture, she couldn't go back to Yazoo City, her hometown. He might never leave her alone. From the tone of his text, he was still obsessed with her. Would it ever end? Now little Sawyer, a sweet angelic child, and Storm, the man she loved, were in Kyle's sick crosshairs.

Wiping the tears from her eyes, she pulled her cell from her pants pocket and started composing a text to Kyle. She had to keep him from going after Storm and Sawyer, no matter the cost to her. One way or another, she'd survive; she always survived. The time for running was over. She'd face him and make him see she'd never be his. If he beat her again, she'd heal. She always healed.

She had a handful of underwear ready to place in an old chest of drawers painted bright orange when someone knocked at her door. She froze. Fear danced up her spine. Had Kyle found her already? She glanced at her revolver lying in plain view where she could grab it. "Who…who is it?"

"Rachel, it's Storm. Let me in, mouse."

Storm? What was he doing here? She threw her clothes in the drawer. Why would he care if she'd left the house? Maybe he wanted to make sure she would still take care of Sunny. She unhooked the security chain, unbolted the lock and gasped when she saw him. One eye was black and blue and partially swollen shut. His nose was badly bruised and swollen. There was a large goose-egg bruise on his jaw.

"Oh no! Did Kyle find you already? Your face. Your wonderful, handsome face."

He stepped in her room and closed the door behind him. Her nurse's training took over. "Is your nose broken?" She placed both hands on his face, feeling, examining. "Oh, I can't bear it. You've been hurt because of me." She knew she was babbling, but she couldn't stop herself. "It was always easier for Kyle to hit than to talk things through. The abusive jerk!" She kept feathering her hands over his face. Before she realized what she was doing, she was breathing kisses on his black eye, chin and swollen jaw.

When his arms encircled her like a velvet vice, drawing her close, she began to cry. "I'm sorry you were hurt because of me. I feel awful. Kyle isn't your problem. He's mine."

"Rachel, love, Kyle didn't do this. Pilar's father landed a few punches to prove a point. Believe me, my face has nothing to do with Kyle. I've come to take you home. Get your gear."

She shook her head. "No, no, don't you understand? I have to protect you and Sawyer. I have to keep you safe."

He cupped her face in his hands. "I'll take care of everything.

Just come back to us where you'll be safer. You belong on the ranch with the family. I'll protect you. Sunny needs your care and friendship. Noella needs you. Sawyer will miss you terribly if you aren't there all the time." A smile briefly softened his features. "Who will call him Superman Sawyer when he charges through the house in that cape you made him? Come home." He pressed his lips to hers. Gentle, feather-light kisses that grew more and more demanding. "Come home, Rach."

He mentioned Sunny and Sawyer needing her. He mentioned Noella, too. What about him? He hadn't said anything about his needing her. Granted, he said he'd protect her, but as an employee, a friend of his sister's, not as a woman he cared for. She felt the acute pain of that omission. Why was this man holding her, kissing her, stirring up so many feelings?

"I can't. No matter how much I want to, I can't move back onto the ranch." Couldn't he see how she felt? Did he think she eagerly went into the arms of every man she met?

"I'm not giving you a choice. Your place is with us." He brushed hair back from her face. Then he cupped her chin and forced her to look at him. "Why didn't you tell me about Kyle?"

Rachel shrugged. "No matter what you claim, you're involved with another woman. I had no business telling you things about my personal life. A woman just doesn't go up to a man, especially one she's attracted to, and start talking about her abusive ex-fiancé."

"You should be able to talk to me about anything, love."

"We don't have that kind of relationship." She wished they did. She wished he loved her. She wished they shared their secrets, their hopes, their fears, but they'd spent so much time and energy fighting their physical attraction to one another, conversations like that rarely happened. He was attracted to her; she didn't doubt that. However, his attraction was a physical one, not one of the heart or the soul.

He cupped a large hand against her cheek. "I was rough with you a couple times. Did I scare you? I'll never hurt you, mouse. Never hit you. Never shove you around. Yes, sometimes I'll yell and rage. That's how I am. But you can yell and rage in return. I won't hurt you for it. Jackson told me about the things your old boyfriend did to you. Look at me, honey, I'm not Kyle."

He splayed his fingers in her hair, smoothing it back from her face, and then locked eyes with hers. "Sometimes passion runs high when a man and woman make love. During those times it can get a little rough. If that makes you uncomfortable, tell me. I'll keep myself in check. I want you to trust me. I will never hurt you."

She returned his steady gaze. What was he suggesting? That they make love? He was still seeing Pilar, engaged or not. Did she want to be used by a man just for the few moments of enjoyment and ecstasy he could give her? He didn't seem like a user, yet appearances could be deceiving. She thought of how he protected Sunny. How he adored Sawyer. How he respected Noella. How he'd been tender with her when she needed it. She did trust him. She loved him and trusted him. She wanted him, wanted to belong to him.

"I know you won't hurt me. I trust you, and that's not easy for me to say about a man."

"Good. I'll take care of you from now on. Now, let's get your things and get out of here." He walked to the open drawer. Reaching in, he grabbed a stack of lingerie and tossed them into her open suitcase sitting on a little round table. A pair of red lace thongs dropped to the floor. Picking them up, he held them out in both hands to study. His gaze swept to hers. "Have you ever worn these around me?"

"Yes. Now kindly stop inspecting my panties." The warmth of a blush crept up her cheeks. She snatched them from his hands and placed them back in the drawer. Meanwhile, he went to the closet and began yanking clothes off hangers. She methodically removed the lingerie he'd just thrown into her suitcase and placed them neatly back into the drawer.

Storm returned with sundresses and skirts bunched in his hands and glanced into the now empty suitcase. He cocked an eyebrow.

She snatched her clothes from his grasp. "I'm staying here. I refuse to put you and Sawyer in jeopardy. I'll be at the ranch tomorrow to work with Sunny. Earlier I sent a text to Kyle telling him where I'm staying. If he wants to find me, he knows where to come."

"You did *what?*" Storm tossed her clothes on the bed, grabbed her arms and shook her. "*Woman*, what in God's name were you thinking? Do you want him to get to you? To hurt you again?"

"I was thinking, *mister-macho-man,* that I would protect two people I care for very much. Now, stop manhandling me. You might push your ex-fiancée, your main squeeze around like this, but you won't order me about. I won't be your girl on the rebound, your honey in the house."

A muscle bunched in his jaw. His eyes narrowed. "Pilar and I are not seeing each other anymore, in any shape or fashion. That fiasco of a relationship is completely over. She tried to commit suicide, but I wouldn't go to her. I called nine-one-one instead, which is what made her dad so angry."

"What happened?"

He drew her to him. "You think I could spend time with Pilar, or any woman for that matter, after holding you, kissing you, touching you? Hell, you've been driving me crazy with need since the moment I set eyes on you." He planted soft kisses over her face and down her neck as he talked. Warm hands held her waist, pulling her near him. Shivers raced over her body. Liquid warmth spread through her.

"You're not seeing her anymore? I'm not someone you're spending time with on the rebound?" She suddenly felt giddy, as if a huge weight had been removed from her chaotic life.

"No. No more Pilar and, for damn sure, no rebound relationship with you. I feel love and devotion and commitment for you. I'd hoped you felt the same thing. Yet you abandoned us." Pain was evident in his voice and his facial expression, and she knew. Instinctively she knew she was facing two Storms—the little boy whose mother abandoned him and the grown man. Both had been battered by life. "You abandoned me."

"No. No, I didn't—"

He pushed her against the wall and kissed her hard. His hands fisted in her hair. His tongue swept over her lips, and she opened for him. She welcomed and accepted the turmoil that poured from his kiss. She sought to soothe and heal, actions they both needed.

Gone was his confident mastery of that first kiss on that deserted country road. Gone were the gentle kisses of comfort and exploration while setting on his horse. Gone, too, was the anger and frustration of the kiss on the back porch and the passion of the kisses they shared on the sofa. This was a kiss of need, a kiss of desire and desperation so keen it nearly brought her to tears.

Rachel placed her hands on his cheeks and looked into his eyes. "Storm, I love you."

"You left me. I can't lose you. I *won't* lose you." He kissed her again, even more needful than before. Although his kiss was almost brutal with its intensity of emotion, she was not afraid. His hands were under her blouse, searching and claiming. "I adore you," he ground out, his breathing labored and his voice rasping as if struggling to regain control. He kissed her again, pulling her into intimate knowledge of his need, his desire. "God help me, but I need you. You've become the very air I breathe. You're mine, mouse. Mine and no one else's."

Rachel tugged on his black T-shirt, pulling it off. Her hands slowly swept up his muscular chest. "You're so magnificent, Storm."

He kissed her with a passion that left her breathless. She gloried in the depth and power of his desire. This strong man had displayed a vulnerability with her. He made her feel in control and immensely sensual. What a turn-on. She stroked her fingers over the ripples of his abdomen. "You're mine, too. No one, Storm. No one touches you, but me." She felt scalding tears tumble from her eyes.

"No one, mouse. No one, but you." With their gazes locked, their hands and fingers touched, traveled and taunted. With lips close, intimately close, all but touching, whispers were shared. Promises made. Breaths mingled. They spoke the language of lovers, making and sharing vows of devotion and promises of forever.

Her lips forged a trail of kisses and gentle bites from his neck, down his hard chest to his nipple. "This is what I want you to do to me." She slowly ran her tongue around his nipple and then across it. Storm groaned. When she took his nipple into her mouth and suckled hard, she rubbed her hand up and down his erection.

"My God, woman!" He grabbed the lapels of her blouse and ripped it open. Buttons zinged across the room. "No man can bear that without going mad." He shoved her blouse aside and unhooked the front clasp of her bra. His hands held her full breasts and his thumbs rubbed over them. "You're so beautiful. I'll be damned if I'll ever let any man touch you again."

When he kissed her, the passion was back. His calloused hands abraded her soft skin, and it felt wonderful, exciting, and glorious. It felt…right. His lips, hot and hungry, rained scorching kisses across her jaw and down her neck. At times he grazed her with his teeth, sending chills of pleasure up and down her body. At others, he bit her gently while his fingers did wicked things to her body. She was so hot, so wild with her need for him that she yanked on his belt, unzipped his fly and shoved fabric aside.

She rubbed her breasts against his chest and watched his eyes go dark. He groaned again when her hand found and encircled his thick erection. She stroked him and sweat beaded on his face. He muttered words in a language she didn't understand—Comanche, perhaps. He was so large with his need for her, she wondered briefly if she could take him and then smiled, imagining how good it would feel when she did. He opened her zipper and shoved down her slacks and thong so he could touch her. Quickly she stepped out of her clothes. She moaned when his expert fingers found her core and stroked her.

"You're so beautiful, mouse." He kissed her again, his lips and hands growing urgent. He lifted her to him.

She wrapped her legs around his waist and locked her eyes on his. "Here! Now!"

Both were blind with need. Both sought the release only the other could bring. He plunged into her. She threw her head back and reveled in the glory of wild, unbridled, hot standing-against-the-wall-sex. His hands squeezed her bottom and he bent to capture a nipple. She held his head against her. "Don't stop! Don't stop!"

Tension coiled in her belly, and she began to tremble. Storm's strokes were long and rapid. Her approaching climax was like a knife ready to cut, ready to sever her spirit from herself, binding all the love she felt for him to his very core. A keening sound erupted from deep inside her as she climaxed. A few more strokes and Storm followed, shouting her name as he poured his essence into her.

Storm's harsh, labored breathing filled the silent room—or was it hers? She couldn't tell.

Slowly they both sank to the floor, a tangled mass of arms, legs, clothes and hearts. For a few minutes, neither could speak. As her universe began to coalesce again, Rachel fought the urge to smile and lost. Storm kissed her forehead. "Is that a self-satisfied smirk I see?"

She ran her palm up his chest and across his shoulder. "That was wild."

"Definitely." He kissed her again, delving his tongue into her mouth, searching for and meeting hers. His hand caressed her derriere while he planted kisses on her neck. "Such soft skin. A man could die happy feasting on you." He sat up and tugged off his boots and the jeans tangled around his ankles.

"How did I get naked and you didn't?" She rose onto her elbows to look at him.

"Damned if I know." He glanced over his shoulder at her and smiled. "We got the most important parts naked. That's all that matters." He threw his boots into the corner of the small motel room.

"What language were you speaking a few minutes ago?"

"Comanche. Dad taught us all he knew of the language. I'll teach you a few words, if you want. Later, love, much later." He rolled over onto all fours and began kissing the soles of her feet. "Now that the edge is off, I can take my time." Warmth rushed to her core again. "You have such beautiful, delicate feet. The night you wore those 'ho-red' heels, I nearly went insane."

These were new sensations, having someone slowly pay homage to her feet. She rather liked it. He kissed her instep and then her toes, one by one. "Do I hear you purring, mouse?"

"Whatever it is you're doing, it feels wonderful."

"Did I ever tell you I'm an old football player?" He kissed the top of her foot.

"No." What was he getting at? What did it matter? Who cared as long as he didn't stop.

He chuckled low and sexy. "I am, love. I'm playing football right now, hoping I can make a field goal." He gently bit her ankle, and she giggled. With slow, deliberate movements, he worked his way up both of her legs. By the time he reached the fifty-yard line, his goal post was ready—*touchdown.*

Chapter Sixteen

Later, much later, when Rachel was sound asleep, Storm dressed and carried her out to his truck. Afraid to wake her, he'd merely wrapped the ugly motel bedspread around her naked and sated body. They'd made love four times, each surprisingly better than the last. He gently laid her on the seat and ran back into the motel room for her clothes. Come hell or high water, he was taking her home where she belonged.

He had a feeling if she were awake, she'd fight him every inch of the way. She was determined to protect him and Sawyer. He retrieved her revolver laying on the nightstand; he shuddered at the thought of her having to use it.

Quietly, he opened the door on the driver's side and slid into the truck. When he eased her into a semi-sitting position, she mumbled and snuggled against his shoulder.

Once the truck was running and in gear, he wrapped his arm around her. A sigh of happiness escaped him when her head nestled against his shoulder. He looked both ways before easing the truck onto the dark highway. Rachel's bare arm slipped across his chest and over his shoulder. He gently brought her hand to his lips and kissed it. She smelled of flowers and sex. God help him, he wanted her again. Would probably always want her—her and no one else.

He leaned down and kissed her mussed hair. When she mumbled in her sleep that she loved him, he smiled and rubbed his cheek and chin over her head. "I love you, too, mouse."

As his silver pickup ate up the road, his mind began to wander. He couldn't ever recall feeling this contented. Oh, there'd been plenty of all-night sexual marathons in his younger years, during his college days, and for a spell afterward. While those encounters satisfied his physical needs, they also exposed a barren desert deep within his soul. Soon sex equated with emptiness. The thrill of the chase dimmed.

Mercifully, duties at the ranch stole his desire to party hearty on campus. His father was slowing down due to his ailing heart. He was needed at the Triple-S. Other things took priority. His father's health steadily declined, and then he passed. Sawyer was born, and Sunny needed help with the child.

Then he met Pilar. For some reason, she chased him. He'd been flattered by that, flattered enough to keep the relationship going, even though he didn't really love her. He'd probably always feel a degree of guilt about that. Hurting someone's feelings as deeply as he'd hurt Pilar wasn't something he took pride in. Still, a man couldn't make himself love on demand. Love just happened when the conditions were right—like lightning.

He glanced down at the blonde bundle wrapped around him. Who'd have believed he could fall in love at first sight? A smile spread as he looked out the side window for a beat and snorted. If he lived to be a hundred, he'd remember the way her blue eyes sparked when she declared, "Stop hiding behind that big ol' Stetson. From what I saw, a French beret would do the job." A French beret! Damned if he wouldn't buy her a dozen of them. He remembered her shaking her fist under his nose the first night she was at the ranch, and rubbed his cheek over her hair. Lord, but he loved her spirit.

A scowl erased the smile. He'd keep this woman he loved safe from Kyle, or die trying. She shifted and sighed his name again. He tightened his arm around her shoulders, feeling fiercely protective. Love. He was in love. Frankly, he hadn't expected to feel this—ever.

Love for his family was easy, as was loyalty and devotion. Little Sawyer had taught him the joys of loving a child. A child. He glanced down at Rachel. Did she want a baby? Could he have the children he so desperately craved with her?

She was probably on the pill. Maybe with a little convincing, he could talk her into going off birth control. Marriage. He'd dreaded marrying Pilar, his only reason being Sawyer, making sure he had a strong claim to the child if something happened to Sunny. Marriage to Rachel, though, would be a sweet life, challenging at times, but he was always ready for a challenge. She was his now in every way, except legally. Staring into the darkness of the night, he began to plan for a proposal.

He cracked the window to let in the refreshing night air, hoping to stay alert. Home was just a few blessed miles away.

****

Rachel stretched slowly and smiled her way to wakefulness.

She'd been Cleopatra in her dream. Cleopatra rolled up naked in an orange and pink carpet and carried up a staircase by a handsome slave. The slave very carefully rolled her out onto a bed of rose petals before Julius Caesar—or was it Marc Antony? She stretched again and sighed. Only she wasn't Cleopatra, was she? No, she was a nurse sacked out naked in a frumpy motel. Naked? Her eyes flew open.

"I've never seen anyone wake up smiling." Storm was propped up on one elbow, twirling her hair around his finger. His eyes exuded warmth, and his dimples were deep as he smiled. "Are you always so beautiful in the morning, or is this the face of a woman who's been well-loved?" His black hair was disheveled, and he needed a shave.

"Good mornin', my beloved mouse," he whispered as he kissed her forehead, her nose and her lips. Her eyes fluttered shut on a sigh. *I'm dreaming. I was Cleopatra in the last dream; who am I in this one?* His erection poked her hip, breaking through the fog of her mental haze.

This was *no* dream. This was reality; she was naked in bed with Storm Blackhawk. Rachel was wide awake now, awake and sore from being loved. Memories returned, and she groaned. Her eyes slid to the smiling, smug man leaning over her. They'd had sex multiple times. He'd come to her motel to convince her to go back to the ranch. Instead, they'd made love, over and over.

She'd been like a wanton hussy with him. Her hands trembled when they pushed back her unruly hair. What had possessed her to behave that way? Her gaze darted around the unfamiliar room. The orange and pink floral bedspread from her deluxe room at the Dew Drop Inn was in a heap on the floor.

"Where am I? This isn't my hotel room." She sat up in bed, and Storm ran fingertips down her back. Shivers, warm and cold, skated up and down her spine. The room was decidedly masculine—just like the man beside her, his muscular leg thrown possessively over hers. Her eyes narrowed when she glared over her shoulder at the man who was equally as naked as she. "Tell me this isn't your bedroom."

He studied her. "I'd say it's *our* bedroom now, love."

She held the navy blue sheet to her throat in an effort to cover her nakedness. "How? How did you get me here, and why don't I remember it? Did you drug me?"

He tugged her back down and began kissing her neck, at times grazing it with his teeth. Her eyes crossed and her nipples peaked. "I drugged you with sex." His voice sounded husky, deep, and very sensual. He ran his hand up her side, stopping to cup her breast. "You fell asleep. I wrapped the bedspread around you and carried you to my truck. Brought you home." His expert fingertips were teasing her nipple, and damned if her nipple wasn't sitting up and doing the happy dance.

"You kidnapped me?" She was getting a headache. No doubt it was from concentrating so hard to mentally shift into bitch mode when her body was humming "You Make My Dreams Come True."

He chuckled. "I merely brought you home." His tongue flicked across her nipple. "Home where you belong, my sweet mouse." His large hand slid from her hip to her waist.

A flash of anger sparked and took hold. She pushed at his bare chest. "Where I belong? Why, you're no better than Kyle." She was tired of men telling her what to do and where she belonged, as if she were a potted plant and men controlled all the windows.

A muscle bunched in Storm's jaw; he was evidently grinding his back molars again. His hand tightened on her waist. "Easy now. I don't take kindly to bein' compared to a woman beater."

"Kyle wants me to come home to Yazoo City where *he* says I belong. You want me to come home to the ranch, where *you* say I belong. He's coming after me to take me home, by force if necessary. You came to the motel, got me drunk on sex until I passed out, and then you rolled me up in a damned motel bedspread and hauled me back here." She was gathering up steam now, ready for a good old-fashioned yelling match. Both hands swept back her hair, and she sat up. "You tell me, what's the difference?"

His eyes narrowed. "The difference is you belong to me."

She jerked the sheet up to her chin, covering her needy body, for it was begging for more of Storm Blackhawk. "Belong to you? I certainly do not!"

He smiled that slow, dangerous smile she loved. She struggled to resist the pull of his masculine charm. "Honey, you've been mine since that first kiss on Longhorn Road."

"So you say." Her lower lip came out in a petulant pout.

Storm growled and jerked her back down beside him. He kissed her slowly and thoroughly until her toes curled. His fingers found her core and started to stroke, his gaze intent on hers. "So I know. Think back, darlin'. Think back to that first kiss. Didn't you feel anything?"

"No." She would not give in. Her bitch gene was rearing its beautiful, foul-mouthed head. "I didn't feel a damned thing out there on that ol' road." Oh God, if he didn't stop touching her like that, she was going to explode into a million pieces.

He bent and kissed her breasts while his fingers circled and stroked. "Wanna know what I felt?"

Her voice hitched an octave higher when his finger slipped into her. "No."

A slow, self-satisfied male chuckle rumbled from his chest. "I felt lightning strike."

"For Pete's sake, there wasn't a flash of lightning in the sky that night. A full moon was shining. Oh…" She wanted to beg him not to stop, but she wouldn't give him the satisfaction.

"True, but I was hit by lightning just the same. Reckon it fried every brain cell I had, 'cause since then I haven't been able to think of anything but you." He rolled on top of her and slipped into her in one smooth stroke. Twining his fingers with hers, he pressed their joined hands into the pillow on either side of her head.

"If you don't want me, Rachel," he said through clenched teeth as he moved within her, "all you have to do is say so. I'll stop and leave you alone, though it'll kill me to do it. Open your eyes, love. Look at me. Tell me you don't want me, tell me you don't want this."

She was already soaring, soaring beyond speech, beyond reason, beyond self. For this, no words were necessary. With their eyes locked, they moved in that sensual dance lovers know and flew over the edge, hand-in-hand, heart-to-heart—together.

Water was running in the bathroom. Storm was humming "The Yellow Rose of Texas." Rachel was curled into a ball, the sheet over her head, trying to deal with her confused emotions. She'd just been thoroughly loved by a handsome man, a man who seemed to genuinely care for her. Yet she hated being manipulated and told where she belonged. Kyle had controlled her that way, and she wouldn't be controlled by another man, even if she did love him.

"Rachel?" Storm stood in front of her, wearing a pair of faded navy sweatpants, slung low on the hips. Concern marred his handsome face. "You okay?" He lifted her from the tangle of sheets, walked to a navy leather wing-backed chair and sat. He snuggled her close and trailed a finger down her cheek. "Talk to me, mouse. Have I hurt you? I got a little crazy earlier. Was I too rough?"

She shrugged and looked away. He could be so tender, so caring. "No. It's not you…yes, it is you…it's my whole life and the mess it's become. I can't go *home* because of Kyle. I shouldn't be *here* because of Kyle."

"I'll take care of Kyle, and that's a promise. Me and Jackson'll take care of things. You're not alone anymore. You have family to rely on. I won't let Kyle or anyone hurt you ever again."

"You don't seem to understand how dangerous he might be." Didn't he get it?

"I understand the bastard's a bully. A bully who picks on people smaller than him. We'll see how brave he is against men his own size." He gently cupped her chin and turned her face to his. "I'll protect you, love. A man takes care of his woman." He smiled wryly. "That is, if I can get you to admit that you *are* my woman. That we're in a relationship."

"Are we in a relationship?" She needed, required some assurances from this man.

He laughed gruffly. "What happened between us earlier pretty much seals the deal, don't you think?"

"So, we're in a sexual relationship?" She slipped off his lap and placed her hands on her hips.

Storm looked her up and down. "God, woman, you're beautiful." She rolled her eyes and huffed out a breath. "Look, what we have is more than sex, and you know it. We're in a permanent, loving relationship." He stood and smiled. "Your bath is prepared, madam." He gave a wave of his hand and bowed, humor glinting in his eyes.

"My bath? I thought you were taking a shower."

He picked her up as if she weighed no more than a kitten. "Noella raised me to be a Texas gentleman. Ladies first. I've been pretty rough on you. I hope I haven't made you sore. Perhaps a long, hot bubble bath is in order for the woman I love."

Storm carried her into his bathroom and then turned so she could see a mound of fragrant bubbles in the huge Jacuzzi. "You…you did this for me? You drew me a bath?"

He leaned over and placed her in the warm water. "Every woman deserves a little pampering." He kissed her forehead. "Relax, darlin'. Mind if I shave while you soak?"

She lifted handfuls of bubbles up and spread them over her shoulders, simply delighted with his consideration. "No. No, go ahead." The hot water felt good on her sore muscles when she slid down. She sighed. "This feels marvelous. Thank you."

He wiggled his eyebrows. "Anytime, ma'am."

Watching Storm shave was a very erotic experience. This new intimacy between them was both strange and unexpected. Yesterday she'd moved out of the ranch to protect him and Sawyer. Today she was well loved, taking a bubble bath in his private bathroom.

"Where did the bubbles come from? You don't strike me as a bubble bath kinda guy."

Storm chuckled and held his razor under water. "They were a birthday gift from Sunny last year. Claimed I needed to get in touch with my feminine side." He turned to her and asked with a sneer, "Look at me. Do I look like I have a feminine side to you?"

She giggled and rubbed her arm with a pink bath pouf. "No, not hardly." He was all male; she had proof of that. A contented smile blossomed.

He ran the razor down his rugged face. "Sunny gave me a basket with a book called *Real Men Like Pink, Too,* pink bubble bath and that pink puffy thing you're using." He ran the razor under running water again. "And a pair of black boxers with pink roses plastered all over 'em." He shook his head. "Damn, fool woman. She claimed I wasn't sensitive to a woman's feelings."

"What did you say to that?" His back was tanned and lean. Muscles rippled as he moved. She could watch him all day.

"Told her I didn't need to be sensitive. Women had to learn to accept a man the way he was."

"Uh-huh. And did you read the book?" She fought back a smile.

He turned and glared at her for a beat and then grinned. "Parts of it." He rinsed off his face and towel dried. Then he pushed down his sweatpants and gave her a lusty look. "Slide forward, mouse, make room."

"What? You don't mean..."

"The hell I don't. Why can't a man take a bath with his woman?" He stepped in behind her, and she slid forward to make room for him. Perhaps this was more intimate than she cared to get.

"Lean back, I'll wash your hair." She glanced over her shoulder to see if he was serious. He held a cup full of water. "Lean back, love." She did, and he poured water over her hair. He squeezed shampoo in his palm. "Hope you don't mind my shampoo."

"It's not pink, is it?"

He tugged a strand of her hair. "Brat." He gently rubbed in the shampoo, working it into a lather and massaging her scalp. Her toes curled under the surface of the bubbly water and her eyes drifted shut. This very masculine man was shampooing her hair. "Are you feeling all right? No feelings like your sugar levels are low?"

"No. I'm fine. I don't think I'll run this morning. Doubt my legs could hold me." Storm's gentle chuckling warmed her.

He was running fingertips over her scalp and down the length of her hair. The whole slow process was very sensual, and she loved it. His comment broke through her thoughts. "I've never seen anyone with hair as long as yours. Guess it takes a lot of care."

She leaned her hair back so he could rinse it. "I'm thinking of getting it cut."

His hands stilled. Would he tell her not to? Would he dictate how she should wear her hair? Kyle had. "Really?"

"Yeah. I'm thinking of donating it to Locks of Love, a charity that makes wigs for children with cancer and other medical conditions."

He kissed first one shoulder and then the other. "I think that's a very noble, caring gesture. Some child would be very lucky to get your hair. Maybe I'll do that, too. How long does your hair have to be?"

"Ten inches." She turned to gauge his expression. "You'd be interested in doing that?"

"To help a kid somewhere? Sure. Seems like such a simple thing to do. I'd have to let my hair grow longer. I'm proud of you for thinking of doing it. You're a very caring person, Nurse Rachel."

She turned to face him and tilted her head to the side and studied this rugged, very handsome man with the surprisingly tender heart. A man who would consider growing his hair long for Locks of Love was a treasure. He was watching her, too, his one eyebrow cocked. "You're very special, cowboy." She placed her wet hands on either side of his face and kissed him, really kissed him.

Storm's hands slid up her back. She rose to her knees and intensified the kiss. Her tongue flicked over his lips, and he groaned. "I want you again, mouse." He laid his forehead against hers and took a deep breath. "I don't want to make you sore, so I'm going to ask for a rain check. I seem to lose my head when I make love to you. Passion takes over. I'm afraid I get a little rough."

She studied his midnight eyes, windows to his soul, a soul she was beginning to know and love with a sweet fierceness. The evidence of his arousal was blatant, yet he was putting her comfort ahead of his needs. Her heart dipped a little more into the chocolate swirl of love. "Sure, I'll give you a rain check." She kissed him. "Any time, big guy."

"Turn around, mouse, I'll wash your back."

She settled in front of him again and sighed in contentment when he ran warm soapy hands over her skin. "A girl could get used to this."

"I'm hoping." He lifted her wet hair and kissed the back of her neck. Warm, soft kisses. Her nipples tightened. "After breakfast, I'll empty out some drawers and make room in the closet for your clothes."

"Are you suggesting I move into your bedroom?"

His hands stilled at the tone of her voice. "Haven't you?"

She gazed over her shoulder. His eyebrows were furrowed. "No. This is your family's home. There's a child here. We can't just shack up."

"Shack up?" His voice held a deathly quiet tone. "Is that what you think this is?" His wet hands were on her shoulders. "Haven't I shown you how I feel about you? How much you mean to me? You said you love me."

"I do." Her tongue darted out to lick her lower lip. She saw his eyes flicker to that movement and darken.

Storm stood and stepped out of the tub. He grabbed a towel, wrapping it around his waist. His anger was palpable. The evidence of his erection was visible under the towel.

She stood, too, and reached for a towel. "What would Noella think?"

He ran a hand through his hair. "Noella already knows. I told her last night, after I put you to bed, that I'd brought you home. That you were staying with me." He jerked his head toward the bed. "Here, in my bedroom. I didn't go into specifics, but I'm sure she put two and two together."

Her hands stilled. She'd been towel drying her hair. "You did what? You…you told Noella? What must she think of me? You had no right to tell anyone!"

She watched his eyes narrow and his control snap. He yanked the towel from her hand and snatched the one she'd just wrapped around her body. Anger and frustration hardened his features. "No right? I had no right?" He lifted her and carried her to his bed. "I'll show you *what* gives me the right, and you damned well *will* move in here with me."

Chapter Seventeen

When Rachel and Storm stepped into the kitchen, Noella was making pancakes. She set her bowl down and hugged Rachel. "Master Storm brought you back to us, *sí?* You'll be safer here, little one. We're having a big family breakfast to celebrate your coming home." She turned and flipped the pancakes on the griddle.

"Thank you." Rachel shot Storm a look. "I'm not sure if I'm happy I'm back or not."

Storm ran his hand up Rachel's back, unable to break physical contact with her. "You're staying, right?"

She raised an eyebrow, her expression determined. "Yes, I'm staying, but in *my* bedroom. Just like we discussed earlier."

Storm raised both hands in a surrender gesture. "I'll keep you any way I can, mouse. I meant what I said upstairs. I won't try to run your life any more than you'd try to run mine." He was slowly learning he couldn't ride roughshod over this little woman. She was every bit as strong willed as he was.

Their most recent lovemaking had been fierce and passionate. Her scratch marks on his back burned. Yet, *what* had she said when at last she was able to talk? That she was still moving into her old bedroom. Damn hardheaded, adorable woman. *God, how I love her.*

Still, he understood the explanations she'd made upstairs. Kyle had commanded her to live her life the way he wanted. He'd controlled her. Once she broke free of that control, she promised herself she'd take charge of her own life. Storm respected her for that. It took a real strength of character to break the cycle of abuse. Most women couldn't break the cycle. Not like his Rachel. No, his Rachel had shown grit. She'd taken charge of her life. How could a man *not* love a woman like that? She'd dug deep in her soul, found a kernel of strength and nurtured it, nurtured it until it became a viable part of her persona.

If he expected to be a part of her life—and he sure as hell did—he would have to support her in whatever decisions she made. A man would never use her for a doormat, not any more. That fact pleased him. He'd lived with emotionally strong women, Noella and Sunny, and loved and depended on their strength. He could depend on Rachel's, too. A man was lucky if he had a woman that strong in his life. *Damned lucky.*

So he helped her put her clothes away in her bedroom before they came down for breakfast. The act was a small concession if it pleased her. She could keep her clothes anywhere she liked, but when it came to loving and holding and sleeping, well, they were doing it together. He'd see to that. His room, her room, it made no difference.

Now, obviously pleased, Rachel wrapped her arms around his waist and smiled up at him. "Thank you for not bossing me around. Not that I would stand for it for one moment."

He tugged her tight against him and kissed her hair. "What man wouldn't move heaven and earth to see his woman smile at him like that? There's not a Texas sunrise that could out-dazzle your smile. Noella, have you ever noticed how Rachel's eyes are as blue as our Blue Bonnets?"

Noella placed pancakes on a platter. "You sound like a man in love."

Storm kissed Rachel's nose. "You mean it shows?" Both women laughed.

Rachel pulled out of the embrace. "I need to get my car back. It's still at the Dew Drop Inn."

"We'll send the men for it after we eat." Noella pulled bacon from the oven and set the platter on the table. "Master Storm, Jackson is out on the back porch talking on the phone. Tell him breakfast is ready, please."

Jackson turned at the sounds of Storm's footsteps. He ended his call and shoved the phone into his uniform shirt pocket. "We've got a problem."

"What?" He was enjoying a great afterglow from his recent lovemaking session with Rachel. He hated to face any problem, big or small.

The chief of police exhaled an audible sigh. "Someone torched Rachel's car. It's totaled."

For a minute he stared at his best friend, trying to absorb the incredulity of what Jackson had just told him. "Damn Kyle Benson," Storm bit out. He shot a glance over his shoulder to make sure Rachel hadn't followed him outside. "Anyone see anything?"

"Nora Mae was on duty at the desk at the Dew Drop Inn. She

said Rachel's brother came in looking for her. Said he'd gone to room one-o-six where Rachel said she'd be, but there was no answer. Asked if she'd already checked out to go visit their sick momma?"

Storm ran a hand through his hair. "Brother? Sick momma? He's one slick bastard. Bet Nora Mae spilled her guts."

"Yeah. Asked him if Rachel's cute red bug was still parked out there. That she'd seen the silver pickup, with the Triple-S decal on the side, parked there for a few hours. Maybe Rachel left with you. He thanked her, all polite and all. Then he left. Not more than five minutes later, she heard the explosion."

Storm's temper flared. Rachel's new car was destroyed. "We're dealing with a maniac."

Jackson crossed his arms and studied his boots. "The women and the boy have to be kept safe. Do we send them off somewhere or hunker in here?"

"I'm for keeping them here. I'll hire some security people so we aren't using all your deputies' time."

Jackson nodded his agreement. "Bill Franklin over in Austin has a good firm. Ex-Marines and ex-Rangers." He flipped open his phone and dialed. "Noella have breakfast ready?" Storm nodded. "I'll be in as soon as I make arrangements."

Storm grabbed Jackson's arm. "I don't care how much it costs. You hear? Everyone I love could be in danger." He turned and stepped inside. He'd need his revolver. How did he keep himself armed with a curious youngster around?

"Unkie Storm! Will you take me horseback riding after breakfast?" Little Sawyer ran into his arms and hugged him tight. His eyes closed as he held the boy to him. He hadn't taken Kyle's threats that seriously. Now? Now, he was on alert mode. He *would* protect those he held dear.

"What if we set up your train and play with it? I bet Rachel likes trains. What do ya think? Should we let a girl play with us guys?"

Sawyer stuck a chubby finger in his mouth and turned to Rachel. "Are…are you a girl, Wachel?"

Storm laughed. "Oh yeah, she's a girl all right." Rachel and Noella both scowled a warning. Sunny smiled a knowing smile, her twin radar obviously picking up vibes this morning.

"Oh. Do you like twains, Wachel? I'll share wif you."

Rachel laughed and, for a moment, his soul warmed, yearned, dreamed. He dreamed of Rachel big with his child. Their eyes connected across the kitchen. "I love you," she mouthed. "You, too," he mouthed in return.

He'd die before he allowed anything to happen to her. This was how a man should love a woman—totally, fiercely, eternally. His mind touched down on the memory of his father. Sawyer Blackhawk had loved the mother of his children the same way; understanding flowed in, forming a posthumous connection from son to father.

Jackson came inside. "Lordy, but something smells good!"

"It's me, Unkie Jack." The boy held out his arm. "Mommy sprayed some of her pa-fume on me."

Storm's gaze slid over to Jackson. "The boy needs a sister for Sunny to spoil."

Noella cleared her throat, her stance prim and proper. "I feel too much testosterone in my kitchen. There are correct steps that must be taken. I'll stand for no less for my girls." She waved a hand to Sunny and Rachel. "They deserve the best."

"You'll get no argument from me, Momma Noella." Storm set Sawyer in his booster seat. He glanced at Jackson. Would he tell Rachel about her car, or should he? Now or after breakfast? "Jackson, let's enjoy these pancakes. We'll talk later. Okay?"

Noella had outdone herself with breakfast—eggs, pancakes, bacon, fried steak, home fries, red-eye gravy, fried apples, biscuits with homemade plum jam. Rachel indulged in a little of everything. Storm watched her every movement, the way she engaged everyone in conversation, her smile, her low sultry laughter. This was the first of many such breakfasts, he'd see to it. First, Kyle Benson had to be arrested and locked away for a long time. Then, and only then, could he relax and enjoy this new happiness that had suddenly colored his world.

After the breakfast dishes were loaded into the dishwasher, Noella took Sawyer upstairs to pull the boxed train from his closet.

Sunny raised the cup of green tea Rachel had brewed for her to her lips. "Okay, you two, out with it. You've been shooting looks at each other all through breakfast."

Jackson squirmed in his seat and stared into his coffee mug for a beat. “There was some trouble at the Dew Drop Inn a couple hours ago.” His gaze swung to Rachel. “Your car was torched.”

“What?” Rachel’s eyes opened wide.

Jackson lifted his gaze to hers and took a sip. “Destroyed, I’m afraid.”

She paled. “Kyle?”

“Nora Mae described him as five-eight, five-nine. Good-looking, short blond hair.”

Rachel nodded, her face an expression of terror. “Yes, that’s him. He’s here in Rosefire. I need…I need…" She started to rise. Her breathing was rapid, and she was obviously fighting for control.

Sunny stood. “I’m going upstairs with my baby. Brother, Jackson”—she shot both men a hard look—“you two do whatever it takes to keep us safe. I want this psycho caught, drawn and quartered.” She punctured the air with her finger as she spoke, then turned, and hurried upstairs.

Storm reached out and tugged Rachel onto his lap. If there was one thing he’d learned earlier today, she wouldn’t be pushed or ordered about. Probably the best thing was to engage her in their protection efforts. “You know Kyle. How does he think? Does he know how to use firearms?”

She pushed back her hair and focused those big blue eyes on him. “He thinks he’s smart and he is.” She grabbed the lapels of his chambray shirt. “He…he blew up my car!”

“I know, mouse. We’ll get you another one. We’ll contact your insurance company. Get that process started. Tell me more about him, the way he thinks.” *Stay focused, sweetheart—don’t fall apart on me.*

Her frantic gaze darted from window to window as if she expected to see him there watching her. Was this how this son of a bitch had terrorized her before? What things had she endured alone at the mercy of this maniac? “Ah…he…he’s very mechanical, good with his hands. He’s a member of the NRA and uses guns easily.”

He loosened his hold on her, much as he wanted to hold her tight. “Good, very good. Does he prefer rifles or revolvers?”

“Revolvers and”—she shuddered slightly, an almost imperceptive gesture—“knives.”

Storm's mind went back to loving her last night. That was when he'd first noticed the pale scar over her right breast—a thin, straight scar. He drew her closer and whispered in her ear. "That scar above your breast?" She nodded and expelled a gigantic sob. She burrowed against him, as if to immerse herself into his being. He drew her closer.

Fury like he'd never known raged through him; raged like a wild bronco charging first one side of the corral fence and then turning and charging the other. It took great restraint to stay in that chair, holding her, when he wanted to jump up and tear something apart in anger and frustration. His woman had been cut; cut and terrorized by a madman. "Sweetheart, never again. You're with me now. He'll never touch you again."

She sat up and looked at him. He sensed fear in her eyes. With his gaze locked on hers, he willed strength and courage into her. Slowly, her color returned. She began blinking again. "I don't want him to hurt anyone else. Now do you understand? If I stay here, danger will come."

"And I'll damn well put a bullet between danger's eyes." His gaze remained locked on hers and his voice deathly calm. "I promise you no one will ever hurt you again."

She placed ice-cold hands on his cheeks. "Storm, let me go."

"Never! I need you too much, love you too much." He wrapped strong arms around her and drew her close. "Jackson, when are those security guys coming?"

"They were supposed to leave Austin thirty minutes ago."

"How many?" He kept his hand moving up and down Rachel's back, slowly, hoping to calm and comfort. Would she try to leave him again? How could he convince her to stay?

"Eight. They'll work in four teams of two, riding in Jeeps."

"Good. That's good." He kissed Rachel's hair. "I've hired a security team to come and patrol the property, love. I'm doing everything I can to keep the family safe. You're part of my family now. You do know that, don't you?" She nodded against his neck and kissed him there. He took comfort in that small gesture.

"Rachel, why don't you go upstairs and play trains with Sawyer? Tell him I had ranch business I had to attend to and I'll play with him later. I need to alert Red and the rest of the hands to what's going on."

"Okay. You'll be careful, won't you?" She pressed a hand to his cheek. It was icy cold as if all the warmth of her body had been scared out of her. He cursed Kyle Benson for that, too.

"Yes, most definitely." He looked at her fear-filled eyes. "If ever a man wanted a future, it's me." He kissed this woman he loved, trying his best to convey assurance that he'd make everything all right. She slid off his lap and left the kitchen.

Someone rapped on the back door. Storm rose and looked out the screen door. "Come in, Red."

Red stepped inside and looked around the kitchen. "Mornin' Boss, Chief." He nodded at both of the men. "Boss, Randy was checkin' the fence line along Longhorn Road when he saw smoke. Someone cut the fence and drove through. Probably kids lookin' for a place to party. Found where they built a campfire along Stoney Creek. Bad thing is whoever it was was pretty careless. Fire spread to two trees. We got the fire out. Boys are keepin' an eye on it."

Storm looked at Jackson. "It's started."

Jackson pressed a key on his cell. "Travis, you, Hector, Clyde and Sam head out to the Triple-S. Bring rifles, high-powered scopes, bulletproof vests and all our night vision gear. Prepare to be here for a few days. I want you here five minutes ago. Is that clear?" He shoved his phone into his shirt pocket.

Red looked from one man to the other. "What in blue blazes is goin' on?"

Storm reached for a mug from the cabinet. "Grab a seat and have a cup of coffee while we fill you in. Trouble's come and we've got to deal with it." He set a mug of steaming coffee in front of his ranch foreman. In a matter of minutes, he had Red filled in on all the events.

Red ran a hand across the back of his sun-beaten, weathered neck. "Holy hell," he breathed. "We can't let him get to Miz Rachel or little Sawyer." He glanced at Storm. "Or you, for that matter."

The foreman had worked on the ranch since Storm and Sunny were ten years old. He was a man both their father, when alive, and now Storm trusted implicitly. The man may have been rough around the edges, but he was intelligent, intuitive and determined. The ranch ran smoothly because Red followed orders, but mainly because he saw all the little details were taken care of so Storm could focus on the big picture.

Jackson, used to making himself at home in Noella's kitchen, stood and made a fresh pot of coffee. "Storm, it would make things easier if the women and Sawyer were gone for the day. I could concentrate on the job at hand without worrying about Sunny and the boy. I'll be busy positioning men, setting up surveillance. If I know they're away from this mess, I can focus."

"I'm not letting Rachel out of my sight." He speared his best friend an unwavering stare.

"Then go with them. Take them shopping or something. Keep them out of harm's way until we have a chance to make sure things are safe here. The guys can set up cameras and sniper blinds."

"Snipers?" Red drained his cup. "Damn, you ain't foolin' around, are ya, son?"

"Snipers don't always go for the kill shot. They can aim for a leg as well as a head. I just want him incapacitated."

"Bastard's already taken a knife to Rachel. He's beaten her, broken her wrist. He deserves whatever he gets and then some. I'd kill him in a minute." Storm locked eyes with Jackson. "That's why you want me out of here, isn't it? You're afraid I'll do something stupid." God help him, he would, too. Cold, hard truth slammed into him—he'd kill for Rachel.

"I'm sworn to uphold the law, buddy. Take the women and Sawyer and give them an outing. Let them run up your charge card. I'll call. Let you know how we're progressing with security and such. We'll get the slimy bastard. Mark my words."

"I'll do it. I don't like it, but I'll do it. Feel like my place is here, doing something to help."

"You don't figure keeping the women and the boy safe is a helluva help? Seems to me that's the most important thing you *can* do." Jackson always could zero in on the heart of the matter.

Storm nodded and then turned to Red. "You and the boys make yourselves available to Jackson. Do whatever he says."

Red refilled his coffee mug. "Sure thing, boss. You're taking Noella, too, aren't you? She's a fine woman. Would hate for anything to happen to her."

Storm stared at Red for a minute. He hadn't expected that from him. Was he interested in Mama Noella? "Is there something I should know about?"

The foreman lifted his mug and blew on it. "I wish."

He'd have to think about this later. For now, there were too many other things to consider. "Hope I can talk those three women into going to the mall."

Red barked a snort of laughter. "First time I ever heard of forcin' women to shop."

Storm smiled. "Yeah, well, you've never tried getting my Rachel to do something she doesn't want to do."

Red looked at Jackson and wiggled his eyebrows. "*My* Rachel. Well, now, don't that beat all?"

****

Rachel was trying to pay attention to Sawyer's excited chatter, really she was. Only panic had set in and had its icy cold fingers coiled around her heart, twisting, slapping and tearing at it. Then for good measure, fear did the Mexican hat dance around her stomach. Kyle had torched her car, her pretty red convertible barely three months old. What would he do to Storm or this sweet child clapping with glee as the two trains passed on the metal tracks?

Leaving would be agonizingly hard now that she and Storm had grown close, intimately close. A smile crossed her features until fear chased it away. If she left, she'd be protecting him. Kyle was a very real and dangerous menace. Still, Storm and she had declared themselves to each other, made promises, sweet, enduring promises. No, she couldn't leave the man she'd come to love. She belonged with Storm.

Noella was changing the sheets on Sawyer's bed, probably trying to keep busy. Sunny told the housekeeper, in whispers, what had happened to Rachel's car. Noella had crossed herself and then hugged Rachel.

"Wachel, when dat twain gets at the station, stop it. Okay?"

"Okay, Mr. Conductor." She gave a salute and the child giggled.

"Well, well, don't you have a nice helper…and pretty, too." Storm had a shoulder leaning against the frame of the doorway and appeared nonchalant. Rachel knew him well enough to see the telltale signs: the clenched jaw and the smile that didn't soften his eyes. He pushed away from the doorway and entered the room, squatting beside Sawyer.

"Wachel helped me. She made the twains go two diffewent ways."

Storm studied the track for a little. "Know what you need, partner?"

Sawyer slid over beside Storm and then shifted into a squatting position, mirroring his uncle. "What, Unkie Storm?" What an adorable child. What a handsome man, squatting with his large hand on the child's small back.

"I think you need some bridges, so your train can go over houses and trees." He made a sweeping gesture with his large, tanned hand.

"Yeah, dat would be somefin. How do I get a bwidge?"

"At a train store." Storm glanced over his shoulder at Sunny sitting on the rocker. "Don't they have a model train store in that big mall in Austin? That mall you like."

She stopped rocking. "Yes. Next to that clothing boutique Pilar's friend owns."

"What do you say we all get in Noella's SUV and head to that mall? Sawyer and I could buy some train stuff while you women shop. Rachel could get her hair cut like she talked about in the tub this morning."

"You saw Wachel take a baf?"

For the first time, Rachel saw Storm blush. He hung his head and shook it once, obviously embarrassed by the slip.

Sunny quickly saved the day. "Unkie Storm said shrubs. He heard Rachel talk about getting her hair cut when she was standing near the shrubs this morning."

"Oh. Can we go, Mommy? Please?" He ran to his mother and took her hand. "Come on, it'll be fun."

Storm stood. "How soon can you ladies be ready?"

"I'm not really in the mood to go shopping." Rachel stood, too. A maniac was closing in on her, and Storm wanted her to shop? What was going on? She stepped in front of him and ran a hand up his chambray shirt, feeling his hard muscles underneath. "What's going on?" she whispered in hushed tones.

He enveloped her in an embrace. "Jackson says it'll be easier to put safety measures into place if the house is empty. Plus, he won't have the distraction of worrying over Sunny and Sawyer, knowing they'll be safe at the mall with me." That made sense. "You could get your hair cut for your donation to Locks of Love. Buy something pretty for me. A nightie, perhaps."

"You wear nightgowns, Storm Blackhawk?" She batted her eyes at him.

He leaned down, gently bit her lower lip and slowly smiled when her breathing hitched a beat. "Everyone be at the front door in ten minutes. You too, Noella. I might even buy you a pretty skirt to wear at the barbeque. Something to turn Red's eye." He winked at the housekeeper.

Sunny and Rachel chimed in unison, "Red, the foreman?" Both ladies turned to stare at the housekeeper.

Noella patted the bun at the back of her head. "And why not? I've still got some moves, but I say nothing." She held her head high and sashayed out of the room.

Before they left for the mall, Rachel checked her phone. She'd turned it off the night before after sending Kyle a text that she was staying at the Dew Drop Inn. She couldn't handle his constant calls and threatening texts.

Storm placed a hand at the small of her back. "Any missed calls or texts?"

"Twelve missed calls and thirty-six texts." She looked up at him. "You know this is all going to come to a terrible head."

"A suggestion, love. Maybe if you give Jackson your phone, he can trace it somehow. Use a GPS to find Kyle's location."

She handed the phone to Storm. "If it'll help, sure. I'll be glad to be out of his reach."

Chapter Eighteen

It was nearing lunchtime when they reached the mall. Rachel pricked her finger to check her glucose levels. With all the worry about Kyle, she knew her reading would be off.

"What's a normal range? I don't know a thing about diabetes." Storm leaned over in the SUV, watching her quick and efficient movements.

"Normal on an empty stomach is between eighty and one twenty. It's been two hours since I ate, so we can expect it to be around one fifty."

"If it's not?" He absently twirled a finger around a strand of her hair.

"If it's too low, I eat or drink something to bring it up. If it's a little high, I exercise. If it's really high, I give myself a dose of insulin. The amount I inject depends on how high my reading is."

"Sounds complicated."

She shrugged. "It's a way of life. I have type-one diabetes. Have since I was nine. I'm used to the routine. When I'm extra active or under stress, I keep a closer eye on my readings." She looked at Storm. "In life, we do what we have to."

Storm gave a low whistle when her reading popped up on the glucometer display. "What now?" He cast worried eyes on her.

She rummaged in her cavernous purse, pulling out her insulin pen and an alcohol wipe in foil. "Watch and learn, cowboy." She opened the foil packet and wiped the saturated gauze over a spot on her thigh. She inserted a needle into her insulin pen, turned the dial for the number of units she needed and pressed the needle into her leg. "Done."

Storm's gaze locked on hers for a beat. Then he leaned over and kissed the injection site on her thigh.

From the back seat came an excited statement. "Unkie Storm kissed Wachel's boo-boo on her weg!"

"That's right, partner. Here's your first lesson in being a man. A man always takes care of his woman." Storm shifted in his seat to regard the child.

"Is Wachel your woman?"

"Yes, son, she is." Storm captured Rachel's hand in his.

“Wachel’s my woman, too.” The child nodded with the sage wisdom of children. Gentle adult laughter filled the vehicle.

Rachel placed her glucometer and insulin pen back in her purse. “You’ve got some stiff competition, cowboy.”

Once inside the large mall, Rachel encouraged Sunny to use a wheelchair. Sawyer saw it as a ride and insisted on sitting on his mommy’s lap. Sunny, being the doting mother she was, wrapped her arms around him and encouraged his “zoom, zoom” noises. Rachel shook her head and smiled.

“First, Master Storm is going to buy me an outfit he promised for the barbeque.” Noella shot her boss a challenging look. “We’ll see if his charge card backs up his words. Then, I need some books, so we’ll head to the bookstore. After that, I’ll take Miss Sunny and little Sawyer to the train store.”

Rachel looked at Storm, who shrugged that uncomfortable shrug men give in shopping malls, grumbling that he hoped Noella wouldn’t take all day making up her mind about that outfit.

“I want to get my hair cut for Locks of Love. I’ll meet you at the train store.”

“Go do your noble deed, love.” Storm gave her a quick kiss before manning the handles of the wheelchair.

Rachel had to admit she had some qualms about cutting so much off the length of her hair. Still, she knew it was for a good cause.

With the weight of her long hair removed, it bounced into curls around her face. Rachel studied herself in the mirror. She looked younger with all those big, loose curls. Maybe Storm wouldn’t like her hair this short, although it almost reached her shoulders.

She found the mall directory and looked for the location of the train store. When she was almost there, she saw Storm with his shoulder leaning against a store window, talking to a tall, slender woman with sleek, chin-length auburn hair.

Storm reached out and tucked the auburn hair behind the woman’s ear. Rachel narrowed her eyes at the intimate gesture. When he ran his hand down the woman’s arm of the very attractive, almost exotic woman, Rachel’s stomach dropped. *Who* was that? She approached and saw Storm glance her way. His face paled.

“Storm.” Rachel stood, waiting for him to introduce her to the woman before she belted him a good shot. Anger vibrated in her like a tight string on a cheap guitar.

He gave her a hard look, and for an instant, she wanted to shrink back. No, she wouldn't be intimidated by a man. Never again. She angled her chin in defiance and glared at him.

The woman in an expensive turquoise pantsuit raised a finely waxed eyebrow. "Stormy, who is this?" She ran a manicured hand up his chest as if she had every right to touch him, an engagement diamond glistening under the glare of the overhead lights.

"Pilar, this is Rachel Dennison, Sunny's new nurse." No signs of affection, no touching. In fact, he was downright standoffish. Why was he acting this way? As if she meant nothing to him. Dawning registered. No, dear God, no. He couldn't have been pretending all this time.

"*And*..." Rachel tilted her head to the side. For two cents, she'd kick him. Hadn't he told her he'd broken up with Pilar? For a jilted fiancée, the woman was acting awfully proprietary. Had he lied to her?

He glared at her as if trying to convey some silent message. "*And* she's staying at the ranch, getting Sunny stronger for her next round of chemo."

The impeccably dressed woman gave her the once-over as if she were a nasty bug under a microscope. She wished she'd worn something better than khaki shorts and a navy tank top, but there hadn't been time to change. No doubt the woman found her lacking. She cut her eyes to Storm. Evidently he did, too, in the presence of tall, tailored, trim Pilar. Fact was, he made her feel like a bump on the underbelly of a pickle.

Her time with Storm had meant the world to her. Now, feeling as though she'd been duped, the cold, ruthless reality hit her—she'd been lied to and used. The sensation of ice water replacing warm blood in her veins chilled her to her very core. Pain, acute, knifing pain, stabbed her heart repeatedly as if it were a crazed murderer. She struggled to take in air, wondering how she could be so easily deceived—again.

"I'm going to the train store to see how my patient's doing." She never waited for an acknowledgment of her statement, marching down the corridor of the mall, anger mounting in her system. She had to draw on anger, for if she allowed the pain to surface, she'd crumble. This man wouldn't see her cry.

She ducked into a little store, feigning interest in the rack of jeans. Her eyes filled with tears. Okay, she'd give herself five minutes to fall apart before she pulled herself together and showed that lying, cheating jerk he was pond scum.

Lies. It was all a lie. All of it. Storm was not through with Pilar. The woman was still wearing a diamond, a big flashy diamond. She sneered as she shoved hangers of jeans back and forth. He'd lied to her, and she'd fallen right into his arms. She rolled her eyes heavenward. He'd told her he loved her, and she'd believed that, too. What a moron she was! What a sap! What a pitiful…

"Can I help you? We're having a great sale today. Clothes have been jumping off the racks." A cheery, pregnant salesgirl with spiky bleached blonde hair, wearing a nametag that read "LaKeesha" saddled up to her side. "Oh honey, don't cry. Believe me, I know how hard it is to grow out of your regular clothes, but the baby's worth it." She placed a hand on Rachel's abdomen. "You gotta embrace the bump, girlfriend."

"Oh, I'm not pregnant." She sniffed and rummaged in her purse for a tissue. Her hand stilled. When had she taken her last birth control pill? Not today—yet. Nor yesterday. Oh no, she'd forgotten her pill yesterday with all the drama over Kyle finding out where she was. She'd take one as soon as she got back to the ranch. Missing one pill certainly wouldn't…

She swallowed. Last week she'd forgotten one, too. That was the day she and Storm had their sensual interlude on the sofa, the one Noella had walked in on. She'd been so upset that night she'd forgotten her pill. Her stomach clenched. She'd had unprotected sex with that lying, cheating pond scum six times. *Dear God.*

"Sorry, I didn't realize this was a maternity clothing store." She wiped her eyes, looked at the girl, then started sobbing in earnest.

The strange salesgirl wrapped her arms around Rachel. "Mercy me!" LaKeesha patted Rachel's back. "What is it?"

"He…he lied to me." More tears flowed. Sobs racked her body.

"Men. Can't live with 'em, can't shoot 'em," LaKeesha added, with the appropriate amount of female commiseration. "But we can cut their peckers off."

"Rachel? Sweetheart, what's wrong?" Storm tugged on her arm. "I saw you come in here."

She whirled around to face the man who had shattered her heart. "Liar! You told me you broke off your engagement."

"I did, but…"

"She's still wearing her diamond." She swiped angrily at an errant tear.

He glanced at LaKeesha, who clearly wasn't going to give them any privacy. "Do you mind?" he barked.

"I'm here for moral support." The salesgirl laid a protective arm across Rachel's shoulders. "I'm not leaving unless my new BFF wants me to."

"What the hell is a BFF?"

LaKeesha sighed as if he were the most stupid man on the face of the earth. "Best friend forever."

Rachel leaned into her. "Yeah, LaKeesha knows how I feel, you lying, cheating mass of horse shit."

He placed fisted hands on his narrow hips. "Horse shit?"

"You heard the lady." LaKeesha pointed a finger at him. Two more pregnant women ambled over, their expressions questioning.

"Rachel, can we please go someplace private so I can explain?"

"Explain? You mean explain how it was a lie when you told me this morning, in your bed, I might add, that I was yours and would be yours forever? Or perhaps you could explain to me how you could promise, when we were having hot standing-up-against-the-wall sex last night, you would never allow another woman to touch you? Maybe you want to claim that was a figment of my imagination." Her voice rose with agitation. She was trembling, trembling and crumbling into a thousand pieces.

"Hunh," LaKeesha chimed in. "Don't see how one could *imagine* having standing-up-against-the-wall-sex. Fanaticize about it, sure, but you'd definitely know if you were havin' it or not." The two pregnant onlookers were joined by another.

"Then today, I see you all but kissing Pilar here in the mall, tucking her hair behind her ear, running your hand up her arm, and leaning in to whisper to her."

"I can explain all that." His gaze darted to the group of pregnant woman who'd moved a step closer to him, whispering, and sneering.

Rachel wiped her nose and waved the hand clutching a wadded tissue. "I suppose you can explain how you could introduce me as your sister's nurse!" There was a collective gasp among the eavesdropping women, as if they'd all sucked in air at the same time. Narrowed eyes swept from Rachel to Storm.

"Suppose *you* stop being childish about this!" More sucking air by the pregnant mob. Two called him foul names. One asked if he'd like to sing soprano for the rest of his life.

"Childish?" Rachel drew a fist and socked him in his rock-hard stomach, nearly breaking her wrist. "I'll show you childish."

He grabbed her by the elbow and looked at LaKeesha. "You got someplace private we can talk? A dressing room, maybe?"

"Oh no! I'm not letting you use *my* dressing room. What if you end up having up-against-the-wall—"

"For God's sake!" Storm tightened his hold on Rachel's elbow and all but dragged her out of the store. "I'll explain everything to you as soon as we get one damn moment alone," he vowed through clenched teeth.

She tried to jerk her arm free, but his grip was too tight. "Let go of me! I don't want you touching me ever again. I can smell her perfume on you. You cheating, low-life pond scum." She struggled as he led her across the mall corridor to the train store. Strains of Nazareth belting out "Love Hurts" blared from the mall's loudspeakers. Indeed it did.

"Yeah, we've covered that ground already. I didn't lie to you, you hell-cat. Now would you just calm down."

"Unkie Storm, Unkie Storm! I got two bwidges. One weally big bwidge and one wittle bwidge and a tunnel and two new cars to make my twain bigger."

The angry couple turned, their fake smiles in place. Storm squatted in front of the excited boy. "Need help carrying that bag, partner? Looks pretty heavy." Sawyer nodded and handed the bag to his uncle.

Rachel walked to the window of a nearby store, pretending to look at the display. She dabbed her eyes and blew her nose. Coming to Texas was the biggest mistake of her life, the biggest error of her heart.

Sunny stepped up and gently shouldered her. "Don't yell at me for walking—it's the first time I've been out of that chair all afternoon. You want to tell me what's going on between you two?"

"Ask your brother. Or better yet, ask Pilar, the woman he was all over a few minutes ago. Look, I need to be alone. I'll meet you at the car." She turned and rushed off.

By the time everyone else made it to the dark green SUV, Rachel had made four trips around it, working up more steam, digging into a heavy dose of resolve as if it were a quart of Ben and Jerry's Chunky Monkey. She wouldn't stay here. She would hire another nurse for Sunny, another nurse for Storm to take on moonlight rides, to watch sunrises with…to lie to.

Storm walked to her. "Have you calmed down yet?"

She turned to Noella. "Would you please tell Master Storm to stop barking at me and that I have nothing to say to him. Also, I'd prefer riding in the back with you and Sawyer."

"For God's sake! You wanna act like that? Fine." He opened the back door and waved a hand for her to get into the vehicle. She was more than happy to oblige.

The silent ride home took forever. She tried ignoring the many times Storm glanced at her in the rearview mirror. She tried not to remember the silent communication they'd shared on the way to the mall when they'd held hands, shared smiles and spoken volumes with their eyes. Lies, so many lies.

At least catching Storm with Pilar had gotten her mind off Kyle for a few moments. Which was worse? Worrying over a crazed man finding her or going crazy worrying about the character of another? She had to get out of Texas. Had to.

When Storm pulled in front of the ranch house, Rachel was the first one to barrel out of the SUV. Before she'd made it a dozen steps, Storm grabbed her and threw her over his shoulder like a bag of grain. "Put me down, you lunatic!"

"Like hell." He stormed into the house, his boots echoing off the hardwood floors of the large foyer. "We're going to have this out right now. I'm tired of you peeling my hide with your accusations."

Jackson rushed out of the den into the large hallway. "Storm? What the hell?"

Storm had one hand on the doorknob to his office. "You got all the security measures in place? Anything that demands my immediate attention?"

"Put me down this instant, you…you caveman cowboy!" He smacked her bottom. She yelped. Once he put her down, she was going to tear him apart, limb by cheating limb.

Jackson had a hand over his mouth to hide his laughter. "Have at it, buddy. I've done my job." He took a sleeping Sawyer from Noella. "Sunny and I will put tiger here to bed."

Storm opened the door to his office, waiting until the couple had the sleeping boy upstairs before he yelled his announcement so the entire first floor could hear: "Anyone who knocks on this door before Rachel and I have worked things out takes their life in their hands. Is that clear?" He slammed the door shut behind them and turned the lock before setting Rachel down on the floor.

She was so incensed, so humiliated, so livid she couldn't speak. She kicked him in the shin with her sneakered foot. Storm winced before stalking over to the liquor cabinet.

He poured himself two fingers of whiskey, neat, and downed it. He poured another and downed it, too. He hung his head, his hands fisted on the cabinet. "You can make me so damned mad I can't see straight. No one has *ever* pushed me over the edge the way you do."

She fisted her hands on her hips, hiked her chin, and glared at him. "Yeah, well, I'd like to slap you into next week, you lying, cheating, poor excuse of a man. You told me things. You told me you loved me. I surrendered to you. I had unprotected sex with you."

"Would you just listen to me for five damn minutes?" He turned to face her and ran both hands through his hair, a sign of frustration.

She folded her arms. "Okay, but this better be good."

He looked away for a beat and sighed before he spoke. "The night after I told Pilar we *really* were through—dating, phone calls, texts and all—she took an overdose of pills. She called me and I told her I wouldn't come. But I did call nine-one-one."

She wouldn't let the nurse part of her surface. Refused it. Better to let the bitch part of her run rampant and rule. She let Bitch Rachel fuel her actions. One eyebrow hiked in question. "This is important, because…?"

Storm walked to his desk and sat in the large leather chair behind it. "Because it shows how fragile she is emotionally, more so than I ever imagined. Hell, she'd never told her father our engagement was off and had been for weeks. Once she was out of the hospital, old man Fontaine came here and took his displeasure out on my face."

He's lying, Bitch Rachel hissed into her ear as if she were perched on one of her shoulders. The bitch had a good point, she had to admit. How did she know he was being truthful? Although he had mentioned Pilar's father hitting him. The bruises were still evident.

"When I ran into her at the mall today, she seemed so delicate." He ran a hand through his hair again and then placed his forearms on his desk. "See, I never told her why I couldn't work things out. I said I wasn't the man for her, that I felt more comfortable on the ranch than in her glitzy, glossy world. I never told her I'd fallen in love with someone else."

Bitch Rachel jumped onto her shoulder again and hissed into her ear. *See how he treats you?* She folded her arms under her breasts again and tapped a foot in annoyance. "And just why not?"

"I hurt her enough, don't you think? What good would it do to batter her ego further by telling her I'd given my heart to another woman?"

She started pacing in front of his desk. "So you were protecting her feelings." He nodded. "You were protecting her feelings today when you pretended I meant nothing to you, when you introduced me as Sunny's nurse."

"Yes. You are Sunny's nurse, after all." The man was clueless. Her temper rose another notch.

When she stopped pacing, she placed her hands on the edge of his desk and leaned toward him. "So, *her* feelings mean more to you than mine."

"I never said that."

"No, you showed me that. You showed me her feelings still mean more to you than mine ever will." She pointed her finger at him. "Make up with her. Marry her and forget me. I'm outta here. Off the Triple-S, out of your life and out of Texas."

He slowly stood, his eyebrows furrowed. "Forget you?" He looked menacing for a minute, but she didn't care. Her anger was just as strong, if not more so.

She turned and headed for the door. "That's right, forget about me, you clueless jerk, just like I'm going to forget about you."

In a few long strides, he reached her and swung her around. He slapped both hands against the door on either side of her head. "Forget about you? Suppose you tell me just what I should forget." He leaned in and smelled her neck. She shivered at his proximity. "Should I forget about the way you smell? That enticing mix of flowers and sensual woman.

"Or maybe I should forget about the texture of your hair—silk and curls. Sexy haircut, by the way." He ran his fingers through her hair, his gaze locked on hers. Her stomach quivered.

He pressed gentle kisses to her face. "Or maybe I should forget about the smattering of freckles that dot your nose. Hmm?"

Bitch Rachel hissed, "Tell him your freckles are none of his damned business."

He ran his tongue around her ear and drew her earlobe into his mouth and gently bit it. Her breathing hitched. "Or maybe I should forget the way your breathing gets all funny when I do that. Should I, love?" Damn him. He knew her weak spots.

"Tell me," he whispered, as his teeth grazed her neck, "should I forget the way my blood stirs when I do this and you groan? Her nipples peaked.

He took her hand and pressed a kiss to her palm. "Should I forget the way your eyes go soft when I kiss you here?" He kissed a gentle trail of kisses from her wrist to the inside of her elbow. "Or forget the softness of your skin here and here? Tell, me love, what shall I forget?"

His eyes were dark when he looked at her again, dark and sensually dangerous. She was a goner. His hands slid inside her tank top and yanked it off. She covered the cups of her bra with her hands. He shoved them aside and unfastened the front clasp of her red lacy bra. "Should I forget the way your breasts fill my hands?" He plucked her nipples with his fingertips, and she was lost. "Or should I forget how responsive you are to my touch? Tell me, love, what shall I forget?"

He bent his head and suckled on her nipple. Her hands fisted in his hair, and she whimpered. He withdrew for a moment and reached over his shoulder with one hand to tug his shirt over his head while it was still buttoned and threw it across the room. He banded a strong arm around her waist and fisted a hand in her curls, jerking her head back and grazing his teeth and tongue up the slender column of her neck before touching her lips. "Tell me, love, should I forget the way you taste?"

He kissed her slowly, taking his sweet time nipping at her lips, his tongue delving in the moistness of her mouth, destroying her final line of resistance.

"I'm telling you, Rachel," he groaned in desperation, "I'll never forget you." With that, he pressed her against his erection and kissed her with fierceness, reclaiming her completely. Without breaking the kiss, he lifted her off the floor and walked over to his desk. He kept one arm banded around her, holding her to him as his tongue dueled with hers. With his other arm, he made a wide sweeping motion, knocking everything off his giant oak desk.

He laid her upon the desk and unzipped her shorts, sliding them off. When he saw she was wearing the red thong he'd held at the motel, his control seemed to snap. He tore it from her and unzipped his jeans, releasing his heavy erection. She wrapped her legs around his waist and he dove into her, muttering in Comanche while he pushed them both to a mind-numbing, unbelievable climax.

Jagged, rasping breaths filled the office. She held him to her, wondering if this would be the last time they'd make love. The problem still existed—Pilar. Emotions conflicted, how could she stay with a man who valued another woman's feelings more than hers? Yet, how could she leave a man she loved so desperately?

Chapter Nineteen

"**I** don't like it when you're quiet." Storm was putting his shirt back on. "Makes me wonder what that beautiful mind of yours is thinking. Here's your tank top. Though it's a shame to cover that pretty red bra." His dimples winked, and her heart melted a tad. She loved his smile, the way the hard planes of his face softened with it.

She tugged her tank top over her head and then ran fingers through her curls, trying to restore some order. "It'll take me a while to get used to this shorter hair."

He tucked his shirttails into his jeans. "Looks good on you. Come here, love." He pulled her into his arms and kissed her. "I have something for you."

"Again? So soon?"

He chuckled and gently bit her earlobe. "Minx. My stubble rubbed you a little raw here. Sorry. I hate leaving marks on your beautiful skin." He unsnapped a chest pocket on his chambray shirt and pulled out a thin jeweler's box. "I got this for you while you were getting your hair cut." He shyly handed it to her.

His giving her little gifts was always a tender surprise. He placed his hands at her waist and slid them around to the small of her back, drawing her closer. "Open it."

She snapped open the lid to find a silver charm bracelet. She fingered the charms: a map of Texas, the word "Dream," a cowboy hat, a pair of boots, a mouse, a horse, and the words "I love you." Charms that meant something to both of them. He lifted the chain from its blue satin nest and held it up. "Give me your wrist."

She extended her hand. "Thank you. I love it." It was such a sweet gesture. She was touched beyond words.

"Promise you won't take it off until I put a wedding band on your finger. Promise me."

A wedding ring? Was this a proposal? She glanced at the bracelet, turning her wrist. "Are you proposing, cowboy?"

"Not yet. I'm trying to get you accustomed to the idea of being with me forever." He ran fingertips down her cheek. "I *can* promise you a proposal is coming. Will you keep my bracelet on and stay with me?"

Marriage. He loved her and wanted to marry her. "Is this really happening? Are you being honest with me about Pilar?"

"Don't you trust me?" His dark eyes pierced hers. Did she trust him?

She rested a hand on his cheek. "You have to know that after Kyle, trusting a man's not easy for me to do. I will say I *want* to trust you." She shrugged. To say anything more wouldn't be completely honest. "Guess I'm not completely convinced you're through with Pilar."

He wrapped his arms around her and kissed her gently. "In time, you'll believe. I was expecting you to ask about the 'Dream' charm."

"It did strike me as a little whimsical for you, but then I remembered what you told me about your having vision dreams like your father did."

"I dreamed about you before I met you."

She leaned back in his arms and looked into his dark eyes. "You did?"

"I dreamed of your blue eyes and the sound of your laughter for three nights before I met you out on Longhorn Road. I think I knew in my heart, the moment I laid eyes on you, we were fated to be together."

"That's why you made that remark about my eyes that night. I thought there was something wrong with them."

He placed both hands on her bottom and squeezed. "Rachel Dennison, there's not a single thing wrong with you. You're perfect." They walked out of his office arm-in-arm.

"I'd better go talk to Jackson, find out what all's been going on. Why don't you lie down until dinner? Rest for later tonight." He winked and kissed her palm.

Rachel stuck her tongue out at him before dashing up the steps to the sound of his laughter. Storm's boots echoed off the wooden floor as he strode down the hallway toward the den.

A bath. She needed a long, hot bath to help unwind and put her thoughts into some form of order. For just a few minutes, she wanted privacy.

She entered her bedroom and turned on her CD player. Smiling, she slipped in the disc Storm had burned for her; he could be so sweet at times. Then she went into her private bath and turned on the faucets. She poured in a generous amount of lavender bubble bath. To further relax, she lit a lavender scented candle. At her dresser, she removed a black bra and matching sheer panties from a drawer.

When Bonnie Tyler's "Holding out for a Hero" floated from her stereo speakers, she turned up the volume to enjoy the effects of the drums in the song. Pretending she was pounding the drums with imaginary drumsticks, she turned to open the closet door to choose something to wear to dinner —and gasped a silent scream.

Kyle stood before her.

Silent.

Ominous.

Menacing.

Her mind tried to accept what her eyes saw—and couldn't. She wanted to scream, but fear, cruel and strong, jumped up and grabbed her by the throat, squeezing and blocking air to her lungs. A squeak escaped, but before it morphed into a scream, Kyle had one hand over her mouth and the other around her windpipe. She hit, scratched and kicked, but all were futile attempts, for he easily overpowered her. "Surprised to see me, *bitch?"* he hissed in her ear. "Didn't I tell you I'd come for you?"

In the midst of their struggles, they fell to the floor. She rolled over in an attempt to escape. "Storm!" Damn those drums! No one could hear her over them. Kyle grabbed her ankle and twisted it. Pain ripped up her leg like a buzz saw. He was going to dislocate her knee. She rolled over, easing the pain. He struck her face. Another scream escaped seconds before he covered her mouth again. He punched her stomach, momentarily knocking the air from her.

With one hand over her mouth and his other clamped around her arm, he yanked her from the floor and tossed her onto the bed, where he held her down with brute force. She tried to break free, but his hold was too strong. Could anyone hear their grappling over Bonnie Tyler singing and all those pounding drums? If only she hadn't turned up the volume.

She struggled to escape, battled to live. He straddled her, his eyes full of maniacal rage. She pushed and hit. "You've become a fighter, I see. I wasn't expecting that. I'll show you what happens when a woman fights back." He circled his iron-like fingers around her throat and slowly began to choke her. Then he reached into his back pocket for a roll of electrical tape, bit off a strip and pressed it to her mouth. She'd seen this expression of madness before and knew what was coming.

How would anyone hear the beating she was about to receive over the volume of the music? Why hadn't she played Brahms or Mozart? His hold over her windpipe tightened. He punched her in the eye, and she saw a shooting shower of stars. His second blow landed on her jaw. Her lip split. Blood trickled down her chin. Through his beating, her mind raced, trying to come to grips with the shock of finding him in her closet. How had he gotten inside the ranch house? Didn't anyone search her room?

He leaned toward her and hissed, "I'm going to kill you." He sniffed. "You smell of sex, slut. Were you screwing the cowboy? Didn't I tell you you'd always belong to *me*? I'll kill you for letting another man have you."

His hand tightened on her trachea. Her vision narrowed. He was strangling her. Fear numbed her mind—or was it loss of oxygen? He fingered a piece of rope pulled from his pocket, rolled her over and yanked her arms behind her back to tie her wrists together. Now his hands were off her throat, she breathed in air. Air, blessed air. If she could open her mouth, she'd gulp it like a starving person.

That's when he noticed the charm bracelet. "Well, well, what do we have here?"

She could feel him finger the charms. His breathing became more rapid with anger. "Your new boyfriend give you this?"

He grabbed her hair and snapped her head back. "Answer me!"

Tears ran down her face, and she nodded.

"What's with the haircut? Didn't I forbid you to cut your hair?" He jerked her head to punctuate each word. "No one defies me!"

She would die. She'd never see Storm again. Never have a marriage to him. Never bear his children. Never grow old with him. Today was her last day of life. Death had come in camouflage clothes, with a ruthless heart and a sick mind.

Kyle slipped a Bowie knife from the leather scabbard on his belt. He pierced her wrist when he slid the knife under the sterling chain. "So, tell me, Rachel, which edge do I have against the chain? The blade? Or is the blade against your skin? Chain…skin…chain…skin. Will I cut you, or not?"

The cold, razor-sharp steel sliced her wrist, and she closed her eyes in resignation. Blood flowed. Then he turned the Bowie knife and cut the sterling chain.

When he rolled her over, his mouth formed a twisted evil grin. "Oops!" He stood, dragged her off the bed and kicked her several times in the small of her back. "I'll make sure you never see that new boyfriend again. So, who do I kill? The cowboy or you?"

Her last coherent fragment of awareness was of his holding an ether-soaked cloth over her face until she passed out.

****

Noella was bustling around the kitchen, putting supper on the table. With all the men she had to feed, she was setting food and plates out on the kitchen table in buffet style. There were policemen, security personnel, and ranch hands in addition to her family.

"Need any help, Miss Noella?" Red grabbed two potholders and lifted a large baking dish of baked beans. "Any special place you want me to put these here beans?"

"Next to the meatloaf, please. I hope everyone likes what I've prepared. I cooked in such a rush." She pulled two large pans of biscuits from the oven. "Red, if you want, you can remove the ears of corn from the boiling water and stack them on that white platter. I hope I made enough food."

Storm was setting out clean mugs next to the coffeemaker. He was surprised at how the crude ranch foreman looked at home in this kitchen, helping Momma Noella. The man was definitely showing his polite side.

"Stop yer frettin', Miss Noella. These freeloaders ought to feel mighty obliged you went to all this bother. Looks like a feast to me." Red picked up the tongs and began removing the corn from the steaming pot.

Noella placed the hot biscuits in a large basket. "Oh, I almost forgot Rachel's salad."

"I'll get it." Storm went to the refrigerator and pulled out a large glass bowl packed with a vibrantly colored salad. He set it on the large table. "What else, Momma?"

"You can go out and ring the dinner gong." She removed several bottles of dressing from the refrigerator.

Storm stepped out onto the back porch and grabbed the striker hanging by a rope next to the old metal triangle. He hit the sides of the triangle with it, the same way cooks had for generations, calling men to dinner with its jarring, gonging sound.

Pistol whined, and Storm gathered up the dog's water and kibble bowls. "Be back in a sec, buddy." The old dog wiggled in ecstasy when freshly filled bowls were set before him.

When Storm stepped inside, the housekeeper and foreman were standing side-by-side watching the noisy gang of deputies, security personnel, ranch hands, and family grabbing the food. "You yahoos best show some sense grabbing for them vittles. Mind yer manners and show Miss Noella here some gratitude for her hard work."

Storm smiled at Red's complimentary remark. He had to hand it to the old goat; he was trying. "I'll go up and get Rachel. She was taking a nap before dinner." He took the stairs two steps at a time, eager to steal a kiss or two from Rachel. He couldn't remember ever being this happy.

He was whistling when he rapped on Rachel's bedroom door. "Rachel, dinner's ready. Come on down and put on the feedbag." The music coming from her room was so loud, he had to yell. When he got no response, he opened the door. He stepped into the stillness of her room and stopped, his eyes scanned the messed-up bed and the open window. Sounds of bath water running caught his attention. His smile broadened. This might work out just fine.

"Mouse? Need your back washed?" He poked his head into the bathroom. The water was overflowing the tub in the empty bath. "What the…?" He rushed to turn off the spigots. The rugs were soaked. A candle was burning, and he blew it out. He looked around. No Rachel. His heart stopped for a beat, and he broke out in a cold sweat.

The woman he loved was gone.

"Jackson! Jackson!" Storm hurried out to the hallway, bellowing as he went. "Get up here, pronto."

Jackson ran, charging up the steps. "What's wrong?"

"She's gone! Rachel's gone." Storm ran his hands through his hair. She'd promised him she'd stay. Promised him. How could she desert him after all they'd been through? After all the times they'd made love.

Jackson shouldered his way around his momentarily paralyzed

friend. “She has to be here. She can’t leave, she doesn’t have a car.” He walked into her bedroom, and Storm followed. Jackson surveyed his surroundings. “Was that window open when you came in?” He walked to the open closet door. “Her clothes are still hanging in here.” He turned and walked to the bed.

“You didn’t touch anything in here, did you?” He retrieved a pair of latex gloves from his pocket and snapped them on.

“No. Well, except for turning off the stereo. It was blaring. The tub was overflowing and I turned the water off. Blew out a burning candle.” Why did Jackson put on gloves? What was he looking at so intently? A wave of cold terror blew over him like a tsunami. He leaned down beside the police chief. “Is that blood?”

Jackson was running evidence swabs over the bloodstains on the rumpled bed and carefully tucking them into plastic evidence bags. “Yeah.” He labeled the bag and then hunkered down beside more stains, repeating the same process with them. He pulled out his cell and pressed a number. “Clyde, get my camera outta the glove box in my squad car and the fingerprint kit from the trunk. I’ve got a crime scene up here. Want you to keep everyone downstairs and in view of each other. You hear?”

“You think Benson took her.” Storm’s words were a statement, not a question. Dread was slowly seeping into his system, grave, overwhelming dread. Rachel hadn’t left of her own free will—she’d been taken.

“I saw a couple candy bar wrappers on the closet floor.” Jackson pointed his thumb in the direction of the closet. “Rachel’s too strict with her diet to eat candy. My guess is Benson was hiding in her closet. She turned on the bathwater and lit a candle. There’s clean underwear next to the pillow. She probably went to the closet to grab some clothes, and Benson was waiting.”

“My God.” Storm ran his hands through his hair. “He must have scared the hell out of her.” Then something sparkled in the light filtering in through the windows. “Her bracelet. I just got it for her today. She promised she’d never take it off.” He bent to retrieve it.

“Stop! Don’t touch it!” Jackson picked it up in his gloved hand and slowly turned it, examining the cut edges. “It’s been cut. Looks like he used a knife. There’s dried blood on the chain.” He looked at Storm for a beat before reaching in his pocket for another plastic evidence bag.

Panic pulsated in Storm's heart, forcing an erratic beat of alarm. He could barely breathe. "Rachel told me Benson likes to use a knife. She has a two-inch scar over her breast where he cut her before." Fear and the power of his rage brought murder to mind. He shook with loathing. His fists clenched and his vision field slowly turned red. "I'll kill him. If he's hurt her, I'll kill him."

"That's not the kind of remark you want to make to the chief of police, although I'd feel the same way if it were Sunny's blood I was looking at. We'll find her, don't you worry." Jackson walked over to the open window and looked out. "Sunny's escape tree she used as a teenager when she would sneak out to meet me. Benson dragged Rachel out and down the tree, by the looks of the blood trail."

"Chief, here's the stuff you wanted." Clyde was out of breath. Jackson had complained to Storm many times about Clyde's lazy work habits.

"Stay where you are. I don't want a bunch of feet destroying any possible evidence." Jackson strode to Clyde and took the offered items. "Who searched the upstairs?"

Clyde scratched his neck. "I did."

"Did you give all the rooms up here a thorough search?"

"Well, yeah. I looked in every room, every bathroom. Went up in the attic."

Jackson stared hard at his deputy. "Did you check in the closets? Be honest, now."

Clyde's face turned bright crimson. "Well, no, Chief. No, I didn't."

"What? You didn't think a maniac would hide in a closet?" Storm advanced on the deputy. He'd tear him apart.

Jackson extended a hand in a stop gesture. "I don't harangue your ranch hands, Storm. Don't think you're going to berate my men. Is that clear?" He turned his attentions to Clyde. "You were severely derelict in carrying out my orders. More than likely Benson was hiding in that closet and attacked Miss Dennison. Unless you act like a damned hero in the next twenty-four hours, you'll be suspended from duty pending further investigation."

Clyde's gaze shifted to Storm for a beat. "I'm sorry. It's just most women's closets are so jammed packed with clothes a cat couldn't hide in there, much less a man."

"Send up Mick Vasquez. Keep everyone else downstairs. You hear me?" Jackson turned and powered up the camera, taking pictures in rapid-fire succession.

Storm pivoted and stood at the open door of Rachel's closet. Two candy wrappers were crumpled on the floor. Extra blankets and some of her clothes were spread out on the closet floor, as if Benson had made himself a bed to lie in wait for his victim. He tried to imagine Rachel's fear when she opened the door and found him there. Had she screamed? Had she fought? Dear God, was the woman he loved still alive?

Chapter Twenty

Rachel's head throbbed. It hurt to swallow. What was wrong? Where was she? Why was it so dark? Pain. She was in a lot of pain. Awareness slowly crept back, entering her muddled mind, sweeping away the cobwebs of confusion with the bristly broom of reality. Kyle had beaten her again. Calm. She must stay calm.

She took a minute to do a mental inventory of her body. She ached all over. Her left eye was swollen shut. Her lips and jaw were sore. Swallowing was very painful, almost to the point of impossible. Her knee throbbed, and the small of her back ached where Kyle had kicked her. The cuts on her wrist stung.

A few minutes later, she started trembling—a sign of low blood sugar. So was the sweating and mental confusion. Or did that come from the chemical Kyle used on the rag he'd held over her nose and mouth? Tired. She was so tired. Drawing on all her remaining energy, she focused on her present situation.

With her non-swollen eye, she surveyed her surroundings. Even though the room was dark, she could tell she was on a wooden floor. As her remaining good eye adjusted to the dimness, she could discern large shapes and many boxes. This was some kind of storage area. With keen ears, she listened and relaxed. She was obviously alone. For the time being, Kyle was gone.

Now what? With her hands tied behind her back and her feet banded with plastic tie-strips, she could hardly escape or investigate her storage prison. The wide tape across her mouth prevented her from calling out for help. Her trembling increased. She needed food.

She had to fight off terror; she'd fall apart if she didn't. In such a situation, one had to focus on the positive. Tears burned her eyes. Long, slow breaths calmed her. She would *not* give into terror. She simply wouldn't. Hadn't she promised herself, after she escaped to the mountains of Colorado, she'd be strong? That she'd never give into the fear of a man again?

A prickle of pride surfaced. She'd fought back this time. She'd surprised Kyle. With any luck, she left some marks on him for a change. Let the bruises and scratches remind him Rachel Dennison was no longer a doormat. Granted, she was beaten and tied up in a storage area, but she hadn't gone quietly or easily. When things got worse, and they probably would, she'd dwell on this one empowering fact. She was no longer a docile doormat.

Gathering resolve, she focused on finding positives in this horrifying situation. If she dwelt on her fears, her pain, or on all the what-ifs, that futile process would only put her into a state of panic. Something she could ill afford. Since Kyle had her, Storm and little Sawyer were safe. She exhaled a shaky sigh. Although she was in peril, those she loved weren't.

She took comfort and dwelled on the fact her loved ones wouldn't be harmed, no matter what happened to her. For sure, her life was ebbing away. If Kyle didn't kill her using a knife, his fists, or a gun, with no food or insulin, her diabetes would probably take her. In her weakened state, she reconciled herself to that fact and prayed, thanking God those she loved were safe.

****

Storm and Jackson bent over the shoulders of a man with military bearing, sitting in a chair, reviewing security tapes on the monitors in a well-equipped van. Mick Vasquez had filled Storm in on the positions of all the surveillance cameras. One was on the entrance to both the stables and the barn, one at the front and back doors of the house and one at each of the windows on the ground floor.

Mick shook his head. "Nothing. I see nothing here on these tapes. I'm thinking the perp was already inside the house by the time we arrived."

Storm ran his hands through his hair in agitation and disbelief. "Are you kidding me?" This maniac had been inside his home all day, and no one *knew* about it? This was one sneaky bastard. Now this sneaky sombitch had his hands on the woman who was Storm's whole world. He swore under his breath.

Jackson shot him a sidelong glance. "Easy now. You won't do Rachel any good if you don't keep a cool head."

The side door to the van slid open. "Mick, here are the tapes from the barn and stable cameras. That's the last of them." A tall, lanky man in his early twenties passed the two tapes to his supervisor.

"Thanks, Harley. You and Smitty do a continual patrol of the buildings' perimeters." Mick slid the door shut, turned and shoved one of the tapes into the bottom of the monitor.

He was ten minutes into viewing the tape from the barn when a figure appeared onscreen, carrying something wrapped in a dark blanket. "There!" He pointed at the screen.

Storm thought he'd prepared himself for seeing the proof Kyle had abducted Rachel. But how did one get ready for seeing such a thing? He pressed the heel of his hand against his heart, hoping to ease the pain there. That maniac had come on his ranch and entered his home, his home where one expected family to be safe. Kyle had taken away the person he cherished most in this world. He knew he loved Rachel, yet he'd had no concept of the depth of his love until that very moment.

"You okay?" Jackson elbowed him, concern shadowing his features. "You're lookin' pale."

For the life of him, he couldn't talk. He nodded. How could he possibly be okay? This woman, his happiness, his future, his *everything* was in peril. He swallowed and closed his eyes.

Jackson clasped Storm's shoulder. "Keep the faith, man. We'll get her back."

Would they? Suddenly a memory washed over him, making him sick with fear—Rachel passing out when her sugar levels dropped. Would Kyle feed her? What about her insulin? He ran both hands through his long hair. "She needs insulin and food."

Jackson nodded. "I know. Time is critical. How long since she's eaten?"

"Not since breakfast. She had her last dose of insulin when we got to the mall. I'm still learning how this whole diabetes thing works."

Mick commented, never taking his eyes off the monitor. "My kid sister's got it. Takes a lot of monitoring. I know that much. When she's sick or stressed, her sugar levels go berserk. If your woman's losing blood in addition to the stress of being abducted, she could have a real problem. Could be fatal."

"Fatal?" Storm's heart felt as if it were being ripped apart by two hungry, snarling coyotes. *Fatal.*

"Easy, fella. We're doing everything we can." Jackson glanced at his watch. "So Rachel last ate thirteen hours ago?"

Storm nodded, still trying to come to grips with the severity of this situation. He could very well lose Rachel. Someone knocked on the van door behind him. He turned and opened it. "Momma, shouldn't you be resting?"

"Who can rest with our Rachel missing? Here." Noella held out a plate of food and two thermoses of coffee. "Meatloaf sandwiches. You and Jackson haven't had supper. You must keep up your strength to find her." She glared at him for a beat. "Don't bring me that plate back until it's empty. Noella wants you to eat, son. You mind me now. *Sí?*"

Storm almost smiled. The woman who stood before him was one of the great constants in his life. He could depend on her for so much. "You're the best. Thanks."

Tears pooled in her eyes. "You find my little one. *Sí?*"

"I will."

She patted her apron pocket. "If I see that sidewinder first, I shoot him dead."

Storm rolled his eyes heavenward. Noella was packing.

Jackson turned and took one of the thermos bottles from Storm. He glared at Noella. "Do you have a gun in your apron pocket? I want you to put it away. My men and the security team we hired will take care of this."

Noella reared back and squared her shoulders in that stance both Jackson and Storm had learned to fear growing up. "Your men? Those security people?" She spat onto the gravel driveway. "Worthless, all of them! They couldn't keep that awful man out of our home. Couldn't keep my little one safe. Idiots, every one. I will *not* put my gun away. Someone with some common sense has to protect this family." She turned on her heel and marched toward the house, ranting at the top of her lungs in Spanish.

"God help Kyle Benson if she finds him before we do." Jackson reached for one of the sandwiches.

"He's on another tape, too. Twice." Mick pointed to the screen. "He's alone this time."

"Show me." Jackson sat again and poured his coffee.

Mick rewound that segment of the tape. "This is the tape from the stable. See, he's coming toward the house again. Note the time in the upper corner: eight sixteen. Now, he's going back the way he came: eight thirty. Both times his arms are empty."

Storm swallowed a bite of sandwich. "It's like he's toying with us."

"Put in that tape from the barn where he's carrying Rachel."

Mick inserted the previous tape and queued it up. "Here he is. The time on this is eight-o-four. So he had to get to wherever he put Rachel and then get to where the security camera at the stable could pick him up in twelve minutes."

"Rewind that part again." Jackson leaned in as if he were analyzing, measuring every movement. "I swear, he knows he's being watched. Look how he turns toward the camera here." He pointed to the monitor. "Bastard is smirking."

Storm swore. His fists clenched. Murderous rage, scalding hot, pumped through his veins. How did one outsmart such an opponent?

"Look at his face, all scratched to hell. Rachel put up a struggle, that's for sure. Play it again, Mick. Something doesn't set right with me." The police chief took a long gulp of coffee.

****

Rachel heard a sound and slowly opened her eye. The room spun; her sugars were definitely low. She blinked several times in hopes of clearing her vision, but it remained blurry. She was shivering. A man leaned over her, his shadowy form slowly coming into focus.

"Storm?" She was shocked at the rasp of her voice. She sounded as if she'd gargled with gravel.

The crack of an opened hand slapping her cheek intensified her headache. "You bitch! Can't you see? He's not coming for you."

Kyle. It was Kyle. So close to her. She was unable to muster enough emotion to be afraid. He crouched next to her and yanked the tape from her mouth. Stinging pain registered; however, she had a more pressing need. "Fo…food." Her teeth chattered. She was cold, so very cold.

Her captor smiled and waved a candy bar in front of her face. "I could share this with you, darling." He tore it open. "But we both know candy's not good for you. Wasn't I always sensitive to your diabetes? Didn't I take good care of you?" He grabbed her hair and yanked her face up to his. "Didn't I?" he hissed, his eyes cat-eye slits.

"Yes," she croaked. Her mouth was so dry. "Wa…water."

He bit off a chunk of candy bar and chewed, his head tilted as if he were thinking. "Now if I give you water, you'll only need to pee." He glanced around and smirked. "Sorry, there's no bathroom facilities here. Gee, bet this wood floor is a bitch to sleep on. I'll try to make you more comfortable. Good ol' Kyle, once more looking out for sweet, gullible Rachel's best interests."

The man was insane. She drifted into unconsciousness again. There was a feeling of being lifted and moved. Her eyelids were too heavy to open. She was tired and so very cold.

****

Jackson was on his fifth viewing of the tape segment in which Kyle carried Rachel away. "Storm, look at this."

"I can't. Not again." It was just too damned painful. He kept thinking that this image might be the last one he'd have of Rachel.

"Stop it right there, Mick." Jackson leaned closer. "Can you zero in on his biceps?"

"Biceps? Sure." Mick made a few clicks with the mouse to pan in on Kyle's arms.

"If he was holding a woman…" He turned to Storm. "How much does Rachel weigh, would you say?"

He shrugged. "About a hundred twenty, hundred thirty."

"Right. That's what I'd estimate, too. Now look at his biceps. Do they look strained to you? There's no evidence of flexing like there should be if he's carrying that much weight. No matter how strong a man is, a hundred pounds, or more, would strain the biceps."

This time Storm took a look. Jackson was right. Kyle's arm muscles weren't tensed. His biceps were flat. "So what are you thinking?"

"My guess is he's carrying an empty rolled-up blanket. Probably has something in it to look like a body, another blanket maybe."

Storm turned his gaze to Jackson. "Why? Why would he go through a pretense like that and risk getting caught?"

Jackson stood. "Because he wants us to think he's taken her from the house. I'm betting he has her hid somewhere inside. Come on."

Both men scrambled out of the van, running through the

darkness of the night for the ranch house.

****

"**D**rink this." The command came from far away as if through a tunnel, yet she could feel something at her lips. Her mouth opened obediently and, after many attempts, she sipped. Swallowing was extremely painful. She choked several times, yet she knew she must take in as much as she could. Orange juice. Orange juice would elevate her sugar levels. She greedily gulped all that was offered. Would it be enough?

She was so confused. Would Storm come for her? No, he was with Pilar. Time to give Sunny her acupuncture treatment. No, she'd done that already, hadn't she? Maybe… Was that Sunny calling her? "Co…coming, Sunny."

Kyle grunted. "Don't bet on it."

She drank more juice. Several minutes later, she felt her system regain a sense of normalcy. The trembling slowed a little. The mental fog lifted. Her non-swollen eye opened and she looked around.

She was lying in some type of hammock contraption. A rope was tied around her ankles. The other end of the rope was knotted around a wooden post, as was the blanket she was lying on. Her arms were extended above her head, also tied to a rope that was probably secured to another wooden post. "Where…where am I?"

"Had to get you off the floor so you couldn't thump on it and alert the people below you."

What did he mean, below her? She was in so much pain now.

Kyle yanked on the knot. "There, these knots'll hold you." He tore off a strip of tape and pressed it against her mouth. "You see, you're in your boyfriend's attic. Imagine his surprise when he finds you up here. Dead." He winked and gave a maniacal chuckle. "That's why I gave you the juice, sweetheart. So you can lie here and think about his finding you. About how he'll never be able to come up here again. Hell, maybe he won't even be able to live here any longer. Wouldn't that be a damn shame?"

He waved his fingers and made a ghost-like sound. "The haunted ranch house. Hey, he could give tours on Halloween. Make a few bucks."

Floorboards creaked. Kyle spun around, his back toward

Rachel. "Well, change of plans. If it isn't the new lover boy to the rescue." His hand reached behind him to the revolver stuck in the back of his camouflage pants. "Who do I shoot first?"

"Rachel? I'm here, mouse." Storm stepped up from the wooden stairway onto the floor of the attic. He was holding a gun. "Move away from her, Benson."

Both men held their revolvers, glaring at each other. *Dear God,* what would happen now?

"How will you help her if you're dead, lover boy?" Rachel watched in horror as Kyle fired two shots and Storm collapsed onto the floor. The reverberations of the loud gunfire echoed off the rafters, lending gruesome sound effects to the nightmarish scene in front of her. Blood flowed from Storm's body. He fired a shot, hitting Kyle's shoulder before he passed out. Three more shots were fired, and Kyle dropped like a sack of potatoes.

Rachel turned frantic eyes on the woman who rose from her hiding spot. Noella had evidently followed Storm up the steps and crouched low so Kyle wouldn't see her. "My son!" she cried, rushing to Storm's side and kneeling to see to his wounds. There was a cacophony of footsteps and voices as police, security personnel and Sunny rushed up the attic steps. Suddenly, Rachel's world turned black.

Chapter Twenty-One

Rachel regained consciousness in the ambulance. The siren was piercing the night. She had a sense of speed from the jostling emergency vehicle. Noella held her hand. "Don't talk. I'm here with you, little one." Concern and caring tinged her words.

"Storm." Between the dryness of her mouth and her sore throat, Rachel could barely croak his name. The man she loved had been shot. She had to know how he was doing.

"He went in the first ambulance. Sunny's with him." Noella crossed herself.

"Fir…first…am…" Talking was extremely difficult; she suspected damage to her trachea, which would account for her labored breathing even though she was on oxygen. She noted she was hooked up to an IV, probably saline solution since she was dehydrated.

"Don't speak. The EMT said you weren't to talk. Noella will tell you everything, *sí?* Storm went in the first ambulance. When Storm and Jackson came barreling into the house to look for you, Storm ordered Sunny to call for an ambulance. Said you still had to be in the house.

"Jackson went to the basement and Storm to the attic. Red followed Jackson for backup. I followed Storm."

The vision of Noella holding her revolver in both hands as she stood from her crouched position on the steps played out in Rachel's mind. That whole horrendous scene, mere seconds really, of Storm charging up the attic steps, gun in hand, only to be shot by Kyle was a dreadful nightmare—the fear, sounds of firing guns, the acrid smell of gunpowder, blood, and silent dread.

Noella kept talking, and Rachel suspected it was out of nervousness. Shooting a man wouldn't come easy for a gentle woman like her. "Many years ago, when the twins were very small, their father taught me how to shoot. Said I should know how to protect them against snakes and such." Noella shifted her shoulders, then nodded once to emphasize her words.

"That's what I did tonight. I protected Master Storm from a terrible sidewinder." She crossed herself again, and a ragged sob escaped. Noella was obviously rationalizing her actions, actions that normally she would have loathed.

Rachel lifted her hand and caressed the older woman's cheek.

Noella reached to cover Rachel's hand as it lay against her face in an affectionate gesture. "From now on, you call me Momma Noella like my other children. *Sí?* I didn't bear them, nor you, but in my heart, the three of you are mine."

What a generous heart this woman had. No wonder Storm and Sunny adored her. She nodded. "K…Kyle?"

"Shhhh, mustn't talk. Kyle's in the third ambulance." Noella crossed herself. "Father Thomas says praying for one's enemies is good, but difficult. He's right. It is hard. To hate is easier, is it not? But to love, even when the person is unlovable, is very difficult."

Rachel was glad Kyle was still alive. This kind woman wouldn't have the death of a man, no matter how cruel and evil, on her conscious. "St…Storm? How?"

"He was shot once in the stomach." Noella pressed a finger to her body to show the position of the wound. "Once in the shoulder. Here. He lost a lot of blood, my Storm."

Rachel digested that information. Storm had been shot at close range, about ten feet if she could judge distance correctly with one eye. Did either of the bullets go straight through? She was concerned about the stomach wound. Had the bullet lodged against the spine? Were any organs injured? As soon as she got to the hospital, she was going to find him. She had to see for herself the man she loved would recover. "How long…ago did—"

Noella placed a finger over Rachel's lips and chuckled. "Shush, little one. Are you his doctor now? Conserve your energy. Master Storm won't like it if you don't recover quickly. He'll need you to take care of him? *Sí?* Quiet now. Noella sing for you."

Rachel listened to the lullaby Noella sang and wondered if it was one of Storm's favorites as a child. She prayed for his recovery as she drifted off to sleep.

When the back doors of the ambulance swung open, Rachel awoke. Noella jumped out so medical aides could remove Rachel, rushing her gurney inside the emergency room. The next few hours were a flurry of activity. Bright lights, hurried questions, examinations, blood work, medications, stitches all became a blur as Rachel, heavily medicated, drifted off.

The room was dark when Rachel slowly opened her eyes. She recognized the nighttime hush of the medical world: rubber-soled shoes squeaking in the hallway, sporadic intercom pages and the lonely beeping of monitors. In this case, the monitors were hooked up to her.

A cool hand stroked hers, and a face came into her limited vision field. "Mom?" How did her mom know she'd been hurt? How could she have gotten from Las Vegas to Rosefire, Texas so fast? Wait, was she even in Rosefire?

"Shhh, Rachel. You mustn't try to talk. You're in a hospital. You've had some serious injuries. You're in the ICU." Twin tears ran down her mom's face. "Oh, jellybean, how did you ever get mixed up with that crazy man? He nearly killed you." Rachel responded to the anguish in her mom's voice. The two embraced and, for a brief moment, the patient comforted the visitor.

Her mom dabbed her eyes with a tissue. "When the chief of police called and told me what happened, I nearly died. I caught the next flight here. Rest, jellybean. I'll be here when you wake up again." Jellybean. No one called her that but her mom. Hearing the pet name was the best medicine; it meant normalcy and safety had returned. Her mom was here.

"Storm." With tubes in her nose and mouth, it hurt to talk, but she had to know.

"I talked to his sister an hour ago. He survived surgery and is stable. Close your eyes now. The best thing for you is rest."

The sun was shining the next time Rachel surfaced from her drug-induced sleep. Her mom was dozing in the chair next to her bed. A nurse, mid-forties by Rachel's estimation, entered her room. "How are we doing this morning?"

Her mom stirred and yawned. "You're awake." She stood and kissed Rachel's forehead. "While the nurse does her thing, I'm going to the cafeteria for some coffee and a Danish." Sonya Asher smiled at her daughter. "I love you, jellybean. I'll be back in a few minutes." Her mom blew her a kiss before stepping into the hallway.

"What hospital is this?" Surely someone had told her, but she couldn't remember.

The nurse pushed the wheeled stand holding a laptop over to Rachel's bed. "You're in Hill Country Memorial in Fredericksburg.

Can you tell me your name and date of birth, please?" After Rachel answered, the nurse—Caroline McBaine, Nursing Supervisor, her nametag read—tapped a few keys on the laptop. She inserted the thermometer into a plastic sleeve and placed it in Rachel's mouth. She entered data into the laptop.

Caroline leaned a hip against Rachel's bed and crossed her arms. "I understand you have a Masters in Nursing." Rachel nodded.

"So, I can be frank."

"Yes, please."

"You've been here for two days. We've kept you under heavy sedation so your body has a chance to heal. You've been through the wringer. I can tell you that. Best you not look at your face just yet, if you're the vain type. You've got four stitches in your lip. Several contusions causing severe bruising elsewhere on your face. A humdinger of a shiner on your right eye."

Caroline pulled a tiny tape recorder from her pocket and pressed a button. "Get ice pack for Rachel Dennison's eye." She shot Rachel a chagrinned look. "Short term memory loss—menopause."

Rachel smiled and winced at the pain that movement caused. She liked this woman.

The nurse snapped on latex gloves and unwrapped the bandage at Rachel's wrist. "You've had sixteen stitches here. Surgeon had to repair a nick to your artery." She continued talking as she examined the wound and changed the dressing. "There are severe contusions on your back where you were repeatedly kicked. We're awaiting tests results to see if you've had kidney damage. You've got a catheter.

"Our main concern is the damage to your larynx. Your airway has been compromised due to traumatic edema to your larynx and the supraglottic tissue. The whites of your eyes are bloodshot because the strangulation forced blood into the whites. In time, as you know, it'll go away. The bruises at your neck will take two weeks or so to heal. Your voice will be raspy for at least a month. Frankly, you're lucky to be alive. Now—"

Just then another medical professional breezed in, interrupting Caroline's medical report, and introduced himself as the respiratory specialist, He asked Rachel some questions and checked her records on the laptop. He asked Caroline to close the curtain so he could remove the breathing tube. As soon as his job was done, he was gone.

Caroline handed Rachel a cup of ice water. "The man is good, but his bedside manner is rather remote."

Rachel sipped and nodded. She knew the type. The cold water felt great on her throat.

"As medical professionals, we're learning to recognize the signs and severity of strangulation in cases of violent attacks. I don't need to tell you the danger signs to watch for in your breathing. Be cognizant of them for the next week until the swelling in your airway is gone." She patted Rachel's shoulder. "At least you weren't raped by that beast. So many victims of domestic violence are."

"No, thank God." If there was any silver lining in this whole nightmare, it was that Kyle hadn't touched her sexually. "My boyfriend, Storm Blackhawk. Do you know about his condition?"

Caroline raised the head of the bed. "Not much. Just that he's recovering. Last time we checked your sugars, they were better. Not great, but better. Dr. Ulmelda wants you kept on the monitors for another twenty-four hours. You can try eating this evening. I'll order your meal. Liquid diet, of course, since swallowing will be difficult for a few days. My best advice is to sleep."

Rachel nodded while she slowly sipped at the ice water. "Thanks."

Eating her supper was more difficult than Rachel had expected. Although the cool fruit juice went down easily enough, her throat couldn't handle the hot broth. She choked. Her mom, frantic, ran into the hallway yelling for a nurse. She was jostled and handled until the emergency passed.

Because her times of wakefulness were brief, she suspected the medications were strong. Frankly, she was getting tired of giving her name and date of birth every time a medical professional came into her room. For sure, she was tired of the mental haze from the medications. She was also *damned* tired of using a bedpan. Okay, so nurses made poor patients. So, sue her.

The following day, she was unhooked from the monitors and moved to a private room. Her catheter was removed and she was encouraged to walk around her room. Rachel felt like she'd escaped prison.

"You've already been out of bed twice, jellybean. Do you think you should overdo?"

"The more I move around, the quicker I'll heal. What day is it anyway? I've lost so much time."

Before her mom could answer, the door opened partway and Noella popped her head in. "May I come in, little one? Noella brought you a bouquet of roses and daisies from her garden."

Rachel made introductions, and the two women warily regarded each other. She suspected both knew the other was encroaching on her private turf. "Have you seen Storm?"

"Yes, he's healing. The surgery was hard on him. They had to repair his 'oh-leek' muscle— "

"Do you mean his oblique muscle?" Rachel ran her hand along her side to indicate the muscle's position.

Noella nodded. "Yes, I don't know this word, so I say it wrong. Oblique, they repaired his oblique muscle and removed his kidney. It was too damaged by the bullet."

"He lost a kidney? Oh no!" She turned and walked to the window. Because of her, Storm, that wonderfully strong man, was minus a kidney. He'd lead a normal life with monitoring. She'd see to it. "Is he in much pain?"

"They give him strong medicine. He sleeps and when he's awake, he asks for you. You're doing better, *sí?* You're looking better than you did in the ambulance."

"Yes, I'm feeling much improved. My voice sounds awful and will for a few weeks. Healing will take time." She crawled back into her bed. "I do tire quickly, though."

"Then I should leave. Oh, before I forget…" Noella opened her purse and pulled out a paper. "Little Sawyer drew this for you. He says it's you and him in the swimming pool."

Rachel held the crayon drawing with two stick figures standing in blue crayon streaks and smiled. "Tell him I love it. Kiss him for me."

"*Sí,* I will do this. Mrs. Asher, it was a pleasure meeting you. How long will you be staying in Texas?"

"I have a flight early tomorrow morning. I wish I were taking my daughter home with me." Rachel's mom reached out to rub her daughter's shoulder, a proprietary gesture.

Noella drew herself up and squared her shoulders. "Oh, but *our* Rachel belongs here with us now. With Storm." The two women glared at one another. Noella patted Rachel's hand. "Tomorrow when I come, little one, I bring you a robe and slippers. Do you need your makeup?"

"She shouldn't be using that stuff on her face until it heals," her mom snapped.

Noella leaned toward Rachel and whispered, "I bring it anyhow."

Five minutes after Noella left, her mom left, too, promising to return shortly.

The next time Rachel awoke, her lunch was being delivered. More juice and broth. A lovely vision of a crisp salad came to mind. Maybe in a couple of weeks she could eat one. For today, it was apple juice and beef bouillon. Yuck.

While she was eating, a hospital volunteer brought in a bouquet of red roses with a balloon that said, "I love you." They were from Storm.

Rachel's lunch tray had just been whisked away when her mom strode in carrying an arrangement of tiger lilies and pink carnations and several shopping bags. "What have you been up to, Mom? You've got that self-satisfied look on your face."

Her mom set the flowers down next to Storm's. "I bought you the prettiest bathrobe." She opened a bag and removed a silky pink robe. "Look at the floral bouquets embroidered on it. Aren't they darling? It's edged in delicate black lace." She reached in the bag again. "Here's the matching nightie you can wear once you're out of here. Oh, and here are little slipper scuffs in the same shade of pink."

Obviously, Mom felt threatened by Noella and wanted to beat her to the punch with the bathrobe delivery. She wouldn't hurt her mom's feelings for the world. Their loving relationship, although strained for years after Drew's death and her parents' divorce, was very important.

She held the robe to her. "It's beautiful. Thanks, Mom. What's in the other bag?"

Her mom chuckled. "Greedy girl. I got you some lotions and other toiletries since I know the brands you prefer. Oh, and a juicy romance novel and two magazines." She looked at Rachel, her expression a little sad. "I just wanted to make sure you had everything you need before I leave. My boss is demanding I come back, or I'd stay longer."

Rachel held out her hand and her mom took it in hers. "Having you here for a few days was the best medicine. I loved our talks."

"Yes. I'm glad I came. Tell me, did you choke when you ate your lunch?"

"I had five or six spoonfuls of bouillon. Was afraid to risk anymore. Imagine how long it'll be before I can have a steak."

"I hope that fiend, Kyle Benson, rots in jail for what he did to you." Her mom was rubbing some of the body lotion she'd bought Rachel onto her hands. She held her hands to her nose and inhaled. "Such a delicate floral fragrance. No wonder you like it."

An idea was forming in Rachel's mind. After her mom left tonight, she'd go to Storm. His room number had been noted on the card with the roses. She'd wear her pretty new nightie and robe. "Mom, would you mind helping me take a bath? A real bath with the stuff you bought me. There's a shower in my bathroom."

"Do you think it would be allowed?" Her mom glanced over her shoulder as if to make sure no nurses would hear and object.

"Why not? I've got my mom here to help me. You got me shampoo, right?" She rummaged through the bag, pulling it out. "My hair hasn't been washed in days." She wanted to look her best for Storm. Well, as good as she could with a black-and-blue face and stitches at her mouth.

Someone rapped on the doorframe of her hospital room. Both women's heads whipped around as if they'd been caught doing something bad. Jackson smiled and strolled in, holding out his hand. "You must be Rachel's mother, Sonya Asher. I'm Jackson Cole, the man who called you a few days ago. I must say, I don't know who's prettier—mother or daughter."

Oh, he could pour on the charm, Jackson could. Rachel watched her mom respond with feminine delight at his compliment. "Why, yes, I'm her mother. Thank you so much for contacting me right away."

Jackson turned to Rachel. "How you doin' today? Feel up to some questions? Afraid I'm here in a professional capacity."

"Should I leave?" Her mom reached for her purse.

"Stay, Mom. I want every minute I can with you."

Her mom smiled, obviously delighted. "Okay, I'll sit on this little chair here in the corner, quiet as a church mouse. You go right ahead, Mr. Cole."

"Jackson, please, ma'am. Rachel and I are friends. You see, I'm dating Sunny, Storm's twin sister. The three of us, Sunny, Storm and me, have been best friends since we were six."

"I see." Her mom sat and pulled a paperback from her purse. "I'll just read while you two talk. You won't even know I'm here." She held a hushing finger to her lips. "Quiet as a church mouse, just like I said."

Jackson folded his long frame into the bedside chair and sighed. "What a week. Rachel, honey, I need to ask you some questions for your official statement." He tugged a notebook and pen from his chest pocket. "Tell me what happened after you left Storm and went upstairs."

She closed her eyes for a minute, drawing on inner strength to relive the horrific episode. "I started drawing water for a bath, got clean underwear out of my drawer, and when I opened the closet door to get some clothes, Kyle was standing there." She closed her eyes and shuddered. Seeing him was the last thing she'd ever expected. The fear that shot through her, back at the ranch, had nearly buckled her knees. "He clamped his hand over my mouth to cover my scream."

"So you did scream?" He glanced at her.

"Yes, for all the good it did me. I had the stereo up so loud the music drowned me out."

Her mom was tsking in the corner, her head buried in her book. Jackson glanced at her mom, then at Rachel, and winked. "Go on."

"I was playing a CD Storm had made for me. The song playing was Bonnie Tyler's 'Holding out for a Hero.' "

Jackson nodded. "Great drums in that song. No wonder we couldn't hear anything."

"She always did play her music too loud," the church mouse in the corner remarked.

Rachel rolled her eyes. "I fought, but he overpowered me and threw me on the bed."

"Were you sexually assaulted?" Jackson looked at her, and his voice gentled. "Sorry, my friend, I have to ask."

She shook her head. "No, thank God. He…he sensed … I'd just been with Storm. Storm and I had just made up after our argument…and…ah…"

The church mouse in the corner gasped.

"That's okay, honey. Tell me about Kyle and his behavior."

She shot her mom a look and breathed a sigh of relief. Sharing that Kyle smelled Storm's sex on her was too embarrassing. "Well, he got angry and called me names. He hit me several times. He strangled me." She gestured to her face and neck. Jackson's jaw visibly clenched. "I was struggling, and that's when he saw my new charm bracelet. He pulled a Bowie knife from a scabbard on his belt and cut the bracelet off me, but first he made sure he cut me." She ran fingers over her bandaged wrist.

"Contemptible bastard." Evidently the church mouse had no compunction about cursing.

Jackson hung his head, hiding a smile. "I heard you required sixteen stitches. I'm sorry about that, my friend. There was blood on the bedspread and floor. Storm nearly lost his mind when he saw it. I can't recall ever seeing him like that." He shook his head once. "There was also blood on the windowsill. Go on."

The church mouse in the corner sniffed and blew her nose.

"He dragged me off the bed and kicked me in the kidney area several times. Then he held a cloth to my face. I smelled ether before I passed out."

"That must have been when he carried you up to the attic. Best as I can tell, he smeared your blood on the windowsill to throw us off the track, so we'd think he carried you out that way."

"I can't tell you if he did or not. When I woke up, I was on the attic floor. Only at the time, I thought it was some kind of storage facility. It never occurred to me I was still in the house."

"Did he say what he was going to do with you? Where he was going to take you next?"

"Nowhere."

Jackson gaze shot to hers. "Excuse me?"

"He made a hammock out of old blankets or something and tied me to it so I couldn't make any noise on the floor to alert people below. My sugar levels had dropped dangerously low. I was suffering mental confusion and having problems staying conscious. He gave me enough orange juice to bring them up long enough to tell me what was going to happen."

"Which was?" His pen stilled.

"He was going to leave me there to die."

"Heartless piece of monkey shit," the church mouse chirped.

Jackson was obviously getting a charge out of her mom. He pinched the bridge of his nose with his thumb and forefinger while he grinned. "Now I know where you get that spirit."

"You're *damned* right."

"Mom!"

"What? I'm being quiet as a church mouse over here." Her mom shot her an indignant scowl. "See how I'm reading?"

Rachel chose to ignore that erroneous remark. "Kyle laughed as he bragged about Storm finding me in the attic—dead. Then Storm showed up."

"Who fired their gun first?"

"Kyle fired twice at Storm. Storm collapsed in a heap on the floor. He fired once at Kyle before passing out." She expelled a shaky sob and swiped at a tear. "Then Noella fired three times at Kyle. She saved my life. Storm's, too. Will she be in trouble for shooting him?"

Jackson slapped his notebook shut and slipped it in his pocket. "Not if I have anything to do with it." He stood and leaned down to kiss her forehead. "Get some rest. I have a feeling one day we'll be family. I'm asking Sunny to marry me soon." He leaned in and whispered, "Already bought her a diamond. That's between us, now."

Rachel grinned. "I'm thrilled for you two. I'm so encouraged by how much stronger she is. She'll beat this cancer."

"Cancer or no cancer, I want her for my wife. Once Storm gets off his lazy duff and proposes, just think, I'll be your big brother." He grinned. "Kinda neat, isn't it? The six of us—family." He winked. "Can't forget Sawyer and Noella."

"Wish I could forget Noella," the church mouse interjected.

At Jackson's raised eyebrows, Rachel said, "Don't ask. It's a mother thing."

Chapter Twenty-Two

Rachel had to admit she hadn't been prepared for seeing herself in the mirror. Although most of the swelling had gone down in her eye, it was vividly purple. Most of her face was bruised. The whites of her eyes were bright red. She looked like a wild-eyed, raging purple demon. Thank goodness little Sawyer couldn't see her. He'd have nightmares for a month.

After her shower, her mom combed her hair while she rubbed body lotion on her arms. "I like this shorter hairstyle. You know, I'd forgotten how curly your hair is. Your hair hasn't been this length since you were in the eighth grade."

"I have to admit, it takes some getting used to. My hair was long for so long, since high school. Storm says he likes it."

"Tell me about Storm, this man who's obviously captured your heart. You *are* on the pill, aren't you?"

"My birth control pills!" Her hand flew to her mouth. "Oh no…"

Her mom's hand stopped combing. "What?"

"I haven't had a birth control pill for three days, no wait, five since I've been here for three." Her voice was so raspy. "I also missed one the week before."

Her mom came to stand in front of her. "Oh, honey!" She didn't look pleased.

"Don't lecture me, Mom. Once I found out Kyle knew where I was and he was coming for me, I forgot the pills. I went into panic mode." She tried to mentally calculate where she was in her cycle. The timing couldn't be worse.

"If you've missed that many pills, shouldn't your period have started? I mean, even if it's early, with no pills, shouldn't it have started?"

She shrugged. "Under normal circumstances, yes, but with all the terror and pain and medications, I'm probably all screwed up schedule-wise."

Her mom reached out and took her chin in her cool hand. "Jellybean, 'all screwed up' is a poor choice of words right now."

"Mom!" She felt a blush rising on her neck and cheeks. She couldn't be pregnant. She couldn't be. Storm would probably be thrilled, but an unplanned pregnancy was not the way she wanted to get married.

Her mom started combing her hair again. "Perhaps when you go see him tonight, you should talk to him about this. You *are* going to see him, aren't you? I mean, that's why the shower and lotion and new nightie, right?" Rachel shot her a surprised look over her shoulder. "What? You didn't think your old mom could read between the lines?"

The quiet night ritual of the hospital had begun. Visitors left. Saying good-bye to her mom was bittersweet. She promised to travel to Las Vegas once she was up to it. Nighttime meds were given. Lights dimmed. She roamed her room, waiting for the right time to sneak up to the next floor.

Had Storm been serious about wanting to marry her? Did she want to be his wife? Her head nodded slightly. Oh yeah, she wanted that. She wanted to be the only woman in Storm's life, to be his bride, his best friend, his lover, his partner. She wanted to carry his children and build a life with him on the ranch, a place where grandchildren would come for spoiling and lessons on life. A sigh escaped; she wanted to fall asleep in his arms every night.

The question remained. Did Storm truly want her? On one hand, he acted like it; on the other hand, he was still very protective of Pilar's feelings. A very small part of her respected him for caring about an ex-fiancée's emotions; most men wouldn't. Still, a large part of her wanted to come before Pilar in all things, in all ways. What woman wanted to be number two on a man's priority list?

He'd given her that beautiful charm bracelet and asked her to wear it until he could place a wedding band on her finger. She hoped the bracelet was still in her bedroom. She'd have a jeweler repair the delicate chain and wear it forever.

The quiet on the floor had deepened. Nurses would be doing paperwork. Slowly she opened her door and peered out into the dim, deserted hallway, taking note of the stairway exit light. In seconds, she'd scampered down the hall and onto the stairway.

When Rachel slowly opened the door to Storm's room, blinking lights on monitors illuminated its dimness with an eerie glow. Heartbeat rhythms, blood pressure, pulse rates, oxygen levels and body temperature were all flashing and beeping in the quiet of his room. With a trained eye, she scanned all the numbers and registered their meaning before padding over to Storm in her new slippers.

She took his hand and felt for his pulse, even though she could see it on the monitor. He was sleeping, his pulse steady and strong just like the man it belonged to. His left arm was in a sling, no doubt to keep it immobilized after the surgery to his shoulder. The nurse in her had to look at his wounds. She gently pulled back the sheet and examined the bandages, wishing she could remove them without waking him, yet knowing that was impossible. Bending her head, she kissed the bandage on his shoulder and then the one on the side of his abdomen.

"I have a boo-boo lower, too. *Much* lower, mouse," the patient whispered.

She smiled against his bandage. If he were stronger, she'd certainly oblige. She straightened and gazed into dark eyes. "Bet you say that to all the nurses, cowboy."

"How are you?" His gaze was locked on hers, his black hair in stark contrast to his paleness and the white sheets. "Dear God, your face!" He reached out to touch her. "I hope the bastard rots in hell for hurting you."

"I'll be fine. Lots of bruises and stitches, but nothing serious."

"Your voice."

"Kind of raspy, isn't it? One of the side effects of strangulation. Raspy voice, bloodshot eyes and broken capillaries under the eyes. Healing takes time. Kyle hurt you worse." It would be a couple of months before Storm completely recovered. She felt a strong sense of guilt for his injuries. Because of her, danger had come to his home and into his life. "How's your pain level?" She started to cover him again with the sheet.

"No." Her hand stilled at his request. "Lie down with me. Get in, mouse. Rest with me for a while." He pushed the button on his morphine drip.

"I'm sure that's against hospital policy." She almost laughed at the primness in her voice.

"The hell with hospital policy. Get in." His eyes were starting to get heavy, and his voice thickened. The meds were taking him under again. "Please."

She knew better, really she did, but she needed to be near him, too. She untied her robe as she walked around to the other side of the bed, the side opposite his injuries. Slipping her robe off, she lowered the railing, lifted the sheet and crawled in. She positioned herself on her side and raised the railing again behind her so she wouldn't fall out if she fell asleep. Then she snuggled in beside him.

He was warm. Her eyes slid to the monitor, which indicated his body temperature was ninety-nine point nine. Low grade fever. Normal after the surgery he'd had.

"Kiss me, love."

She kissed his forehead, his eyes, his cheeks and listened to his breathing deepen. He was asleep. She laid her head on his good shoulder, exhaled a contented sigh and drifted off.

A cool hand jostling her shoulder stirred Rachel from sleep. "Wake up. You can't sleep here."

"Hunh?" Rachel rubbed her eyes, looking into a pair of cold hazel eyes. "Oh, dear, I must have fallen asleep." Embarrassed at being found in another patient's bed, she started to sit up.

"Let her stay." Rachel glanced at Storm. His eyes were open, lucid and determined. "I feel better with her here."

"This is against hospital policy." The nurse—Desiree Hackett, her nametag read—was obviously not pleased.

"She stays." Storm extended his good arm, drawing Rachel next to his body again. "Now, do what you have to do, nurse, and get out." He pushed his drip button, obviously in pain.

"I simply must insist. Are you Rachel Dennison? The missing patient in two twenty-seven? Security's looking for you. I'll have to notify them of where you are." The attractive brunette pulled a cell from the pocket of her purple scrubs. "This is Desiree Hackett in room three-twelve. Rachel Dennison, your missing patient, is here. Please send security." She snapped the phone shut and slipped it back in her pocket. She raised an imperial brow over those cold hazel eyes. "As soon as you're gone, I'll tend to my patient."

"She stays." Storm's hold tightened.

Rachel rose onto her elbow and peered into his determined eyes. "We'd both rest better in separate beds. I don't want to cause trouble."

"We were resting quite well before Nurse Godzilla stormed in. Lie down, love, and sleep."

Caroline McBaine, Rachel's nurse, pushed an empty wheelchair into Storm's room. "Here you are. When I came on duty ten minutes ago, the whole floor was in a tizzy."

"I'm sorry for all the trouble."

She tried to get up, but Storm's hold held her to his side. "She stays."

Nurse Desiree put her hands on her hips. "This is a hospital, not an open pajama party where folks can sleep together willy-nilly. I need to change your bandages and your IV bag."

"Work around her. She's small…she's staying."

Rachel noted on the monitor his heart rate and blood pressure had increased dramatically. Perhaps her staying and all the drama that would create might harm him and impede his recovery in some way. "Storm, I have to go. I'll be back later. I promise. Let's not make trouble." She kissed him, crawled out of the bed, and slipped on her robe and slippers.

She could sense his eyes on her when her nurse, Caroline, wheeled her out. She felt bereft of his presence and warmth. He'd been right. They'd both slept better snuggled in the same bed.

Caroline pushed Rachel's wheelchair onto the waiting elevator. The doors whispered shut, and she pressed a button. "Your man is quite commanding. Those eyes of his are something else. He devours you with them. Lucky you. My Harold quit looking at me like that years ago."

"Does he really look at me like that?"

"Oh, honey, that man's got it bad for you." The elevator doors opened, and Caroline pushed her down the hall. "If he's as virile as he looks, you'll be in our maternity ward next year." The nurse curved the wheelchair into Rachel's room. Sooner than that if she didn't have her period in the next few days. Rachel crawled into bed, and Caroline proceeded to take her patient's vitals. "Looks like your little late-night rendezvous didn't hurt you. Need anything?" She fussed with Rachel's covers and lifted the security railing. "Now, the next time I pop my head in here, you'd better be in this bed. Hear?"

Rachel smiled. "Yes. Sorry to be a bother."

Caroline waved her hand. "Oh, honey, we've come across worse things than two people sleeping in the same bed." She leaned in and wiggled her eyebrows. "You *were* sleeping, weren't you?"

Rachel could feel the heat of a blush dance across her face. "Of course."

Jackson strolled into Rachel's room shortly before noon, carrying a bag of clothes. "At last I get to break someone out of a joint instead of putting them in. Like I said on the phone, I figured the doc would want to keep you in here for another day after all you've been through."

"Doctor says I'm fine. I'm healing. No signs of infection and my sugars are down. Are those the clothes you bought me?"

He laid the bag on the bed. "Yep. Don't know if you'll like what I gotcha, but you're lookin' at a man who'd sooner take a beating than set foot in a store. Sunny talked me through the process over the phone."

Rachel laughed. "I'm sure they'll be fine. Thanks for doing me the favors. Buying me clothes and taking me home…er…to the ranch, I mean." She cast shy eyes on him. She'd had to give him her sizes and everything.

Jackson scratched the side of his face. "Buying a bra turned into more of an embarrassment than I care to admit. Was my first time. Never knew it was wires that held those things up." A blush crept up his neck. "Sunny liked to die laughing on her end of the phone." He gathered her flowers in his arms. "I'll take these down to the car while you get dressed."

Poor Jackson. Chief of police goes on a lingerie-buying spree. She opened the bag to see what he'd bought. She laughed when she pulled the items out: a plain white underwire bra and bikinis. No lace. No frills. A female version of "tightie whities." There was also a white and pink flowered blouse and a pair of jeans. Pink flip-flops were at the bottom of the bag.

She'd have to thank Sunny for talking him through his buying spree. Once she got back to the ranch, she'd write Jackson a check to cover what he'd spent. More than ready to get out of there, she hoped to make a detour by Storm's room on her way out.

****

Storm closed his eyes and sighed. He was dog tired—too many doctors poking and prodding. He had the energy of roadkill right now. He pressed the button twice on the morphine drip. Within minutes, he was asleep.

She was kissing him. Warm, sweet kisses gently placed on his forehead, his cheeks, his mouth. Instinctively his arm banded around her, drawing her close. She smelled of Armani Code. Pilar. His eyes shot open.

"Darling, I came as soon as Desiree called."

"Desiree?" Nurse Godzilla? She knew Pilar?

"I brought you red and yellow roses." She waved her hand toward a vase sitting on a stand next to his bed.

He tried sitting up and winced. "Flowers are very nice. Much obliged. How'd you know I was here?" He was trying not to show his irritation.

She sat and crossed her legs. "Your nurse, Desiree, is a sorority sister of mine. We've known each other since college. She called me this morning when she got off work. I was shocked to say the least. To be shot in your own attic; why, it just doesn't bear thinking about."

He shrugged his good shoulder. "One of those things."

"I've had my mind on you for days, on all the things you said to me, the gentleness you showed me at the mall." She opened her purse, removed a linen handkerchief and blotted her eyes. "I'd like another chance. I'll do whatever it takes to get you back." Her chin quivered.

"Now, we talked about this at the mall." This was definitely the last conversation he wanted to have right now, when he was so tired. A wave of pain washed over him and he winced, breathing through his teeth. He pressed the button on his morphine drip again.

Pilar stood and leaned over him; twin tears spilled onto her cheeks. "Please. I can't live without you." She kissed his neck. "You know I've always been good to you."

He did know that, which played on his guilt. She'd treated him well except for the cheating and being born Pilar Fontaine instead of Rachel Dennison.

She sat on the edge of his bed and lay next to him. "Please hug me. Hold me." She sniffed back a sob and laid her head on his shoulder. "What will my life be like without you? Who is this Rachel person? Don't you care for me at all?"

His arm slid around her waist. The morphine was making him

sleepy. If only he could get her to leave so he could slip into oblivion. A stab of pain slammed into his side, and he pressed the button again for another dose. "Don't worry about Rachel. Of course I care for you. You'll be fine. We'll go on with our lives, me and..." Darkness swallowed him.

****

Rachel held her hand up. "Stop. Please stop!"

The elderly volunteer brought the wheelchair to a halt. "What's wrong?"

Wrong? *Everything*. Everything was wrong. "I've changed my mind. I'm not going in that room. He has company." She was going to be sick. Her heart had shattered into a million pieces on her lap. Pilar was in his bed, in his arms, just as she had been during the night. Now Storm was telling Pilar not to worry about Rachel, that *they'd* be fine. She crossed her arms over her chest. When would she learn not to trust what he said? "Let's go, please."

The volunteer turned the wheelchair around. "Just as well. My job is to take you directly to the entrance of the hospital to meet your ride. I didn't feel right about making this little side trip." The white-haired woman pushed the elevator button, obviously eager to be rid of her troublesome charge.

Visitors stepped onto the elevator with them. "Kate, did I see you talking to Pilar Fontaine?"

"Yes, she was on her way to visit her fiancé. He was shot, you know. Poor dear was frantic."

"I heard about it on the news. Some nut had abducted his sister's nurse. There are a lot of wackos out there, you ask me. When's their wedding?"

"Pilar said as badly as he was hurt, they might have to postpone for several months. Poor man lost a kidney."

Thankfully the elevator reached the lobby before Rachel dissolved into tears or a screaming fit. She wasn't sure which. What she really desired was fresh air and distance away from Rosefire, Texas.

Jackson was waiting at the curb with the passenger door of his cruiser open.

"Here's your young lady." The volunteer leaned over to put the locks on the wheels. Rachel stood, eager to be on her way.

“Ready to head to the Triple-S?” He helped her in the car and hurried around to his side. “You up to stopping by the office first to sign your statement? Our secretary should have it typed up, ready for your signature.”

“Sure. I’m feeling great. Glad to get that big bandage off.” She held out her arm to show off her smaller bandage. “Then I need to make a stop at a car rental agency. I need a car for a few days until I buy one to replace my little Beetle.” She had to convince him she was good enough to drive. She had to stay perky and chipper, no matter how much she wanted to fall apart.

He glanced in the rearview mirror before easing out onto the street. “What kind of car are you thinking of buying? Another convertible?”

“Don’t know. I’ll have to think about it.” She leaned her head back and closed her eyes, willing herself not to cry. Twice Storm had turned to Pilar after swearing his love for her. She stared out the side window, her vision blurred by tears. In a couple hours, she’d be on her way out of Texas and away from Storm Blackhawk.

Chapter Twenty-Three

Three days later, sweat beaded on Storm's brow. He leaned on the physical therapist while slowly walking back and forth across the therapy room. He had to make two trips, according to her no nonsense orders. The physical therapy session had been easy, yet grueling. In other words, his little nephew could have breezed through it, while he groaned and grunted with every movement.

Would his shaky legs hold him? Damn the pain. He could have sworn the room grew bigger the longer he shuffled, and shuffling was what he was doing. There was no way one could classify this as walking. Finally, having made the required number of trips, he collapsed into the wheelchair. "That was harder than I expected." What a humiliating experience.

When the therapist wheeled him back into his room, he could have sworn his bed blinked a neon "welcome." The therapist helped him lift his legs onto the mattress and covered him. "I'll get you some fresh ice water." She refilled his container and then hurried out, presumably to her next patient.

Sunny knocked on his open door. "Hi there, how are you today?" She came in carrying a small bag. "Noella sent a couple banana nut muffins." She bent to kiss him. "You're sweating." She pressed a hand against his forehead, probably checking to see if he had a fever.

"I've just had a torture session, otherwise known as physical therapy." He narrowed his eyes. "You want to tell me why I haven't had any visitors for three days except Pastor Quinley?" She shrugged a reply. "Why does Rachel only come see me in the middle of the night? Why won't the hospital allow her to come down here during the day?"

"Rachel comes here at night?" Sunny's eyebrows rose.

"Yes, but never during the day. It's the *damndest* thing. Why is it when I call you or Noella or Jackson, all I get are runarounds? You won't even let me talk to Sawyer." He was whining. He knew it and hated it, but he had a strong feeling something was going on.

"Was Rachel here last night? What did she say?"

"Same thing she says every night. She crawls in bed next to me, whispers in my ear that she loves me, and then we both fall asleep."

What was wrong with Sunny? She acted like she didn't believe him.

She slowly set the bag of muffins on a table. "Is she here when you wake up?" Her eyes were locked on his.

"No, and I can't figure out why. How come you're looking at me as if I've spent too many hours out in the hot sun?"

She sighed and fiddled with the handles of her purse. "I think you've been dreaming her visits, brother."

"What do you mean?"

"Has Pilar been here to see you?" She shot him a look.

"Yeah, the other day." He touched two fingers to his forehead as if to pull out the answer. "Two…three days ago."

"Did she get in the bed with you?" She rested a cool hand on his arm.

"Well, yes…" His eyes probed hers, and then he closed them as if to block out the truth. "Tell me Rachel didn't see Pilar in my bed." How else would Sunny know?

Sunny crossed her arms. "Storm, what are you doing playing one woman against the other as if you couldn't give a tinker's damn about either one? I can't believe you'd do this."

She really sounded angry with him, and that stung. "What did Rachel say?" *Not again. Don't tell me she caught me with Pilar again.* Couldn't he catch a break? Wasn't it bad enough he'd been shot and lost a kidney? That he was laid up here in this hospital instead of at home taking care of the ranch? "Tell me everything."

Sunny sat and sighed. "When she left the hospital—"

"She's been discharged? Why am I just now hearing this? Wait…she's been here every night…" Or was Sunny right? Truth be told, his recollection of the first few days after his surgery was muddled—too much pain medication. He'd been sure Rachel was coming to him every night. Had he been dreaming that? Had the morphine driven him to hallucinations? He glanced at Sunny. His sister wouldn't lie to him; they'd always been honest with each other. "When did she leave the hospital?"

"The day Pilar was here. Rachel asked the volunteer, who was taking her out in a wheelchair, to come by your room so she could see you for a few minutes before she left."

Dread grabbed his stomach, twisting and pulling. "She saw Pilar in bed with me?"

Sunny nodded. "She heard you tell Pilar 'that of course you cared for her, that she should forget about Rachel, that you'd both be fine.'"

Storm ran a hand through his hair. "Dammit!" His gaze roamed the room before landing on Sunny. Understanding ebbed in and chilled his heart. "She's gone, isn't she? Rachel's left the Triple-S."

"Can you blame her? She rented a car, came to the ranch and packed her stuff. She was distraught and angry, going from ranting to crying and back to ranting. She feels you've been lying to her all along. Her heart is broken." Sunny glanced away and sighed. "No, worse—shattered."

"Oh, mouse." He groaned. When would she start trusting him? For that matter, when would women he loved stop leaving him? That never-ending feeling of abandonment walked into his heart and set up camp. He exhaled a long, slow breath. "Where is she now?"

Sunny shrugged. "I don't know. I don't think even she knew where she was going. She was in flight mode, not think mode, trying to get away before she completely fell apart. When she called Jackson, she told him she'd keep in touch."

"Jackson? Why?" Why would she call Jackson and not him? He fought to suppress an insane jealousy. Never in his life had he been jealous of his best friend; why now? Because he felt insecure with Rachel's leaving. He felt left out because she'd talked to Jackson.

"Rachel asked Jackson some questions about Kyle. Was there a chance he could go free? Was she really and truly safe? Would she need to return for Kyle's trial? Things like that. Guess she felt she owed the chief of police the courtesy of keeping him informed as to her whereabouts. She gave him her cell phone number so he could contact her about Kyle."

"But she didn't tell him where she was going?"

Sunny shook her head. "No." She leaned toward him. "How could you do this to her? Help me understand."

"You condemn me, too, sister?" Women—they always stuck together.

"What am I to think?"

His eyes narrowed. "You don't trust me any more than Rachel, do you? *Why* is it so hard for a woman to trust a man?"

Sunny patted his arm in what he thought was a conciliatory

gesture. "Experience. Once a woman has been hurt, she guards her heart. She looks for fallacies in a man's character and inconsistencies in anything he says. Just like when a small boy is abandoned, he expects others to abandon him, too." She cocked her head to the side and regarded him, waiting, he supposed, for her words to sink in.

He contemplated her words. First, his mother. Now, Rachel. He exhaled a deep sigh of pain and…emptiness. The woman he loved was gone. Suddenly, the colorful light floated out of his life. He saw things in muted shades of grays.

"Two nights after my surgery, Rachel came to me." He shot a glance at his sister. "For real. I didn't dream this. She crawled in bed with me and slept. A nurse found her in the morning. Turned out the nurse was a sorority sister of Pilar's. She couldn't wait to call Pilar to fill her in."

Sunny nodded, finishing Storm's retelling of the facts. "And Pilar came charging over with her usual dose of drama."

"Yeah. I was in a lot of pain and using the morphine drip pretty heavily. I was more than half out of it and thought she was Rachel at first, until I inhaled the expensive perfume I'd bought Pilar for her birthday. Pilar was crying. I was pressing the button on my morphine drip." He ran a hand through his hair. "Lord only knows what all I said."

"Which woman do you really want?"

He exhaled a harsh bark of laughter. "You really need to ask? Rachel, hands down."

"Then tell Pilar, in no uncertain terms, she's to stay away. Tell her you love Rachel."

"I've done that already to a degree. I didn't mention Rachel, though, because I've hurt Pilar so much already."

"So Pilar's feelings take precedence over Rachel's." She gave him a look of disgust.

"Hell, no! You're as bad as Rachel. She said the same thing after seeing me with Pilar at the mall." His twin stared at him as if he were an idiot. He shifted in the bed and looked away. Was it wrong to keep from hurting another person's feelings? He'd dated the woman for two years; didn't he owe her a measure of kindness? He thought of his gut reaction when he'd heard Rachel gave Jackson her phone number, a purely jealous reaction. Maybe, just maybe, he was making the woman he loved feel the same way by protecting Pilar.

"Rachel's feelings come before Pilar's."

Sunny pulled her cell from her purse and handed it to him. "Then call Pilar and tell her. Make the first step in getting Rachel back, because I assure you, no woman wants to play second fiddle to another. It's what drove Jackson and me apart years ago." He hesitated, and she shook the phone at him. "Sometimes you have to be cruel to be kind."

He took the phone and dialed his ex-fiancée's number. "Pilar, it's Storm."

"Storm, darling, I was just getting ready to come see you." The woman knew how to put the purr in her voice, he'd give her that. How had he ever endured such phoniness?

"Don't come."

"Pardon?"

"I hate hurting you, but I don't know how else to get through to you." He took a deep breath. "I'm in love with Rachel Dennison. I fell in love with her the moment I laid eyes on her. I plan on marrying her if she'll have me. Please don't contact me again. I want you to have a good life, but without me."

"You bastard!" she screamed.

"Good-bye. Don't contact me again. I love someone else." He disconnected the call. "Was I clear enough?"

"For the average woman, yeah. But Pilar can be persistent. You may have to repeat it a few times, no matter how much she whines and cries and yells." Sunny took the cell phone from him and slipped it in her purse.

"Do you think Rachel went back to Yazoo City?" He'd go get her if he was able, but right now he could barely walk across the room. Hell, he still had a catheter shoved up his penis. Wouldn't he make a romantic sight hobbling to her front door, with one arm hanging in a sling and dragging a bag of urine with his other hand? He ran a hand over his eyes as if to rub away that image of himself. No man liked being weak, least of all him.

"Maybe not right away, brother, but I'm thinking she'll go back to her home after a few days. She's too numb right now to think clearly."

"Do you know her number?" Why didn't he? Because they hadn't been away from each other long enough to need to call—until now.

Sunny reached for her phone again and waved it at him. "Speed-dial nine. Don't be surprised if she hangs up on you as soon as she hears your voice."

He looked at her for a few beats. Knowing Rachel as he did, he had no doubt she'd hang up, but not before giving him a piece of her mind. Was calling wise? Would that put him on the same level as Kyle, harassing her by phone? He speed-dialed nine and waited for her to answer, suddenly realizing how much he hungered for the sound of her voice.

"Hello." He closed his eyes, willing himself to say the right thing. "Hello?"

He took a deep breath and willed her to hear him out. "I don't care how much you cuss at me, what names you call me, just so long as I get to hear your voice." All he heard was sobbing. "Mouse, talk to me." Lord, he felt like a heel hearing her cry.

"Haven't you hurt me enough? Leave me alone, you lying, conceited, manipulative, cheating snake. You spawn of the devil. You yellow-bellied, blue-balled weasel."

A smile creased Storm's face. "See, that's why I love you. Just a few minutes ago when I called Pilar and told her I was in love with you and had been since the moment I laid eyes on you, all she could think to call me was 'bastard.' You're much more inventive." He heard more sobbing. "Where are you, love?"

"None of your damned business! You louse. You used me on the rebound after breaking up with Pilar. I was nothing more to you than a challenge, you callous cretin cowboy!"

He could see her in his mind: her eyes blazing, her cheeks blushed with anger and her pointy chin hiked the way it did when she was pissed. God, she was beautiful like that. "I love you, too, sweetheart."

"Well, I don't love you!" she shouted. Then she broke down and cried again. The sound of her despair caused an ache so severe in his heart it nearly took his breath away. He simply couldn't bear being the cause of her tears. The urge to gather her close and murmur reassuring words to her was strong.

"Don't cry, love. I'm sorry. I'll do whatever it takes to get you back. Are…are you taking care of yourself?" Silence. Total silence. His Rachel was thinking. "May I call you again tomorrow?"

"No. No, I need time. Please leave me alone. Talking to you hurts too much. I can't endure it." Rachel ended the call. They were in love, yet they were destroying each other. He squeezed the bridge of his nose between his thumb and forefinger. Face it, Blackhawk—you brought this on yourself by not making things clear to Pilar. If you'd been upfront with her about meeting another woman, she wouldn't have come to the hospital, and Rachel wouldn't be crying right now.

"Seems I've got some groveling to do. I've really messed things up."

"I'm surprised she gave you that long to talk. I'd love to know what she called you." Sunny's lips twitched as if she were amused. No doubt she was trying to lighten his mood.

"A 'yellow-bellied, blue-balled weasel,' for one. God, I love that woman. I never told you I dreamed of Rachel's eyes and her laughter for three nights before I met her out on Longhorn Road."

"Really? Wait. You've been having dreams like Daddy used to? How long? Why haven't you told me?"

"The night after Dad died, I dreamed of you crying. Somehow I could sense your heart was broken. That's why I pushed you so hard after his funeral to find out what was happening with your marriage."

Storm reached for her hand and intertwined his fingers with hers just as they'd done as children whenever they were going to share confidences; just as he suspected they'd probably done in the womb. His dark eyes turned toward hers. "I dreamed about your cancer, too." Sunny's eyes filled with tears. "Dreamed of you being thin, frail, and bald."

"Is that why you insisted I see the doctor when I was so tired all the time and had that weird feeling of fullness under my ribs? That's why you made me promise to ask for a complete blood work-up, isn't it?"

"Yes." He squeezed her hand, brought it to his lips and kissed her knuckles. "Those were scary times." She nodded and swiped at a tear. Her diagnosis was his diagnosis, too, for to lose his twin would be to lose a large part of himself.

Sunny cast dark, dewy eyes on him. "I *will* beat this, you know.""How are you feeling, sister?" She looked so much better since Rachel's arrival. Her skin had a healthy glow to it, her eyes were bright again and her hair was slowly growing back. Her scalp was almost completely covered now. "How will Rachel's leaving affect you?"

"I don't think it will at all, physically. Even though she was in a hurry to leave, she went over a daily schedule for me for the next month."

"She's a very caring person. That's one of the many things I love about her—her devotion to her patients."

Sunny nodded. "Rachel's the best. She promised she'd send another nurse. We still e-mail each other every day. I'm handling her leaving fair enough, but poor Sawyer is so sad with his Unkie Storm and his Wachel gone. He doesn't understand. Bedtime has turned into a nightmare again."

"After his bath tonight, have him call me. I'll talk to him and then tell him a bedtime story until he falls asleep." He smiled. "E-mail Nurse Rachel, see if you can hire her to take care of me so I can come home as soon as possible for Sawyer."

"You'd use a child to get her back?""I'd use anything. You're looking at a desperate man."

Sunny laughed and slapped his arm. "Big jerk!" Storm winked at her. He'd missed their talks and shared confidences. She really was looking like her old self, which relieved him greatly. She seemed happier, no doubt because she and Jackson seemed closer than ever. He enjoyed seeing her more animated and beaming a smile. "Tell me about the dreams you had of Rachel, brother."

Their hands were joined again, fingers intertwined—their sharing position. "They started three nights before I saw her out on Longhorn Road. Same dream three times." He slid his gaze to hers. "Did Rachel tell you we'd met before she arrived at the ranch?"

Her eyes twinkled with mirth. "The naked cowboy? The kiss? Oh yeah. Your behavior that night was so out of character for you. I couldn't believe it when she told me."

"I'd been so tied up in knots over my reoccurring dream of this blue-eyed, blonde-haired woman with those full, sensuous lips laughing in that low, sultry way Rachel has…"

"Only you didn't know at the time who you were dreaming of."

"Right. When I walked over to her car that night, and those big blue eyes looked up at me, I couldn't believe it. Same eyes, same enticing lips. Same long hair, only she had it in a braid that night. I made a remark that pissed her off and she drove away. I felt like a part of me was leaving and I just stood there watching her go, not knowing what to do. I willed her to come back. Chanted an old Comanche prayer Dad taught me."

"What happened?"

"She turned the car around and came back. Soon as she stopped, I grabbed her arm as if I could keep her with me. At that moment, my recent breakup with Pilar was the farthest thing from my mind. There was only the blue-eyed stranger." He looked away. "Since then, there's only been her."

Chapter Twenty-Four

Four days and forty million tears later, Rachel eased her new silver Rogue next to the curb in front of sixteen-twelve Calvin Court in Yazoo City. She was home. Comfort was here. So was the realtor, she noted, seeing the realtor logo on a black Mercedes parked in the driveway, which was a good thing. This would save her a call. She wanted to take the house off the market.

Now that Kyle was no longer a threat, she could move home again. She'd close down her Web site for a while, stop doing private nursing and apply at a couple of nearby hospitals. Maybe she'd eventually look into teaching some nursing classes.

Then again, maybe she'd just lock the doors, go to bed and pull the covers over her head until next June or July, maybe forever. Right now, she didn't care about much of anything. Depression had moved into her heart with a five-piece set of luggage.

She slammed the door on her mini-SUV and surveyed the yard. Some of the shrubbery needed trimming. She sighed. Yeah, like she cared.

"Rachel, what perfect timing!" The realtor strode down the sidewalk, her face beaming. Behind her were a dazed woman and three bouncing children. "We have a contract on the house."

"You do?" This couldn't be happening.

"Yes. Isn't that great? This is Anna Beth Richardson, who loves the house. Anna Beth, this is Rachel Dennison, the owner."

"Nice to meet you, Anna Beth." Rachel shook her hand. Her gaze traveled to the three children running through the yard. "So you like the house?"

"It's perfect. I've been saving every penny I can for a down payment, which hasn't been easy with my son's asthma. His medicine's been so expensive. Still, this is doable. I can swing this, and the yard and schools are great. I've been looking at houses like crazy, hoping I could get us moved before school starts."

Rachel stared into the woman's eyes and sensed she was a good person, a hardworking woman, and better still, a good mother. She made a snap decision. After all, not all memories here were good ones. Kyle had beaten her several times in this house. There was new drywall in the living room where he'd run his fist through it in a rage.

"I know you'll love it here. This is where I grew up." Her eyes focused on her bedroom window; snippets of childhood memories flashed by. "It's a family house."

After accepting Anna Beth's offer and agreeing to a settlement date, she got back in her car and sat. She'd just signed a contract to sell her home. The tears started, and she laid her head over the steering wheel and sobbed. *Why doesn't anything turn out the way I plan? My career's a mess. I have no home. The guy I love is...* Her phone rang, interrupting her crying jag, and she snatched it from her purse. "Hello." She wiped her nose with the back of her hand and sniffed.

"Mouse, what's wrong? I just got this sudden feeling. Are you okay?" It was Storm. She should tell him her life was none of his concern. The jerk. If he'd been the man she'd thought he was, this wouldn't be an issue. She'd be with him, Sawyer, and the whole family on the ranch she'd come to love.

"No, I'm *not* okay. You broke my heart. Haven't I asked you not to call me?"

"This is only my second call, Rachel. I'm trying to honor your wishes, but it's damn hard." Tension was evident in his voice. "I'm worried about you."

She pressed the disconnect button and tossed the phone out onto the street. Before she knew she was going to do it, she started her SUV and drove over the phone. Then just for good measure, she shoved the gearshift into reverse and backed over it again. She was getting a new phone number and a new job and a new place to live. Wasn't that just fine and dandy?

An hour later she was ringing Grace's doorbell.

"Hey, come in." Grace's eyes widened. "What have you brought?"

"Chinese and cheesecake. You can't come to a slumber party without food and drinks and stuff." She breezed into the tidy apartment. "You do still have off tonight, don't you?"

"Yes. I'm off for three days, then back on for four." Grace started rummaging through the bags Rachel had deposited on the kitchen counter. "Diet soda, cookies, pudding cups, taco chips and salsa. What Chinese food did you get?"

"Your favorites, of course." She planted a kiss on Grace's cheek. "Won-ton soup for me."

Her friend opened the bag of chips and popped a couple in her mouth. "Good girl," she mumbled with her mouth full. "We haven't had a feast like this since…"

Rachel slung her arm across her best friend's shoulders. "Since before Kyle." She opened a pudding cup and reached for a spoon. "I have a contract on my house."

"I thought you were going to take it off the market." Grace pulled plates and silverware out of the cabinets and drawers. "Where will you live? Hey, you want to move in with me? I've got a spare bedroom. It'd be like old times."

She licked chocolate pudding off the back of the spoon. "Could I? Just for a couple months, until I decide what I'm going to do with my life. I need to make plans and hunt for another house. Oh, before I forget, I have a new number."

Grace reached for her cell. Her finger was poised over the keyboard. "Let me have it." Once she had the data saved, she put a hand on Rachel's arm. "Now, suppose you tell me why you got another number. You don't have to worry about Kyle anymore, the lousy creep. Do you know he pawned my grandma's ring? Thank goodness the police have it now. I'll get it back—eventually." She carried plates to her coffee table. Rachel brought drinks and the bag of Chinese.

"Storm called me this afternoon. At the time, I was crying, upset over the house selling and realizing I'd have to deal with one more upset in my life. My cell rang and it was Storm. Wondered if I was okay. Said he got a bad feeling about me, so he called."

Grace spooned fried rice onto her plate. "A bad feeling? What, is he psychic?" She opened a container of sweet and sour chicken.

Rachel tugged the lid off her soup. "He's half Native American and says he has dreams sometimes about the future. Claimed he dreamed about me before he ever laid eyes on me, if you can believe that. 'Course he said he loved me, too. The cheating cowboy said a lot of things. He said he was through with Pilar. He said he wanted to marry me."

"Oh, this is so good." Grace held a piece of chicken at her lips. "Tell me about him. What is it about this guy that attracts you?"

“Everything.” Rachel lifted a spoon of broth to her mouth, remembering. “It’s more than his looks. He’s earthy, in tune with his ranch and animals.” She laughed. “He talks to his horses like they’re his best buddies. The ranch is doing well, so he obviously knows what he’s doing. His ranch hands are very loyal because he treats them well. You should have seen him when Eduardo got hurt. He even went by the man’s mother’s house to take her to the hospital. He’s one of the most caring men I know.” She set her soup down, her appetite suddenly gone. “I miss him so much I think I’ll lose my mind.”

“Then go to him. Work things out. How do you think he feels about you?”

“When I’m with him, he makes me feel like I’m a pitcher of iced tea and he’s a man dying of thirst. He’s so intense, so focused. He can go from fierce to tender in a heartbeat. You should see him with his nephew.” She wiped a falling tear. Every part of her wanted Storm Blackhawk, desired him beyond all else. Could she believe what he’d said, that he’d told Pilar about her? Was it truly over between Storm and the cool, sophisticated woman?

She looked at Grace. “I may have another problem.”

“Oh?” Grace was clearly enjoying her food. She’d always been able to tell Grace anything. How would she react to this possible development?

“I might be pregnant.”

Grace’s head whipped up, her brown eyes widened in surprise.

“I’ve got a home pregnancy test in one of the bags in the kitchen.”

Two pairs of apprehensive eyes watched for results on the plastic stick. “Why is it taking so long?” Rachel felt as if her heart were doing a drum solo. The rest of her life hinged on the results.

“I see something.” Grace was leaning over Rachel’s shoulder to get a better view. She turned her head and looked at Rachel. “Congratulations, girlfriend. You’re pregnant.”

“Help me sit down. I don’t think my legs will work.” Pregnant. She’d missed six pills and now she was pregnant. A seemingly intelligent woman, twenty-seven years old with a master’s degree, no less, was dumb enough to get pregnant. No job. No home. No husband. And a baby on the way. “I need chocolate.”

"You're a diabetic, remember?"

She collapsed onto the commode lid and grabbed Grace's hand. "I'm pregnant and I want chocolate. Do you hear me?"

****

Storm's eyes snapped open. The clock on his nightstand read two twenty-two. He smiled at the significance. He'd just dreamed of Rachel. She was awkwardly walking toward him, her eyes shining and her abdomen large with her pregnancy. She was carrying his twins.

He wanted to call her, just to hear her voice. But she'd asked him not to. If he didn't honor her request, he'd be no better than Kyle. Yet what was he to do? He had to keep her mind on him; had to let her know his mind was on her.

The brief e-mail he sent her every morning was all he dared do without crossing the line she'd drawn in the sand. He had to respect the boundaries she'd set, even if it was killing him. His hand reached out, and he slid his palm over the pillow he'd come to think of as hers. Memories flooded back of the morning they'd loved each other here in this bed. He hardened with need for her and groaned her name.

Slowly he got out of bed; a twinge of pain from his incision snagged his attention for a moment, taking it off the pain of unfulfilled sexual desire. "Rachel, love, come home to me." He shook his head once and wondered how many times his dad had uttered the same request for his wife, Sunny's and his mother. Life played cruel tricks sometimes. Love was never easy.

He donned a pair of old sweatpants and opened his bedroom door to the hallway. Maybe if he got something to eat, he could fall back to sleep. He would dream of Rachel and his babies again.

It was good to be home. Storm padded into the kitchen and looked into the refrigerator. Hospital food had taken a good twenty pounds off his frame. The overhead light snapped on, and he pivoted. "Momma Noella, I'm sorry. Did I waken you?"

She tugged on the ties of her bathrobe. "I was awake, writing an e-mail to my sister." She shrugged. "Thinking of the little one. Worrying."

Storm pushed a bowl of salad aside to reach a slab of roast beef left over from supper. "She won't be the little one for long." He turned and wiggled his eyebrows. "I had a dream."

Noella tugged a bag of rolls from the breadbox and set about making them both a sandwich. "You and your dreams. You sound just like your father." He snatched a slice of roast beef from the roll. She slapped his hand, and he smiled that cheeky grin he knew, from years of experience, would rankle her.

"I dreamed Rachel was pregnant with twins." He shoved in the slice of meat and chewed.

"You dreamed she was pregnant? No!" She regarded him with a raised eyebrow. "You have much work to do, young man. I want my little one back. She belongs here with us, her family. I want you married first."

Storm slung an arm over Noella's shoulder. "I want us married, too. I ache with need for her. I need to see her smile, to see her chin hike up when she gets riled, to hear her laughter, and watch her with Sawyer. She'll make a great mom, won't she? Just think, two little bambinos for you to spoil. My bambinos." He wanted Rachel here with him with fierceness akin to his need for air. Just how was he going to achieve his objective?

****

Rachel was still coming to grips with everything, especially impending motherhood. A baby. She smiled. Something she'd found herself doing a lot in the past twenty-four hours, now that she'd gotten over the shock. For all its complications, having a baby pleased her on some deep level. There were decisions that required her attention, but with a baby on the way, she had to think things through carefully and logically.

She powered up her laptop and checked for e-mails. There was one from her mother and one from Noella. She clicked on it; maybe she had news of Storm.

Little One, I miss you. When will you come home with your family who cares for you? Storm is out of the hospital, but he is sad without you. He finally told Pilar he's in love with you. He took too long to do that, but I say nothing. He wants me to inquire about your health. Are you taking care of yourself? Sawyer frets for you. Don't forget our bar-b-q next week. You helped plan it. Now you must attend. Noella will make your bedroom all fresh for you, sí? Come.

The birthday barbeque—Rachel had forgotten all about it.

Storm and Sunny would turn thirty. She read the e-mail again. So Storm was home. On her fourth reading of it, her stomach dropped. Storm was inquiring about her health, asking if she was taking care of herself. He knew. He knew about the baby. *Him and his dreams.* He'd probably know the sex of the child before she would.

Dreams. She'd had a few of them herself over the years. Hard work and determination brought a few of them to fruition. Her nursing degree, for one.

She'd been giving thought lately to writing a book about her integrated form of health care for cancer patients. With her research and work experience, she certainly had enough material. In fact, she'd consulted with an expert in oncology regarding her idea. He'd given her a few suggestions and an offer to assist in any way he could. Maybe she'd e-mail a respected hematologist she'd once worked with on a case; she made a note to that effect and smiled. This was a dream with a very real possibility of coming true.

Still, there was one dream that consistently enveloped her like a warm snuggly blanket—a family. Storm, her, and the baby. If she pursued the dream, she'd have to be sure he was through with Pilar. She'd also have to trust he wouldn't revert to his old domineering ways. He hadn't overwhelmed her with phone calls before she'd gotten her new number. She'd give him that. She'd told him not to call and, for the most part, he'd honored her request.

There was his daily e-mail telling her he loved her. Just that, nothing more. Three words. Why didn't he write more? Her eyes filled with tears. Maybe those three words were just lip service, a way of controlling her.

She stood and walked to the window. These raging pregnancy hormones were going to drive her crazy. One minute she was smiling and the next, she was in tears. Who was she kidding? This pie in the sky dream of her and Storm and happily ever after wasn't going to happen. She swiped at her tear-drenched cheeks and then placed a hand over her abdomen. "It's just you and me, baby, but we'll be all right. Mommy promises. We'll make our own dreams, just the two of us."

She wasn't planning to keep news of the pregnancy from Storm. She was just giving herself time to adjust and get her life in order. Why throw another problem into the mix? Because once Storm

Blackhawk knew he had a child somewhere, he'd demand to be part of his or her life.

That would mean seeing him on a regular basis when he came for visitation. Could she endure that? For the sake of the child, she'd have to. She'd seen too many children emotionally scarred by one parent using the child as a weapon to hurt the other parent. Her child wouldn't be hurt that way. A strong protectiveness raged through her, and a smile blossomed. Goodness, she was feeling maternal. How glorious.

She returned to the chair and began a response to Noella's e-mail.

Chapter Twenty-Five

Rachel sat at the iron gates of the Triple-S ranch, her hand poised above the security code keypad and her stomach alternately fluttering and clenching. For sixty long seconds, she didn't think she could go through with it. A wave of nausea lapped at her ankles like cold seawater before rising to officially disturb her stomach. "Oh, not now, baby. We don't want to puke in front of anyone."

A truck pulled up behind her. The driver leaned out of the window and honked the horn. "You all right up there, little lady?" She glanced in her rearview mirror, wishing the truck would disappear. Before she thought it through, she yanked on the steering wheel and made a U-turn. She couldn't go through with it. Her heart pounded and sweat formed on her brow. The nausea…

Why was she putting herself through this? Granted, she needed to tell Storm, but wouldn't an e-mail be better? A giggle escaped. She could start it *Dear Daddy...* With her hormone levels fluctuating, she was bouncing from giggles to tears with every beat of her heart.

No, she wouldn't run. She wanted to see the expression on his face and hear his response. She'd write every part of Storm's reaction in the baby book Grace had given her yesterday. There was a page for Daddy's response to the good news. Her child deserved to read it one day.

She made another U-turn and headed once more for the Triple-S. Should she give the baby a name starting with "S"? Didn't her child merit that bit of paternal family tradition? Samuel or Summer? How about Sterling or Sylvia? No, not Sterling. Scott, perhaps. Did she want a boy or a girl? A boy with Storm's personality. She groaned. Could she handle him? Was she strong enough to raise a mini-Storm?

Rachel's heart was beating wildly when she eased her SUV to a stop along the gravel driveway of the ranch. Cars and trucks were parked along the drive. Many of the guests had already arrived. The air was filled with Mexican music. Noella would be dancing in the new skirt Storm had bought her. She smiled at the thought as she checked her appearance in the sun-visor mirror.

Her bruises were now a mottled yellow. She'd thought about

covering them with makeup, but since she doubted she could get through the day without crying, she'd decided against it. Tear tracks through makeup would only make her look worse than she did without it. Her eyes were minimally bloodshot. The stitches were gone from her lip. In a week, she expected she'd look normal again. She fussed with her hair and freshened her lipstick.

Rachel took a deep breath, got out of her vehicle and reached for the gift bags. She straightened her skirt. Her stomach felt queasy again, and she placed her hand on it. She'd taken great pains with her appearance today, trying to look dazzling, yet casual.

She'd borrowed a denim sundress from Grace with spaghetti straps and a slim skirt that had a ruffle at the hemline. A red stretch belt was at her waist and red hoops at her ears. Just for spite, she'd worn those "ho-red" heels Storm seemed so taken with. Now, if only she could keep from throwing up so her breath wouldn't reek of… She shuddered; how disgusting.

"Well, baby, let's go see Daddy and get today over with." She headed for the party. Smells of barbeque wafted in the still, hot air. Red and Eduardo were manning the grills and barbeque pits.

"Miss Rachel! How good to see you." Eduardo motioned to a lovely, dark-haired woman. "Maria, come meet Miss Rachel, the angel who took care of me before the ambulance arrived."

"How are you doing?" He looked pale and had lost a lot of weight. She noticed he'd been sitting before he slowly stood to greet her.

"The doctors say I was very lucky. I will heal in time." He took Maria's hand. "This is my Maria."

The woman smiled shyly. "I am honored to meet you. You saved my Eduardo's life. The doctors tell us this. You had his terrible wound cleaned so well, he had no infection."

"Thank you. I'm glad I was here to help."

"You're needed here, Miss Rachel. The boss, he misses you like a man misses air." Her stomach did flip-flops. Could Eduardo be right?

"Guess you ain't got no hug for ol' Red." She turned and laughed. Red stood there in a clean white Western shirt and jeans, wearing one of Noella's orange flowered aprons. He hugged her and whispered in her ear, "Thank God you've come. Boss has been like a lion with a sore paw. He reaches out to take a swipe at us from time to time. Ain't been hisself without you, and that's a fact."

"Patients who've undergone surgery sometimes are emotional afterward. Going under anesthesia and the surgery itself is a shock to the nervous system. Be patient with him. He'll soon get over it."

"He won't get over it until you've moved back here. What in the world happened 'tween you two? He liked to go mad when that crazy feller had you. Yet you left. Can't you two work things out?" Red peered at her with a questioning gaze. Maybe coming was a mistake. She felt she was being tugged where she didn't want to be tugged—into Storm's arms. "Now, you go on and find him. Set things to rights." He gave her a gentle push.

Oh dear. She glanced back the driveway to her SUV and made a step in that direction. Her nerves were wound so tight they were starting to frazzle. Leaving would be so easy. Still, she had to face him sometime. He deserved to hear about the baby from her lips.

"Wachel! Wachel!" Sawyer ran toward her and leaped into her arms. He hugged her tight. "I miss you so much." He planted loud, smacking kisses over her face.

Tears sprung to her eyes. She'd missed this sweet child. "How's my Superman Sawyer?"

"I got new boots on. Put me down, and I show you." When she set him on the ground, he grinned and pointed to his gray boots. "Ain't dey somefin'? Unkie Jackson got dem for me, and guess what?" He looked up at her.

She smiled. "What?"

"I'm getting a new Daddy!" He jumped up and down.

"You are?" How she loved this child.

"Yup. Guess who he is?"

"I don't know. Who?" Jackson must have popped the question. Better still, Sunny must have accepted.

"Unkie Jackson! And we're getting a new house, too. Come. I show you." He held out his chubby little hand, and Rachel took it. He led her to a spot near the orchard. Sawyer ran to an area marked by stakes. "Here! Our new house will be wight here. Ain't dat somefin'?" His arms spread wide to show her the area. "My woom will be wight heah." He skipped to a spot and jumped into it, pointing with pride at a little stake with a sign that read, "Sawyer's room". He placed his hands on his hips. "Ain't dis a nice place faw a house? My new daddy said he wants it next to the awchawd where he kissed Mommy the fawst time."

Rachel laughed. "Where is your mommy?" A lot had happened since she'd been gone.

"She's talking to people by the pool." Another little boy came running over. "You go see Mommy. I have to mingle."

Rachel laughed again. "Mingle?" Where had this three-year-old learned that word?

He flashed a smile. "Unkie Storm said a good host mingles." The child sighed. "It means move around and talk to evwybody. He says I'm good at dat." Off Sawyer and the other boy ran.

She turned and headed for the pool area behind the ranch house. Would Storm be there? Could she keep from crying the moment she saw him?

Although some of the guests were congregated near the grills, Rachel found the majority of the thirty or so invited guests were at the patio by the pool. Some were in the water to escape the nearly hundred-degree heat. Pepe and his band were playing salsa music. Colorful Japanese lanterns were hung everywhere, and the bartenders were doing a brisk business. Festivity and laughter were in the air.

Sunny was sitting on a chair beneath an umbrella sipping from a cup. Rachel walked up behind her and leaned over her former patient. "That better be green tea in that cup."

Sunny jumped from the chair, squealing and giggling. "You're here! I was so afraid you'd chicken out at the last minute." She enveloped Rachel in a hug. "Oh, sweetie, you've been missed so much."

"Let me see this diamond Jackson swore me to secrecy about." Sunny extended her hand. "Oh, it's breathtaking. Congratulations. Have you set a date?"

"Yes, but it's a secret for a little while yet. Will you be my maid of honor? Say yes!"

Tears stung Rachel's eyes. "Are you sure you want me? What about family or friends from college? How soon is the wedding?" She might have to waddle up the aisle in a maternity gown.

Sunny slung her arm around Rachel's shoulders. "The wedding

will be soon, and you *are* family. Please say yes!"

How could she refuse Sunny? She wanted her friend to embrace life and marry. She wanted to see her smile like this every day. Rachel laughed and nodded. "Okay. I'd be honored."

"My little one, you're here!" Rachel spun and was quickly embraced by Noella.

She stepped back and gave the older woman the once-over. Her sleek, dark hair was down, hanging to her waist; there was a red flower above her ear. Noella wore a white peasant top with one shoulder exposed. The red taffeta full skirt Storm had bought her was topped with a wide black stretch belt. The skirt was pulled up at one point, its gathers secured with a black feather pin. This exposed a few inches of black crinolines. She wore black strappy heels. "Momma Noella, you look fabulous!"

Noella's smile beamed and she preened, which was so unlike the conservative dresser. "I look like a young flower with dew still on the bloom, *sí?"* She batted her eyes. All three women laughed.

****

He'd felt her presence for the last ten minutes, that telltale prickling on the back of his neck, a fluttering in his stomach and a heaviness in his groin, not enough to be noticeable—thank God—seeing as how he was playing host to a lot of guests, but enough to make it hard to concentrate on polite conversation. That is, if one could call conversation between ranchers about a new artificial insemination company from Ireland as "polite."

Storm took a sip of his ice water and surveyed the patio and poolside, wishing he had something stronger to steady his nerves. Unfortunately, his surgeon didn't approve of drinking mass quantities of alcohol with only one kidney. For now, he'd behave himself. There were more important things to think of than beer and whiskey, like Rachel. Where was she? She must be talking to someone. He sipped again and ordered himself to be patient.

His eyes riveted to her as soon as she finally came through the gate to the patio area. The sight of her caused him to take in several long gulps of air. She was glowing, glowing with her pregnancy. The smile on her face when she leaned over Sunny to whisper in her ear caused him to smile in return. Sweet heaven, she was even more beautiful than he remembered.

His eyes took in everything. Her tawny blonde hair was in sexy loose curls. Little straps held up her dress, a dress that showcased her full breasts and trim figure. He narrowed his eyes in concentration. Was her waist thickening? Surely he was imagining it. He took another sip of water as his gaze traveled down her tight skirt to her legs—he choked. She was wearing those "ho-red" heels. He shook his head once; the woman had a way of delighting him. A predatory smile flashed across his features. He was going to take those "ho-red" heels off her tonight with his teeth.

"Who's the *fierce* looker in the denim dress talking to your sister?" Shawn Masters, owner of the Irish artificial insemination company, leered at the mother of Storm's children. His blood ran hot with possession.

"That's the woman I'm about to propose to." He wasn't so sure he liked this Irishman.

Shawn narrowed his eyes, studying Rachel. "Well now, doesn't that make you a *jammy* person? May the sun shine on both of you and bless your union with many little ones."

Storm smiled, his gaze never once leaving the woman he loved. "Thank you, Shawn."

Sunny embraced Rachel. No doubt she'd agreed to be Sunny's maid of honor. Noella came onto the patio area just then and hugged Rachel. If he were a better man, he'd wait and give the women time to exchange a few words. He set his empty glass on a nearby table. The hell with waiting. The time for waiting was over.

****

Noella cupped Rachel's cheek in her hand. "Noella has your room all ready for you. How long will you be staying with us?"

Suddenly the hairs on the back of Rachel's neck and arms stood up. Her nipples peaked and she knew—

"Forever. She's staying forever." A voice, deep, dark and sexy as black satin, washed over her. She took a deep breath before she slowly turned around. She'd reassured herself she could handle seeing Storm, but she hadn't been prepared for the whirligig ride her emotions would take when she did. Tears filled her eyes and she clasped them shut.

Storm's hand went to the small of Rachel's back, and he pulled her into an embrace. The man was warmth and security…and *home*.

He bent down and kissed her on the top of her head. "Momma Noella, Rachel and I need some privacy. After we talk, we'll be out to join the party."

"Ten minutes, Master Storm. You have guests."

"Thirty minutes, and to hell with the guests." He took Rachel by the elbow and led her inside. "You look exquisite today, mouse." He opened the door and escorted her to his office. Once he closed and locked the door, he pushed her flat against the door. He grasped her upper arms and stared at her as if he were drinking in everything about her appearance. She couldn't stop trembling. They stared at one another, speaking volumes with their silence.

Rachel swiped at falling tears. The time to tell him about the baby had come. "How…how are you recuperating?" He looked wan and pale. She wanted to reach out and touch him with every fiber of her being. Once she told him about the baby, he might not want her to touch him.

"Well enough. I think I'd recover quicker if I had a good nurse." He leaned down and kissed away her tears. "Know where I can get one?" He placed a kiss on her neck. Her stomach quivered. Their thighs touched.

"Do you want a nurse short term or long term?" God, he smelled so good.

He brushed his lips across hers, and her breathing hitched. "Most definitely long term. I mean, I'll have to live the rest of my life with only one kidney. Stands to reason I'd need looking after, don't you think?" His tongue swept across her lips, his dark eyes intent on hers. She was losing the battle.

She fidgeted with a button on his shirt. "You must know how sorry I am you lost a kidney protecting me. I feel terrible about that."

"It was nothing." He took her wrist and looked at her scar. "Your stitches are out."

He placed a gentle kiss on the scar, and her knees nearly buckled. "How can you say losing a kidney is nothing?" She'd relived the shooting scene a hundred times in her mind and in her dreams.

"Mouse, when a man loves a woman the way I love you, he'd die for her. So losing a kidney was nothing. Nothing compared to losing you." He planted soft, gentle, quick kisses on her lips. Someone moaned, and she was surprised to realize it was her.

Storm leaned in, and she felt his arousal. Her gaze flicked to his desk, the desk where they'd made love and, for all she knew, where they'd created a child. He glanced over his shoulder, in the direction of her gaze. "You remember, too, don't you? I can't sit at that desk without remembering how we made love there." He groaned. "How good you felt around me. Your legs wrapped around my waist." He captured her lips, and she opened for him. His tongue did wondrous things to hers. "I love you so much, honey.

"I have something for you." He reached into the pocket of his pale blue Western shirt and pulled out a silver bracelet. "This is not the original one. It's still being held for evidence. Besides"—he looked at her with determination in his eyes—I don't want you wearing anything that man touched. He fastened it around her wrist. "I had the jeweler make you a new one with a few more charms on it."

She fingered the charms: the map of Texas, the word "Dream," a cowboy hat and boots, a horse, a mouse, the words "I love you," an engagement ring, and two baby shoes. Her eyes swept upward to his. She opened and closed her mouth twice; nothing would come out.

He removed a black box from his pants pocket. "I'm afraid I can't get down on my knees to propose."

Her eyes filled with tears. Could this really be happening? First she had to tell him about the pregnancy.

"If you'll have me, I promise to adore you the rest of my life the way I do at this very moment." He opened the box to reveal a square-cut diamond flanked by blue sapphires. "I love you and I hope to God you'll marry me."

"I can't. There's something you should know first." She had to tell him about the baby.

"Whatever it is, we'll discuss it after the proposal. One thing has nothing to do with the other. I'm asking you to marry me because I love you above all others, because I need you like I need air to breathe, and because I want to grow old with you." He took her hand and set the ring box in her palm. "Please say 'yes' and put me out of my misery. I've loved you from the moment I first dreamed about you. I'll love you until eternity ends."

Rachel *did* love this man. How could she possibly accept his proposal with a secret between them? A secret that might cause his mind to change about marrying her. Lots of men didn't want a baby right away. They wanted time alone with their wives first. "Before I accept, I have to tell you something. I have a secret."

"Love, once you put on my ring and agree to marry me, I'll be glad to hear whatever you have to say. One thing at a time. First the proposal, then we'll talk." She shook her head. "Don't you love me?" He kissed each corner of her mouth softly. "Tell me. Tell me you love me." His next kiss was fierce and demanding, as if he were driving all rational thought from her mind. His hands swept up her sides and his thumbs flicked over her nipples. "Tell me."

"Yes. Yes, I love you."

His teeth grazed her neck the way he knew she liked. Her knees went weak. "Now, tell me," he groaned. "Tell me you'll marry me." It seemed his hands were everywhere, igniting little fires. No other man could touch her soul like this.

"Yes, I'll marry you." She hoped with every ounce of her being that all would be well once she told him he was soon to be a father.

He slipped on the ring, folded her in his arms and kissed her, a kiss of love and promise and adoration. She was breathless when Storm ended the kiss. He placed his forehead against hers and stared into her eyes. "I hope you don't mind a short engagement, love."

"How short?" Would he want to get married before she had the baby?

"I have a plane scheduled to fly the whole family to Vegas in the morning. We're having a double wedding. You and me and Sunny and Jackson."

Her head was whirling. "A double wedding? In Vegas?" Dawning registered. "Is that why Sunny wouldn't tell me when her wedding date was? Because she knew about all this? She knows about your plans to fly to Vegas tomorrow? Vegas? My mom lives in Vegas. Does she know? Mom asked me what size dress I wore. It was the strangest e-mail…"

Storm feathered kisses across her face. "Is that a yes, love?"

She laughed and nodded against his neck.

"So, we're through with the proposal? Everything is set?"

"Yes." She'd be married tomorrow. Ready or not, she'd be Mrs. Storm Blackhawk.

His hands covered her abdomen. "So tell me, how are my babies?"

"Babies?"

"Yes." His smile broadened. "As in twins."

"Oh no, you're wrong." She couldn't be having twins. Granted her clothes were tight on her already, but…

"I had a dream." He kissed her neck, the heat from his hands warming her abdomen as if he were sending a love message to his babies.

"A dream?"

"Yes, love. A dream where you were carrying twins."

She narrowed her eyes and glared at him. "Your dreams are never wrong, I suppose."

"Never." His hands were making slow circles over her abdomen.

"Twins." This just couldn't be. She was barely prepared for motherhood, much less twins.

He smiled and nodded.

"Did the dream tell you the sex of the babies?"

A dazzling smile spread. "Yes, love, I know their sex."

Sex as in singular, not one of each like Storm and Sunny. "Wait. Tell me I am *not* carrying twin boys."

Storm pulled back from her and laughed.

"Storm Blackhawk!"

He took her hand and pulled her toward the door. "Come on. We've got an engagement announcement to make to our guests."

"You didn't answer me." How could she ever handle twin boys as ornery and determined to have their way as their father?

Storm held the office door open, turned dark eyes to her and winked.

Epilogue
Six Months Later

Lisa, the nurse on the hospital's maternity floor, removed the blood pressure cuff from Rachel's arm. "Looks like you came through childbirth just fine. Your husband, on the other hand, looks shell shocked."

Rachel regarded Storm and smiled. He looked pole-axed, as Red would say. She thought of how Storm had coached her through her long night of labor, telling her how marvelous she was doing and how beautiful she was.

During the difficult time of labor, when she asked him for what had to be the hundredth time over the past few months if she still had feet, his eyebrow arched. "Whose toenails have I been painting every week for the last three months?" He kissed her forehead. "And, yes, they're blue today to welcome the boys."

In her opinion, he was simply the best husband in the entire universe. He was passionate about everything in his life, and he was already passionate about their children.

"It's a good expression for him, don't you think?" Rachel winked at Lisa, and the nurse smirked.

Lisa patted Storm's shoulder while she looked at the tiny boys in his arms. "You have some handsome sons there, Mr. Blackhawk."

Storm's voice was full of emotion when he thanks her. "My wife does good work, don't you think? His gaze swept over Rachel. "Although she is a bit of an overachiever."

Rachel glanced at the little girl snuggled against her breast. "Oh, stop it. She wanted to surprise her daddy, is all. That's why she hid during the sonograms." Triplets. The whole idea was more than a tad overwhelming. Thank goodness they had Noella to help and Sunny, too, now that she was in remission.

Storm laughed. "Well, she certainly did that. I was never so shocked in my life as I was when she popped out. We have a bit of a naming problem, mouse. We've got these two big fellas taken care of, but what about her? I'm drawing a blank on a girl's name.

Rachel lifted her daughter and pressed a gentle kiss to her silky forehead. The tiny baby groaned and stretched, her little arms peeking out of the pink blanket. "I know. I've been rolling names around in my mind, trying to come up with something. She was just so unexpected. I still can't believe we have three babies." She rubbed a fingertip over the girl's downy cheek. "She's our little secret joy."

She'd been excited about the boys' impending birth, once she'd gotten used to the idea of twins. As her due date slowly approached, her happiness expanded almost as quickly as her waistline. The blue nursery at the Triple-S, decorated with a border of horses and filled with two of everything, was testament to her enthusiasm. Yet she still longed for a daughter. Sensing this, Storm had suggested they try for a little girl in two years.

Little did they know she was carrying triplets. No wonder she'd been on bed rest for over a month. Dr. Fetterhoff said it was rare that a third baby wasn't seen in the sonograms or its heartbeat unheard, but with multiple births, it *did* sometimes happen. During her long days in bed, Rachel had read books on Native American lore. She was more inclined to believe this adorable girl was a gift.

Because she wanted to enjoy this day, Rachel refused to think about midnight feedings and diaper changes and colic and teething. She simply wanted to enjoy the moment and give thanks.

When the nurse opened the door to leave, she glanced back over her shoulder. "You have a gang of people waiting out here to get a look at these babies. They can stay for five minutes. Then I'll be back to shoo them out, don't you worry about that. I want to get the babies settled into their incubators, especially the smallest one."

Lisa repeated her orders to those standing in the hallway. Rachel's mother was the first one to enter, carrying two teddy bears. Sunny and Jackson followed along with Sawyer, as did Noella and Red. Tears and much oohing and aahing were shared as the visitors looked from one baby to the next.

"Which one is my new cousin, Unkie Storm?"

"They're all yours, partner. But for now, you have to be very gentle with them just like we were with you after you were born."

"What do I call dem?" Sawyer reached with his index finger to touch the dark hair on one of the boy's heads.

"Daddy, why don't you introduce your children?" Rachel's heart was so full of love and happiness, it ached with a desire to draw her loved ones close. Her gaze swept around the crowded hospital room at all the people she loved with a sweet fierceness.

"Sure thing, love." Storm unfolded from the chair and moved to stand next to the head of Rachel's bed. He proudly extended the babe in his right arm. "Folks, this is our firstborn, Samuel Storm Blackhawk. He weighed in at five pounds one ounce." He held out his left arm. "This pudgy fella weighed in at five pounds six ounces and was named Sloane Drew Blackhawk."

Rachel's mother dabbed a wadded tissue to her tear-filled eyes. "You named him after our Drew? How sweet of you to do that."

"I thought it would be nice to honor my brother." Rachel reached for a tissue and wiped her eyes, too.

Rachel is holding the cagey one of the bunch. We've decided…" Storm's gaze swept to Rachel and held for a beat… "to name her exactly what she is for us—Secret Joy Blackhawk."

"Storm, that's so perfect." Rachel blotted another tear. How did one contain so much happiness?

"Secret only weights four pounds twelve ounces. Seems she's the runt of the litter." Storm rocked back on his heels. Rachel knew him well enough to realize he was waiting on Momma Noella's reaction. He didn't have to wait long.

Noella clucked her tongue. "Storm, that will not do, calling our little Secret Joy a runt, but I say nothing."

Storm laughed and bent over to kiss his daughter. "Yeah, well, she might be small but she's got my heart in her little hand. I have a feeling she'll grow up to be a strong woman, just like her momma."

Secret decided to howl at that particular moment. Both of her brothers turned their heads in her direction, as if to listen to her very vocal demands.

Rachel laughed. "That's right, Secret. Show your big brothers who's the boss of this outfit."

Joyous laughter and tears filled the room. The nurse entered the room, pushing an incubator and placed Secret in it before pushing her back out. Storm handed Sammy to Momma Noella and Sloane to Rachel's mother so they could cuddle them before the nurse returned with another incubator.

Storm leaned over and whispered in Rachel's ear. "I'll love you forever and a day, mouse." His kiss was warm and gentle. "Thank you for my children," he murmured against her lips.

Rachel sighed, feeling incredibly fortunate and exhausted at the same time. “Look around, honey. There’s so much love in this room. We are so blessed.” She took his hand and squeezed it before laying it over her breast. “My heart is overflowing with love. A lifetime of love…for you. Especially for you.”

COMING SOON:
More of *Rosefire, Texas romances*

Visit Vonnie Davis at her website:
www.vonniedavis.com
where you can sign up for her newsletter to stay in the know of new releases and be eligible for special prizes.

About the Author:

Vonnie Davis is an award-winning, international author who writes mainly contemporary and paranormal romance, often with strong elements of suspense and dashes of humor. She likens herself to a croissant: warm, crusty, wrinkled, a tad flaky—and best served with strong coffee. Vonnie lives in southern Virginia with her hero and author husband, Calvin Davis. She's been blessed by six fantastic grandchildren and three grown children, who take pride in the fact Mom is finally pursuing her life-long dream of writing.

Printed in Great Britain
by Amazon

18504712R00153